W9-BED-934

A TREASURY
of REGRETS

A TREASURY
of REGRETS

Susanne Alleyn

THOMAS DUNNE BOOKS
ST. MARTIN'S MINOTAUR
NEW YORK

THOMAS DUNNE BOOKS.
An imprint of St. Martin's Press.

A TREASURY OF REGRETS. Copyright © 2007 by Susanne Alleyn. All rights reserved. Printed in the United States of America. No part of this book may be used or reproduced in any manner whatsoever without written permission except in the case of brief quotations embodied in critical articles or reviews. For information, address St. Martin's Press, 175 Fifth Avenue, New York, N.Y. 10010.

www.thomasdunnebooks.com
www.stmartins.com

ISBN-10: 0-312-34371-X
ISBN-13: 978-0-312-34371-2

First Edition: April 2007

10 9 8 7 6 5 4 3 2 1

To Don Congdon, with deepest affection

and appreciation

C'est une dangereuse espergne

D'amasser tresor de regrés;

Qui de son cueur les tient trop prés,

Il couvient que mal lui en preigne.

Veu qu'ilz sont si oultre l'enseigne,

Non pas assez nuysans, mais trés,

C'est une dangereuse espergne

D'amasser tresor de regrés.

CHARLES D'ORLÉANS, 1391-1465

FOREWORD

Married and widowed women in France, while they bear their husbands' surnames socially, are always referred to in official proceedings and documents by their maiden names; thus Madame Blanc is officially either "Marie Noir, wife of Blanc" or "Marie Noir, widow Blanc."

North American readers may find the distinction between "dinner" and "supper" confusing. For the middle and upper classes in eighteenth-century French society, the midday dinner was the main meal of the day, served anytime between one and four o'clock, though usually the more fashionable and wealthy the diners, the later and more formal the meal. Supper was a light and simple evening meal for the bourgeois family, or—for the elegant set who met after balls or theatrical performances—a lavish, but informal and usually intimate repast that might be served as late as one or two o'clock in the morning.

I have followed general European practice in the naming of floors in buildings; the first floor is one flight up from the ground floor, and so on.

———

Much of the tangle of medieval streets in the heart of Paris disappeared during Baron Haussmann's extensive rebuilding of the city in the 1860s. Many other streets have had their names, or the spelling of their names, changed during the past two centuries. To make matters even more confusing, many street names still in use today were temporarily changed or altered during the most radical phase of the Revolution to eliminate references to royalty, aristocracy, or Christianity. All streets and street names mentioned in this novel, however, existed in the 1790s.

TERMS

Commissaire: A local official of the eighteenth-century Parisian police force, who combined the approximate functions of precinct commander and chief investigator.

Commissariat: Police headquarters for a Parisian section.

Décade: The ten-day week of the republican calendar.

Décadi: Tenth day of the week in the republican calendar and the official day off.

Faubourg: A suburb or, less precisely, a neighborhood; areas of Paris such as the faubourg St. Germain, the faubourg St. Marcel, and so on were so named in the Middle Ages, when they were parishes lying outside the twelfth-century walls, but by the eighteenth century they were well within the city limits.

Frimaire: Third month of the French Revolutionary calendar, corresponding to November 21–December 20 of the Christian calendar.

Hôtel: Can mean a hostelry, a large public building (*hôtel de ville,* city hall; *hôtel-Dieu,* hospital), or a large private town house or mansion *(hôtel particulier).* I have used the French form, with the circumflex over the *o,* whenever referring to a mansion or municipal hall, and the unaccented English word when referring to public accommodations.

Inspector: A low-level police officer roughly corresponding to a uniformed "beat cop" in a modern police force.

Jacobin: A member of the republican Club of the Friends of the Constitution, which met in the former monastery of the Jacobin Brothers; or, less specifically, a radical republican.

Nivôse: Fourth month of the French Revolutionary calendar, corresponding to December 21–January 19 of the Christian calendar.

Notary: The equivalent, in France, of a British solicitor: an attorney who deals in contracts, transactions, wills, property, legal issues, and the like, but who is not licensed to plead in court in criminal cases.

Palais-Égalité: In the 1780s the Duc d'Orléans built the Palais-Royal, an enclosure of elegant buildings with ground-floor shopping arcades, to surround the extensive gardens of his family's Paris mansion, and opened it to the public. It was temporarily renamed during the Revolution to follow republican fashion. Though quiet today, in the eighteenth and nineteenth centuries the Palais-Royal was the center of racy, fashionable social life, chic shopping, and expensive debauchery.

Peace officer: A police official with powers and responsibilities lying somewhere between those of the inspectors and those of the commissaires.

Police: The duties of the police of eighteenth-century Paris extended far beyond the prevention and investigation of crime and the maintenance of public order. Essentially city administrators, they supervised all kinds of public affairs that today, in a large European or American city, would be managed by various Departments of Health, Sanitation, Public Welfare, and even Public Morals.

Republican calendar or French Revolutionary calendar: Used officially in France from 1793 to 1809. It consisted of twelve months with three ten-day weeks in each, and five additional festival days (six in leap years) completing the calendar. The republican year began on September 22 of the Gregorian calendar and was dated from September 22, 1792.

Section: One of forty-eight administrative districts of Paris, consisting of a few square blocks in the heart of the city, and a wider area in the more sparsely populated outer quarters. The sections were created in 1790 to replace the twenty-four districts of the prerevolutionary regime. Not equivalent to the modern arrondissements.

Thermidor: The eleventh month of the French Revolutionary calendar, corresponding to July 20–August 19 of the Christian calendar. Also a general term for the events of 9–11 Thermidor, Year II (July 27–29, 1794), which resulted in the overthrow of Robespierre and the Jacobin government and the beginnings of the political reaction that led to the establishment of the Directory a year later.

Ventôse: Sixth month of the French Revolutionary calendar, corresponding to February 19–March 20 of the Christian calendar.

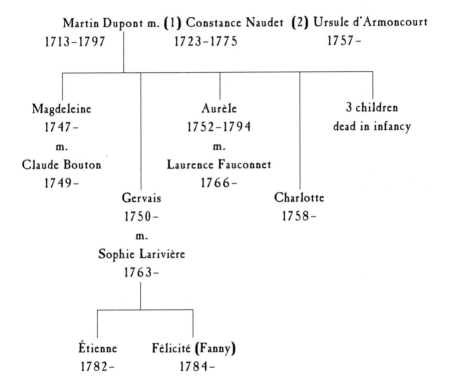

Martin Dupont m. (1) Constance Naudet (2) Ursule d'Armoncourt
1713–1797   1723–1775   1757–

Magdeleine
1747–
m.
Claude Bouton
1749–

Aurèle
1752–1794
m.
Laurence Fauconnet
1766–

3 children
dead in infancy

Gervais
1750–
m.
Sophie Larivière
1763–

Charlotte
1758–

Étienne
1782–

Félicité (Fanny)
1784–

A TREASURY
of REGRETS

1

16 Ventôse, Year V of the Republic
(March 6, 1797)

Since the twenty-fourth of Frimaire, Aristide Ravel had dreamed at least a dozen times of the guillotine.

This time it was Mathieu. He saw Mathieu as he always did, as he had last seen him, hands bound behind his back, waiting in the rain in the center of the Place de la Révolution. They called it the Place de la Concorde now—Harmony Square—but for those who had known Paris three or four years ago, in 1793 and 1794, it would forever remain the Place de la Révolution, the place of the scaffold.

Sometimes, he thought, lying wide awake in the dark, your dreams were bizarre or grotesque, altogether divorced from reality; at other times they reflected a fantastic, distorted version of your everyday existence. This dream had been neither. It had played the scene as he had remembered it far too often over the course of the past three and a half years, not a word or movement out of place.

Five carts—four for the living and one for the dead. One cart bringing up the rear for Valazé, who had had the supreme impertinence to stab himself in the very hall of the Revolutionary Tribunal as the sentence of death was read out, as if denying the right of the Republic to take his life. Four carts for the living, for the twenty-one who had not thought to smuggle a dagger into the Tribunal, who had clung to the faint hope of acquittal.

Mathieu had known better. He had never been such a starry-eyed and earnest optimist as some of the others with whom he was to die, had always had the saving grace of a gentle cynicism and a sharp and roguish sense of humor. He was still making jokes when they sent him to his death. Though Aristide could not hear the words he spoke on the long journey beneath a bleak, chilly sky, he could see the smile on Mathieu's face and the feverish sparkle in his eyes. Was he jesting for the sake of keeping up his companions' courage, or his own? One or two of them smiled with him, even as the guillotine loomed into view through the fine October rain, even as the carts swayed to a halt and the executioner's assistants called their names and sorted them into a line, the most famous toward the end, to please the crowd.

Mathieu was sixth in the line, small fry among men like Bishop Fauchet, Vergniaud, Brissot. Perhaps the careful arrangement of the order in which they were to die had been the subject of his final jest. A glance up at the guillotine, at the thing that had, with a muted rattle and thud, just devoured Sillery, and then Mathieu turned to the man beside him and murmured a few words that made them both smile for an instant.

Thud. Two.

Mathieu had not looked about him since they arrived in the square, he in the executioner's cart, Aristide following. Then at last, perhaps sensing his time was ebbing fast, Mathieu glanced over his shoulder toward the watching crowd. Their eyes met.

Thud.

Three.

What do you say to your oldest friend when they are the last words you will ever exchange?

In the midst of the staring crowd, of course, and with fifteen feet between them, they could say nothing. Perhaps there was nothing to be said. Aristide saw Mathieu's lips move, murmuring a few words; then Mathieu merely gave him a quick grin, and the slightest of nods, and turned away, but not before Aristide saw him swallow hard.

Four.

A pool of blood had already collected under the scaffold, and a muddy crimson rivulet trickled away between the cobbles, dissolving beneath the pattering rain.

And suddenly Mathieu was at the head of the line, and above him an assistant executioner was guiding a man up the steep steps while another heaved a bucketful of water over the seesaw-plank. A third, with the list in his hand, approached Mathieu, reached for his elbow.

Aristide turned away, suddenly tasting acid bile at the back of his throat, and shouldered his way past those behind him. A moment later he heard the blade fall once again—*five*—and he increased his pace, running almost through the fringes of the crowd toward the stony road that led out to the Champs-Élysées—anything to avoid hearing the sound of the blade as it fell for the sixth time.

He had walked blindly for an hour through the meadows until he was nearly at the barrier, as the rain thinned out to a drizzle. It was only then that he had wondered if, at the last instant, Mathieu had glanced over his shoulder again, searching for a friend, and found no one.

He woke on the morning of the sixteenth of Ventôse, well before dawn. He had not dreamed of Mathieu's death for months, and had hoped that finally he was free of it. Rising at last, he threw on his clothes in the gloom before the servant girl could arrive with the usual candle and jug of hot water, and spent an hour walking aimlessly as he had on that rainy morning three and a half years before, wrapped in dark thoughts and memories.

According to the old calendar, it was early March, almost spring, well into the new year 1797; but there was little cheer in the narrow back streets of the Right Bank, where the poor felt the bite of poverty grow ever harsher while the nouveaux-riches of the Directory squandered their fortunes at the opulent cafés, gaming dens, and brothels of the Palais-Égalité a few streets away. Paris, lying beneath heavy clouds for days on end, seemed washed with charcoal gray.

At a few minutes to eight, as the lamplighters snuffed the last of the oil lamps that hung from ropes stretched from house to house, he wandered toward Rue Traversine and the police commissariat of the Section de la Butte-des-Moulins. Inspector Didier, meticulously writing a report at the raised desk in the antechamber where local folk waited to report a crime, air a grievance, or file a complaint with Commissaire Brasseur, cast him a sour glance.

"He's not in yet."

Aristide raised an eyebrow. Commissaires were supposed to be more or less on duty from eight in the morning to ten in the evening, and Brasseur was ordinarily quite punctual.

"Where *is* the commissaire, if you please?" demanded a pale, black-clad young woman who was seated on one of the empty benches, a small bundle at her feet.

"He'll be in, citizeness," said Didier, without glancing up again from his report. "Any time now."

"But it's quarter past eight."

"His mother-in-law's been visiting from the country," Aristide said, moving toward the young woman. "I gather it's not the jolliest of times for Brasseur."

She turned. "Well, it's not the jolliest time for us, either!" Scowling, she abruptly checked herself instead of continuing in the same acrimonious fashion. "Pardon me. Your colleague here"—she cast a scorching glance at Didier—"already knows why I'm here, and why I want an interview with the commissaire."

"This fellow's no colleague of mine," said Didier, waspishly. "He has no official standing here; do you, Ravel?"

Aristide leaned against the wall, folded his arms, and looked at him, without bothering to reply. Didier and he had always got along about as well as a pair of tomcats.

The young woman examined Aristide more thoroughly, taking in his shabby black suit, well-worn top boots, lank dark hair threaded with gray. "I suppose you must be a police spy," she said at last, coldly. "I've heard of people like you."

"I'm an agent of the police, citizeness."

"Same thing, isn't it?" Didier remarked.

Aristide suppressed a sharp retort; he did not care to satisfy Didier by taking offense. Although most people would insist a police spy was what Aristide was, he detested the term, which for a century and a half had been a synonym for "informer." He had made a modestly profitable career of investigating matters, usually criminal in nature, when the mood took him, and if many of those matters were investigated on behalf of the police, it was because Brasseur was a friend and trusted his competence.

He turned his back to Didier and added, to the young woman, "The two are not necessarily one and the same. I happen to be a friend of the commissaire."

That was a jab at Didier, who was no friend to Brasseur. But because he was the senior inspector at the Butte-des-Moulins section commissariat, Didier (who had always been of the opinion that it should have been he and not Brasseur who was elected commissaire back in 1790) could not simply be discharged. Didier would never understand that his complete lack of imagination was what would keep him—unless he made powerful friends—from rising higher in the ranks of the police. No doubt he could, however, out of sheer spite, accuse Brasseur of royalism or some such ludicrous offense if he were ever to be sacked, and cause Brasseur a great deal of unnecessary and undeserved trouble.

Didier shut his teeth on a snappish retort as Brasseur flung open the door and strode inside, shaking droplets of mist from his hat and broad shoulders. "My faith," he announced to no one in particular, "I've had enough of that old cow! If she doesn't go back to Nevers pretty soon, I'll murder her myself!" His glance alighted on Aristide and he grinned. "Morning, Ravel. Don't take me at my word."

Aristide nodded a good morning as Brasseur turned to Didier. "All right, what should I know about?"

They disappeared into the corridor that led to Brasseur's office. "They shouldn't be long," Aristide said to the young woman. "Brasseur wasn't here yesterday, so—"

"I *know* he wasn't here yesterday," she interrupted him impatiently. "That's why I'm here now. If he'd been here as he's supposed to be, perhaps none of this nonsense would have happened."

"What nonsense?"

"That inspector," she said, with a glance down the corridor, "made a dreadful mistake yesterday, and I've come to speak to the commissaire in the hope that he can clear it all up."

"I'm sure he can," said Aristide. "Brasseur's a just, conscientious man."

She looked dubious but said nothing more. They waited in silence, as peddlers raucously cried their wares outside in the street, until Didier returned from Brasseur's office. Aristide gestured her to her feet. "Come on, citizeness. Second door on the left."

"The commissaire didn't say anything about seeing the citizeness now," Didier snapped as they passed.

"That wouldn't be because you didn't mention it to him, would it?" said Aristide, without pausing. He opened Brasseur's door without bothering to knock and ushered the young woman inside. "Brasseur, this citizeness claims she needs your help. Since she says it's something to do with Didier, I imagine she's right."

Brasseur sighed and rubbed his eyes. "All right, citizeness, sit down and tell me what's the matter." Settling himself more comfortably in the hard wooden chair at his desk, which creaked under his solid weight, he eyed her with an inquisitive scowl.

"I suppose it's in one of the reports in front of you," she said, taking a chair. "A charge of poisoning against a girl named Jeannette Moineau. She's one of our servants and the whole thing is absurd. Of course she didn't poison anybody."

"Poisoning?" He leafed through the reports. "Right, here it is. 'Took the citizeness Jeannette Moineau, domestic official, age nineteen, employed at the house of the citizen Dupont on Rue des Moulins, into custody to answer charges of eight counts of poisoning' . . . *eight counts?* . . . 'and to await interrogation by the justice of the peace. Complaint against the said citizeness Moineau lodged by the citizeness Magdeleine Dupont, wife of Bouton.' Hmm. A couple of statements . . . not much here. Why don't you tell me more, citizeness? First of all, who are you?"

"Laurence Dupont. Citizeness Bouton is my sister-in-law."

"Dupont, Dupont," Brasseur muttered. He rose and ran a finger along one of the shelves of cardboard folders behind him. "Yes, here we are. Martin Dupont . . . man of finance, residing at the house belonging to him on Rue des Moulins, by all accounts a solid citizen, pays his taxes, police know nothing against him . . ."

"My father-in-law. But he's just died, so my brother-in-law Gervais Dupont is now head of the family."

"What's this about eight counts of poisoning, citizeness?" Brasseur inquired.

"It's completely ridiculous," said Laurence. "My father-in-law died two days ago, on Saturday the fourth . . . the fourteenth, I mean," she hastily corrected herself, and darted a quick glance at Brasseur to see if her use of the Christian calendar had irritated him. He said nothing and she continued. "He died on the fourteenth of Ventôse, in the evening, of a violent colic. Then something we ate at dinner yesterday, the fifteenth, had evidently gone bad, and nearly all of us who dined were taken a little ill. One of our dinner guests, a surgeon, said sometimes unbalanced servants might try to poison their employers; something of the sort had happened in his family once, years ago."

"Don't you trust your servants?" Aristide inquired.

"As much as anyone does, but the kitchenmaid—Jeannette—had only been with us a month. So Citizen Hébert, the surgeon, told us she ought to be investigated. Then my sister-in-law Magdeleine—Citizeness Bouton—seized on the notion that Jeannette had not only poisoned us, but also murdered old Martin. They searched Jeannette's room and right away found some sort of powdery, gritty, light-colored stuff in her apron pocket, and a little packet of the same stuff in her drawer. Citizen Hébert thought it could be arsenic, and of course Magdeleine was so worked up she was ready to believe him, even though Citizen Hébert is really something of a fool." She paused for breath and Brasseur glanced in Aristide's direction.

"So the citizeness sent for the police?" Aristide said.

Laurence nodded. "Yes. Though Maître Frochot advised against it, since it was all very circumstantial and he thought it was probably just tainted food, but Hébert insisted."

"Who's Frochot?"

"A family friend, a notary. He's the Old Man's—he *was* the Old Man's legal adviser and man of affairs."

" 'The Old Man?' " Brasseur echoed her.

"My father-in-law—Martin Dupont. 'The Old Man' is what Gervais calls him. Citizen Commissaire, this whole affair has been blown completely out of proportion. We ate something that didn't agree with us, and Martin must have eaten it previously, and died of it. I've seen enough of this maidservant to be quite sure she's no more than an ordinary, honest, stupid country girl. The thought that she could poison anyone is ludicrous. I doubt she would even know what arsenic is."

Brasseur leaned forward on his desk, interlocking his fingers, and fixed Laurence with a hard stare. "So you insist no one deliberately poisoned anybody?"

"Of course."

"Are you absolutely sure, then, citizeness, that this was just a bout of tainted food?"

She blinked. "But it must have been. If you knew the family, you couldn't remotely imagine any of them poisoning someone."

"I understand you're reluctant to think this could be a case of murder," he told her, "but do you honestly believe that all of you, including old Citizen Dupont, managed to eat the same bad food, on two different days, and that somehow the food he ate killed him, while what the rest of you ate—a day later, when the food would have spoiled even more—only gave you a stomachache?" He continued to stare at her, unsmiling. "Citizeness, this may be more serious than you think it is, or than you want to believe. I want you to try very hard to remember what you all ate for twenty-four hours before Citizen Dupont fell ill. On the thirteenth, did he eat anything that could have made him ill, and that none of you ate? And then did any of you take the same dish at dinner on the fifteenth? Something that might have spoiled?"

Laurence frowned and was silent for a moment, while Aristide glanced with an inquisitively raised eyebrow at Brasseur. "Well, citizeness?" Brasseur said at last.

"You're right," she admitted. "It goes beyond belief that the Old Man could have died from something we all shared. It's a horrible thought, but . . . how long would poison take to make you mortally ill? Less than a day?"

"No more than a couple of hours, probably," Aristide said, "if he seemed healthy at breakfast time and the dose was large enough to kill him by nightfall."

"Then it couldn't have been something he'd eaten the day before. . . ." Laurence raised her head and gazed at Brasseur, and Aristide saw, for the first time, real fear in her eyes. "We all ate the same thing that day—Friday, I mean—cabbage soup and braised skate, which was fresh from the fish market. It must have been something in his breakfast on Saturday morning, the day he died, and he only took porridge, and coffee with milk . . . nothing that had been kept, and could have gone bad. . . ."

"Was he the only one who ate porridge for breakfast?"

Laurence nodded, as if she did not trust her voice.

"Can you explain what Citizen Hébert found?" Brasseur inquired. "White powder, at the bottom of the girl's pocket?"

"Well, we don't even know what it is," Laurence said, with a flash of her former asperity. "It could be anything. Maybe it's salt. Or maybe Jeannette had a stomachache last week and went to the apothecary for a remedy. Why not ask her what it was?"

"Oh, you can be sure I'll do that," Brasseur said. "Didier doesn't mention this white powder in his report, by the way."

"Citizen Hébert took it with him for safekeeping before the police arrived. He should be coming here with it soon—"

"After a whole night in which he, or anyone else, had the opportunity to doctor it as he pleased?" Aristide said. "That's completely irregular, citizeness. It should have been given to the police right away."

"I did protest, you know," Laurence retorted, turning toward him, "but who in that house ever pays attention to the poor relation?"

"I thought you said you were the late Citizen Dupont's daughter-in-law."

"I am. I'm his younger son's widow. I'm also a distant cousin and the poorest of poor relations, so I have nowhere else to go. Are you satisfied, citizen?"

"Oh, please, continue."

They inspected each other, stonily, each taking the other's measure. Aristide knew she was unimpressed by what she saw: a tall, thin, unsmiling young man, not so young really, no longer in his first youth, but at thirty-eight not quite middle-aged. He cut an indifferent figure, he knew, in his shabby black costume, the telltale sign of a man of the professional classes who, for whatever reason, could afford only one suit of clothes.

Laurence Dupont had an interesting face, he thought, though the plain black mourning gown she wore did little to soften her looks. She might have been moderately pretty at sixteen, in the freshness of youth; but now, at about thirty, her dark brows were too heavy and too sharply angled, the unsmiling mouth was too wide, the jaw too strong for beauty. Yet it was a face of character, lively with a wry and bitter intelligence.

Something about her seemed familiar, though he could not guess how they might have met before, except by passing each other in the street. Perhaps, he thought, it was her manner—something about the gaze, alert and intense, that reminded him of someone, or the slender, restless hands that clutched at the bundle she had brought with her.

"That's all, I suppose," Laurence said, turning back once more to Brasseur. "Magdeleine lodged a complaint and your inspector out there came over with a couple of others, and asked silly, useless questions of everyone and finally took Jeannette away with him. Oh, and he took all the dishes and cooking pots from yesterday's dinner and made Magdeleine lock them in a cupboard, and said someone would be over this morning to fetch them away and look for arsenic in the soup tureen." She paused, frowned, and continued. "Citizen Commissaire, it's probably not my place to say it, but that inspector is an ass."

"You needn't tell me that, citizeness," Brasseur said, with a sigh. "Dautry!"

"Commissaire?" said his secretary, flashing Aristide a grin as he thrust his head out the door that led to his own tiny office.

"We have a girl in custody?"

"Yes, Commissaire. Since last evening. Kitchenmaid suspected of poisoning the family."

"Send Didier in here, will you?"

2

"Only Didier," Aristide said as Dautry hurried down the corridor toward the front chamber, "would think a locked cupboard was sufficient to hold evidence overnight, and that in a house where obviously at least one person wants to cast blame on another."

Brasseur grimaced but said nothing as he set a fresh sheet of paper on his blotter and sharpened a quill. "Citizeness, we can look at the section records, of course, but perhaps you'd tell me just who are the members of this household. The residents are you, and your sister-in-law and her husband, Citizen Bouton . . . any children?"

"No," she said. "No children."

"Then there's Citizen Gervais Dupont, your brother-in-law?"

"Yes. I don't know if you're aware that Gervais is the actor and playwright known as Hauteroche."

"Hauteroche!" Aristide echoed her. Hauteroche had been a leading player at the Comédie-Française for the past decade and a half, perhaps more famous for his interpretations of Molière's characters than for his own efforts at authorship. A few years ago he had left the Comédie in order to form his own company in a newly renovated theater by the boulevards.

"Well, well," said Brasseur, adding a note. "Gervais Dupont, called Hauteroche."

"And his two children, Étienne and Félicité."

"Two minor children . . . that right? Yes? What about their mother? Is she his wife, or . . . ?" He paused delicately. Long considered godless vagabonds, professional performers in France had officially been forbidden the sacraments until 1790. Most, in past centuries, had never bothered to secure the necessary dispensations—obtainable through confession to a sympathetic priest and a few discreet bribes—that would have allowed them to marry with the blessing of the Church, and so the immorality of actors had become notorious.

"Sophie Larivière, the actress," said Laurence. "They're married. But she's been touring in the South for weeks; she can't have had anything to do with this."

Brasseur nodded and continued to write. "Go on."

"Citizeness Charlotte Dupont, Gervais and Magdeleine's sister, and Citizeness Ursule Dupont, née Armoncourt. Ursule is Martin's widow—Gervais and Magdeleine and Charlotte's, er, stepmother. Martin married for a second time rather late in life, and married a woman half his age."

"Well, old gentlemen will have their fancies, won't they?" Brasseur said, with a tolerant smile. "And you are Citizeness Laurence Dupont."

"Born Laurence Fauconnet."

"Any children?"

"No."

"And that's all of the family?"

"I imagine you ought to include Citizen Jullien, my late father-in-law's secretary, who lives in the house. He also tutors the children."

Brasseur nodded. "Servants?"

"Thérèse Huteau, the cook; Zélie Nicolay, the chambermaid; Antoine Bernardin, man of all work. Citizeness Chuquet, who came in to lay out the Old Man, she lives in the quarter."

"Yes, she's well-known in the neighborhood," said Brasseur. "Did you have her in to nurse Citizen Dupont?"

"No, he died before we needed an extra hand, and there was little she could have done. We only hired her to lay him out."

"And lastly Citizeness Moineau, of course . . . kitchenmaid and maid of all work?"

"Yes, that's everyone," said Laurence. "Commissaire, may I go, then, and see Jeannette? I've brought some warm clothes for her, and a little food."

Brasseur gestured to her to stay seated. "Let's hear what Didier has to say first."

Didier arrived shortly and drew himself up in front of Brasseur's desk, arms hanging stiffly at his sides and jaw clenched. Aristide leaned more comfortably against the wall, hands in his pockets, as Brasseur cleared his throat.

"All right, Didier, what's all this about poisoning on Rue des Moulins?"

"You have my report, citizen, and the witnesses' statements."

"How about a few details? The citizeness here," Brasseur said, "claims this girl was no poisoner."

"Citizeness Bouton accused the maidservant of poisoning the household, and causing the death of Citizen Dupont, in order to distract them while she stole certain items of value," said Didier. "The items were found in the maid's room before we arrived."

Brasseur glanced at the next page of the report and looked at Laurence. "A gold watch and some small items of gold and silver. You didn't say anything about stealing. Where would a servant girl get gold or silver jewelry, if she didn't steal it?"

Aristide saw her jaw set at a stubborn angle. "I didn't speak of it," she said, "because I refuse to believe Jeannette is any more capable of stealing from an employer than she is of poisoning the soup. Commissaire, the kitchenmaid's room doesn't even have a lock on the door. Nothing could be easier than to go into Jeannette's room and put those things, and the powder, in the first place anyone would look!"

"That's none of my affair," Didier declared, at a sour glance from Brasseur. "We were called in, we questioned the witnesses, and were presented with credible evidence of wrongdoing, and on the basis of the evidence I took the girl into custody. She can explain herself before the justice of the peace."

"Death of the devil," Brasseur muttered. He took up the statements and read through them before raising his head and glancing again at Didier. "All right, that's enough. Tell Chesnais and Thomas to wait for me out front. Oh, and fetch Dr. Prunelle and tell him to meet us at the house of Citizen Dupont, on Rue des Moulins, opposite the sign of the Great Turk."

"Commissaire." Didier inclined his head in the slightest of nods and left the room.

"You're going to see for yourself, Commissaire?" Laurence asked.

"Yes, yes, obviously Didier's made a botch of things." Brasseur rose with a sigh. "Citizeness, I'm going to talk to your maid first. You come along and give her what you brought." He led the way to the lockup at the back of the commissariat, where disruptive drunkards were usually held until they sobered up. The room, bare except for a straw mattress, a stool, and a bucket, was unlit and cold. A girl lay huddled on the mattress, shivering beneath a tattered, dirty blanket and a thin shawl.

"Citizeness, I'm Commissaire Brasseur. Stand up, please."

She scrambled to her feet and bobbed a curtsy, then stood blinking and rubbing at the tears on her face with the back of her hand. Aristide looked her over. According to the police report, she was nineteen years old, but no doubt a poor diet and hard farmwork in her childhood had left her thin and undersized; he would have taken her for no more than fourteen. Nevertheless, she might have been pretty if it were not for the dark circles of exhaustion beneath eyes reddened and puffy from crying. Another uneducated country girl come to find work in Paris, he immediately thought: merely one of the thousands who were scraping together a tiny dowry, and imagined they would find an easier and more lively existence in the city than in the endless dull drudgery of peasant life. And like most of them, she seemed as ignorant, transparent, and eager to please her betters as a child of five or six.

"Your name, citizeness?" Brasseur said.

"Marie-Jeannette Moineau, monsieur—citizen," she said, with a nervous glance at his tricolor sash.

"And what have you to say for yourself about all this?"

She glanced from him to Aristide, and then to Laurence, standing behind them in the doorway. "I—I don't know, citizen."

"You don't know? What don't you know about?"

"I don't understand. The mistress and everybody kept shouting at me, and saying I'd gone and done something to the dinner, and I don't know what they meant. I didn't do nothing I shouldn't have."

"The mistress," Brasseur echoed her, with a glance at the list of names Laurence had given him. "You mean Citizeness Dupont, the old man's wife?"

"Oh no, she doesn't do any housekeeping. Thérèse, that's the cook, she told me Citizeness Dupont was an aristo before the Revolution," she added, with a hint of pride. "Aristos don't work. It's Citizeness Bouton who runs the household."

"Citizeness Moineau, your mistress has brought a very grave charge against you. A charge of poisoning, theft, and murder. Do you understand? What do you have to say for yourself?"

"But I don't know what you mean, monsieur—citizen."

"Wasn't it you who prepared the family's dinner yesterday?"

She stared at him. "No, monsieur. Leastways, I did a little, but it was the mistress—Citizeness Bouton—and Madame Laurence who cooked dinner, 'cause I fell asleep. They cooked the soup and dressed the duck and got it into the oven to roast. I just peeled some potatoes and turnips, and basted the duck once or twice, and laid the table."

"Citizeness Dupont," Brasseur said, turning to Laurence, "Citizeness Bouton's statement claims the maid cooked the meal."

"Then Magdeleine was embroidering the truth," Laurence said. "Jeannette did a little, just as she says, but she certainly didn't cook all of it. She had helped to nurse my father-in-law the day before, and then kept vigil all night beside his body. And then in the morning, because the cook had the vapors, Jeannette was expected to return to the kitchen and provide breakfast and prepare dinner! Of course she fell asleep at the kitchen table. Magdeleine and I prepared dinner, because Jeannette wouldn't have been any use in such a condition—she'd have left everything to burn, probably—and she assisted us when she woke up. We were in and out, all three of us, with various errands."

"So you couldn't have noticed whether or not the maidservant slipped something in the soup?"

"No," she admitted. "Nobody could have noticed."

"So you laid the table," Brasseur said to Jeannette, "and then I suppose you served the soup? What kind of soup was it?"

"It was cabbage soup, monsieur, what they have every day for the first course. I served it in the tureen, and then I went back to the kitchen and Citizeness Chuquet, the woman who came in to lay out the poor old gentleman's body proper, she had a bit of soup with me and Zélie and Antoine in the kitchen."

"The other servants," Laurence interposed.

"The same soup?" Aristide said when Brasseur merely gestured to Jeannette to go on. "From the same kettle?"

Jeannette shook her head. "No, citizen. There was two pots of soup."

"One for the family and one for the servants," said Laurence. "Magdeleine made fresh stock for our own soup, with meat in it, and used the old leftover stock in the pantry, with some vegetables, for the servants. She said it was quite good enough still."

"Two pots," Brasseur repeated. "So somebody might have dropped something into one kettle and not the other. Now Inspector Didier locked up the dirty dishes, correct?"

Jeannette nodded. "Yes, citizen, they was still in the scullery, where I put them when we cleared the table after the main course. Zélie and me, I mean. We weren't finished with our dinner yet. And then Madame—I mean Citizeness Bouton—she came in with the others shouting all kinds of things, and saying they'd been poisoned. I tried to tell them there wasn't nothing in the dinner that could have been off, no undercooked meat or raw eggs or mayonnaises or such, but nobody listened."

"Didn't your mistress say to you," Brasseur continued, glancing through the report, "that she could smell burned arsenic in the kitchen?"

"She did, m'sieur," Jeannette said, "but I don't know what that is. I didn't put nothing on the fire but another stick of wood." From

Aristide's position he could see her eyes were wet with tears, whether of fear, or frustration at her ignorance and helplessness, he could not guess.

"Brasseur," he said, "do you think this Citizeness Bouton has conducted so many scientific experiments that she can immediately recognize the fumes of burned arsenic in the air?" He saw Laurence's lips curve in a small, bitter smile. "Personally, it's been a long time since I've attended a test for arsenic, and I don't really recall what it smells like."

Brasseur grunted. "No, I wasn't putting too much trust in her scientific knowledge. Citizeness Dupont, was a doctor called in?"

"No," said Laurence. "You'd think they would fetch the doctor, wouldn't you? But they'd already paid a doctor to see to the Old Man the day before—not that it did any good—and I imagine they didn't want to pay another fee for what was no worse than a stomachache. They did call in Citizen Thierry, the apothecary, who lives nearby."

"And what did he have to say about it?"

"He examined all the plates and the tureen, just as the inspector did, and stirred up the ashes in the kitchen hearth, and didn't seem to be able to find a thing out of place. And it's very odd indeed," she added, "that he, of all people, couldn't make out any smell of burned arsenic in the kitchen. Don't you think it would be his business to know exactly what it smelled like?"

"So he couldn't find anything the matter?"

Laurence shrugged. "We did all have stomach cramps that afternoon, and Gervais was doubled over in misery, but Citizen Thierry didn't discover anything wrong in the kitchen. Magdeleine insisted the man must be incompetent. All he did was to ask Jeannette if she knew anything about it."

"What did you tell the citizen apothecary?" Brasseur asked, turning to Jeannette, who had sunk onto the stool and was hugging herself, hunched over, eyes darting fearfully from one person to another.

"I said as I didn't know anything about it, or why they was all shouting at me. And then they all shouted louder, and started asking me questions all together, and called me wicked names, and I didn't know what they meant, and—and I was so tired, m'sieur. . . ." Her voice trailed off and again Aristide caught the glint of tears in her eyes.

"She burst into tears and had a fit of hysterics," said Laurence sharply, "as anyone might have in such a situation. I took her into her room, gave her some water, and left her there to collect herself. I suppose I ought to have stayed with her," she continued, her voice softening a trifle, "but there was such an uproar in the house, what with stomachaches, and Gervais declaring he was dying, and Magdeleine telling all the neighbors how we had been poisoned, that I thought I'd better try to keep matters from falling into complete chaos."

Brasseur sighed. "Oh, lord, anything for a quiet life . . . all right, Citizeness Dupont, we'll go along to your house now and look into it."

"If I may ask you one favor, Commissaire . . . don't tell them I came to you. Magdeleine thinks I've gone to the baker and the market, nothing more."

"As you like, citizeness."

They left her with Jeannette under the watchful eye of a junior inspector and returned to the antechamber of the commissariat, where two black-clad inspectors awaited them. Aristide said little as they walked out to Rue Traversine. How many members of the Dupont household, he wondered, clung to the expedient theory that their kitchenmaid had attempted to murder them? And how many others might already sense the ugly web of suspicion, distrust, and fear that would be closing in around them?

3

The Section de la Butte-des-Moulins encompassed the long rectangle of the Palais-Égalité and the maze of narrow, congested streets and alleys just west of it and north of the former church of St. Roch. They strode along Rue Traversine through the crowds of shouting peddlers, hurrying pedestrians, and lumbering farm carts, one driver cracking his whip and swearing at a bony horse that had collapsed in the shafts and probably would never rise again.

At Rue des Moulins, a linen-draper's shop boasted an enormous sign in the shape of a robed and turbaned Turk. Opposite the shop stood a nondescript five-story bourgeois house, all its curtains drawn to indicate a household in mourning. The house, probably a century and a half old, was a jumble of architectural styles, with seventeenth-century timbering on one side and more-recent masonry and stucco on the other. Though the stucco was weathered, discolored, and chipped, betraying a certain lack of care, the house seemed large and solid.

Aristide and Dautry paused a moment for coffee from a hawker on the corner, grimacing at the taste of what was probably one-fourth coffee and three-fourths chicory and roasted barley, with yesterday's milk. A few minutes later Dr. Prunelle, the police surgeon, appeared. Avoiding the aggressive coffee seller, who tried to wave a steaming pewter cup under his nose, he straightened his wig, stifled a yawn, and shook hands with Brasseur. "Morning, Brasseur, Ravel. You're up early."

"Duty calls," Aristide said.

Prunelle smothered another yawn. "Oh, indeed, though you might have allowed me my sleep, Brasseur," he added, over his shoulder. "A corpse isn't going anywhere."

Brasseur eyed him sadly. "Regulations. The judge has to interrogate the suspect within twenty-four hours of our taking him in for questioning, and this particular suspect was detained last night. I daresay the suspect is innocent, but I don't like the sound of things, and since that fool Didier's set this damned process in motion, we'd better see if there really was foul play here."

"So what is it today?"

"Poisoning. Half a dozen sick to their stomachs, one dead."

"Poisoning!" Prunelle exclaimed with relish, immediately looking more awake. "Well, that'll make for an interesting change, won't it?"

Brasseur cast him a dubious look but said nothing as he pulled the bell-chain at the front door of the house opposite. A moment later a slender, handsome young man of thirty-odd, dressed in a respectable, though modest, suit of clothes in brown and fawn, answered the bell and stared at Brasseur, large, solid, and official in his black suit and tricolor sash.

"Citizen," Brasseur began, "we've come to conduct further investigations into the matter of poisoning that—"

The young man straightened. "Oh, the fuss last night. That way, citizen. You should talk to Citizen Dupont or Citizeness Bouton, I suppose. She'll be in the kitchen." He pointed the way and Aristide noticed the black armband he wore.

"Are you a relative?" he inquired.

The young man shook his head. "Charles Jullien. Secretary to the old master, Martin Dupont. Died day before yesterday. Citizeness Bouton is clamoring now that *he* was poisoned, too . . . but I suppose that's what you're here about?"

Jullien led them through a whitewashed foyer with a single high-backed wooden bench to a severely clean and spartan salon, ornamented only by a clavichord, a pair of dour family portraits, and an intricate, wrought-metal crucifix. A tiny fire smoldered in the hearth. The salon opened onto another, smaller room with an empty dining-table covered by a rough linen cloth, where shelves of glazed earthen-ware jugs and shining brass chargers ornamented the plaster walls. "I'll fetch Citizeness Bouton for you," he told Brasseur, and hurried away.

The door to the foyer opened an instant later and Aristide turned to discover a girl of fourteen or fifteen staring at them, round-eyed. "Are you the police again?" she demanded, with a glance at Brasseur's tri-color sash. "Because you need to find out who poisoned Grandfather right away, or else we'll never get any more servants."

"Don't you think the kitchenmaid did it?" Aristide said, taking a step toward her. She was a pretty child, dainty in a high-waisted white gown whose former sash, probably blue to match her eyes, had been exchanged for one in black taffeta.

"No, I don't!"

"Why not?"

The girl shrugged. "She's much too stupid to do anything like that. She doesn't have the brains to poison anybody."

Aristide exchanged a glance with Brasseur. He suspected the girl was right. What would an ignorant, unlettered peasant like Jeannette know of poisons beyond the rustic ones of field and forest? Hemlock or nightshade she might recognize, but arsenic, never.

"What did you mean by 'we'll never get any more servants'?" Brasseur asked her.

"Oh, Antoine and Zélie ran off last night, after the inspector left! They said they weren't going to stay here and be poisoned. So Thérèse is all alone in the kitchen, and Aunt Laurence and Aunt Magdeleine have to help her with the cooking, and Aunt Magdeleine is furious!" She looked delighted at the prospect.

A lean, middle-aged woman, dressed in an unbecoming gown of rusty black, swept into the room and glared suspiciously at the assembly of police. "Citizen Commissaire? I am Magdeleine Bouton. I suppose you're here to fetch away the dishes? Come this way, if you please."

"I'm here for more than that, citizeness," Brasseur interrupted her as she turned toward the door. "I understand the master of the house died day before yesterday, under suspicious circumstances. We'll have to look into that first of all."

"But we were *all* poisoned," she said, indignant. "To one degree or another. We're barely recovered, as you can see. We haven't any dishes left over from Father's last meal, but the plates from yesterday—"

"You look in good health to me, citizeness," Brasseur said, looking her up and down. "So does the young demoiselle here. Nobody else dead, or rolling about in agony on the floor?"

"Citizen Commissaire, I'll have you know that yesterday afternoon, shortly after dinner, I had a violent stomachache, and my brother Gervais was bent over a basin for an hour at least, sick as a dog."

"Papa looked *disgusting*!" the girl chimed in.

"If that's not poisoning," Magdeleine concluded, with a baleful glance at her niece, "I don't know what is."

Aristide covertly looked her over. Magdeleine Bouton seemed perfectly well, though she was tense and angry, which did not improve her appearance, and her mourning gown did not suit her sallow complexion. She was perhaps fifty, with gray-streaked hair, sharp, intelligent eyes, and a tight mouth.

"We'll look into the matter of your father-in-law's death, but are you sure that you yourself didn't just eat a bad bit of fish, citizeness," Brasseur continued, "or something undercooked?"

"Certainly not. My niece"—she gestured to the girl—"she noticed something strange in the soup. Something gritty. And so did I."

"I noticed it, too," said a tall, good-looking man, entering the room in time to hear the last of the exchange. The newcomer, who seemed oddly familiar to Aristide, did look unnaturally pale. An instant later Aristide realized this must be Hauteroche, the actor, whom he had seen half a dozen times, made up and padded in various disguises, on the boards of the Comédie-Française. Stripped of the elaborate makeup he wore in his comic roles, Gervais was about forty-five, sturdily built with a strong profile and a head of wavy dark hair. "And I certainly felt the effects," the actor continued. "I was bent over a basin—"

"Wait a moment!" Brasseur thundered. "You can all have your say, citizens, but first we have to take a look at the late citizen Dupont's remains. If someone would kindly show us where the body's been laid out—"

"I'll show you!" the girl said, and scurried out of the room. Aristide followed her, Brasseur and the others trailing them.

"I'm Félicité Dupont," the girl added, over her shoulder, as she started up the staircase to the first floor, "but you can call me Fanny; everybody does. My papa is Hauteroche, you know," she added with a smirk. "The famous actor. That was him just now. There," she added, pointing down the corridor, as they reached the first-floor landing. "That's Grandfather's room, the door at the end. Step-Grandmamma's with him. Are you going to cut him open to find the poison?"

She grimaced at Prunelle's solemn nod and bobbed a dutiful but coquettish curtsy before speeding down the stairs again. Aristide made a mental note to speak to the girl alone; in his experience, children often noticed things their elders did not, and the girl seemed intelligent enough, if perhaps more than a trifle spoiled and conceited.

Brasseur knocked on the door and then, without waiting for answer or invitation, pulled it open. A slender, fair-haired woman rose to her feet from a chair beside the big bed where the corpse lay in semidarkness.

"What's the meaning of this?" she demanded, scowling, as she attempted to hide rosary beads in the folds of her elegant black gown.

"Police, citizeness," said Brasseur. "You'd be Ursule Dupont, the late citizen's widow, I suppose? I'm afraid you'll have to leave now."

"Leave! I'm keeping vigil beside my husband's body, Inspector."

"Commissaire," Brasseur rumbled, "if you please. And the police surgeon has to take a look at him, so if you'll kindly step outside, citizeness, we'll be about our business." He took Ursule's elbow and politely, but firmly, escorted her out the door.

Dr. Prunelle tut-tutted impatiently and threw open the curtains to flood the room with the thin sunshine of early spring. Aristide joined the doctor as he turned back the sheet that draped the corpse up to the chin. Martin Dupont had been a vigorous man of strong will and character, he thought, studying the gaunt, harsh old face, still forceful in death despite the marks of suffering in the drawn cheeks. The old man, alive, must have been the picture of rude health, wearing his years lightly; he had

the teeth of a man of thirty and a full head of thick, long white hair. Here
was a man who needed no horsehair wig to cover a bald pate.

He squinted at the profile, with its great hawkish beak of a nose,
and recognized traces of Gervais Dupont, though the actor's nose, fortunately for him, was far less pronounced than his father's. He thought
of Gervais, in his middle forties, and estimated his father's age to be
about seventy. "How old was he, do you think?"

"Eighty-four, according to his wife," said Brasseur, returning.

"Eighty-four!"

"A robust old bird," Prunelle said irreverently, echoing Aristide's
thought. "It's rare to live to such an age, but those who do, they're usually tough as shoe-leather. Never see a day's illness beyond a few inevitable aches and pains."

"Not a man to suddenly die of a violent colic?" said Aristide.

"Bah! From the looks of him, he might have lived another five years,
I imagine, or even more. Ravel's quite right, Brasseur; such people don't
suddenly up and die of a stomachache, even from food gone bad. I
wouldn't be surprised if someone did help him along." The doctor
glanced about. "Hmm . . . nothing here to lay him on . . . let's have the
dining-table up here, citizens."

The two inspectors went out. "Know why it's the custom to keep
vigil for a couple of days over a dead body?" Prunelle added. "For fear of
premature burial—just in case the corpse comes to life again. I suppose
if they still look dead after two or three days, then it's safe to hold the funeral. Of course, the scalpel is really the best way to tell; dead bodies
don't bleed, despite the lingering superstition, among some people, that
a murdered man's wounds will bleed if his killer touches his corpse. . . ."

The inspectors returned with the trestles and broad, smoothly planed
planks that, as in many wealthy households, composed a dining-table
that could be dismantled and stored away if the dining salon was wanted
for another purpose. The table set up, they hoisted the old man's body
onto it and drew back.

Prunelle set to work with his scalpel. Aristide hurriedly excused
himself and retreated into the hallway. A freshly dead corpse was one
thing, and he had seen his share of them, but he would have been the

first to confess to a certain squeamishness when confronted with the handiwork of the anatomist.

Brasseur joined him a moment later and beckoned him downstairs to the salon, where Gervais Dupont and Magdeleine Bouton waited impatiently by the meager fire. "All right, all right, citizen," he said, raising a hand as Gervais began to speak, "first things first. Your full names, if you please, for my secretary's notes." He gestured to Dautry, who seated himself in a corner and unobtrusively opened his notebook. "You, citizen?"

"My name is Gervais-Jean-Baptiste Dupont," said the actor, throwing his shoulders back and smoothing his thick, wavy hair. "Though I expect you will know me better," he added complacently, "as Hauteroche."

"I don't have much time to go to the theater myself," said Brasseur, "but I understand you're quite famous, citizen. So this is your family's home? You and your family live here?"

Gervais nodded. "My son and daughter, Étienne and Félicité—you've already met Fanny—and my wife and I. My wife—my wife is out of Paris, however."

"Our extended family lives here," Magdeleine interrupted him impatiently. "Gervais's family; my husband and I; our younger sister, Charlotte, a spinster; our sister-in-law Laurence; and our late father and his wife, or his widow, I should say now. And somebody has tried to poison and rob all of us," she added, glaring at Brasseur, "starting, I shouldn't be surprised, with our poor father! It seems quite clear we've been the victims of a ruthless thief!"

"I'm sorry to hear about your father's death," Brasseur said perfunctorily, "but attempted murder with theft's a serious charge. You still claim your kitchenmaid did it?"

"Certainly I do. Do you take me for a fool? My father was never ill. And yesterday, as soon as we finished our dinner, we could tell something was wrong. Some of us were taken worse than others."

"Like me," Gervais interrupted. "I was—"

"—And I tell you, Commissaire, when I went back into the kitchen, I smelled a distinct odor of burned arsenic in the air!"

"You never suspected your cook of having poisoned you, then?" Aristide said.

"The cook? Of course not. Do give me credit for some intelligence, Citizen Inspector," she told him, drawing herself up and fixing him with a steely glare. He opened his mouth, ready to tell her he was not an official member of the police, but thought better of it. The police customarily wore plain black suits, as he did by habit, but if she had not observed that he wore no tricolor rosette or sash on his own coat as Brasseur and Didier did, then it was none of his affair.

"Thérèse has been with us for twenty-eight years," Magdeleine continued. "Besides, she was quite overcome at poor Father's death, and took to her bed. It was the new maidservant, Jeannette, who cooked the dinner yesterday, with some help from my sister-in-law. That wretched girl must have done it—I only engaged her a month ago."

"And you suspect her merely because she's only been employed here a month?"

"The other servants have been with us for some time. I think I can speak for their honesty. She was the only one who was an unknown quantity. So when my friend Citizen Hébert, the surgeon, suggested that it looked like poisoning and that a servant was the most likely culprit, we went to her room and Citizen Hébert searched her apron pockets while I looked among her—her body linen, and straightaway I found my watch, which I'd missed for two or three days, and a silver brooch belonging to my father's wife, and other things as well! My husband came with us and he'll attest to what we found."

"Perhaps Citizen Bouton should confirm your statement?" Brasseur suggested mildly.

"Certainly." Magdeleine flung open the door, shouted for Fanny, and ordered her to run and fetch Uncle Claude. A few minutes later a thin, gray-haired man sidled into the room. Magdeleine repeated her statement, and Claude Bouton nodded. "I was there, Citizen Commissaire."

"So you searched the maid's pockets and her linen," said Brasseur. "With her consent?"

"Of course," Magdeleine said, interrupting her husband as he opened his mouth to speak. "The miserable girl was right there. She had the gall to hand over her apron to Citizen Hébert as soon as he proposed searching her! As if she thought we wouldn't find the proof of her wickedness!"

"And why didn't you just send for the police straightaway?" Brasseur inquired as Dautry scribbled down notes as quickly as he could. "This has all been managed in the most irregular fashion, citizeness. You ought to have left the stuff where it was, and sent for us immediately."

"I didn't know what I ought to do," she retorted. "What with Father dead, and all of us at death's door—"

"We were *not* at death's door," Laurence interrupted her from the doorway. She strode in, still clutching a four-pound loaf of bread under her arm. "At worst we were ill for an hour or two. I felt a few stomach cramps and now I'm more or less recovered."

"What about me?" demanded Gervais, wheeling about. "I was deathly ill, you know. Vomiting for—"

"Gervais," said Magdeleine, "kindly stop referring to such an indelicate subject—"

"It probably did you good," Laurence snapped, with a glance at his middle. Gervais, while handsome and well built, was undeniably beginning to run to fat. "At the rate you're going, soon you won't fit into your costumes."

"Are you a member of the household, citizeness?" Brasseur said, with no indication that he had ever before met Laurence. "Your name?"

"Laurence Dupont, née Fauconnet."

"Our sister-in-law," said Gervais. "My younger brother's widow."

Magdeleine coughed. "Aren't you going to ask me what we found in the girl's pockets, Citizen Commissaire?"

"I know what you claim to have found, citizeness; it's here in the inspector's report. Some bits of white dust that could have been anything. And since your friend seems to have taken it away with him, there's no proof that what we'll get from him, if we ever do, is what you found in the maid's pockets."

"Commissaire, we found bits of white dust and grit, coarse and metallic looking, and it certainly wasn't salt! I tasted a single grain of it before Citizen Hébert wrapped it up and it's the same gritty stuff that was in our soup. What could it be but arsenic? The brazen wench. It was right there for anybody to find, in the pocket of her Sunday apron, hanging over a chair. You saw Hébert find it, didn't you, Claude?"

Her husband nodded again. "Yes, Citizen Commissaire, I saw it myself. Couldn't have been mistaken."

"And then we found some of our valuables hidden among her linen," Magdeleine continued. She darted out of the room and soon returned with a small bundle, wrapped in a square of coarse cloth, which she thrust at Brasseur. "See for yourself. My own watch! You see, Commissaire? It *must* have been that miserable, thieving creature who murdered my father, and tried to poison us. No doubt she imagined she could steal us blind during the uproar, and get away scot-free."

"Sister-in-law," said Laurence, "how is it you're so familiar with arsenic?"

Magdeleine sniffed. "Citizen Hébert *said* it could very well be arsenic, and Father could have been poisoned. He knew as well as you do that Father had always enjoyed the best of health. And he's a surgeon; he ought to know about poison!"

"The science of the physician and the science of the surgeon," Aristide said, "are two different things, and what's known by one, such as the identification and action of deadly drugs, may not be so familiar to the other."

Brasseur raised a hand as Magdeleine began to retort. "So it was then, after you found the white dust and the valuables in the girl's room, that you sent for the police?"

"Yes, Citizen Hébert insisted it was a matter for the law."

"Maître Frochot disagreed," Laurence said. "He seemed to think it was only a case of spoiled food, and nothing to fetch the police over."

"And he was at this dinner with you?"

"Yes indeed," Magdeleine said, with a venomous glance at Laurence. "He was feeling ill himself."

Brasseur grunted and unwrapped the folds of cloth. "I won't believe Jeannette took any of this," Laurence declared as she and Aristide crowded about him to see. "That girl's not a thief!"

Aristide looked over the contents of the rag: a gold ring, a single earring, a pair of silk handkerchiefs, and a dainty lady's watch. The watch seemed intact and in good order, but the ring, set with amethysts and tiny pearls, was missing a few of its gems. The single silver earring was heavily tarnished and the two handkerchiefs showed signs of wear.

"Do you know whose the other pieces are?" Brasseur asked Laurence. She slowly nodded.

"The ring is Ursule's, but she hasn't worn it in some time, because of the missing pearls. The Old Man was probably unwilling to spend the money to replace them. The handkerchiefs belong to Gervais, and the earring is mine."

"Why only one earring?"

"I had only one. I lost the other, months ago, long before Jeannette was engaged here."

"Where'd you keep it, citizeness?"

"In my jewelry case, of course. Not that I have much to keep in it at the best of times. Martin told me I should sell the earring back to the silversmith, but . . . well, my husband had given them to me."

"At a guess," Aristide said, "if Jeannette really did steal these items, she began by taking only small items that still had some value but wouldn't be missed: an odd earring, a ring with stones missing—things that could be sold to a jeweler—and a pair of handkerchiefs that needed some mending but would still fetch a few sous from an old-clothes dealer. Then perhaps she grew bolder."

"Or someone wanted to make it look that way," Laurence said. "I still don't believe it. Someone could have planted these things in her room, you know, just as easily as they planted the powder Magdeleine and Dr. Hébert found. Rolled in linen at the back of her drawer—it's a silly, obvious hiding place. How could somebody not find that, once they looked for it?"

"Are you suggesting one of the family could have done this, and poisoned Father?" Magdeleine demanded, dull red patches rising in her cheeks. "This is the thanks we get, for giving you a home—to be accused of parricide—"

"Ladies!" Brasseur thundered before Laurence could reply and the brewing quarrel get out of hand. "That's enough. You'll be able to tell us everything you know, and give us your opinions, when we take your official statements. Now, where's the kitchen, and this maidservant's room?"

4

Magdeleine, still flushed with rage, pointed toward the rear of the house and set off. Laurence trailed them as Brasseur, Aristide, and the two inspectors followed Magdeleine. The kitchenmaid's bedroom was a tiny, bare chamber off the corridor to the kitchen, scarcely larger than the narrow cot and small chest of drawers that filled it. A simple but bright calico dress, evidently Jeannette's Sunday gown, hung from a peg on the wall.

Brasseur set Inspector Thomas to searching the room for any evidence that had been overlooked. Then he strode out again, shaking his head. "The kitchen is this way, I suppose, citizeness? Where are these soiled dishes we're talking about?"

Magdeleine led him into the kitchen, a long room with stone walls and floor, warm from the fire in the broad hearth, and pointed at a door. Brasseur gazed at it gloomily.

"Not even sealed. What was Didier thinking?"

"He did lock it, and he took the key away with him," said Magdeleine.

"And you have a duplicate key handy, of course, citizeness?"

"Naturally," said Magdeleine. "My brother has the other set of household keys."

"Anyone else?"

"Certainly not. How are you supposed to stop the servants from stealing all the provisions unless you keep them locked away?" She pulled out a ring of keys from beneath her apron and unlocked the door. A clay terrine or roasting vessel, an iron soup kettle, a greasy platter, several neat stacks of soiled dishes, and a tureen stood together on a shelf beneath rows of glazed, covered earthenware crocks and a few cheeses and smoked sausages.

Brasseur dutifully looked the dishes over, more, Aristide guessed, for the sake of placating Magdeleine Bouton than in the hope of finding any evidence. The dinner plates, having been wiped clean with bread at table by the diners, in a perfectly normal fashion, had nothing on them but traces of grease from the last of the gravy. The soup plates contained only a few drops of liquid. Brasseur concluded by lifting the lid of the tureen.

"I'm sure that's how I smelled burned arsenic," Magdeleine announced as he opened his mouth to speak. "The wretch must have thrown the last of the soup onto the fire in order to do away with the evidence of her crime."

"But we ate all the soup, Sister-in-law," Laurence reminded her, her tone deceptively gentle. "Don't you remember? Jeannette served us all, then went off to have her own dinner with old Mother Chuquet and the other servants in the kitchen. Étienne wanted another helping, and so did Gervais, so Gervais served out the last of it to Étienne and himself. He was scraping the bottom of the tureen with the ladle; there couldn't have been more than a spoonful left when Jeannette cleared the table and took the tureen back to the scullery."

"It might have collected at the bottom of the tureen," Magdeleine insisted, grimly. "Citizen Hébert says arsenic is a sort of metal, so it must be heavy. The remains of it could have sunk to the bottom."

Aristide took the opportunity, while the women argued, to lift the lid of the tureen himself and take a quick look inside. A tablespoonful or two of brownish broth did remain at the bottom, which seemed to contradict Magdeleine's assertion that the maid must have thrown the last of the dregs on the fire.

"Citizen Thierry already looked at all that!" Magdeleine snapped, indignant, as she caught sight of him examining the tureen. He replaced the lid and moved away, wondering as he did so why Magdeleine Bouton was so intent upon blaming the inoffensive kitchenmaid.

"Citizeness," Brasseur rumbled, "I've seen all I need to see, I think. My men will take away the dishes and cooking vessels. Go back to the salon, if you please, and finish giving your statement to my secretary."

"But I—"

"*Now*, citizeness."

She pursed her lips and cast him an indignant glance before retreating. Brasseur pulled out a handkerchief and mopped his brow. "Saints, what a mess! And damn Didier! He should never have taken the girl in for questioning in the first place. But all in all there's something fishy about this matter. Dupont's wife and his daughter both swear old Dupont was in perfect health, that he was never ill. Then he suddenly dies of a stomachache? It's not natural, not at all."

"But you can't honestly believe that servant girl poisoned anybody," Aristide said.

Brasseur shrugged. "Of course not. But my hands are tied. She's in police custody, and that shrew has filed a formal complaint against her, so now we have to take her in front of the magistrate whether we want to or not, and then concentrate upon the real task at hand, which is to discover how old Dupont actually died."

"And when you dismiss the complaint against Jeannette," Laurence said, behind them, "if the doctor says the Old Man didn't die of natural causes . . ."

"Then someone else in this household certainly poisoned him," Brasseur concluded for her, turning to face her. "I don't suppose you know who might have wanted to murder the citizen?"

"You ought to ask who *didn't* want to murder him," she retorted. She shrugged as she saw Brasseur's ill-concealed start. "Wanting to do it, and actually doing it, are two different matters, of course. But he was a moneylender, and he was rich. Where there is a great deal of money, there are always people who want to get their hands on it."

"What about yourself?" Brasseur asked bluntly.

She gave him a fleeting, wry smile. "I'm probably the only one here who doesn't profit by his death."

Brasseur opened his mouth to speak but Inspector Thomas, appearing at the door, interrupted him. "Commissaire? I'm done searching the maid's room. There was nothing that oughtn't to have been there."

"You see?" Laurence said after Brasseur had dismissed the inspector. "She's nothing more than she seems. Someone's trying to entrap her."

"I have to agree," Aristide said. "*Why* would the girl want to murder the old man? It makes no sense. If she really did put something in the food to make everyone ill, with the intention of stealing valuables and then running off in the uproar, surely that would be enough for her purposes. Killing old Dupont wouldn't have helped her much—"

"Jeannette sat with him and tended him for hours," Laurence interrupted. "She volunteered—nobody asked her to do it. Why would she have done that instead of making off with her stolen goods during the fuss?"

"But we still could make a pretty good case against her," Brasseur said, frowning. "She might have been about to bolt with the goods just as Citizeness Bouton lodged the complaint and summoned the police. Servants do that sometimes," he added apologetically.

"But Jeannette isn't that sort," she insisted. "She hasn't an ounce of guile in her. The idea that she could come up with something as clever and malicious as poisoning her employers—it's simply ridiculous. And on the other hand, I can think of a motive for murder for everyone in this quarter who owed him money. People hated my father-in-law, Commissaire; he probably made a few hundred enemies over the past fifty years."

"I don't suppose anyone outside the house had the opportunity to poison him, though," said Brasseur. "Poisoning's an intimate crime, citizeness. You can't do it from a distance."

"Citizeness," Aristide said, "if I were a police official, it would probably be improper of me to ask you this, but since I'm not, I will. If you were to speculate who in this household might have murdered Martin Dupont . . ."

Laurence suddenly shivered. "That's a horrible thought, that it could be one of us. You really don't think it could have been bad food. . . ."

Brasseur shook his head. "No, citizeness."

"Well, I suppose if I had to guess, I would say—" She stopped abruptly. "No, it's not fair. The police are right—you shouldn't ask me that. But if it's spiteful gossip you want," she added, with a glint in her eye, "you may as well sit down with me here, where we can be more comfortable. I've had no breakfast yet. Have you? Take some morning coffee with me, and I'll tell you everything I know while you're waiting on the doctor upstairs." She gestured them to seats at the well-scrubbed wooden table. "I'm afraid we haven't had any butter for the past several days. But there will be decent bread, and preserves."

Aristide shrugged, thinking of the pallid, slightly rancid lard that his landlady usually scraped across his breakfast bread when butter was scarce. The door leading outside to the garden opened and a heavyset, red-haired woman of forty-five entered with a bucket of water. She gave Aristide and Brasseur a suspicious glance before setting the bucket down by the hearth.

"Citizen Commissaire," Laurence said, "this is Thérèse Huteau, the cook. Coffee, please, Thérèse, and something to eat for the gentlemen. Commissaire, Thérèse may be able to tell you something about Martin's death, though she can't help you with the other matter, since she wasn't present when we prepared yesterday's dinner."

"If I'd been here where I should have been," Thérèse said as she laid down a rough linen cloth and coffee bowls and plates for three, "none of these horrid goings-on might have happened. Oh, I could just cry for vexation! But there was the poor old master all of a sudden dead and gone, and me knowing him these twenty-eight years, since I was kitchenmaid myself, and I just couldn't seem to do a thing but cry into my pillow, like he was my own father. Ma'm'selle Magdeleine, she understood."

"Citizeness Huteau," Aristide said, "what did you think of Jeannette?"

"Oh, that wicked girl!" Thérèse exclaimed, slapping down frayed napkins for them. "To think I let her cook anything in my kitchen!"

"So you think she did it?" Brasseur inquired. "You think she poisoned Citizen Dupont?"

"Well, Ma'm'selle Magdeleine thinks so—that's Citizeness Bouton, begging your pardon—and she wouldn't think so if she didn't have good reason to, would she?" the cook said. "Besides, the old master was never ill in his life. A colic wouldn't have carried him off." She bustled away and returned with a small pot of coffee and a jug of steaming milk that had been keeping warm by the fire. "There you are, then, and I'll just cut a bit off the loaf for you."

Aristide poured hot milk into his coffee and sipped at it. It was better than any Clotilde, his landlady, had sent up to her lodgers for years. "Excellent coffee this. Thank you."

Laurence pushed a small box of sugar his way but he shook his head. He had had to alter his tastes when the price of sugar had risen to dizzying heights four years before, during the first food shortages of 1793. "You seem to eat well enough here," he remarked as Thérèse returned with several slices of bread on a plate, and a pot of preserves.

Laurence shrugged. "They're quite rich, though the Old Man was always the first one to cry poverty when somebody in the family asked him for money. Magdeleine can afford to pass the baker a few extra sous in silver, to be sure he'll reserve a decent loaf for us every day."

Aristide eyed the sliced bread, guessing it was wheat, at worst mixed with good rye or millet, rather than the heavy, sour bread sold by unscrupulous bakers in the poorer quarters, made of various rancid, weevil-ridden flours, often mixed with moldy peas, sawdust, and even mud. "Was that what Citizen Dupont ate for breakfast?"

"No, for breakfast he always took wheaten porridge, and a bowl of white coffee. Said porridge was good for the digestion." Suddenly she paused, in the midst of stirring hot milk into her own coffee bowl, and met his gaze. "That's what it was in, wasn't it? The porridge?"

"He ate nothing else in the morning?" said Brasseur.

"Sometimes he had a little fruit, in season. But there's no fruit in March except Spanish oranges, and who can afford those?"

"Did he take sugar in his coffee, or his porridge?"

"Sugar? No. He claimed it was an unnecessary expense," she added dryly, "and he was forever lecturing those of us who prefer our coffee sugared."

"His stomach pains came on at about nine o'clock in the morning," Brasseur mused, rereading Didier's report, "after he'd eaten breakfast at seven, as he always did. Yes, I fear it was either the porridge or the coffee, probably the porridge."

After a few more grateful swallows of coffee and a slice of bread, dark but fresh, and layered with thick, tart quince preserves, Aristide pulled out his notebook again. Brasseur cleared his throat and gestured to Thérèse to join them at the table. "Very well then, tell us, if you please, ladies, what you remember of Citizen Dupont's death."

"That's what is so horrible. . . . It was just like any other day." Laurence thought for a moment as she spread preserves on her own bread. "I rose, dressed, everything as usual, and then I took my breakfast. I had woken a little early and breakfasted in the kitchen. Those of us who don't breakfast in our rooms, like Ursule, take it in the dining room, where it's served between seven and half past seven. At any other time you'll have to fetch your own breakfast in the kitchen and eat it there."

"Ursule prefers to be waited on?" said Aristide.

"Oh, she puts on airs because she came from some impoverished aristocratic family that had, as Gervais says, a name more ancient than illustrious."

"That one," Thérèse sniffed. "Breakfast in bed, if you please, like a duchess. Because she had a 'de' in front of her name once, she's far too fine to have anything to do with the kitchen. But the truth is her father'd borrowed money from the master and couldn't pay it back, so finally she married him. Master Martin had been a widower for years, of course."

An old story, Aristide thought. No doubt Martin Dupont had thought it amusing to bed a gently bred woman half his age in exchange for a bad debt.

"But if she could stoop to marrying the master," Thérèse continued, "him being a bourgeois and old enough to be her grandsire, then I'd wager she used to set her hand to cooking more often than not, back at her family's château. Château! More like a jumped-up farmhouse is *my* guess."

Brasseur took a sheet of paper from his pocketbook and handed it to Laurence. "This is the list of the members of the household that I've put together. Is everybody accounted for?"

Laurence glanced over the list and made a few corrections with the pencil Brasseur handed her. "So, since Citizeness Dupont, the master's wife, never lent a hand with the cooking," Aristide asked Thérèse, "you could swear she was never in the kitchen on the morning he died?"

The cook opened her mouth and shut it again, scowling. Apparently, he thought, she would have been quite pleased if the supercilious Ursule had been found guilty of the poisoning.

"That's so," she admitted at last. "She was never about in the morning. But she could have gone into the master's bedroom easy enough and slipped something into his breakfast," she hastened to add. "There's a door between, of course."

"No," he agreed, "we can't yet discount Ursule."

Laurence passed the list back to Brasseur and Aristide glanced over at the names.

THE DUPONT FAMILY

Gervais Dupont (called Hauteroche), surviving son of Martin Dupont
Étienne, his son, aged 15
Félicité (Fanny), his daughter, aged 12
Sophie Larivière, his wife (touring in the provinces for the past three months)
Ursule d'Armoncourt, widow of M.D. (second wife)
Magdeleine Dupont, wife of Bouton, elder daughter of M.D.
Claude Bouton, Magdeleine's husband
Charlotte Dupont, younger daughter of M.D.
Laurence Fauconnet, widow Dupont, daughter-in-law of M.D.

SERVANTS AND EMPLOYEES

Charles Jullien, private secretary to M.D. and tutor to Étienne and Fanny
Thérèse Huteau, cook

Zélie Nicolay, maidservant (chambermaid)
Antoine Bernardin, manservant (man of all work and valet)
Jeannette Moineau, maidservant (maid of all work and kitchenmaid)

"So," said Brasseur, "you took your breakfast in the kitchen. When was this?"

"About twenty minutes to seven. Thérèse was hurrying about, and Jeannette was making the Old Man's porridge."

"Jeannette cooked it?"

Laurence frowned. "I fear so. That was one of her regular tasks."

"Did you see her cooking it?"

"I must have, while I was eating, but I can't remember anything out of the ordinary. There's always such a hustle and bustle in the kitchen in the morning; the maid is running out to the market or to the milk-woman's cart, and preparing breakfast, and making the coffee, while Thérèse is already fussing with dinner preparations, and perhaps the man selling firewood or vinegar or brooms is knocking on the door. I just barely noticed Jeannette spooning out the porridge into a bowl and setting up the tray. Then she took it—no, wait a moment. Charlotte took it upstairs that morning. She said something like: 'Thérèse is so busy, Jeannette, you stay here and help her with the cooking. I'll take this up to Father.' It's true Thérèse was very busy, because we were to have those guests at dinner the next day and there was all the market-ing and cooking to be done, and you know it's harder than ever to find decent foodstuffs at any sort of reasonable price. Charlotte left the kitchen with the tray and that's the last I saw of it."

"A little before seven o'clock . . . Jeannette cooks Martin Dupont's porridge and Charlotte takes it upstairs to him shortly afterward," Aristide murmured, noting it down.

"At about half past eight Ursule announced she wanted a bath, and since poor Jeannette was so burdened with tasks, I helped Zélie, the other maid, to fetch the water from the well in the garden, and heat it for her. By the time we'd filled the tub and set up a screen around it, I think Martin was beginning to complain of stomach pains."

He nodded. "Now, did Charlotte take the breakfast tray straight up to her father, I wonder, or did she pause on the way, and lay the tray down, where someone could have tampered with it?"

"I wouldn't be a bit surprised if she did set it down for a moment," Thérèse said. "She's a good soul, Ma'm'selle Charlotte is, but she's the sort who'd be distracted by the first thing she saw, and stop in the middle of a task."

"Could anyone have tampered with the food after Charlotte had left it with Citizen Dupont in his bedchamber?" Brasseur asked Laurence.

"I suppose they could have. Magdeleine often went in to exchange the news of the morning while he was eating his breakfast. Or, as Thérèse said, Ursule could have gone into his room through the communicating door and no one would have seen her."

"I'd have my suspicions when an old man with a young wife ups and dies suddenly," Thérèse said darkly as she bustled back to the hearth to stir a simmering pot of broth.

Aristide nodded. "Yes, when a married man or woman succumbs to poison, I fear the spouse is the first person the police suspect. Could she have wanted him out of the way?"

Laurence shrugged. "I expect she'd grown tired of being chained to an old man, no matter how vigorous he was, and had longed for a free and wealthy widowhood." She sighed suddenly. "I'm being completely malicious, but there it is. I ought to tell you I don't like her much. Nobody does. If you were to discover that she was the one who poisoned Martin, I think it would please everyone."

"Just as blaming the maidservant pleases everyone?"

"Well . . . yes." She reddened. "Magdeleine, Charlotte, Gervais— they'll all refuse to believe any of them could have done it. They'd much prefer it was someone who didn't matter, like a servant, or somebody they don't like, an outsider like Ursule."

"Or you?"

"I suppose so," she said with a grimace. "Though I don't profit by his death."

"Has Ursule profited by his death?"

"I expect Martin arranged to leave her a respectable sum when they drew up the marriage contract, since she had no dowry. But more than that, now nothing stands between Ursule and Citizen Jullien."

"Martin's secretary?" Brasseur said, glancing at the list of names.

"Yes. That very good-looking young man who goes about the house looking as demure as a boarder in a convent. Ursule," Laurence added, significantly, "also thinks he is very good-looking. She's barely forty, you know, not ancient by any means, and they're very friendly together."

"That gives Jullien a motive, too. If the old man was dead, Jullien could marry the widow."

"And enjoy her legacy," Aristide said. He finished another slice of bread, savoring the indulgence of preserves at a time when all such luxuries had grown impossibly expensive, far beyond his modest income. "Citizeness, tell us more about Magdeleine and Charlotte."

Laurence shrugged again, with a brief wry smile. "I've been told the Old Man, besides being an astute man of business, was very handsome in his day. Well, Magdeleine inherited his brains, and Gervais inherited his looks, and Charlotte inherited neither."

"Magdeleine is clever?"

"She's far brighter than Gervais, though Gervais would never admit that. She'll be the one taking over the Old Man's business and managing the household finances as well, not he . . . not that Gervais would wish to."

"And Charlotte?"

"Charlotte is a very generous, kindhearted person," she said, "but an utter nitwit. If I were her husband I fear I'd murder her within a month!"

"'Murder'?" said Brasseur. Laurence drew a sharp breath and fell silent, cheeks crimsoning.

5

"Murder?" Brasseur repeated blandly.

Laurence sighed. "I fear that wasn't the tactful thing to say, under the circumstances. But truly Charlotte can be exasperating."

Aristide could not help smiling, for he found Laurence's tart tongue amused him. She raised her gaze and eyed him narrowly. "So you do know how to smile, after all. I was wondering."

"Yes, I smile once in a while," he said, thinking of another woman who had said much the same thing to him.

"You ought to—especially if you customarily go about in black. People are likely to mistake you for an undertaker."

"The police have been wearing black suits for more than a century, citizeness," Brasseur told her with a grin.

"But Citizen Ravel isn't an inspector of police, is he?"

Aristide glanced down at his redingote and waistcoat. Wearing only black, besides saving him money on his wardrobe, spared him the nuisance of having to decide what to wear. At most times he was indifferent to fashion and to the state of his costume; for everyday use, he owned two suits of clothes and three waistcoats in various stages of repair (or disrepair), all of them unadorned black in a restrained cut that the young dandies, known as *incroyables,* of the modish cafés would have dismissed as hopelessly passé.

"Tell us more about Charlotte, if you feel so strongly about her," he said. "Has she a husband?"

"No, she's a spinster. She had a fiancé, years ago—about 1782, I think it was. But he died of a fever and she decided her heart was broken forever, so she went off to a convent and took vows."

"A nun," he said, making more notes. "But she had to come home again when they closed the convents." The abolition of legally binding religious vows, and then the eventual closing of the monasteries and convents in 1790, had suddenly denied the pious a refuge from the world. Though religious houses had long had a reputation for being both prisons and hotbeds of vice, they had always served as homes for the many surplus, unmarried, dowerless women who, lacking families to support them, would otherwise have lived their lives in lonely poverty.

Laurence nodded. "Yes. It's too bad they did, because that would have been the perfect life for her. Undemanding daily labor—she's not afraid of hard work, I'll give her that much credit—and a nice safe spiritual outlet for her sentimental yearnings, where she could indulge herself as she pleased, and no harm done. Sentimentality and gullibility—it's a dangerous combination. Let alone, she's likely to give everything she owns to the first charlatan who can convince her he's a sorcerer or a saint."

"You sound as if something of the sort has already happened," Aristide said. He drank the last of his cooling coffee and Laurence poured him more.

"The Old Man knew better than to give her more than a stingy dress allowance, of course, but lately she's been borrowing pocket money from all of us, and I can guess where it's going. There is a man. . . . He calls himself the Chevalier Cavalcanti and claims he's an alchemist, a sorcerer, an astrologer, and the prophet of some new mystical religion. He can also speak to the dead." Brasseur snorted and she added, "Oh, he's a clever mountebank with a bit of book-learning and a persuasive way about him. But Charlotte thinks he is the Baptist returned to earth."

"A sort of Oriental cult, I suppose," Aristide said, "with trances and mysterious rites drawn from Hebrew and Arabian lore?" Such fads were nothing new; Mesmerism and animal magnetism, mystics and founders of new spiritual sciences, persuasive humbugs who expertly dazzled and fleeced a bored, gullible aristocracy eager for some new diversion, had been in fashion long before the Revolution.

Now the Revolution had attempted to do away with Catholicism as the established religion and dozens of eccentric sects had sprung up, the most infamous of which was probably that of mad old Catherine Théot, who had called herself "the Mother of God" in the weeks just before Robespierre's fall. Even some members of the government, including Director La Revellière-Lépeaux himself, who loathed the power of the pope, supported a few of the newer "religions."

"Charlotte: motive: might want money to give to religious fraud," Aristide scribbled in his notebook. "What did you think of Martin?" he continued as he poured the last of the hot milk into his bowl. "Sometimes one can learn a great deal about how and why a murder was committed by learning more about the victim. Did you like him?"

"As much as I like anybody of the family. He could be a kindly old grandfather one moment and a petulant tyrant the next. He seemed always very fond of me, but I suppose that was merely because I was his son's widow."

He heard a slight catch in her voice as she spoke of her dead husband. "How did Martin get on with the rest of the family?"

"He and Gervais were always at odds. I'm told he was furious when Gervais declared he was going to be a playwright and run a theatrical troupe, and it was even worse when they learned Gervais had gone on the stage himself, and was living with an actress! Martin considered himself a good son of the Church and he was convinced Gervais was setting himself up for damnation; and besides, it's no way to get rich. Even when Gervais joined the Comédie and became quite famous, there was no pleasing Martin. He always used to hold my husband up as a model for Gervais. 'Why can't you be like your brother?' and so on. Of course, that made Gervais even more determined to go his own way."

"Yet your brother-in-law and his family still live in the house?"

"They came to live with us in 'ninety-four . . . after my husband died. My father-in-law swallowed his pride and asked Gervais and his family to come back and live with him, now that Gervais was the only surviving son," she continued, her voice a little unsteady. "Gervais was restoring his theater and was rather badly in debt, so he was glad enough to sell his furniture and dismiss his servants and live here rent-free."

"Did your father-in-law still quarrel with Gervais?"

"I wouldn't call it quarreling. More like endless faultfinding and carping. I think it became almost a malicious contest between them, seeing which one could irritate the other the most. Don't most men try to outdo their fathers, if they can?"

"I wouldn't know," Aristide said. He thrust aside the memory of his own long-dead parents, his mother murdered with her lover, his father broken alive for his crime.

"You said most of the family would have had a motive to see Martin Dupont dead," said Brasseur. "Tell me a bit more about that, if you please. Who would have profited by his death, and why?"

Laurence thought a moment and ticked the names off on her fingers, one by one. "There's Ursule, as I said, who would get her legacy and be free to marry Jullien, or at least to amuse herself with him; there's Jullien himself, obviously; Gervais, who'll inherit a third of the Old Man's fortune, and who needs the money quite badly; Magdeleine and Claude, who might have grown tired of waiting for Magdeleine's inheritance. . . ."

"Inheritance? What about her dowry?"

"Martin wouldn't give her a dowry, or so I've been told. He claimed women scarcely ever had any sense when it came to marrying, and he didn't see why he should give away part of his hard-earned money to some fortune hunter. He declared his daughters would receive no dowries, but that they and their husbands and families could live under the Old Man's roof for as long as they wished, and at his death they would inherit part of his fortune. And now, since they've changed the inheritance laws, Magdeleine will get about a third of Martin's estate, even more than he probably would have left her before. Claude's patience evidently paid off."

"In other words," Brasseur said, "old Dupont wasn't going to watch any son-in-law of his spend his money, but they could do as they pleased with it after he was dead?"

"Yes, that's it exactly."

"Is Claude Bouton a fortune hunter?"

"I expect so, in a small, petty way. He's one of those people who manages to take everything he can for himself while doing as little work as possible. Though I think he's really quite harmless."

"Couldn't have poisoned his father-in-law?"

Slowly Laurence shook her head. "By 'harmless' I meant inoffensive. Indolent and ingratiating, content to let Magdeleine manage everything, including him. His only interest is Italian opera, and playing the violin—unfortunately not very well. Nobody really dislikes him; it's more of a tolerant contempt . . . aside from Charlotte, who always believes the best of everyone. But I suppose if Claude needed that inheritance badly enough, he wouldn't shrink at murder."

"And Magdeleine herself?"

"I can't see her callously poisoning the Old Man—she was quite fond of him, in her way, because they were so much alike. But if she made up her mind to murder somebody, she'd do it very efficiently and very cleverly."

"Interesting," Aristide said. He glanced over his notes. "So . . . Ursule, Jullien, Gervais, Magdeleine, Claude. Then there are Gervais's two children."

"Yes, Étienne, who's fifteen, and Fanny, who's twelve, though you would think she was twenty. You'll see more of them, never fear. You can scarcely avoid Fanny, wherever you may go. You can't imagine *they* could have a motive, can you? Or that they could do such a thing?"

"Children aren't so innocent as you might suppose, citizeness," Brasseur told her. "If you'd seen what I've seen over the years . . . well, it's unlikely, to be sure; but you can't eliminate them altogether. Magdeleine and Claude haven't any children?"

"No. Though sometimes Magdeleine says Charlotte is her 'child.' Charlotte has no more common sense than a twelve-year-old. Less, in fact; of the two of them, Fanny is probably the more levelheaded.

Fanny is the sort of clever, spoiled child who knows exactly what she wants and exactly how to get it!"

"Indeed," Aristide said, scribbling a few more notes. "What about Charlotte? Why haven't we seen her yet?"

Laurence frowned. "Well, she had hysterics when she learned the Old Man was dead, and fled to her room and locked herself in, and she's been crying her eyes out for hours. She still won't come out of her room. But she's the last person I would suspect of poisoning anyone. She's the kindest person imaginable; she coos over other people's babies, and nurses injured stray cats and puppies from off the street, and all that. Why on earth would she do it?"

"Well," Aristide said, "people commit murder for just a few principal reasons: gain, self-preservation, revenge, jealousy, love."

"Old Martin had quite a large fortune," said Brasseur, "so let's begin with gain. Gervais, Magdeleine, and Charlotte each inherit a third of their father's fortune."

"Yes, but I'm sure he would have tied it up somehow to keep it safe from Charlotte. The Old Man used to say she was the silliest woman he'd ever known, and that if you gave her money beyond a mere dress allowance, she would just fritter it away on foolishness, let it slip through her fingers. He would never have left her an unconditional legacy and trusted her to manage her own affairs."

"What if she'd married?"

"She's scarcely likely to marry now, is she?" said Laurence. "She's thirty-nine, after all, and she was a nun. The Old Man certainly didn't think it was right that she should marry, and of course there would be no dowry. But if he did give his permission, probably he would have first made sure her husband controlled the money, and was a man of some honesty and sense."

Aristide suddenly smiled. "I was just thinking of Molière's *The Miser*. You recall, when Harpagon is speaking of marrying his daughter to a wealthy older man . . . he concludes by saying gleefully, 'And he will take her without a dowry—'"

"'*Without a dowry!*'" Laurence chimed in, laughing. "That was the role that made Gervais famous, you know," she added. "His performance as Harpagon was the most brutally perfect portrait of his father you could imagine."

"I suppose a third of his fortune might be a fine motive to do away with the old man," Brasseur said, scribbling more notes. "And Charlotte did take the porridge up to him that day."

Laurence sat thinking for a moment, then at last frowned and shook her head. "Oh, it's possible, I suppose . . . but honestly I don't think Charlotte would have the brains or the nerve to commit murder. Or if she did it, she'd never be callous enough to cast the blame on an innocent servant. What about that mysterious white powder in Jeannette's apron pocket? If it *is* poison, someone had to have put it there. But I can't see Charlotte doing something as wicked as that."

"Might she not have done it if she suddenly panicked, if her only thought was to divert suspicion from herself, without pausing to realize it would necessarily put Jeannette's life in danger?"

"She might," Laurence said uncertainly. "She's featherheaded enough for that, I suppose. But she couldn't have been the one who put something in the soup yesterday; she hasn't been out of her room for a day and a half."

Aristide clapped his notebook shut, sighing. "So almost anyone in this house could have murdered old Martin, but the one who had the best opportunity had no opportunity at all to poison the soup. Damn."

He was beginning to form an image of the Dupont family. Caged together, kept short of money under the benevolent tyranny of a capricious, miserly old patriarch, many of them must have come, over the years, to silently loathe each other.

"Nearly anyone in the house could have murdered him," he repeated, "and I suspect everyone might have wanted to." He paused for a moment and then added: "Even you."

Laurence blinked. "I!"

"Martin Dupont sounds as if he was a very strong, dominating, selfish personality. Was it he who wanted you to stay here?"

She nodded. "He wouldn't hear of my leaving. He said I was all that remained of Aurèle, that I belonged here with—"

"Aurèle?" he echoed her.

Aurèle Dupont?

"My husband," she said. "Martin said I belonged here with his family, as Aurèle's widow. I suppose he was right. And I don't know where I'd have gone. I'm an orphan, and I have no money of my own."

Aurèle Dupont? he repeated to himself, staring at her. *Dupont . . . it's such a common name . . . but I might have seen it. . . .*

"Citizen?"

"But with Martin dead," he continued, collecting himself, "at least one of the chains that binds you to this house is broken."

"I don't know how you can possibly imagine I might have done it!" Laurence exclaimed.

"I'm only pointing out that there are motives aplenty in this affair."

Brasseur nodded. "No doubt we'd have come to that conclusion last night, if I'd been here instead of that imbecile Didier—blame my witch of a mother-in-law—and if somebody hadn't led Didier so conveniently toward the maid."

A distant bell clanged and he glanced at his watch. "Eleven already. We'd better be seeing what Dr. Prunelle has found out. I thank you for the breakfast, citizeness."

6

Brasseur rose and Aristide made to follow him, but Laurence reached out and touched Aristide's elbow.

"Citizen, you recognized his name; did you know my husband?"

Three years, four; has it been so long already?

Aristide thought back, remembering a tall, handsome man with black hair scarcely touched by gray, and brilliant black eyes and a warm smile. "No, I can't say I knew him well at all; though I met him several times. He . . . he knew Mathieu Alexandre?"

Her expression changed, her pale face becoming suddenly lively with a fond memory, though he thought he saw the glint of tears in her eyes. "Yes. Yes, they—we all—were good friends, inseparable for a time. We did everything together. Did you know Citizen Alexandre?"

"We were friends for many years . . . schoolmates, and beyond."

"He—I was horrified—Aurèle and I both were—to learn of his death, and that of the others. Aurèle was never the same afterward."

"Yes," Aristide said, "it was a dreadful waste . . . of life, and youth, and talent."

"I'm sorry. I'm very sorry for—for the loss of a friend we both cared for. Citizen Alexandre was a delightful person. I liked him very much." She seemed about to say something more, but thought better of it, smiled briefly, and turned to assist Thérèse at the hearth. With a backward glance at her, Aristide left the kitchen and followed Brasseur to the salon, where the tiny fire had burned itself out.

"So," Brasseur said, rubbing chilled hands together, "it's going to be the devil of a time finding out who could have poisoned that porridge, if that was what it was."

Aristide nodded, scarcely hearing him, for he was thinking instead of Mathieu, and how little he had seen of him that last year, despite their promises. He had ascribed it to his own ceaseless occupations during the uneasy months after France had so unwisely declared war on Austria in the spring of 1792; and of course Mathieu had been a member of the government, a deputy from Bordeaux, occupied with political matters and the endless factional squabbling that had erupted even before Louis XVI's headless body was laid in its anonymous grave. Yet they might have seen more of each other, he thought, despite all.

Of course, there had been Delphine to distract him. How was it possible he had nearly forgotten Delphine?

Because she was forgettable, said the mocking little voice of reason inside his head; *because she cared nothing for you, and you know it.* She meant nothing to him any longer—he could look back dispassionately now, as if watching a poor play—but during that chaotic summer he had endured a brief moment, six weeks, of madness before she had run off with her wealthy protector and left him stunned and bewildered as a schoolboy.

Better he should have spent that precious time with Mathieu, he thought, with a stab of regret, especially during those last weeks in the autumn of 1793, when Mathieu had been held under house arrest, before he and the other Brissotin deputies had been subjected to the mockery of a trial and sentenced to death. He suddenly realized he had never known the extent of Mathieu's friendship with Aurèle Dupont, and felt a twinge of irrational jealousy that he should have had to share his oldest and best friend with a stranger.

"Ravel," Brasseur said, "are you listening to a word I'm saying?"

He returned to the present with a start, and an apologetic nod. "I fear not."

"I said, if old Dupont was poisoned, we're going to have a hard time discovering who did it, or how, or where. In the kitchen, on the way up-stairs, in the old man's bedchamber—anybody at all, I'm thinking!"

"I think we ought not to approach it chiefly from the angle of op-portunity," Aristide began, but got no further as the door opened and Dr. Prunelle joined them. One of Brasseur's inspectors followed him, looking pale.

"Well, I can tell you he was poisoned with something or other," the doctor announced, with a hint of satisfaction, as he set down his medical valise on a writing-desk and adjusted his wig. Opening the valise, he took out a small flask containing a cup or so of dark, reddish liquid, re-sembling the lees at the bottom of a wine bottle. "This isn't normal, not at all. No colic did this to him. The mucous membrane of the stomach was detached in some places, and its internal surface was corroded—you could see it with the naked eye—and there's a fine, crystallized sedi-ment here in—"

"For God's sake, Prunelle, put it away," Brasseur growled, realizing in the same instant as Aristide that the murky, brick-colored liquid must have come from the late Martin Dupont's stomach. "I'll take your word for it."

"Definitely not normal," Prunelle repeated as he thrust the little flask out of sight. "I'll have to take it to a colleague who knows more about analyzing for poison than I do, before I can say what it was, but I can swear right now you have a poisoner here, Brasseur. And from Di-dier's report from last night, I'd guess the same poison, though a very much smaller dose, just enough to make you sick for a few hours, went into yesterday's soup. The gritty, whitish, metallic substance they found in the maid's pocket could be arsenic, all right. The crystallized matter I found in Dupont's stomach might be the same thing. I don't suppose any of the family thought to save a sample of their vomitus?"

"I'll ask them," said Brasseur, rolling his eyes, "but don't get your hopes up. There's the soup tureen, of course; we're taking all the soiled plates and serving dishes over to headquarters."

"Well, I'm done here," said Prunelle. "Send a messenger around to my surgery when they want my statement for the magistrate. I'll have my friend look at the stomach contents, meanwhile, and perhaps he can determine in a day or two what it was that killed old Dupont."

He brushed off his sleeves, shook hands with Brasseur, and strode out. Brasseur cast Aristide a resigned glance. "Arsenic. Seems likely enough. And I'd guess at least half the household had the opportunity to use it!"

"I was going to say, before Prunelle came in," Aristide said, "that we ought not to approach this affair merely from the angle of opportunity but rather to study motive and personality. Citizeness Laurence Dupont seems like a good judge of character to me. If she says Charlotte, for example, doesn't have the brains or the character of a poisoner, I'm inclined to believe her."

"Charlotte," Brasseur echoed him. "That's the one who's still locked in her room, having crying fits? All right then, it's time she came out of it. Citizeness Bouton!"

Magdeleine soon thrust her head into the salon in response to Brasseur's baritone roar. "Commissaire? What is it?"

"I'll see your sister now, the one who went to pieces and who isn't showing her face."

"I'd prefer she weren't disturbed so soon—" Magdeleine began, but he interrupted her.

"Damn it, woman, I'm an officer of the law, and I have to ask her certain questions. She's a grown woman, isn't she? I won't eat her."

"Commissaire, I insist you let her rest for at least one more hour. She's had a terrible shock. Let me speak to her, and try to get her into a calmer frame of mind, and then you may ask her whatever you wish. About noon, say?"

"Talk to her if you must," Brasseur said with a sigh, "but I'll have to send one of my men with you. I can't have you influencing the witness. Go ahead, and I'll take formal statements from the rest of the household. If you'd send your husband to me."

She nodded, lips compressed in annoyance, and swept out. Brasseur turned to Aristide.

"I can handle this lot. It'll only be the usual questions and Dautry'll take all the notes I need."

"What do you want me to do, then?"

"What you do best. Slouch about the house and ask innocuous

questions; look around and see what you can see; discover what's out of place and who isn't behaving as he should. You know."

Aristide nodded and left the room, passing Claude Bouton as he did so. Claude was now wearing a rather shabby wig over his sparse hair and Aristide observed a little crease of worry between his graying eyebrows. "You wished to see me, Citizen Commissaire?"

If one was studying motive and personality, then the first, and often most important, personality to be considered was that of the victim. Aristide retraced his steps to the first floor and Martin Dupont's bedchamber.

Martin's body was back on the bed, a sheet covering him, two candles burning by his head. A handsome teenaged boy was sitting in a nearby chair, a set of rosary beads dangling from his fingers, though he was not muttering prayers but staring gloomily out the window through a crack between the drawn curtains. Turning sharply as Aristide entered, he gave him an appraising glance, half-suspicious, half-contemptuous, through the gloom. "Who are you?"

"I work for Commissaire Brasseur. And you? You must be Citizen Dupont's grandson, Étienne."

"Yes."

"It's generous of you to stand vigil over your grandfather's body. Were you fond of him?"

The boy shrugged. "Not really. There's nobody else to do it. They're all too busy. Except for Aunt Charlotte and Step-Grandmamma, but Aunt Charlotte's having hysterics and Step-Grandmamma says she's had enough of it and has a headache. And my sister," he added scornfully, "who's too *sensitive* to keep vigil over a corpse."

"When is the funeral to be?"

"Tomorrow, I suppose. Aunt Magdeleine sent for the undertaker."

The makeshift examining table had been taken back downstairs and all traces of Dr. Prunelle's presence were gone, save for a few smudges of drying blood that had not been wiped from the floorboards. Aristide paced about the room, watching for anything out of the ordinary as he did so. The boy eyed him, without speaking. Nothing caught Aristide's attention beyond the plainness of the furnishings—bed, wardrobe, chest of drawers, dressing table, close-stool behind a screen in the corner—and the visible signs of age and wear upon them. The dressing case, containing the usual brushes and combs, was of good quality but unadorned and well worn. The austere chamber, with its bare white plaster walls, reminded him of his own simple room, all he could afford, in Clotilde Prieur's lodging-house on Rue d'Amboise. Beyond a crucifix, a prie-dieu, and a small chalk portrait of a rather vacant-looking young woman dressed in the fashions and hairstyle of forty years ago—Martin's first wife, he guessed—few clues, beyond the severity of the room itself, remained to the old man's personality.

"Your grandfather was a frugal man, despite his wealth?" he asked.

"Tightfisted is more like it," said the boy, unsmiling. "People used to make jokes about him. You know that passage in *The Miser,* where the servant talks about the old man? Something like 'He won't say, "I give you good day"' ?"

"Oh, yes. '*Give* is a word to which he has such an aversion that he never says, "I give you good day," but "I lend you good day." ' He was that stingy, then?"

"That's about right. He hired Citizen Jullien as our tutor as well as his secretary, because it was cheaper than sending me to school. I'd rather have gone away to school. Anything to get out of here." He returned to his gloomy contemplation of the scene outside the window and Aristide joined him, pulling the curtain back a few inches and allowing a shaft of pale spring light to illuminate the room. The window overlooked the muddy back garden, where a dozen chickens scratched beneath a walnut tree that spread leafless branches from a corner. A few limp, frost-killed marigolds from the previous autumn hung their heads in a neat vegetable patch among tiny green shoots. Beyond, a narrow path led to a well, an outdoor privy, the chicken coop, a small gardener's shack, and a gate in the high wall.

"You're not happy here?" Aristide said, thinking of Laurence.

The boy turned and fixed him once more with a sulky glare from beneath a curtain of thick, untidy dark hair. "I don't see that it's any of your business, but why shouldn't I hate them? Step-Grandmother looks at you as if you're something she picked up on her shoe in the street, and Aunt Magdeleine's as mean as Grandfather was."

"Surely your Aunt Charlotte and Aunt Laurence are kind."

He waved a hand dismissively. "Oh, Aunt Charlotte's decent, but she's such an idiot. I told her once I'd heard voices, like Jeanne d'Arc, telling me I ought to be given a second helping of roast pork that Sunday dinner, and she believed me. And of course, just like everyone else, she flaps and coos all over that brat because she's such a pretty, clever little thing."

"Your sister?"

"Spoiled little bitch. And Father lets her have everything her own way," he burst out abruptly, "while nothing I ever do is right. No matter what I do, it's never *enough*! I work and work at my lessons, and she gets to do nothing but read plays and stories, and act out the parts because she's such a clever *actress*, just like Mamma, and I may not be much of an actor but I'm better at my studies than she is, but does he ever give me credit for it? I'm only his *son*, you know!"

"I'm sorry," Aristide said.

"I don't suppose *you* know what it's like," he snapped, retreating once more into sullenness. "You probably had a father who thought you were perfectly splendid, and who told you how proud he was of you when you won a school prize or something."

"Both my parents died when I was a child," Aristide told him. The boy flushed hotly and Aristide spared him further embarrassment by trying the handle of a door that led to an adjoining room, which proved to be bolted on the other side. "What does this door lead to?"

"That? That's Step-Grandmother's bedroom. She's back in there, I suppose." He cast a venomous glance at the door and continued, without lowering his voice. "Admiring herself in the mirror and pretending she's sorry he's dead."

"And this door?" Aristide inquired, pointing to the door in the opposite wall. "Where does it lead?"

"Grandfather's study," said Étienne. "Jullien's probably there, tending to business, since there won't be any lessons today."

"Thanks." Aristide wondered briefly if a solitary and sometimes lonely existence was, indeed, as Brasseur often grumbled when dealing with his mother-in-law, far less taxing than the demands of relatives whom one was arbitrarily expected to love. He tried the door and went into the study.

7

He found himself in a small, shelf-lined room whose tidy severity was even more pronounced than that of the bedchamber. Jullien, seated at the smaller of the two desks, a large ledger open in front of him, glanced up as he entered.

"Inspector? Can I help you?"

"This is where Citizen Dupont conducted his business?" Aristide inquired, without bothering to correct the secretary's misapprehension about his status.

"Some of it."

"You only deal with matters relating to his household, and his other financial concerns, his investments, and so on?"

"That's right."

"What sort of business did he conduct, aside from usury?"

"I don't see what that has to do with anything," Jullien said. "He *was* poisoned, wasn't he? By that servant girl?"

"He may have been." He forestalled Jullien's next question. "What sort of business was Citizen Dupont involved in?"

"Various sorts of investments, mostly. Moneylending to the wealthy, with *great* discretion a specialty; buying and selling. In 1790 he speculated in some Church lands, and resold most of them at a good price."

"He didn't keep them in order to rent them, or have them worked for his own profit?"

"Him? No. He preferred money in the hand, not farm property out somewhere that he'd never visit. He also dealt in annuities for a while, up until about 'ninety-two, when people stopped buying them."

"Annuities?" Aristide said. He was not well acquainted with the intricacies of finance; "annuity" had always, to him, seemed synonymous with "pension." "That's paying out an income for life to someone, isn't it?"

"In exchange for a large initial sum of money, which is signed over in perpetuity to the issuer of the annuity. The state started doing it at least a hundred years ago, but speculators issue annuities, too."

Aristide looked puzzled and Jullien sighed and said, in a somewhat patronizing tone, "Look, have a seat and I'll spell it out for you. A life annuity is a gamble," he continued as Aristide sat down in the other chair, "just like any other investment, but with an annuity the issuer is wagering on how long somebody is going to live. He's hoping the annuitant, the buyer, won't live long, and the annuitant is hoping he will. Say you had twenty thousand livres to invest—"

Aristide could not help smiling. "When hens have teeth!"

Jullien grinned, his features softening boyishly for an instant. "Yes, well, imagine you do, and that you haven't any heirs you wish to leave it to. And imagine you're older, about sixty, and perhaps you don't look as if you're in terribly good health, and that it's ten years ago, when a livre was worth a livre . . . all right?"

"Very well."

"All right." He carefully closed the ledger and busied himself with cutting a handful of quills as he continued. "You have twenty thousand livres to invest. You go to Citizen Dupont and tell him you hear he's selling annuities and you'd like a nice steady income from your twenty thousand. He takes a look at you and says to himself, 'Hmm, a fellow about sixty, probably has eight or ten years to live if he's lucky. So what percent interest can I offer him that will give him back about ten or twelve thousand over the course of the next ten years, and allow me to keep at least eight thousand?' He works it out and says to you, 'I can offer you a rate of six and a half percent annually, which will give you an assured income of thirteen hundred livres a year.' Thirteen hundred a year for ten years will mean he's paying out thirteen thousand altogether and, at your expected death at seventy, or before, he'll pocket the last seven thousand or more. Are you following me?"

"I believe so. I pay over my twenty thousand, permanently, in exchange for an annual income of six and a half percent of that twenty thousand."

"Exactly."

"And if I should live longer?"

"Well, while *he* thinks you're not going to live past seventy, *you*, on the other hand, are feeling very well, thank you; and you expect you'll live to seventy-five at least. So fifteen years of income, instead of ten, will work out to . . . nineteen thousand five hundred livres. If you're sixty and you live to seventy-six or beyond, you'll have taken in more money than you invested."

"To Citizen Dupont's loss."

"Yes. If you should be lucky enough to live to eighty, he'll have paid out a total of twenty-six thousand to you, which he has to do, by law, because he's contracted to do so. On the other hand, if you buy your annuity, then a year later come down with the smallpox and die, Citizen Dupont has done very well on his gamble, for he's only paid out thirteen hundred livres in exchange for your initial sum of twenty thousand. It's a wager, as I said; there's a fairly large chance you'll live just as long as he thinks you will, and a much smaller chance that you'll live a far greater or far shorter length of time, to the great profit of one or the other of you. But if you do a lot of business in annuities, then the large profits and large losses tend to cancel each other out well enough, leaving a steady profit from the ones who live only as long as you expect them to."

"And did Citizen Dupont earn a good living by selling annuities?" Aristide said.

"Oh, yes. Of course, during the past few years, with the inflation, nobody's been buying them, but on the other hand he scarcely had to pay out anything."

More financial niceties, Aristide thought. He settled himself more comfortably in the chair and said, "Enlighten me."

Looking at him as if he were an especially stupid schoolboy, Jullien shrugged. "It's the assignats, of course. The way they've lost value, because nobody trusts them. Everybody whose fortune is in assignats instead of gold or silver or real property has been ruined by the inflation."

"I certainly know that," Aristide said wryly, thinking how the price of a pair of shoes had gone from five livres in 1790 to two hundred livres in 1795, unless one had silver with which to pay the shoemaker. The paper assignats issued by the government, beginning in 1790, had begun to depreciate almost immediately; aside from being far too easily forged by those determined to undermine the Revolution, the notes were thoroughly distrusted by a population for whom money meant coins and nothing else. By 1796 a gold louis, worth twenty-four livres in silver or copper before the Revolution, could sometimes be exchanged for four or five thousand livres in paper money.

"Shopkeepers aren't hurt quite so badly," Jullien continued, dropping the freshly cut quills in a drawer, "because they simply raise their prices. Outrageously. But anybody with a fixed wage or income is still receiving the same amount of money per day or week or quarter, even though he's probably receiving it in dirty bits of paper nobody wants. Suddenly his hundred livres, which in gold and silver, before the Revolution, would have bought a few weeks' worth of supplies, in paper will barely buy a pound of candles."

"That's nothing I don't know."

"Well, Citizen Dupont, who was immensely clever about such things, saw, early on, how the assignats were losing value, and offered to take them off people's hands. At a ridiculously low rate, of course, but people were just glad to be rid of them. He also had made a few loans to the Royal Treasury in the past, and in 1790 they'd paid him off in assignats, take it or leave it. And now, during the past year or so, when the inflation went sky-high, he had all those worthless assignats—and a few dozen annuitants who were receiving fixed incomes from him. So he paid out their incomes only in assignats, of course."

"Which was completely unscrupulous," Aristide said, understanding, "and yet perfectly legal. He'd taken people's fortunes in gold, perhaps five, ten, twenty years before, and was paying out the interest in paper that was worthless."

Jullien nodded. "Except to the government. The government says a hundred-livre note is just as much a hundred livres as a handful of louis d'or. If you owe somebody a hundred livres and you give him that hundred-livre note in repayment, you've fulfilled your obligations, and there's nothing he can do about it, according to the law."

Aristide thought about it for a moment as Jullien refilled the inkwell. Jullien was quite right; the near-worthless assignats and the inflated prices they had caused had been a boon for debtors, though a disaster for those who had been receiving fixed incomes before the Revolution. Such folk had been utterly unprepared for the brutal inflation of 1795, when the price of a bushel of flour, if paid for in paper currency, had risen to a hundred times what it had been in 1790. During the past two years, Brasseur had discovered more than a dozen starving widows or cripples, reduced to barely a crust of bread a day, who, in despair, had hanged themselves from their own roof beams. Traffic at the Basse-Geôle de la Seine, the city morgue where bodies pulled from the river were taken, had also risen appallingly.

"People must have loathed Dupont for that," Aristide said. "It almost sounds like a motive for murder."

Jullien looked dubious. "Why? Everybody who's paying out fixed incomes or salaries is doing the same thing, even the government. Aren't you getting the same pay from the Ministry of Police that you always did, except now it's in paper, and your week's salary of paper won't buy you a mouthful of bread or a rotten potato?"

Aristide nodded, thoughtful. Like all police agents or spies, he did not receive an official salary from the ministry, but rather a payment for services now and then from the commissariat's petty cash. He was free to accept gratuities from grateful clients, however, whether or not the affair had been a police matter, and asked for gold whenever he judged the client was wealthy enough to spare it.

He had, nevertheless, heard Brasseur complain about his pay often enough. Fortunately Brasseur had a brother not far from Paris who often sent him a hare or a pheasant and a couple of loaves of good country bread, so he and his family were not as badly off as were many.

"People might hate old Dupont's guts for screwing them like that," Jullien continued, "but if you killed him you'd probably regret it eventually. Heirs have a way of being terribly ignorant of records and contracts of that sort—believe me, among the three heirs here, affairs are going to be completely snarled for a while, and I can guess Citizeness Bouton isn't going to let go of a sou more than she has to. Better to take the paper than to have nothing at all. I doubt any of his annuitants would have killed him."

"It's more likely it would have been someone who owed him money, you think?" Aristide said. "Someone whom he'd been bleeding dry?"

"He might have been bleeding people dry five years ago," said Jullien, "but these days debtors don't worry so much about their debts. It's just the same as Citizen Dupont paying out paper on the annuities; people who owe money owe the same amount whether it's in gold or paper. You could practically go out and find a hundred livres in paper in the public privy, if that's what you needed. It wouldn't buy much at the market, but you could legally pay a debt with it. That's about all the paper is good for. Some of his debtors have already paid up in full; better to pay off your debts and start afresh than to spend thirty or forty livres on a pound of butter."

Aristide nodded. "If it wasn't something to do with his loans or investments, then that leaves personal motives for seeing him dead, doesn't it?"

"I don't know what you mean," Jullien said, shrugging, and turned to his desk.

"Don't you?"

"I wouldn't listen to household gossip if I were you."

"But you admit there is gossip?"

"I suppose people gossip every time a man and woman are thrown together, especially if the woman's husband is twice her age."

"I never mentioned a woman," Aristide said.

He watched Jullien for a moment. He thought he could detect a faint pink flush creeping up the young man's neck past his neat cravat, and the hand that reached for a quill was not as steady as it might have been.

The door to the hallway opened and they both turned and rose as Martin Dupont's widow entered. Her cool gaze flicked over Aristide with a bare glimmer of interest, before turning quickly to Jullien.

"Who is that?" she inquired.

"Police," said Jullien. She glanced back at Aristide with more interest and a little worried frown.

"What do you want, then?"

"To discover who murdered your husband," Aristide said.

"Murdered!" Ursule exclaimed.

"The police surgeon found evidence of poison. Was it you who gave it to him?"

She paled, but recovered herself well enough to fix him with a frigid glare. "How dare you suggest such a thing."

"I believe you had the opportunity," he told her. "You could have come through the communicating door to his bedroom, dropped the poison in his breakfast porridge, and no one would have seen you."

"Except for Martin, of course," she snapped. "He wasn't senile, you know."

"But still he was forty years your senior, citizeness."

"What if he was?"

He said nothing, but allowed his glance to wander over to Jullien. The hot flush crept into Jullien's cheeks and Ursule let out an impatient sigh.

"Citizen Inspector, I won't insult your intelligence by trying to convince you I loved my husband. But I was fond of him, and he treated me well, gave me almost anything I asked for. I had no reason to want him dead."

"No?" Aristide said, with another glance at Jullien. "Not with a good-looking young man residing in the house?"

She gave him a superior smile and glanced down at her fashionable, high-waisted gown. Even in mourning dress, she maintained an air of modish elegance. "Do use some common sense. My husband was perfectly aware that a good-looking young man lived in the house."

"If he'd been jealous, he wouldn't have had to keep me on, would he?" said Jullien. "Plenty of hungry scribblers with a bit of education out there looking for work. He could have thrown me out anytime he wanted to."

Ursule nodded. "All he required was that we be discreet. You see, Inspector, Martin didn't really want a wife; he made no demands of that sort on me. What he wanted was a handsome, well-dressed woman at his side whom he could show off to his business associates. Why else do you think he spent money on fine gowns for me? To prove he was prosperous, to impress them, to feed his own vanity. He said to me once that no matter how much you might spend on new gowns for Magdeleine or Charlotte, they would still look like mules dressed up in sacking, so why waste the money. But I—I'm something he could boast of. He was like a man who buys a beautiful painting and invites his friends to see it. I have everything I could want; what would I gain by murdering Martin?"

"Your freedom?" Aristide said, though he suspected she was telling the truth.

She shrugged. "Freedom isn't as important as you people make it out to be, with your 'liberty, equality, fraternity,' and so on. I've had my comforts and my security, and I had to do very little to be sure of them. Freedom only means responsibilities."

"Why don't you come downstairs with me to Commissaire Brasseur and repeat to him what you've told me?" he said. He unlatched the door and gestured them both through.

8

They preceded him down the staircase as a distant bell clanged noon, Ursule cool and confident as ever, Jullien a trifle uneasy. The girl Fanny was just leaving the salon as they approached. "Good morning, Step-Grandmamma," she said, curtsying perfunctorily. "I hope you're feeling better?"

"Quite," said Ursule, sweeping past her. "I can't abide children," she added when the door had closed behind them. "Especially that one."

Aristide privately thought that perhaps Ursule disliked Fanny because they were very much two of a kind, single-mindedly pursuing their own interests. He said nothing, however, and went over to the small writing-desk where Brasseur, despite the chill in the room, was mopping his brow.

"That child talks too much," was all he said. "So what's this?"

"I thought you should next question Citizeness Dupont—the widow Dupont, rather—and Citizen Jullien."

"Very well then, your full name, citizeness?"

Ursule composedly seated herself in the nearest chair and Jullien edged closer to it to rest a hand on her shoulder. "Ursule Marie Adèlaïde d'Armoncourt, wife—widow Dupont."

"Your age, and your place of birth?"

"Forty. I was born at the Château d'Armoncourt near Vouziers."

"How long were you married to Citizen Dupont?"

"Thirteen years."

"And where were you, citizeness, when they were preparing breakfast day before yesterday in the kitchen?"

"I was in my bedroom, as I always am. I take my breakfast in bed at about quarter to eight. Then I went in to bid my husband good morning."

"What time was that?"

She shrugged. "A few minutes past eight, I suppose. Magdeleine was talking with him."

"Was he still eating his breakfast?"

"No, the girl had already taken away the tray."

"And you stayed how long?"

"About a quarter of an hour. You see, Commissaire, I had no opportunity to poison Martin. Nor would I have wished to. Your inspector here," she continued with a swift glance in Aristide's direction, "insinuated that Citizen Jullien and I might have conspired to murder Martin. I assure you nothing could be farther from the truth. My husband was not a jealous man and I have everything I want right here, including Charles's company. Why should I risk that by committing murder?"

"Perhaps you, citizen, were not so complacent about the situation?" Brasseur inquired, turning to Jullien. Jullien paled.

"No! I—that is to say, I have the greatest esteem for the citizeness, but . . ."

"Come now," said Brasseur, "we're all adults here. You were carrying on a love affair with Citizeness Dupont, weren't you?"

"Yes, of course," Ursule said. "An affair that my husband knew about. He was content that I should be happy, in whatever way pleased me, so long as we were discreet about it. And we kept that side of the bargain. I've gained nothing by Martin's death."

"Except a legacy, I think, citizeness?" Brasseur said, watching her.

"I expect so," she said, with another indifferent shrug. "There was something of the sort in the marriage contract. But what could I buy with such an inheritance that I don't already have? I don't imagine the money would be enough for me to live like a duchess in my own household, and besides, establishing and maintaining a household of one's own is a bother. Here I can let Magdeleine run things, which she enjoys doing and does very well. I think I would arrange for a more varied table and certainly a lady's maid of my own, but in all other ways I'm content enough to let her play housekeeper and enjoy myself as I please."

She leaned forward, elbows on the arms of the chair, as her expression grew serious. "Commissaire, my father was no great lord or courtier; he was the fourth son of a viscount, just a shabby country squire. I grew up in a tumbledown farmhouse that they called a château, on a patch of land they called a manor, but my father plowed his own acres, walking behind a team of oxen. We were scarcely wealthier than the peasants whose land adjoined ours. My mother was forever telling us who we were, and what we were, that our ancestors had gone on crusade and fought for the king against the English and all the rest of it, but that didn't hide the fact that we wore sabots and mended our own gowns, over and over again, and boiled our own soap. When the opportunity came to marry Martin Dupont and leave all that behind me, I took it. Would I be so immensely foolish as to jeopardize what I have now?"

Brasseur grunted and made a few notes before suddenly looking over at Jullien. "You, though, it's different for you, isn't it? With the citizeness married, you're nothing but a secretary, not much more than a servant, who sleeps with his master's wife while the master looks the other way. But with the master's wife a widow, and a widow with a legacy, you can look forward, if you play your cards right, to marrying her and enjoying that legacy with her. A much nicer state of affairs for you, isn't it?"

"No!"

"Oh, come now, citizen. Don't tell me the thought hadn't crossed your mind."

"Perhaps it did," Jullien said sullenly, "but I never did a thing to harm the old bastard, and you can't prove I did."

"Describe your movements in the morning, the day before yesterday."

"The same as every day. I rose, washed, dressed, took breakfast in the dining room. The children were there, and Charlotte." He rolled his eyes at the memory. "Prattling about all sorts of nonsense as usual, of course. Then I went back up to Citizen Dupont's study and . . . oh, I remember, I had some letters to copy into his letter-book. I was working on those while waiting for him to come in and set to business. But he never came in, because he was taken ill."

"So you never saw Citizen Dupont that morning?" Brasseur said.

"No."

"That'll do for now, then. Don't go far."

"Are you aware old Dupont's study is next to his bedroom," Aristide asked Brasseur after Ursule and Jullien had left the room, "and that there is a communicating door?"

"Oh, lord," he grumbled. "So he could have slipped in, just like the wife, and nobody'd be the wiser. What do you think of the wife?"

Aristide thrust his hands in his pockets and frowned for a moment before replying. "I think I believe her. She looks like the sort who enjoys her comforts and wants to make the least amount of effort to keep on enjoying them. As she says, if she's content as she is, why would she risk her life by poisoning her husband?"

"The secretary's got a better motive."

"Yes . . . yet he's not stupid. Would *he* take the risk, I wonder? Or would he think it through, and realize that while the lovely Ursule may have no qualms about amusing herself with him, that she'd never marry him if the least cloud hung over his head? Marry him after her husband dies suspiciously, and she'd promptly be suspected of doing away with the old man, or at least of being her lover's accomplice. She's far too fond of herself and her own ease and security to take that chance."

"True." Brasseur glanced over his notes and sighed. "Well, Claude Bouton claims he woke up with a bellyache early that morning . . . seems he's a martyr to indigestion . . . and never went down to breakfast, never left his bedroom until midmorning. Same for Magdeleine, who was fussing over him. She was only in the kitchen for a minute to make him a cup of peppermint tea, and she says it was early, about six, before the girl began cooking the porridge. The cook confirms it. So neither of them could have poisoned the porridge unless they nipped out and did something in the hallway while Charlotte's back was turned."

"What about the two children?" Aristide said.

"Ate breakfast in the dining room, but they admit they were both in and out of the kitchen all morning, cadging food. You know how children are." He grinned. "Mine would eat us out of house and home if Marie didn't lock up the pantry. And decent food the price that it is!"

"What about the servants who ran off? Zélie and Antoine?"

"I sent Thomas to track them down. I doubt either of them did it, though; they've both been with the family for a few years, and they'd have no motive that I can see."

"Unless one of them needed money," Aristide said, "and was expecting a legacy for faithful service in Martin's will?"

"Do you really think the old pinchpenny was the sort to remember servants in his will? Brasseur said. They eyed each other for a moment and simultaneously shook their heads.

"Not likely," he added. "Nor was he the sort to let on what was in his will. Nobody's business but his own, I'm thinking. Any servant who knew him wouldn't have expected so much as a cracked sou." He added a note to the scrawled pages before him. "I suppose this Maître Frochot is the one in charge of the will; we'll have to see that, too."

"Parents have to divide their fortune equally among their children now," Aristide reminded him, referring to the new inheritance laws. "There won't be many surprises."

"Still . . . he could do what he liked with one-tenth of his estate, and if he's as rich as they've been hinting, one-tenth would still be pretty considerable. . . ."

"So," Aristide said, taking up Brasseur's notes, "at six the servants breakfast, then go about their duties. At about quarter to seven Jeannette begins cooking Martin's porridge. At seven o'clock Charlotte takes Martin's porridge and coffee upstairs to him. The poison could have been put in the porridge, or the coffee, in the kitchen, or on its way upstairs, or in his own bedchamber. Jeannette could have done it in the kitchen; Thérèse also; Charlotte could have done it in the kitchen or on the way, although she certainly wasn't the one who poisoned yesterday's soup; also either one of the children. Ursule or Jullien could have done it in Dupont's bedchamber, while he'd been using the close-stool perhaps. Magdeleine and Claude seem to be clear. What about Gervais?"

"The great Hauteroche hasn't condescended to come down yet and speak at length to a mere commissaire of police. Let's get to know him, shall we?" Brasseur gestured to Dautry and the three of them left the salon. Fanny, who was sulkily sweeping the first-floor hall, directed them to Gervais's study, not far from Martin's bedchamber.

"If, at any time, Charlotte put that breakfast tray down and turned her back to it before taking it in to her father," Aristide mused, "Gervais could have come out of this door, seen it, and seized his chance to drop arsenic in the porridge."

"Assuming he already had the arsenic and was planning to use it," said Brasseur.

"Yes, of course. But poisoning isn't a spur-of-the-moment sort of crime; it requires premeditation. If he had it already and was intending to dose his father with it, he might have simply thought it was an ideal opportunity." He scratched on the door and a sonorous voice roared "Enter!"

Aristide followed Brasseur inside to a small study hung with at least a dozen fanciful engravings and pastels, presumably depictions of Gervais Dupont in costume on the stage of the Comédie-Française. A large, pigeonholed desk, where Gervais sat with his back to them, stood squarely in the center of the room. Opposite it hung an oil portrait of a very beautiful woman wearing a fantastic confection of a flounced and hooped gown. She held a Greek theatrical mask in one hand and Aristide guessed that this was Gervais's wife, Sophie.

"Yes?" Gervais glanced up from the papers strewn about the desk, twisted about, and gazed blankly at the three of them. "What the devil is it now?" He rose and gave Brasseur a hearty and thoroughly artificial smile as they shook hands. "I thought you'd be done investigating this business by now? The inspector last evening arrested the kitchenmaid and there's the end of it."

"Not quite, citizen; there's still the question of your father's death. . . ."

"My father!" He frowned and thought about it for a moment. Clearly the idea that Martin Dupont had died of poison had scarcely occurred to him—or else he was making full use of his formidable talents. "What, you think the girl bumped off my father, too?"

"Our condolences for your loss," Brasseur began automatically, with a slight bow. Aristide did the same, only to find, as he straightened, that Gervais was looking him up and down as if he were a prize bull at a country fair.

"Good God," he exclaimed, "what a perfect type. Who are you? Done any acting?"

"No, citizen," Aristide said, after an instant of confusion. It was true that he had not acted upon the stage since boarding school.

"That's a pity. You're a perfect comic servant type—the dolorous ones, the more melancholy the better. Keeps them in stitches. Lord, yes, I can see you in all sorts of comic roles—thin as a rail, and that long face of yours. . . . That would keep you in good bit parts night after night. Put you and Imbert together onstage, you'd be a wild success— I'm always looking for the right people for my company." He seized a lorgnette hanging by a chain from his waistcoat. "No," he continued, half to himself, as he examined Aristide more closely, "no, you're actually not that bad looking—you could do juvenile leads in a pinch; it's the lank hair and the somber expression. . . . Lugubrious fellow, aren't you? Fancy performing on the stage? Any good at memorizing? Though I expect you could carry off comic mutes just as well—"

"Citizen, please," Brasseur protested. "Ravel is my associate, and I don't think he plans on joining the theater anytime soon."

Gervais laughed and offered his hand to Aristide. "I beg your pardon, citizen. I admit it freely—like most stage folk, I'm afraid I have no manners. No offense intended."

"None taken," he said.

"Are you always this solemn?" Gervais added. "Do you ever crack a smile, Ravel?"

"Now and then." Gervais was perfectly right, Aristide thought; both Brasseur and Aristide's colleague François were forever telling him he was far too serious for comfort. He summoned a half smile and

Gervais burst out laughing, good humor illuminating his handsome face.

"Oh, excellent, excellent. Ravel, if you ever tire of—what is it you do?"

"I work for the commissaire. . . ."

"Yes, of course," Gervais said, dismissively. "Well, if you ever grow tired of that *thrilling* profession, come to me. I think your face alone would give you a fine career upon the stage."

"Citizen . . ." Brasseur rumbled. Gervais turned back to him, with an apologetic grin, and, with a gesture to the armchair by the fireplace, threw himself into his chair.

"I am at your disposal, Commissaire. Fire away!"

"Your full name, for the record?"

"Gervais-Jean-Baptiste Dupont, called Hauteroche," he said, turning slightly so his fine profile caught the best light from the window.

They would get little useful information out of the actor, Aristide suspected; Gervais Dupont's type, being thoroughly self-absorbed, made poor witnesses, for they saw nothing that did not directly involve their own persons or interests.

"Your age, place of birth, and condition?"

"Age, forty-six; born . . . here in this very house, or so I've been told. My condition, of course, you know."

"'Actor,'" Brasseur told Dautry, who had paused in his transcription.

"Actor, author, and impresario, if you please," Gervais corrected him, smiling. When the Comédie-Française's monopoly on legitimate plays by long-dead, celebrated authors—Molière, Racine, Corneille, and many others—had been abolished in 1791, ambitious actors and managers had seized their chance to profit by mounting dozens of popular plays that, for a century and more, had been available for performance only by a licensed troupe.

"Yes, you've bought your own theater out just past the Boulevard, haven't you, citizen?"

"Indeed I have. Are you a patron of the theater, Commissaire? Say the word and I'll have them give you a box for any play you wish."

"Well, that's very generous of you, citizen," Brasseur continued imperturbably, "but I'll have to wait to take advantage of your offer until after this affair is over. Meanwhile, perhaps you can tell us your movements in the morning, day before yesterday?"

He waved his hands in an elaborate shrug. "I rose, at about eleven o'clock; I dressed, I took breakfast."

"Where did you take your breakfast?"

"In the dining salon, alone, with a copy of the *Journal de Paris*. I'd been on, the night before, and of course I slept late."

"Did you go into the kitchen?"

"No, why should I have? Thérèse brought me out some coffee and bread and pot cheese she'd kept aside for me. She always does that, after a performance night, and my daughter, Fanny, clears away the breakfast dishes; that's one of her chores. I finished my breakfast and went in here at about half past eleven—"

"Surely you knew your father was ill?" Aristide said.

"Oh, certainly, I heard Father was taken ill, but I didn't think anything of it until he took a turn for the worse, a bit after noon. I was busy with my accounts." Gervais smiled again, with a dramatic sigh. "The life of an impresario is far more tedious than you probably imagine, citizen. It primarily consists of calculating profits and losses, and keeping the bloodsuckers who invested in the building happy, and deciding how best to save money on remounting one old production while spending money on another. If being my own manager didn't afford me the artistic freedom I'd craved, I would throw it up and—well! I mustn't bore you with my little troubles."

"I understand you're rather badly in debt after restoring your new theater?" Aristide said.

"Ah, well, the investors have to get their percentage, you know, and these things can't be paid for in an instant," he said. "But it'll come right, soon enough. The box-office receipts are good. Look about you; Paris is theater-mad! They want to go to a new play every night."

"Now that your father is dead," Brasseur said, "I suppose you'll inherit enough money to pay all your debts?"

"Half a dozen times over, I expect."

Abruptly the genial, insouciant celebrity vanished, to be replaced by a man with hard, mistrustful eyes who bore a sudden startling resemblance to his father. "But I didn't kill the Old Man because of it. What would be the point?"

"Your inheritance," said Brasseur, returning his narrow stare. "Plenty of rich old men have been hastened off before their time by their children."

"Rubbish," said Gervais. "Look here, Commissaire, I think you'd better understand my situation. You know what dealing with money has been like during the past few years—everybody hoarding coin. It's miserable if you want to buy anything, of course, but it's been a stroke of good luck for debtors."

Aristide nodded. After Jullien's little lecture to him on the subject of money, assignats, and debts, he thought he understood what Gervais was about to say.

"He's not as hard up as you might think, Brasseur," he explained. "Ten years ago, if you owed somebody a great deal of money, say ten thousand livres, you owed them ten thousand and that was that. But with this cursed paper money, and the way it's lost value, nowadays you can scrape together ten thousand livres in paper in exchange for a few household objects." He glanced at Gervais.

"I sold my house and all my furniture two years ago when I moved back here with my wife and children," he said. "Got a fair bit for it, though it was all in assignats, of course."

"And your creditors can take the paper you give them or they can demand gold," Aristide continued, "but they can't legally press you for the gold, after all, because you've offered to repay them in all good faith with perfectly legal money off the government printing presses, haven't you?"

"That's exactly what I've done," Gervais declared, "and I'm not worried about being hounded for my debts. I didn't need to murder my father in order to pay off my theater. There was no love lost between us, but I had no pressing reason to want the old bastard dead. You tell that to the examining magistrate, won't you, Commissaire?"

"If you didn't poison your father," Aristide said, "perhaps you have some theories as to who did?"

"The kitchenmaid, I suppose."

"Come, you can do better than that, citizen. You're an actor; your profession is all about interpreting motives. What motive do you think Jeannette Moineau could have had to murder your father, or to make you all ill, for that matter?"

Gervais sighed. "I suppose my dear stepmother—who is six years younger than I, by the way—doesn't mind being a widow. Have you grilled her yet?"

"What about your sisters?" said Brasseur, ignoring the question.

"My sisters?" Gervais chuckled. "You can put it right out of your mind if you think Charlotte bumped off the Old Man. She's far too tenderhearted, and besides, she has no more sense than a hen. She couldn't think that far ahead."

"And Citizeness Bouton?"

"Magdeleine? Perhaps. She'd have the nerve to do it, at least. But I don't know why she would. She and Claude don't want for anything particularly, living here."

"And what about your children?" Aristide said, more to gauge Gervais's reaction than with any real hope of an answer. Gervais colored.

"My children!"

"If you'd not noticed, Étienne is unhappy. He resents his sister and he craves some attention from you, a little consideration. I imagine he might have seen his grandfather's death as a deliverance from an oppressive household; he could go to boarding school, become his own man."

"You're insinuating that my boy could have poisoned my father?" Gervais snapped.

"You know him better than I. Do you think him capable of it?"

His only answer was a scowl. Brasseur rose and gestured Dautry and Aristide to their feet.

"We'll let you be now, citizen; but I need hardly tell you not to leave Paris." They left the study with Gervais glaring sourly after them.

9

A nd now," Brasseur announced, planting his fists on his hips, "I am
going to talk to sister Charlotte if it's the last thing I do. Dautry,
go and find the Bouton woman and tell her I won't be put off any
longer."

"So," Aristide said when Dautry had hurried downstairs, "who
would you stake your money on?"

"Thus far? Magdeleine, I think. I get the impression she could be
pretty ruthless if she had to be. You?"

Aristide nodded. "Magdeleine . . . or Gervais, if either of them already had the poison, and if they came out of their respective bed-
chambers unseen, and if Charlotte had laid the tray down in the
first-floor hall before taking it in to Martin. But that's far too many ifs,
and we know very little yet."

Magdeleine joined them on the landing, looking worried and cross,
and led them upstairs to the second floor. She paused at the end of the
hall and tried the nearest door, which was bolted on the inside, before
rapping softly. "Charlotte, dearest, are you awake? The commissaire
has to ask you some questions."

No one answered, though Aristide thought he could hear a faint sniff
from within the room. "Charlotte," Magdeleine repeated, her voice

much gentler than he had heard it at any other time, "you must come out sometime, you know. You can't hide there forever. No one's going to hurt you. Poor Father is gone, but we have to go on with our lives."

"Citizeness," Brasseur added, to the silent door, "you can't stay locked in that room for the rest of your life, and it's my duty to clear up this matter. You wouldn't want me to fail in my duty, would you?"

"It's *all right*, Charlotte," Magdeleine insisted. "You know I'll take care of you. Do come out and speak to the commissaire. He won't hurt you."

At last the door slowly opened and a woman peered out. Wrapped unbecomingly in a limp peignoir over her linen chemise, she was plump, with light brown hair and large, rather protuberant blue eyes, red-rimmed from crying. Sniffing violently, she dabbed at her nose with a soggy handkerchief and glanced nervously from Magdeleine to Brasseur.

"But I didn't do anything!"

"Of course you didn't," Magdeleine soothed her. "Nobody would believe you would do anything to hurt Father, or any of us. But perhaps you saw or heard something that will help the police. Just tell the citizen what you know."

"I don't know *anything*. . . . "

"Do you think I might come inside, citizeness?" Brasseur asked, lowering his voice to what, for him, was a gentle rumble. Brasseur was a big man, with the shoulders of an ox and two bayonet scars on his cheeks, souvenirs of his years spent soldiering; he could be most intimidating when he wanted to be, though he knew how to handle anxious women well enough.

Charlotte stepped back and Brasseur strode inside with Aristide and Dautry, firmly shutting the door in Magdeleine's face when she made as if to accompany them. "Sorry, citizeness, but questioning is to be done in private."

Aristide had half expected Charlotte's bedchamber to be festooned with the overpretty, painted rococo paneling of the style of Louis XV's reign, or perhaps to be decorated in the newer fashion with wallpaper, quite possibly in a pattern of pink flowers, but the walls were of bare whitewashed plaster like the rest of the house. A few cheap, sentimental colored prints of dainty shepherdesses, implausibly clean, frolicking in woodland groves with their rustic swains, and of virginal saints receiving visions of angels, hung above the chest of drawers and modest dressing table. Charlotte stepped back and gestured vaguely at a chair, then retreated to the rumpled bed in its alcove and continued to mop at her eyes and nose.

Brasseur cleared his throat. "Very well, then, citizeness, I am Commissaire Brasseur, and these are my associate Citizen Ravel, and my secretary, Citizen Dautry. We're very sorry for your loss. Our condolences."

Charlotte sniffed again and nodded. "Now," Brasseur continued, "I understand you were the one who took Citizen Dupont his breakfast?"

"Yes?" she whispered, darting a fearful glance at the door, as if hoping to find Magdeleine there. "I mean, yes, I was . . . citizen . . . but I didn't do anything, honestly I didn't. I only fetched Father's breakfast tray from the kitchen, because the maid was so busy, and brought it up to him."

"Did you set it down anywhere along the way, to talk to someone, perhaps, or to attend to a little task?"

"Oh!" She thought about it for a moment, openmouthed. "Yes, I must have. In fact, I'm sure I did. I set it down on the first-floor landing, near the top of the stairs. Father's room is farther down the hall, you see."

"Why did you do that, citizeness?" Brasseur inquired, patiently.

"Because . . . because one of the maids had left a dusting rag on the little table on the landing. Yes, that was it. I saw the dusting rag, and I set down the tray in order to pick it up, and then I saw that the bench on the landing was quite dusty. Jeannette or Zélie, whichever one it was, she must have been called away in the middle of a task, and left her dusting rag behind, and then forgot to go back and fetch the rag and finish her work. So I thought I'd better dust the bench, as long as I was there, and I had the rag right there in my hand, so I dusted it, and then I went to the window in the sewing room to shake it out. The sewing room's right there, you see; it's the little sitting-room right at the head of the stairs."

"You left the landing and went into the sewing room."

"Yes, I shook the rag out the window, only for a moment of course, because in this weather you'll let all the cold air in if you keep the window open for long—"

"How long did you stay in the sewing room?" Brasseur persisted.

"I . . . oh, I know, I shook out the rag, then I closed the window, and then I realized that the windowsill was a bit dirty, so I gave that a rub, too. And the sewing table that sits in front of the window was rather dusty—ashes and soot, you know. One of the children, not that they're really children any more, are they?—one of them must have left the window open for a while, and you have to be so careful with ashes flying about in this season, when everybody has fires going. So I made sure the table was quite clean, and then I shook the rag out again, and put it in my apron pocket, and then I fetched the tray and took it in to Father."

"So you might have remained five minutes or so in the sewing room, with your back to the door?" Brasseur said, still kindly, though Aristide could tell he was nearly bursting with impatience at her rambling. Brasseur glanced over his shoulder at him. He understood the glance; five minutes was plenty of time for someone, anyone, to creep down the hallway and silently stir a spoonful of powder into the covered dish waiting on the tray.

"Yes . . . five minutes . . . I suppose so." Charlotte gulped back a sob and hurriedly blew her nose into her sodden and crumpled handkerchief. "Poor Father was a little bit annoyed with me because I was a few minutes late with his breakfast. He expected his porridge to be sent up to him every morning at seven o'clock exactly, you know, because he said that punctuality kept things running properly and efficiently, and I *was* a very little bit tardy." She blinked several times and Aristide feared she was about to burst once more into tears. "Oh, it's so sad that I should have made him cross on his very last day on this earth!"

Brasseur sighed and passed Charlotte his own serviceable handkerchief. "Citizeness, I'm sure he's forgiven you. You brought in the porridge, and your father was in his bed just as usual? Nothing seemed abnormal, or out of place?"

"Oh, no. It was all just as usual."

"Was anybody in the bedchamber with him?"

"Oh, no," she said, shaking her head. "He was alone. Ursule hardly ever rises before eight o'clock."

"What about your sister?" Aristide said. "I understand she often visited with your father in the mornings. Did she stop by his room that morning while you were there?"

"No, Magdeleine wasn't with Father when I brought him his tray. Nobody was. I set up the tray and punched up his pillows a little and asked him when he wanted Antoine sent up to him to help him dress—Antoine serves as his valet, you know, as well as doing work about the house—and he said half past eight would do, and I went back downstairs."

Brasseur smiled reassuringly. "There, citizeness, that's all we needed to know. That wasn't so terrifying, was it?"

"Who in the family do you think might have desired your father's death?" Aristide said. She started and stared up at him, her eyes wide and frightened.

"Desired? Oh, *nobody* could have wanted Father to *die*!"

"Someone did, citizeness. Somebody deliberately poisoned him."

Charlotte blinked rapidly as the door flew open and Magdeleine strode in, white-faced. "I think you had all better leave now, Citizen Commissaire," she snapped. "It is inconceivable to me that anyone of our family would have done something as wicked as murdering Father."

There was a faint gasp behind them as Brasseur reached for the door handle and Aristide turned just in time to see Charlotte dissolve at last into noisy tears.

Brasseur and Aristide left Magdeleine to tend to her sister, for they knew they would get nothing more out of Charlotte until she had calmed. "Well?" Brasseur said softly when they had shut the door behind them.

"I wonder," Aristide said.

"Charlotte?"

"Yes."

"She's uneasy about something, that's plain to see."

"I'd swear she knows something."

"Or else she did it herself."

"Or she did it herself," Aristide agreed. "But everyone we've questioned has said Charlotte's no murderess. And on meeting her . . . people don't act against their nature, Brasseur."

Brasseur nodded. "All the same, keep an eye on her. Now . . . I suppose we'd better take a look at old Dupont's records. He was a moneylender, so he may have made some bitter enemies. Let's talk to Jullien a bit more."

Aristide followed him downstairs to Martin's study on the first floor. Jullien, though vexed at being interrupted, ushered them inside and leaned against his desk in an attempt to seem unconcerned. "Yes, Commissaire? How can I help you?"

"I gather Citizen Dupont conducted his business dealings here?"

"A portion of them," Jullien said. "His transactions with—well, with his more genteel clients. He kept an office on Rue du Renard, too, but I can't help you with that. He has a clerk there who tends to that side of affairs, and I have nothing to do with it."

Rue du Renard was in the shabby quarter northeast of the great central provision markets, a quarter where modest tradesmen kept a workshop on the ground floor and lived on the first floor, where journeymen and their families lived on the second and third floors, and where laborers squeezed into squalid furnished rooms on the fourth, fifth, sixth floors, with near paupers in the two uppermost levels of drafty, leaky garrets. It was an ideal location for a usurer's establishment: a neighborhood of poor workers, always needing to borrow to make ends meet when some crisis straitened their slender wages, but not so wretchedly poor that there would be no hope of loans being repaid.

"I suppose he did a lot of his business from Rue du Renard?" said Brasseur, brightening. "The folk in that quarter—that's more the sort of person I can see doing away with the moneylender if things got tight."

"By poisoning him?" said Aristide. "Brasseur, if you're a laborer or a shopkeeper who wants to make away with the usurer who's bleeding you white, it's by far the easiest thing to go to his countinghouse and knock him on the head, or knife him, or burn his brains; you don't poison him from inside his own home."

Jullien nodded. "Besides, what he took in at Rue du Renard was negligible in comparison to the sums of money he dealt with here. He began his business at Rue du Renard, decades ago, but he progressed far beyond that. Lending money to the poor will earn you a living but it won't make you rich. You get rich by lending money to the rich.'"

"Well then," said Brasseur, "I think we'll take a look at the records. Citizen Jullien, you can stay here if you please, but don't try to interfere."

Jullien shrugged. "Commissaire, you're welcome to look inside any box or drawer you can open. Maître Frochot, the notary, has Dupont's keys to the most important records and you'll have to get them from him." He flung himself into a chair. "Search all you like. Though I'd appreciate it if you didn't get the papers mixed up, as I'll still have to answer to the heirs for keeping them all straight."

Brasseur sent for Dautry to assist them and they set to work, Aristide at one cabinet, Brasseur at another, Dautry at a third, as rain began to spatter at the windowpanes. "Don't bother with the files marked 'Paid in Full,'" Brasseur told them. "We're not looking for somebody who's already paid out his debt."

"What about these?" Dautry inquired, turning around with a large metal box marked ANNUITIES in his arms. "It's locked."

"They're not debtors; *he* owed *them* interest," Aristide said. "Correct, Jullien?"

"Yes. No reason for any of them to bump him off."

"Don't bother with it, Dautry. What we're looking for, I would guess," Aristide said, "if he exists, is a man of normally easy circumstances—a merchant or manufacturer—who still owed Dupont a significant sum of money, and who may have had recent financial difficulties, and who probably was about to go bankrupt."

Dautry groaned but turned back to his cabinet. They worked silently and steadily, sifting through papers covered in Martin's bold handwriting and Jullien's meticulous, trained script.

"Well, well," Brasseur muttered twenty minutes later as he pulled out a sheet emblazoned with a large red wax seal. "Citizen Dupont may not have approved of his son becoming an actor, but he wasn't above lending the actor money. Signed and witnessed, June 1792, ten thousand livres at four percent to Gervais Dupont, called Hauteroche, for the purposes of buying and restoring a playhouse near the Boulevard des Italiens."

"Hauteroche won't have to pay back that debt now, will he?" said Dautry. "Though four percent is pretty generous."

"A crumb of family feeling, I suppose." Brasseur grunted. "Oh, no, wait a minute, the old fellow didn't let anything get past him. 'Half or more to be repaid only in gold coin of the realm,' no less. By 'ninety-two he could already see assignats were no good. Well, we'd better keep this in mind."

Half an hour later Aristide had two names to be investigated further, while Dautry had four and Brasseur only one. At last Brasseur yawned and rose to his feet with a glance at Jullien. "All right, citizen, we're going to take these seven files with us, and this record of the loan to Gervais Dupont. Everything else is back where it ought to be." His stomach abruptly rumbled and he glanced at his watch and scowled as he shepherded Aristide and Dautry out of the room.

"Nearly two o'clock. Well, I have to go back to headquarters and start my report, and I want my dinner. I'll send for those keys, and I'll be back as soon as we get an official confirmation on what was inside old Dupont's stomach. Dautry, you come with me; Ravel, stay here and try to become friendly with the family."

"They won't be very forthcoming," said Aristide. "Nobody likes having the police in the house."

Brasseur grinned. "Ah, but you're not a police official, are you? Just an interested bystander. Stay on Laurence Dupont's good side and you should be all right."

"I suppose you want me to concentrate on Charlotte, though?"

"Listen to them all, if you can, but especially that one. Get her talking—which shouldn't be difficult," Brasseur added, with a grimace. "Even if she's innocent as a lamb, she may have seen or heard something, and that sort never thinks through the meaning of anything she's seen. See what spills out of her. Charm her if you have to." Aristide raised an eyebrow at that, but Brasseur elbowed him as Dautry stifled a snicker. "I know you can charm a susceptible woman when you want to, Ravel. Go on. I want to know what she knows—that she doesn't know she knows."

"Heaven help me," Aristide said.

10

Fanny and her broom were nearly at the foot of the staircase as Aristide approached. "Still sweeping?" he said. "I hope you don't have to do this too often."

"I don't," she told him, with a toss of her head. "It's not one of my chores; only Zélie left and Aunt Magdeleine said somebody had to do it." She cocked her head and studied him for a moment. "Are you a real inspector of police? You aren't wearing one of those sashes."

"You're very perceptive," Aristide said with a slight bow. Closely resembling the portrait in Gervais's study, Fanny shared her mother's blue eyes and perfect features and looked, he thought, far more like a coquettish young woman of fifteen than a child of twelve. "I've just had the pleasure of meeting your father, by the way. I've applauded him several times at the Comédie-Française."

"My mamma is Citizeness Larivière," she told him smugly as she flicked the last of the dust and grit from the lowest step onto a cloth laid at the bottom. "She's famous, too. I'm going to be on the stage soon, too, like Mamma and Papa."

"Is your brother Étienne going to be an actor, as well?"

"Probably not." She stifled a giggle. "Once, when I was little, they needed a boy in one of Papa's plays, and Papa put Tienne in the play, and he forgot his lines! *I* wouldn't forget my lines."

"No, I'm sure you wouldn't."

"*Are* you a police inspector? You wear a suit like theirs, but you don't have a tricolored sash like the commissaire who asked me questions, or the inspector who was here last night. I didn't like him very much; he was cross."

"No, I'm not an inspector. I merely assist Commissaire Brasseur with some of his criminal cases."

"Why?"

"Because he's a friend of mine, and because they interest me."

"Why do they interest you?"

"When I was a boy," he said, "someone I loved very much was murdered. I suppose I've spent a good deal of my life trying to learn why people murder other people."

"Did somebody murder Grandfather?"

"I fear so."

She frowned and he braced himself for an onslaught of childish hysterics or at least tears, but she only said, "Why?"

"Probably for money. That's very often why people commit murder."

"Why does the commissaire need your help to solve it? Isn't he good enough?"

"Oh, Brasseur is quite good enough, and most murder cases are really quite simple. But the police have a great many more duties than just the investigation of murders, you see. When you're obliged to patrol the streets, regulate wet-nurses, haul away rubbish and dead horses, test grocers' scales, license peddlers, and so on, you can't always devote all your time and skills to the solving of a complex murder. I, on the other hand, because I am not an official member of the police, can pick and choose how I earn my wages, and spend all my time and effort in solving one case if it pleases me."

That seemed to satisfy her, for she shrugged and turned her attention to gathering up the dust cloth. "Well, the commissaire asked me all kinds of questions about where I was and what I saw."

"And did you see anything?"

She gave him a wide, brilliant smile. "Nothing but Aunt Charlotte. She was taking Grandfather's breakfast tray upstairs. Usually one of the maids does that."

"Is that you, Fanny?" Magdeleine inquired, above them. "Run to the kitchen and fetch a jug of hot water. Your aunt Charlotte is feeling better and wants to freshen up."

"But I have to clear up the sweepings—"

"Take the sweepings outside and then fetch the water. Quick now!"

"All *right*," Fanny said. She gathered up the dust cloth and flounced down the hall toward the kitchen. "Silly old cow," she muttered under her breath.

"Don't you like your aunt?" Aristide said as he followed her.

"Which one?"

"Which one did you mean just now?"

"Both of them! Oh, I suppose Aunt Charlotte's all right. She's very nice, really. She's nicer than Aunt Magdeleine. Aunt Magdeleine's bossy—you saw how she orders people about." They entered the kitchen and Fanny went straight to the door that led out to the garden, flung it open, vigorously shook out the dust cloth, and dropped it by the door. Crossing to the fireplace, she snatched a jug from the mantel, filled it from the steaming kettle at the fire, and stomped out again. "Aunt Charlotte used to buy me gingerbread when we went to the fair. But she's rather stupid."

Aristide could not suppress a slight smile. "Don't you know it's very ill-bred for a child of your age to call an adult stupid?"

"But she *is*. She's the stupidest grown-up I ever met. And she talks *all* the time. She's just like Manon Charcot, who lives across the street. Manon's only ten and she never has anything interesting to say, but all the same she never stops jabbering."

"Let me carry that," he said, taking the water jug from her. "It must be heavy and hot."

Fanny promptly relinquished the jug, with another dazzling smile. If Sophie Dupont, Aristide thought, was half as flirtatious and manipulative as her daughter, then the lovely actress must have had countless men ready to do her bidding.

"So did you see Charlotte with your grandfather's tray on the first-floor landing?" he continued as they began to climb the stairs.

"No, I just saw her taking it up. Right here," she added, pausing on a step. "I was coming downstairs and I passed her."

"And she seemed quite normal, no different from any other day?"

Fanny frowned as they continued up the second flight of stairs. She was silent until they had returned to Charlotte's door and she had knocked and unceremoniously thrust the jug Aristide carried into Magdeleine's hands.

"Well, her cheeks were very pink, I remember," she told him as they retreated back to the landing, "as if she was happy about something, but Aunt Charlotte hasn't been what you would call 'normal' for weeks and weeks!" She plumped herself down on the bench at the head of the stairs and leaned toward him. "She's been even more absentminded than usual. *I* think," she added, in a triumphant whisper, "that she's in love!"

"Do you?" he said, taking a seat beside her.

"Well, she's been completely silly. Smiles a lot, and giggles, and doesn't pay attention to you when you speak to her. And sometimes she just looks very pleased with herself." She thought for a moment and then turned to him again, eyes bright. "She looks just the way Mamma looks when she wants something from Papa. Or after a performance, when one of the rich gentlemen comes backstage to give her presents. It's a little bit disgusting. Aunt Charlotte, I mean, not Mamma. Aunt Charlotte's *old*."

Aristide sighed as he recalled that Charlotte was no more than a year older than he, but Fanny continued, unheeding.

"She's an old maid; and besides, she was a holy sister once. It isn't right that nuns should get married, even if they're not in their convent any more. Grandfather said so."

"Do you think Charlotte might want to marry somebody?"

"Everybody wants to get married," said Fanny, in a tone that suggested he was a fool for even asking such an obvious question. "But if you're a girl you get married when you're eighteen, or twenty, or twenty-five. Not *thirty-nine*."

"But a spinster of thirty-nine," he said, thinking aloud, "would have reason to be a bit smug if she'd become engaged at last, wouldn't she? And act a bit silly, as you say?"

"Aunt Charlotte's always silly," she said dismissively. "She's just been sillier than usual."

He wondered if Charlotte was in love, eager to marry, and desperate for a dowry. Considering Martin Dupont's stinginess in the matter of dowries, and adding to that the old man's reluctance to allow a former nun to forsake her vow of chastity, he suspected she might have far better luck getting a marriage settlement out of her brother than out of her father.

"Fanny, you're a clever girl, and I'm sure you know about everything that goes on in this house."

She smirked, with a complacent little shrug. "Maybe."

"How do you think your father feels toward Aunt Charlotte?"

"He likes her all right. But he thinks she's stupid, too," she added, lowering her voice again.

"Do you think he would give her a great deal of money, if she asked him for it?"

"Father doesn't *have* a great deal of money, not after fixing up the theater. He's always saying so."

"He has your grandfather's money now. And it wouldn't be money for just anything, but for a dowry. I'm sure he would give *you* a handsome dowry, in a few years. Do you think he would give your aunt a generous dowry if she needed one?"

Fanny frowned again. "I suppose he might. Mamma keeps saying he doesn't know how to manage money properly. Of course, she wants him to spend it on *her*! They're always fighting about it."

Charlotte's door opened and Magdeleine stepped into the hall. "What are you doing wasting time, child?" she said, seeing them. "We're two maids short! You'll be wanted in the kitchen to help with dinner. Come along!"

Fanny heaved a deep, melodramatic sigh, rose to her feet, bobbed Aristide a dutiful curtsy, and scampered down the stairs behind Magdeleine. Aristide remained on the bench, wondering suddenly if Gervais could have wanted money badly enough, in order to keep his Sophie happy, to kill for it.

11

Charlotte's door suddenly opened. He rose as Charlotte came out, but, glancing over her shoulder and absorbed in her own thoughts, she did not see him until she had nearly collided with him.

She started violently, with a squeal of surprise. Aristide excused himself but she fluttered her hands at him. "Oh, don't apologize! I wasn't paying attention." She paused and stared at him for a moment, trying to recall who he was. "Are . . . are you the police inspector who came with the commissaire?"

"Ravel," he said, nodding. "Though I'm not a member of the police," he added, guessing he would seem less intimidating as a civilian. "I'm merely a friend of the commissaire's. And you are Citizeness Charlotte Dupont, aren't you?"

She smiled and bobbed him a ladylike little curtsy. Though her eyes were still red-rimmed from crying, she had clearly made an attempt to look presentable, for her thick light brown hair was haphazardly pinned up beneath a linen bonnet and she had changed into a simple dark blue day dress. Few bourgeois women did not possess a black gown of some kind; he wondered if perhaps Magdeleine had not insisted upon a formal mourning gown for fear of upsetting Charlotte once again.

"May I offer you my sincere condolences on the loss of your

father?" he added, curious to see how she might react to the reminder of old Martin's unnatural death.

The overlarge blue eyes widened for an instant and she blinked several times. He braced himself for another rush of tears, but she only dabbed at her eyes with a fresh handkerchief and gamely smiled. "Poor old Father! Thank you for your kind wishes. Though he is in a better place, you know," she hastily continued. "He's very happy. He must be. Quentin has told me so, several times, that the other world is a happy place."

"Quentin?" Aristide said.

She blushed. "You wouldn't know, of course. Quentin—my poor fiancé. I was engaged to be married once," she told him, simpering and casting her gaze toward the floor. "But then he died of a fever—and I just couldn't bear to go on. If I couldn't be Quentin's bride, then I would be the bride of Christ . . . but I shouldn't bore you with all of this; it's only to say that . . . you see, long before any of this, Signor Cavalcanti, a great, great mystic—I'm sure you've heard of him? He's terribly famous. He can speak to the dead and work all sorts of miracles."

"I believe I know of him," Aristide said cautiously, remembering what Laurence had told him about the alchemist and seer who had captured Charlotte's imagination.

"Signor Cavalcanti reaches out to the other world for us and lets us speak to our loved ones, and he found Quentin for me. I've heard his voice many times. Signor Cavalcanti is a true miracle worker—he's comforted me so much. I speak to Quentin quite often, and he assures me that the other world is a lovely, kindly place. He says to me, 'Someday we'll be reunited here.' The old Church would never allow that the dead could speak to the living, would it? I think that's rather heartless. It deprives people of so much comfort, of knowing that their dear ones are happy and not in Purgatory, which is really such a horrible idea, and it can't be true, can it? Not if those who have left us can tell us that they're content and not suffering at all."

Her earnest gaze rested on him for a moment as he attempted to digest the rush of words. "So if Quentin is quite happy and content," she continued, with a little gasp for breath, "and of course my father must be in the same place, mustn't he?—then I'm sure Father is also content. It's *such* a comfort."

"I see," Aristide said, not knowing what else to say. "Well . . . that's good news, I suppose, and comforting indeed. Though don't you think that your father would have liked to live a bit longer? I understand he was quite hale for a man of his age."

"Oh, yes, at first I was so terribly upset, I couldn't stop crying for poor Father . . . but Magdeleine—my sister, you know—she reminded me that I would be able to speak with Father the next time I visited Signor Cavalcanti, and that Father was undoubtedly happy in the other world, and I realized yes, that must be true, so I did feel a little better about it. How can we know how really delightful the other world is until we've arrived there ourselves? I'm sure Father wouldn't wish to return, now that he's there. It's really all for the best. That's what Signor Cavalcanti says: that Fate and Providence have a way of arranging matters so that everything really does work out for the best, even if we can't see it at the time. We are all, after all, in the hands of the Divine," she added brightly.

Another few minutes in Charlotte's company, Aristide thought, and he would either laugh or weep. He stemmed her prattle by offering her his arm, asking her if he could escort her downstairs, and she accepted with a bashful smile.

"It must be nearly time for dinner," she said suddenly, sniffing the air, heavy with the smell of boiled mutton, as they reached the ground floor. "Dear me, I've been so upset over poor Father that I nearly forgot to eat! My sister brought me some broth and gruel yesterday, but I just couldn't touch a thing. I declare I'm really quite hungry now. Won't you stay to dinner, citizen?"

Étienne and Jullien were occupied in setting up the dining salon for a meal as they entered. Étienne, dragging chairs to the table from their places against the wall, gave them a swift glance and returned sullenly to his work. Jullien, whose scowl marred his undeniably handsome features, gave them a barely civil jerk of the head.

"Good day, Citizeness Charlotte."

She simpered again as she bade him good day in return. Evidently, Aristide thought, seeing Jullien's scornful grimace as soon as Charlotte's back was turned, Charlotte had for some time been clumsily attempting to flirt.

"Tienne," she said to the boy, "I've just asked Citizen Ravel to dine with us, so be sure to lay an extra place."

"The police?" sniffed Jullien as Étienne turned a dubious eye toward Charlotte. "You don't ask the police to dinner."

"I'm only a friend of Commissaire Brasseur," Aristide said, "not an inspector." His explanation seemed to satisfy them and Jullien stared gloomily at the bare table.

"Nine at dinner every day . . . I suppose it'll do for ten," he muttered. "Don't fancy taking it apart and adding more boards; I have more important things to do. . . ."

"Oh, no, this will work quite well," Charlotte assured him as she hurried to a linen press and fetched a tablecloth. "I wouldn't dream of putting you to extra effort, Citizen Jullien. Where on earth is Antoine? Why isn't he here?"

Jullien rolled his eyes. "In case you were wondering, citizen," he snapped in Aristide's direction as he inspected the planks of the tabletop, to be sure they were all butting closely together without gaps, "I don't normally do menial work in this household. But in time of emergency or crisis I suppose we must all pitch in. . . ." He straightened, flicking a lock of hair out of his eyes with a casual toss of his head that Aristide imagined he might have practiced in front of a mirror.

"Why, what's the matter?" said Charlotte, turning. "What emergency?"

"Zélie and Antoine," Étienne said, with dismal relish. "Didn't you know? They've up and skipped out, both of them! Took their pay and left last night. Said they didn't want to be poisoned, or taken away by the police. I can't say I blame them."

"You must be quite shorthanded now," Aristide said as Charlotte faintly cried "Oh, dear!" and dropped into the nearest chair.

"Shorthanded indeed," Jullien agreed. "Two servant girls *and* the man of all work gone like that, and all the chores still to be done. And I'll lay you a good bit that Citizeness Bouton won't find so many folk eager to come here and be poisoned, once word gets around. But I'll have them know they can't expect *me* to be doing servants' work for much longer," he added, with a grim glance in Charlotte's direction. "I would have given notice immediately, but I did feel my duty was here, to be sure Citizen Dupont's affairs were wound up properly." He took the tablecloth from Charlotte's limp hands and shook it out over the table.

"Oh, dear," Charlotte repeated. She pushed herself to her feet and vaguely began laying napkins on the tablecloth. "We shall have to hire more servants, and it's so hard to find good ones these days. . . . Domestics have become quite insolent and impossible since the Revolution began, haven't they?"

"It does seem to have lowered standards," Aristide agreed. "And with fewer people willing to go into service, you have to take what you can get. I could tell you stories of my sister's household in Bordeaux. . . ."

The door flew open and Fanny sprinted into the room. "Tienne? Where are you? Aunt Magdeleine says you're to fetch the plates and lay them."

"Why should I?" Étienne demanded. "That's a girl's job."

"Well, Aunt Magdeleine says you're to do it today, because there's nobody else."

"I don't care, it's a task for a girl, or a servant—"

"Aunt Magdeleine said you were to help!" the girl shrieked. "I'll tell her you wouldn't help!"

"Go ahead. See if I care."

"I *will*," she said, thumping down onto the table the basket of forks, knives, and spoons that she carried. "And then Aunt Magdeleine will tell Papa you're being lazy, and you'll catch it!"

"Oh, for God's *sake*," the boy declared, and stalked off.

"I'll tell her you're blaspheming, too!" she cried after him. She glanced about and curtsied perfunctorily to Jullien before her gaze settled on Aristide. "Hello again, citizen."

"Good day, citizeness," he said, recognizing the coy sparkle in her eyes.

"Have you learned anything else? About Grandfather, I mean?"

"Not much."

"I think the commissaire and his secretary left. Are you leaving, too?"

"No, not yet. Aren't you going to ask your aunt how she's feeling?"

"Good day, Aunt Charlotte," she said, turning. "Are you feeling better?" She promptly turned back to Aristide. "I suppose you have lots more questions to ask all of us."

"I might," he said, wondering if the mother was as naturally flirtatious as the daughter.

"And then you'll discover who poisoned Grandfather, won't you? Maybe it was my brother," she added waspishly as Étienne reappeared with a stack of plates in his arms.

"Don't you ever stop yammering?" the boy snapped. He thrust the soup plates at the head of the table, shoved a dinner plate onto each place, and stomped out again. Fanny dropped the handful of spoons she had been clutching and scuttled after him.

"I don't yammer!"

"Oh, dear," Charlotte said once again, "I don't believe he remembered to bring in an extra plate. . . ." She hurried off, shaking her head.

"Those children aren't quite as tiresome as they look," Jullien told Aristide, after a moment's silence, as with a sigh he took up the spoons and set them in their places. "Étienne's quite a bright boy, when he applies himself. And Fanny does very well, as long as you give her a play to read and allow her to act out all the parts. But Heaven help you if you set her to studying any sort of mathematics or natural history."

Aristide joined him in straightening a few chairs. "She's a very handsome child."

"And doesn't she know it! Exactly like her mother. Citizeness Dupont was the celebrated Mademoiselle Larivière before the Revolution, you know. You've probably seen her at the Comédie. Beautiful creature, simply ravishing, vain as a peacock. Though frankly there's not too much talent; she gets by on her looks and . . . well . . . her other talents. It always surprised me that she married Gervais Dupont rather than becoming some duke's mistress. She could have, easily. Maybe it was the lure of respectability."

"Actors didn't become respectable until 'eighty-nine or 'ninety."

"Well then, maybe it was the lure of the family fortune." Jullien set the last chair in place and pushed the hair from his eyes again.

"Not too many actors who have expectations of a fat inheritance, you know."

It takes a sponger to know a sponger, Aristide thought, remembering what they had learned of the relations between Jullien and Martin Dupont's widow, but he said nothing.

12

Magdeleine hurried in, clapping her hands and calling over her shoulder. "Dinner! Tienne, kindly go upstairs and fetch your father. Charlotte, tell Thérèse we're ready. Inspector, may I ask what you're doing here? The commissaire has—"

"Oh, I asked Citizen . . . the citizen to stay to dinner," Charlotte hastily told her.

"You asked someone from the *police* to stay for dinner?" Magdeleine echoed her, sharp eyes raking Aristide from head to foot.

"He's not really from the police—"

"Oh, very well," Magdeleine said, interrupting her, with a last appraising glance at him. "Charlotte, you'll be sitting there, then, to make room for Citizen . . ."

"Ravel, citizeness," Aristide told her, with a slight bow.

Magdeleine, he saw, was placing him opposite Laurence and beside Charlotte, perhaps in the hope, common to guardians of unwed females, of getting either her sister or her sister-in-law married at last, and off her hands. He shuddered inwardly at the thought of marriage to Charlotte as Ursule joined them and took her place at the foot of the table without appearing to notice anyone else in the room.

Gervais strolled in, his two children behind him, and absently reached for a chair near the end of the table before suddenly collecting himself and sitting instead at the head. Magdeleine rang a bell as chairs scraped in around the table. Thérèse soon entered with a steaming tureen.

Martin Dupont, Aristide decided, in keeping with his parsimony, must have decreed that the daily fare in his household was to be modest and economical. He had expected a more elaborate first course than cabbage soup on the table of a prosperous bourgeois family, though it smelled savory enough. The bread, as Laurence had mentioned, was coarse, not the fine wheaten bread that only the rich could afford. He caught another whiff of mutton from the kitchen and smiled to himself as he recalled Molière's miser ordering greasy mutton stew to be served to his guests—"with plenty of dumplings in it, so they get filled up quickly."

Magdeleine coughed. Gervais, who had been gazing at his daughter, a haunted, wistful look in his eyes, came to himself with a start and bowed his head to rattle off the benediction. "Bless us, O Lord, and these thy gifts which we are about to receive from thy bounty, through Christ Our Lord, Amen."

So the Dupont family, like many others, still clung to a discreet Catholicism, just as Jeannette had said. Though perhaps their religious principles did not extend quite so far as forbidding the ex-nun Charlotte to marry.

Ursule began to serve the soup. "As you've probably learned by now, citizen," Magdeleine said to Aristide as she passed the soup plates down the table, "our two other servants have abruptly left us, so there is no one to wait at table today. I apologize and hope you will not find it too inconvenient. Wine, Étienne, if you please."

"I live alone in a lodging-house, citizeness," Aristide said as the boy sulkily rose, fetched the carafes of wine and water from the buffet, and began circling the table with them. "I'm quite accustomed to simple accommodations and taking my meals on a tray or in a chophouse."

"You're unmarried?" she inquired, further confirming his suspicion that she was considering him as a possible husband for either Charlotte or Laurence.

"Yes." He tried the soup, which was hearty enough but a trifle underseasoned for his taste.

"We serve plain fare in modest portions here, citizen," Magdeleine continued, catching his eye as he looked up from his soup plate. "I hope you will find it acceptable."

"Plain indeed," Gervais said, through a mouthful of cabbage. "Might we occasionally have something other than cabbage soup, now that Father's no longer clutching the purse strings and decreeing the menu?"

"Father was a frugal man," Magdeleine said, "and these are straitened times. We could all profit by his example."

"Frugal!" Gervais echoed her, with a snort of laughter. "*Frugal* is scarcely the word. Are you familiar with Molière's *Miser*, Ravel?"

"Of course."

"Well, I've played old Harpagon so many times I've lost count—"

"That was the part that first made him famous at the Comédie," Charlotte hastened to tell Aristide.

"Yes, yes," Gervais continued, "but honestly I can't take much credit for that, because playing the part of a miser comes easy as breathing to me. Stage direction: 'Harpagon sees two candles burning and puts one out.' Father thought of that one all by himself, without any help from Molière."

"Oh, Gervais," Charlotte protested, "you shouldn't speak ill of the dead."

"Especially if they were murdered," Laurence said, speaking for the first time. Beside him, in the sudden silence, Aristide heard Charlotte swiftly draw in a breath. "Isn't that the truth, Citizen Ravel? Somebody did poison him?"

He nodded. "The police think so."

"Oh, well," Gervais muttered, breaking up a lump of dark bread into his soup, "let's not be hypocritical about it. I wouldn't wish poisoning on anybody, but I'm not particularly sorry the old screw's dead."

"Gervais!"

"Oh, don't be so righteous, Magdeleine. It was high time, for God's sake. Did you want him to live to be a hundred? Even if he was our father, he was a cantankerous old skinflint and I don't suppose any of us will miss him much."

"Has the miserable kitchenmaid been charged, I hope?" Ursule said, glancing dubiously down at her soup plate.

"Of course," said Magdeleine. "You needn't worry about that, Step-Mamma. Do you care for more soup?"

"What are they going to do with her?" Fanny inquired suddenly. "I thought she was nice, even if she was a little stupid. I don't believe she poisoned anybody."

"They'll try her for murder, of course," said her brother, beside her.

"But what if she didn't do it?"

"Of course she did it. The *police* aren't stupid. Are they, Citizen Ravel?"

"No, indeed."

"See? So then they'll cut off her head—chop!" He slashed his finger across his throat and made a gurgling noise, tongue lolling. Fanny let out a stifled shriek.

"Stop it! Father, make him stop!"

"Enough, Étienne," Gervais said, without looking at him.

Aristide covertly glanced about him. Fanny and Étienne glared at each other while Gervais, Magdeleine, and Laurence concentrated their gazes on the soup plates in front of them. Charlotte looked troubled and ready to burst into tears once more. Evidently Jeannette's possible fate was an uncomfortable subject no one wanted to discuss. He felt it was high time they did discuss it.

"Nevertheless," he said, "the girl is fortunate this didn't happen ten years ago. Poisoning—that's a particularly diabolical form of murder. Before the Revolution they probably would have sentenced her to be burned alive."

Charlotte gasped. "If she was guilty," she protested.

"Yes, to be sure, if they'd found her guilty."

"Of course she's guilty," snapped Magdeleine. "Didn't we find the poison in her apron pocket?"

"But you don't know yet that the powder you found is poison," Aristide said. "I hope Citizen Hébert has taken it straight to the commissariat so a competent apothecary can analyze it."

"I was the one who found the poison in the soup," Fanny announced.

"It crunched in my teeth, like lettuce that hasn't been washed properly."

"Were you ill from it, too?" he inquired.

"No, I spat it out again and didn't have any more soup. I hate sand in vegetables. Then Aunt Magdeleine said she had some of the stuff in the bottom of her plate, too, and she thought she felt a little funny. Then Papa said he felt funny, too. Then Aunt Magdeleine—"

"Fanny," Magdeleine said, "kindly refrain from being such a chatterbox. The world does not always have to center around *you*. If you can't behave yourself at table, you'll have to eat your dinner in the nursery until you improve your manners."

"But I only wanted to say what happened, so Citizen Ravel can find out who did it. Because I don't think Jeannette poisoned us, or murdered Grandfather, either. Maybe Step-Grandmamma did it."

"How dare you insinuate such a thing," Ursule said icily. "Gervais, I insist that until your daughter has learned some manners—"

"Well," Fanny continued, unheeding, "now you can marry Citizen Jullien. Isn't that what you want?"

"Fanny!" Magdeleine exclaimed.

"But it's true." Fanny looked up and down the table before shrugging. "Nobody wants to say so, is all. And Jeannette was nice. She wouldn't do a thing like that."

"I think Fanny has put it in a nutshell," Laurence remarked in the silence. "Jeannette wouldn't do a thing like that. So which of us would?"

Charlotte sharply drew in her breath as Magdeleine opened her mouth to retort.

"Let's stop hiding from the truth, Sister-in-law," Laurence continued, before Magdeleine could speak. "You all want to believe Jeannette murdered the Old Man, because if you stop believing that, then you'll have to face the fact that it was one of us who killed him, and tried to poison us all."

Charlotte gave a sharp squeak of fright as the Duponts cast sidelong glances about the table.

Why? Aristide suddenly thought. There could have been many reasons to murder old Martin, but why sicken the rest of the family with a trifling dose that the poisoner must have known would not kill? Perhaps the key to the mystery lay not in the facts of Martin Dupont's death, but in the tainted dinner the day afterward.

"Who, exactly, was present at the dinner yesterday?" he said, though he knew the answer already. "All of you, here?"

"Charlotte wasn't," Magdeleine said. "She had been upstairs in her room since the day before. She wasn't fit to receive guests."

Charlotte hastily nodded. "Yes, my sister told me I'd much better lie down and rest until I'd got over the shock of Father's death."

"The rest of us were present," said Claude Bouton. "And the guests: Hébert, and that lawyer fellow, Frochot."

"It's a bit uncommon, I should think, to have guests to dinner the day after one's father has unexpectedly died," Aristide said. Gervais shrugged.

"I think they both offered to come some other time, after hearing about Father's death, but—"

"No," said Magdeleine, "it was only Citizen Hébert who had heard of it, because he lives nearby, and he said he would quite understand if the dinner invitation had to be withdrawn because—"

"The point I'm making," Gervais continued irritably, "is that Magdeleine is such an excellent and efficient housekeeper that she wouldn't hear of them being turned away. She set Zélie to keeping vigil beside the body and insisted they come to dinner anyway, and so they did. It wasn't the most cheerful of gatherings, even before we discovered the stuff in our soup, but never let it be said the Duponts let a little thing like a death in the family interrupt their social obligations!"

"You can't suppose either of them had anything to do with my father-in-law's death," said Laurence. "Neither were anywhere near the house on the previous morning."

"Citizen Hébert likes Aunt Charlotte, though," said Fanny. "I've seen him looking at her sometimes!"

"You must be mistaken, Fanny," Charlotte protested, though her cheeks turned a trifle pink. "Citizen Hébert is your aunt and uncle's friend."

"Maybe, but he comes here to visit you, too, Aunt Charlotte. Are you going to marry him?"

Charlotte abruptly choked on a sip of watered wine and was obliged to hide her face in her napkin for a moment. Fanny continued, unconcerned.

"Because he's *fat*. And I don't think he has any hair at all under his wig. *I* wouldn't want to marry somebody who was fat and bald."

"He's quite well-off, though," Laurence remarked, with a gleam of mischief in her eyes.

Fanny sniffed. "So what? *I'm* going to marry somebody very handsome, and very rich, too."

"I'm sure you will, dear," Laurence murmured.

"Well," said Gervais, grinning, "what about it, Charlotte? Are you going to marry Surgeon Hébert if he asks you? I'll give you a proper dowry, never worry about that."

"He's not going to ask me!" Charlotte exclaimed. "And I don't care a jot about him, really I don't." Without warning, she sucked in a breath and stifled a sob in her napkin. "Oh, dear . . ."

"Whatever is the matter?"

"What you said—it brought it all back to me. . . ."

"What did I say?" Gervais demanded.

"That you would give me a dowry . . . *you*, not Father. Father's dead, and here I am laughing!"

"Charlotte, dear," Magdeleine said, "you mustn't work yourself up so. It's going to be all right."

"But Father . . . and that poor girl—"

"Don't worry yourself another minute about that wretched girl," snapped Magdeleine. "She'll get what she deserves, and there's the end of it!"

"But . . . Citizen Ravel," Charlotte said suddenly, turning to Aristide, "you must know all about these things . . . what will happen to her?"

"If she's found guilty," he said, "they'll execute her. That's the law."

"No exceptions? That's horrible!"

"The law is clear: the penalty for murder, and for attempted murder resulting in grievous injury, is death." He paused, taking stock of them as discreetly as he could. Charlotte's hand, clutching a soup spoon, was visibly trembling. If Charlotte had poisoned her father, she was clearly feeling pangs of remorse. "These days at least the penalty of death is swift and merciful. The guillotine," he continued, thrusting away the memory of the last execution he had so unwillingly attended, "takes only a moment to do its work. It's bloody, to be sure, but they say it's quite painless. And the executioners are decent men—kinder, perhaps, than the mob that comes to watch executions. The worst part of it for the victim is undoubtedly his own knowledge that soon his—or her— life will be extinguished. And perhaps the journey to the Place de Grève . . ."

Charlotte let out a soft moan. "Citizen, *please*," Magdeleine began. Abruptly Laurence shot up from her seat, overturning her glass, thrust away her chair, and fled the room.

13

Aristide blinked as the door slammed shut behind Laurence. She was the one person he had presumed almost beyond suspicion, for if she had murdered old Martin, why would she have lifted a finger in Jeannette's defense?

"I beg your pardon, citizens," he said lamely, realizing eight pairs of eyes were fixed upon him.

"Evidently no one warned you," Magdeleine said at last, breaking the icy hush, "how Laurence's husband, our brother Aurèle, met his end." Mutely Aristide shook his head and she continued. "It's a painful subject, but I suppose you ought to know, in order to avoid any further gaffes. My brother was guillotined on the eleventh of Thermidor in the Year Two, with many other members of the municipal government, because he supported Robespierre. Kindly refrain from raising the subject again while you're in our house."

Aurèle Dupont was executed with the Robespierrists? Aristide said to himself as he murmured a mechanical apology.

He remembered Thermidor with fierce clarity. It had been a vast purge of the Parisian city government. Seventy-eight men: more had died the day after Robespierre's execution, for being faithful to him, than had ever died in one day during what people had begun to call "Robespierre's Terror."

But he had never known, or suspected, that Mathieu's friend had died with them, for Mathieu was long dead already.

What a dreadful waste, he thought once again. *Mathieu, Aurèle, so many, many others, so many dedicated, courageous, gifted men . . . and all for nothing but avarice and hatred and fear . . .*

"Pardon me, citizens." He scraped back his chair and hurried to the door, feeling Magdeleine's gimlet gaze upon him as he threw it open.

He found Laurence at last in the garden, crouched by the vegetable beds, uprooting dead marigolds with swift angry jerks. Unsure how to approach her, he paused. A moment later she caught sight of him and froze.

"I wish to apologize for my tactlessness," he said, after an eon of silence between them. Beyond the garden wall, a baby wailed in an upstairs room and a woman shrilly berated a servant.

"I'm deeply sorry to have caused you such distress. It was entirely unintentional."

"You didn't know?" Laurence said, swiftly looking away again to the earth before her.

"I'd no idea."

She wrenched out another dead stalk. "It brought it all back . . . that horrible day."

"I'm sorry."

"Do you know what it's like, to lose somebody like that?"

"Yes, I do."

She glanced at him, then gathered up the uprooted plants and began crushing the heads between her fingers to loosen the seeds. "Yes . . . Citizen Alexandre was your friend. But Aurèle was my husband."

"I've never married," Aristide said, "so I can't imagine how it must have been to lose a spouse; but you're hardly alone in your grief. I lost more than one friend in 'ninety-three and 'ninety-four, though Mathieu Alexandre was my oldest and dearest."

"It's scarcely the same thing," she retorted, "to lose a friend as to lose someone whom you loved with all your heart, who meant everything in the world to you, whom you would have died for if you could."

"Kindly don't presume to know the nature of someone else's friendship," he said, stung. "Mathieu was like a brother. He protected me, shielded me—" He stopped short as he found himself approaching memories and private matters he did not wish to discuss, least of all with this angry, lonely woman. "He would have done anything for me, and I for him. I think I know the pain of loss as well as you do. Shall we call it a draw, or do you insist upon continuing this contest of 'my suffering is greater than yours'?"

"How dare you!" She flung down the flower heads and faced him, dark eyes glittering. "I didn't just lose my husband—we all lost a dream!"

"What are you talking about?" he said. "What dream?"

"Robespierre!" she told him, in a fierce whisper. "*His* dreams! His dream of what we all could become, what the world could become—if only—"

Suddenly he recognized what it was about Laurence that he had found so familiar that morning in Brasseur's office: it was that same youthful, yearning naïveté and conviction, thwarted energy, frustration, that had sent Mathieu and his friends into the thick of the revolutionary tumult.

"If only his dream hadn't become corrupted?" he said, remembering his last glimpse of Mathieu. "If only the Incorruptible, in his fine dreams for humankind, hadn't lost sight of what it is to be a human being?"

"That's a lie! You know nothing about it!"

"I know what I see around me—that the Revolution is dead and that everyone who tried to shape it to his own ends had a hand in destroying it. The king, the constitutional monarchists, the Brissotins, the Robespierrists." Laurence's chin jerked upward at that but he forged onward, ignoring her.

"Every soul who thought he could use the Revolution to further his own private obsession—whether it was monarchy, or profits, or liberty, or equality—only ended by twisting it until it became something perverted, unrecognizable. Mathieu's friends thought a war would be a good way to unite the nation and turn people in favor of a republic—instead they brought all Europe down upon us."

"And Robespierre was against the war from the beginning!" she interrupted.

"I know that. And I respected him for it. I know he and the Committee inherited an impossible task and a country in crisis. But Robespierre chose to try to impress some vague ideal of social virtue and equality on a mass of people who—nine-tenths of them—want only a solid roof over their heads, enough bread and soup and cheap wine to fill their bellies, and a warm bedmate to amuse them at night, and to the devil with everybody else."

"People have to be educated—enlightened—"

"By force? 'Liberty, Equality, Fraternity, or Death'? 'Be my brother, or I'll kill you'?"

He paused, realizing his voice was rising, and shook his head in frustration. "Citizeness, Robespierre tried to make ignorant peasants and bitter, underpaid, brutalized sansculottes—yes, and greedy bourgeois, too—'virtuous' in some way they couldn't understand, will never understand, and he forced that virtue on them by way of intimidation and the guillotine. If, instead, he'd simply tried to feed the hungry and make peace with the rest of Europe, then he—and many others, including your husband—might still be alive today."

"That's not fair!" Laurence cried. "He was a great man!"

"Yes, I know. That's the tragedy of it."

Aristide said the words without irony and she stared at him, eyes narrow, searching for any sign of mockery. At last she said, "You agree?"

"Robespierre could have been a very great man, if he had ever been able to comprehend that people don't all think alike, and they don't all want the same things. Isn't that the fatal flaw of everyone, from the king and queen on down, who's been devoured by this revolution?" He sighed. "Yes, I admired him for a time. Mathieu Alexandre admired him. *He* said he was a great man. Five months before Robespierre and his committee sent him to his death."

"Robespierre never did that!"

"Perhaps not. But someone did, someone who admired Robespierre just as much as you and your husband did. Because they disagreed on how we should be governed, and what kind of republic we ought to have. Because they couldn't agree how Heaven on earth was to be arranged, twenty-two honorable, gifted, patriotic men had to be given a travesty of a trial and condemned to death in order to please the mob. And I followed them to the Place de la Révolution and watched them die, in order to bid Mathieu farewell. They were among the first, but by no means the last. Is that the work of great men?"

"All right then!" Laurence cried. "They made mistakes! And they paid for them! They all killed each other over trivialities and words, and finally they died for it—for nothing! Aurèle died for nothing but to keep swine like Fréron or Fouché alive! Think of what they wanted to accomplish, and look what kind of scum we have governing us now!" She drew a breath as if to continue, but stopped suddenly, darted to the garden gate, flung it open, and disappeared.

Aristide closed his lips on his angry retort. He and Laurence shared a common contempt for what had come after Robespierre, no matter what differences Aurèle and Mathieu might have had.

He lingered in the garden another twenty minutes, breathing in the scents of warming earth and the first green shoots of early spring. Next door the housewife had ceased shouting at the servant and returned to her kitchen and her squalling baby.

After allowing enough time for the Duponts to finish their dinner and disperse, he returned to the house through the kitchen door. In the foyer he encountered Charlotte, who was hurrying toward the front door while continuing to talk breathlessly over her shoulder.

"I'm sorry—I really can't stay to help you. I—I have to go out."

"Out?" Magdeleine echoed her from the dining salon, a stack of soiled plates in her arms. "Where on earth do you think you have to be?"

"I have to go, truly I do. Signor Cavalcanti—I need to ask his advice. He'll know what to do."

"Don't you give every sou you have to that quack!" Magdeleine called after her. "Mind you keep enough money with you for the fare home. If you find you're short, you'll have to walk again."

Charlotte nodded and, turning, promptly cannoned into Aristide. She gasped, stared at him for an instant as if she were trying to place him, and muttered a vague apology before scuttling out.

Magdeleine shook her head and sighed, like a mother with a

headstrong child, and hurried off toward the kitchen. Aristide turned as he heard Gervais's deep chuckle behind him.

"Citizen Ravel! Had it out with my sister-in-law, have you?"

"Citizeness Laurence is a woman of . . . strong opinions."

Gervais snorted. "You should have met my brother. He and Laurence were all of a piece with their politics; never talked about anything else. But never mind that," he added with a grin. "What would you say to a glass of something? Come up to my study."

"Where you'll try once more to persuade me to join your acting troupe?"

He laughed. "Perhaps."

Aristide followed him upstairs to the study, where Gervais poured out two glasses of Cognac before poking the smoldering fire into a blaze and sinking into an armchair. "Sorry about that bit of unpleasantness at dinner," he said. "I suppose we all thought that, being with the police, you must know everything about us, including Aurèle."

"We know quite a lot, but not everything," Aristide said, thinking back to Thermidor, when he had been occupied with other concerns than Brasseur's police matters. He took a tiny sip of the brandy, which was excellent. Gervais, unlike his father, was evidently willing to indulge himself with certain luxuries. "I felt I should apologize to Citizeness Laurence. I expect the subject of her husband's death is too painful for her to bear, even now."

"Yes, it seems to be . . . but he's been gone almost three years, you know. It's time she put him behind her, instead of always living in the past. Of course, I loved him as much as anyone would love his brother, but I've moved on. We all have . . . even Father, in the end."

Gervais, Aristide thought, was slightly too eager to insist he had loved Aurèle. Might a resentful son, always passed over in favor of a more dutiful brother, finally take his revenge by murdering his father—and inherit a fortune in the process? He decided to prick, like a surgeon with a lancet, at what he suspected was the tenderest spot.

"I gathered from the citizeness's talk that your brother could do no wrong in Citizen Dupont's eyes. Your father must have been devastated at his death."

His probing was rewarded as Gervais shifted uncomfortably in his seat and fidgeted with his glass. "Nearly killed Father, that did. My brother was always the good boy, the obedient son, the handsome, clever lad who could do anything."

"Yes . . . I met him once or twice; I remember."

"Did you? Well then, you know what he was. Aurelius, 'the Golden One' . . . the Old Man certainly always thought of him so. He was the brilliant lawyer who was going to be a magistrate someday, and get a title out of it, and turn the family into nobility at last, so we could forget we were only a lot of filthy moneylenders. Of course," he added, with a shrug, "that hope of a title ended with the Revolution, but still my brother got on. . . . He got a lot of notions in his head from all those books he read, and he joined the Jacobin Club and was friendly with all the up-and-comers. He even clamored for a republic before it was fashionable to. He was Mayor Lescot-Fleuriot's right-hand man, you know. He'd have ended with a seat in the National Convention and maybe even on the Committee of Public Safety, if things had gone on." He added bitterly: "Father was so proud."

"Was Citizen Dupont senior a republican, then?"

Gervais gave a harsh bark of laughter. "Father was for whatever faction would allow him to hold on to his fortune and make more of it. He approved of the Revolution because it freed us from the rules that always gave the aristocracy the upper hand. When Robespierre was in power, he approved of him as much as anyone did . . . until some of the Robespierrists started fulminating against the rich. And once Robespierre was dead, and people were making fortunes in army contracts and land speculation and so on, and that collection of thieves and scoundrels was running things and turning a blind eye toward corruption, Father was all for the thieves and scoundrels."

"It is, perhaps, the politic thing to do," Aristide said. Gervais smiled.

"Keep your head down and swim with the current? Yes, I suppose it is. Aurèle never saw it that way, though. Aurèle had his ideals, and look where it got him. To the scaffold in the Place de la Révolution." He shook his head and gulped down another swallow of brandy.

Aristide leaned forward, with an expression of sympathetic interest. Gervais, he sensed, was famished for a congenial male companion in the comfort of his home; the vain and acerbic Jullien and the taciturn Claude Bouton could scarcely be to his taste. Let people talk, and eventually, whether they meant to or not, they would tell you everything.

"Such a man of principle," Gervais continued. "So much principle he didn't have the sense to see when to drop everything and get out. Sticking with Robespierre even when it was obvious he was finished! They arrested Aurèle in the City Hall, you know. He went there that night, the ninth of Thermidor, to defend Robespierre and the others, and he never came out except to go to prison and the guillotine. Damned fool. And of course to Father he promptly became a martyr, a saint. Aurèle, the golden boy, his father's pride . . . I don't suppose Father would have been nearly as heartsick if it had been I."

"Surely you can't mean that."

"Can't I? I was the elder, the one who ought to have stayed at home like a proper son and followed the family business, and who instead chose to be a dissolute vagabond—at least that's how Father always saw it. He never had a good word to say for theater folk; the Church disapproved of them and so did he. Perhaps if I'd got myself tragically guillotined like Aurèle, Father would have thought more of me."

Suddenly he laughed, a sour chuckle, and tossed back the last of his brandy. "But here I am, the vagabond actor, and I've outlived them both, even though Father showed signs of living forever. Bumped off by a simpleminded servant girl. Who's having the last laugh, I wonder?"

"This servant," Aristide said, "she must be touched in the head."

Gervais shrugged. "I expect so. I never noticed her much, come to think of it. Magdeleine sees to the servants. She seemed normal enough, but why else would a creature like that want to go poisoning us all?"

"We don't know yet what it was, or if the soup was truly poisoned—"

"Oh," he interrupted, "there was something funny in the soup, to be sure. Fine grit of some sort. Luckily Fanny noticed it and complained about it. I had two helpings, though, and I must have got a fair bit of the stuff, considering how ill I was."

"Your daughter was the first to complain about it?"

"Yes, she said something like, 'Ugh, there's sand in my soup,' and right away Magdeleine found something gritty in hers as well. And since everyone was a bit jittery, with Father dying suddenly just the day before, I suppose it's only natural that somebody panicked and declared we were all being poisoned."

Aristide nodded. "So it had already been concluded that Citizen Dupont had died of poison?"

Gervais opened his mouth for a rapid reply, then closed it, frowning. "No, I don't believe so. That's odd. But then it might be a logical conclusion to come to, wouldn't it? My father was in perfect health for a man of his age. He might have lived another ten years, God help us."

"Indeed," Aristide said, thoughtful.

"Then we were all a bit queasy, or worse, by midafternoon. I was supposed to be going on that night, as Tartuffe, but I'd been bending over a basin for most of the afternoon. We had to cancel the performance. *Something* in that soup shouldn't have been there."

"Who was it who first said you were being poisoned?"

"Don't know. We were all so flustered. . . . No, wait. It might have been Hébert—the surgeon, you know. Then Magdeleine joined the chorus."

"Do you suppose she could have had a grudge against the servant girl, for some reason?"

Gervais stared at him. "Good God, why? If she didn't like a servant, she would have let her go. Why on earth would she need to have the wretched girl arrested?"

"Why indeed?" Aristide echoed him. "Because it was expedient?"

"Expedient?"

"Do you fear *she* poisoned your father?"

"Never," said Gervais, shaking his head vigorously. "My sister's no poisoner—though she's poisonous enough herself, I'll grant you," he added with a thin smile. He rose and tossed another log onto the fire. "And *I* didn't do it, though I don't suppose I can prove that—but I certainly never put anything in the soup on Sunday, and nobody can say I ever went near the kitchen. Even, as I said at dinner, even if I honestly can't pretend to be racked with misery that the Old Man's dead."

"Thank you for the brandy," Aristide said, rising to his feet. "And for being so frank with me. You've been most illuminating."

14

Brasseur still had charge of Jeannette at the commissariat, until he could find time to deliver her to the justice of the peace for official questioning, and provide his own statement. "Well?" he said as Aristide rapped perfunctorily on the office door and went inside. "Learned anything in two hours?"

Aristide shook his head and dropped into a chair. "Plenty, I expect, but nothing that'll lead you immediately to a poisoner. And you?"

"Prunelle sent over his report. Nothing we didn't already know, or guess."

Aristide took the pages covered with Dr. Prunelle's meticulous handwriting, glanced past the official, detailed description of the deceased's identifying marks, and turned to the medical report.

"The police surgeon," Prunelle had written, referring to himself in the third person as many people did in formal documents, "in accordance with the suspicious nature of the death, opened the body and examined the contents of the stomach and upper intestines. He found traces of a suspicious substance mingled with remains of food eaten by the deceased. He reserved a quantity of this substance for further analysis, which is shortly to be performed by a highly qualified apothecary. Failing this further analysis, it is the considered opinion of the examining police surgeon that the citizen Martin Dupont, deceased, met his death from the administration of a lethal quantity of arsenic in his food, specifically wheaten porridge or white coffee, on the morning of 14 Ventôse, Year V (4 March 1797, old style)."

"Well, Ravel, if you were going to do away with somebody, where would *you* go to buy arsenic?"

Aristide shrugged. "Any apothecary shop. You'd have to sign for it, of course; not that that means much." An epidemic of poisonings, a century and a half before, had prompted King Louis XIV to pass a decree forbidding apothecaries to sell deadly poisons to anyone except persons known to them. The law also required purchasers to sign a register and state why they needed the poison, but such laws were far too easily circumvented.

"Yes, all you need to do is tell them you want it for rats," Brasseur agreed. "Who's going to disbelieve you?"

Aristide shrugged. Most apothecaries, in these lean and disordered times, were not going to worry too much about the niceties when a stranger asked for "something to kill rats"; a sale was a sale.

"I've got a man on it already," Brasseur continued, "interviewing this neighbor Thierry and any other apothecaries in the section, and the nearby sections, as well. Not that I expect him to turn up anything. The person we want, if they've any brains, will have gone to some shop on the other side of the city. We can interview every apothecary in Paris, I suppose, but it'll take days."

Thorough, patient, tedious questioning was the backbone of a police investigation, and one reason why Aristide had discovered, some years before, that he was not cut out for the life of a police inspector or commissaire. He stifled a yawn.

"Meanwhile," he said, "I did learn one thing. With three servants abruptly gone, the household is painfully shorthanded."

Brasseur grinned. "You want to plant somebody, don't you? Know any likely women?"

"I fear not. Nobody who could pass as a kitchenmaid, at any rate. Actually I was thinking of François."

"A manservant?"

"They've lost one, and in the straits they're in, I expect they'll engage anyone who turns up at the door. We'll need some sort of reference for him, of course. In the name of . . . well, François will do." In the course of three years, he had never learned his friend's surname, but "François" would do for surname as well as Christian name. "I don't know if he's ever posed as a servant before, but these days, most people don't expect the same efficient and deferential service from the domestics as they did before the Revolution." They would, he suspected, tolerate any laxness or inexperience on François's part as one of the inevitable annoyances of modern life in Year V of the Republic.

"Well, we have nothing to lose," Brasseur grunted, making a note. "I'll get a recommendation for him. Send him along first thing in the morning to fetch it; let's get a pair of eyes in there as soon as possible." He sifted through the dossier of the case and glanced up again. "I have to question those guests who dined with the Duponts—the surgeon and the notary. Care to come along?"

"If you can wait a quarter hour. I want to talk to Jeannette."

Aristide left him and went back to the lockup. Jeannette blinked at the light of the lamp he brought back with him like one who had lived in darkness for weeks, though she had been in the cell for less than a day. He squinted at her through the gloom and thought, upon a second look at her, that she might have been pretty enough, in the fresh, artless manner of peasant girls, before she had been abruptly accused of a frightful crime and hauled away to jail.

"They took me on a month before it happened," she told him when he asked her to describe everything she could remember about her life at the Dupont household. "I do as I'm told, monsieur—citizen. The mistress never had anything to complain of."

"Were you happy there? Was the work hard?"

"It was hard, but it wasn't so bad that I'd have gave notice. It's not so easy to find work in service these days, since the aristos all left. And Thérèse was all right. She didn't box my ears like the last one did, back in Rouen."

"How did the Dupont family treat you?"

She looked at him blankly through the feeble lamplight, as if his question had puzzled her. A kitchenmaid or maid of all work was accustomed, he supposed, to being paid no more attention than a dog might receive. "Well enough, citizen," she said at last. "That is, the mistress slapped me once, when I broke a cup, but I've had worse." She stared down at the straw that littered the floor. "The old gentleman spoke nice to me sometimes. He said I was a handsome minx and he'd rather look at me for a change than at his sour-faced daughter, and he hoped she wasn't working me too hard. I'm very sorry he's dead, God rest his soul."

Aristide nodded as she crossed herself. The miserly, autocratic Martin Dupont, who could still take a moment to offer a few kind words to a kitchen drudge, became suddenly more human, less of a caricature. "Tell me more about the family."

"Citizeness Bouton, the mistress, she's the one he called sour-faced. She's very good at the housekeeping. She doesn't take any nonsense and she never lets any of the grocers or such get away with more than she thinks they should have." A smile flickered on her lips for an instant. "The way she bosses her man around, it's something to see."

"What about her sister, Charlotte? Imagine you're gossiping with your best friend."

She thought for a moment. "Well, citizen, the mistress never lets Ma'm'selle—I mean Citizeness—Charlotte deal with the tradesmen because she says they'd steal her blind. Not much sense at business; she'd believe anything they tell her. And I hear Charlotte was ever so pious," Jeannette continued eagerly, "and so she took vows long ago and went to a nunnery, but then they said you couldn't be a nun any longer, so she came home again. But she used to go to Mass every day, like clockwork it was, Thérèse said. That is, she did till two or three years ago, when she went off somewhere else, to a house in the Marais. She goes there almost every day, leaves at half past five. It's not church, if you know what I mean. It's not a proper Mass, not Christian at all, something to do with a foreign gentleman. Thérèse would mutter about it and say Charlotte would give all her money to that heathen foreigner if she wasn't careful."

This must be the mystic, Cavalcanti, Aristide thought, *to whom Charlotte hurried away so precipitously half an hour ago.* He made a note to himself to pay a visit to the man and learn what else he could about Charlotte and what was fretting her.

"Tell me about the day the old gentleman died."

Jeannette shrugged, helplessly. "It was Saturday. . . . They keep to the proper calendar, you see, with Sundays and feast days. It was Saturday, because Thérèse and I had to think about Sunday dinner the next day, when they were having guests to dine."

"Just start at the beginning. What did they eat for breakfast?"

The family took coffee and bread, just like everybody else, and sometimes preserves or salt fish with it, according to taste, and butter with the bread when butter was to be had. Old Martin, however, always took porridge and white coffee in his bedchamber. Jeannette had gone out and found the milkwoman, as she did every day, and brought back the milk and cooked the porridge, and one of the ladies had taken it up to him.

"I would have took it up just like I did every morning," Jeannette added, "but Ma'm'selle Charlotte said I ought to stay in the kitchen and help Thérèse. Then after I'd made the old gentleman's breakfast and washed the crockery I scoured out the porridge kettle. Then the mistress told me it was time to go to Mass with the old gentleman's wife."

"So Citizeness Ursule Dupont attends Mass, does she?" Catholic rites were grudgingly tolerated if they were conducted by priests who had sworn an oath of allegiance to the nation; in addition, many small congregations and fugitive, dissident priests met secretly to worship in garrets or parlors.

"Yes, citizen, every day. Sometimes the mistress goes, too, when she has the time, and even the old gentleman went once or twice a week, I remember. But Madame Dupont is too fine to carry her own traps like her shawl and a prayer-book and a hot stone or a heater when it's cold, and like I said, Ma'm'selle Charlotte wasn't taking communion any more but going to that heathen gentleman's house, so Madame took me along every morning. I didn't mind. I'm a good Catholic, no matter what they tell us."

"When did Martin Dupont finish his porridge?"

"I fetched his tray back at half past seven, just like always, and I washed the porridge bowl and the coffee bowl, and then the rest of the crockery from their breakfast, and the kettle, and then it was time for Mass."

"So you went to Mass, and returned," he said. "Then?"

"I did whatever Thérèse needed, some peeling and chopping and such, and then a bit later on the old gentleman took sick and I had to help with him. I stayed in his room and tried to make him comfortable, much as I could. I was there all the time."

"Surely you had to leave sometimes to answer calls of nature?"

"Well, yes, citizen, except for that."

"You never returned to your own room?"

She shook her head. "It's down by the kitchen, on the other side of the house, and the poor old gentleman was so ill. . . ."

"Did you ever lock the door to your room, Jeannette?"

"No, they never gave me a key for it." She shrugged, with a small, wry smile. "What've I got that anybody would steal?"

"What about a gold ring, and some silk handkerchiefs?" Aristide said suddenly, looking her in the eye. "And a silver brooch and a watch?"

She stared at him, paling. "Monsieur?"

"You took them, didn't you?"

"No, m'sieur!"

"I think you did. Just a few things that wouldn't be readily missed, isn't that right?"

He studied her as she shook her head and repeated her denial. She was undoubtedly telling the truth; a peasant of Jeannette's age and simplicity was rarely a convincing liar.

"No," he said, "it's all right, Jeannette; I didn't really think you'd taken those things. But someone wanted to cast suspicion on you, and hid them in a place where they knew they would be found. Can you think of who would want to do that?"

She mutely shook her head, rubbed at her nose with the back of her hand, and swallowed hard. "I don't know, citizen."

"You have no enemies?" he said, already sure she did not. Someone, he felt certain, had callously chosen Jeannette to be a pawn in a ruthless game. A hard knot of anger was building up in the pit of his stomach, anger that a cold-blooded poisoner had chosen ignorant, defenseless Jeannette to take the blame for his—or her—crimes.

"Look here," he said, "someone has done a very wicked thing. People will say, 'If she's a thief then she may also be a murderer.' So I don't want to discover anything about you that you would be afraid to tell me yourself. Do you have anything at all on your conscience, Jeannette? Any sins you would want to confess to the priest?"

She shook her head. "No, citizen. I swear it. On all the saints."

"Then I'll do my best to help you. I promise."

"Oh, bless you, m'sieur!" She jumped up from the stool on which she had been sitting and seized his hand and kissed it. He took an involuntary step backward, surprised.

"Don't thank me yet," he warned her. "This charge of poisoning is far graver than thievery, and you did have an opportunity to poison Citizen Dupont's breakfast. I don't think you did it," he continued, raising a hand as she opened her mouth to deny it, "but the opportunity was there. And most people haven't the imagination to understand that one needs more than opportunity; one also needs means and motive."

"Motive?"

"A reason to do something. The person who murdered old Citizen Dupont had to have the opportunity to do it, and he or she also had to have the poison in hand, and a reason to do it. Can you think of anyone in the household who would have had a reason to kill the old gentleman?"

She stared at him. "No, citizen." Perhaps, he thought, the idea had never occurred to her. "It must have been a colic carried him off, or a mistake. Maybe he had some stuff from the apothecary and he took too much of it."

"I fear that what probably killed him is not something anyone would take as medicine, Jeannette. It's rat poison."

"But why would anybody poison the old gentleman?"

"Well, he was very rich. Many people murder other people because of money."

Jeannette managed a weak smile. "But his money wouldn't have come to me."

"No," Aristide agreed, "it wouldn't. So we'll have to discover who does profit by his death, won't we?"

He left Jeannette and rejoined Brasseur when Didier arrived to fetch Jeannette away to the justice of the peace. "Just tell the magistrate the truth," he told her as Didier fastened manacles about her wrists. "Answer all the questions he asks you, and tell the truth. You've nothing to fear."

15

They first called on Hébert, who lived not far away, on Rue du Mail near the coaching station at the Place des Victoires. The surgeon proved to be a stout, pink, fussy, bewigged man who looked about fifty-five but was probably younger.

Having promptly gestured Brasseur and Aristide into his consulting room, which was lined with impressive-looking glass cases and specimen jars, he stood tapping the tips of his fingers together, frowning. "A very bad business, citizens," he repeated, several times, over the top of his spectacles. "What can the world be coming to? This wretched kitchenmaid must be touched in the head. Tell me, is Citizeness Dupont—I mean Citizeness Charlotte Dupont—is she all right? I understand her father's death greatly affected her."

"She seems to be much recovered," Aristide said. "She did spend a long time closeted in her bedchamber, but Citizeness Bouton at last persuaded her to rejoin the family for dinner today."

Hébert clucked. "Dear me, yes, that's what her sister said, that Charlotte was prostrated with grief. She didn't join us for Sunday dinner, you know; or come out once from her room, I understand. That means, of course," he added hastily, "that she had no opportunity to poison our meal, if you were even considering it was likely that—"

"I gather you regard her with a certain tenderness, citizen?" Aristide said.

"Well, I admire her greatly, you know; Citizeness Charlotte is a fine woman. Not, perhaps, the most shining intellect," he continued, with a complacent shrug, "but that quality isn't so very necessary in a woman. She's a good creature and an excellent housekeeper; I've admired her ever since she returned from her convent. Really she ought to have a husband."

Fanny, Aristide thought, was quite right: Hébert was plainly imagining himself as a prospective mate for Charlotte and her inheritance.

"Perhaps you can tell me, in your own words, what happened at the dinner yesterday at the Duponts' house," Brasseur said.

"Certainly, certainly, if it will help." Hébert gestured them to chairs and proceeded to repeat what they already knew from members of the Dupont family. "Of course, Citizeness Bouton was most distressed when she realized everyone was feeling ill," he concluded, "so I advised her that—"

"Was Citizeness Bouton ill from the dinner?" Brasseur inquired.

"I think she complained of some stomach cramps. I myself felt some nasty twinges, but was better within the hour. It was Citizen Dupont—Hauteroche, that is, Citizen Dupont the younger—who was affected the most. He suffered some painful cramps and vomited. I was quite worried about him for half an hour or so."

"Could he have been the poisoner's target?" Aristide said, thinking how foolish he sounded as soon as the words had left his lips. "I don't mean that anyone could have poisoned one particular corner of the soup tureen, but perhaps someone might have dropped something into his soup plate without being seen?"

Hébert shook his head. "No, no, we were all sitting about the table; everyone would have noticed. And obviously the poison didn't kill him, did it? The dose wasn't nearly enough to kill, only to sicken; and Gervais Dupont is a big man."

"Yes, I imagine you're right," Aristide said, nodding. "So you suggested to Citizeness Bouton . . ."

"I asked her if she could trust her servants, and she said of course she could, that they'd been with the family for years, except for the new kitchenmaid. Whereupon I told her the maid ought to be investigated. She was dubious at first, but I insisted—a cousin of mine was actually killed, poisoned with hemlock in his coffee, by his cook, who went off his head and suddenly became convinced my cousin was the devil. So at last Citizeness Bouton showed me to the girl's room."

Brasseur coughed. "I understand you took away certain evidence that you found in the room?"

Hébert tut-tutted again. "Yes indeed. Traces of arsenic—I'm sure of it! How an ignorant girl like that could have the wit to obtain arsenic—but perhaps the cook kept rat poison in the house. I found it right in the girl's pocket."

"Citizeness Bouton said you took it away with you, for safekeeping. I'll take that now, if you please."

"Oh, yes, Citizen Commissaire, of course." Hébert crossed the room to a glass-fronted cabinet in the corner and unlocked it. Reaching between a human skull and a jar containing some slimy-looking, unidentifiable substance, he retrieved a small screw of paper—a page of the previous day's *Journal de Paris*, Aristide saw—and carefully untwisted it.

"You see, citizen?"

A pinch or two of a fine, gritty, whitish powder, along with some ordinary gray lint, lay in the creases of the paper. The powder glittered slightly in the light from the window as Hébert tilted the paper. Aristide knew little about poisons but could tell straightaway that the substance was certainly not salt.

"Right in the girl's pocket," Hébert repeated as they bent over it. "The brazen little trollop! She must have been planning to rob the house and run off during the uproar."

"Then why didn't she?" Aristide said.

"I beg your pardon?"

"Why didn't she rob the house? I gather there was certainly uproar enough. She might have stolen what she meant to steal and then made herself scarce before anyone noticed. Instead, she remained right where she was, and nursed Citizen Dupont senior—with great care and devotion, I may add—and allowed you to search her belongings. Are those the actions of a thief?"

Hébert frowned and hastily screwed up the paper again. "That's for the magistrate to decide, I suppose."

"I'd better take this straight back to headquarters," Brasseur said when they were once again outside and elbowing their way past the crowds that swarmed about the waiting stagecoaches in the broad circle of the Place des Victoires. "Looks like rat poison to me, I'm afraid, though I don't know what the shiny stuff in it could be. What about you?"

"I suppose I'd better find François."

"Is he still living in the faubourg Marcel? You might save me the trip and interview Frochot, the notary, on your way back. He's in the Latin Quarter or thereabouts." Brasseur scribbled the address on a scrap of paper and they parted.

François, who was presently living in a dilapidated boardinghouse on Rue Geneviève, near the knackers' district, was a singular character, a young rogue of no more than twenty-three, but possessed of all the cunning, wit, vices, and robust cynicism of a man twice his age. He was also highly observant and a most talented actor (he had run away at thirteen, he had once told Aristide, to briefly join a theatrical troupe): as he cheerfully admitted, the ideal spy.

Aristide found him at home, or rather at the seedy neighborhood tavern on Rue du Pot de Fer to which the sullen maidservant at the boardinghouse directed him. He had taken a glass with François there not long before and now retraced his steps easily enough, to find François sitting alone at a table as near the small, smoky fire as he could manage. A jug of water and a half-empty glass of pinkish wine beside him, he was gloomily playing a round of patience, which Aristide had taught him three years before.

"I suppose this preoccupation with patience and watered wine means you haven't a sou to risk on a hand of cards?" Aristide said as he slid onto a bench across from his friend. François looked up at him and grinned.

"Hello, Ravel. No, curse it, I'm particularly short right now. Lost a bundle at trictrac a few days ago."

"Looking for a job?"

"Anything to pay old Mother Bastien for that hole I live in," he said, cheerfully. "What's doing?"

Aristide told him about Jeannette Moineau and the Dupont household. When he had done, François frowned into his glass and muttered, "Poor kid—what a hell of a life." Aristide nodded, having long suspected François was not quite as cynical as he made himself out to be.

"Would you be willing to pose as a servant to help her?" he said.

"What, serve at table and empty chamber pots? Like I said, what a hell of a life."

"It would be for only a few days, I hope. And," Aristide added, "you'd get your room and board, and perhaps even some pay, on top of what Brasseur would pay you."

François thought about it for a moment, then shrugged. "All right, why not?"

"Go to our commissariat early tomorrow morning; he'll have a reference for you. Then go straight to the Dupont house and get yourself hired. I want to know what they're saying when they don't think the police are listening."

After providing François with the address and with further details about the affair, Aristide turned his steps northward once again. Frochot, the notary, lived in a comfortable second-floor bachelor apartment near the Academy of Surgery. He was just sitting down to a late dinner as Aristide arrived and, learning of his business with him, insisted that Aristide join him.

"I have less appetite today than I might, you know," he told Aristide, "and it's a shame to let my caterer's excellent efforts go to waste. Do sit down—I'm sure you won't be disappointed. Another place setting, Pierre!" he added to the manservant.

Aristide accepted; he had eaten only half of a plate of cabbage soup at the Duponts' table before excusing himself, and these days good dinners were expensive and hard to come by. He took the chair Frochot pointed out to him as the notary fetched another wineglass from a cup-board and thrust it into the ice-filled glass cooler.

His host was perhaps a well-preserved fifty, of medium height but lean and distinguished looking in a silk coat, satin waistcoat, and neatly dressed wig, with the polite, impenetrable smile that Aristide had come to associate with many lawyers. The apartment matched him, its mas-culine elegance obvious, but understated, in the clean lines of the Louis XVI furniture. If he could afford it, Aristide thought, he would live in such a lodging, the refuge of a single, well-to-do professional man with good taste and the resources to indulge it as he pleased.

"I understand," he began, "you advised the family not to fetch the police over what seemed, to you, like a matter of tainted food."

Frochot nodded. "I thought it overreacting, but Citizen Hébert in-sisted it was poison, and he is, of course, a medical man. You never know what you're getting when you take on a new servant, after all. Even with the best of references, sometimes . . ."

The manservant entered and silently laid another place at the table. Frochot gestured to him and he poured two glasses of wine and stood ready with the water carafe.

"I assure you I am very grateful for a supper companion," Frochot continued, "since my wife—my dear wife died three years ago."

"My sympathies," Aristide said, glancing about the room again, cu-rious. He had had no inkling that the notary might be a widower; usu-ally, he thought, one would see some trace of a departed spouse, but here there was none at all, no portrait, no keepsake or memento of a woman's presence. "It must be lonely without her."

Frochot nodded. "Ordinarily I try to dine out when I can, merely for the company of others. Now: what can I tell you?"

"Merely give me, in your own words, your recollection of yester-day's dinner at the Dupont house."

Frochot complied with an account that tallied well enough with Hébert's and with Magdeleine's, while the servant brought in a fricas-see of rabbit and they set to it.

"Were you ill yourself?" Aristide asked, when Frochot had con-cluded his story.

"A few stomach cramps," he said with a dismissive gesture. "Fortunately I was not greedy with my soup!" He pushed away his half-eaten plate of rabbit, gravy, and roasted parsnips. "You begin to wonder, of course, after an experience like yesterday's, what the cook may be slipping into the sauce. No, no," he added as Aristide glanced down at his own plate, "I assure you, my caterer has a sterling reputation, and my servants have been with me for over a year; they're entirely trustworthy. I'm merely feeling . . . not quite myself yet."

"How long have you known the Duponts?" Aristide inquired as he set back to work on the fricassee. It was very good indeed, and he could rarely afford such well-prepared fare at a restaurant.

Frochot leaned back in his chair, pondering. "Let me see. . . . It must be nearly fourteen or fifteen years now. I'm old Martin's legal adviser, you know, and—or I suppose I must say I *was* his legal adviser. Dear me, it's very strange to think he's gone. He showed every sign of being immortal." Smiling a little at his own minor witticism, he went on. "Of course, they've invited me to dine more often since my poor Henriette died. With two single women in the house, I expect Magdeleine, for one, would like to see at least one of them safely married off."

"You are not receptive to the suggestion?" Aristide said, perceiving his slight grimace.

"What a choice! An utter nitwit or a hatchet-faced scold." Frochot straightened in his chair and signaled to the manservant to take away Aristide's empty plate. "Will you take a cordial, or some coffee?"

Aristide chose coffee and they retreated to the sofa as the servant silently cleared the table. "I assume," Aristide said, resuming their conversation, "having met them both, that Citizeness Charlotte Dupont is the nitwit and Laurence the scold."

Frochot nodded. "She is not, precisely, ill-tempered, but she has a sharp tongue and no patience for fools. Whereas Charlotte is her exact opposite—the sort of empty-headed, maudlin woman who spends her leisure either kneeling at her prie-dieu or reading sentimental novels."

"Dr. Hébert seems to think her quite amiable," Aristide said. Frochot gave a delicate shudder.

"There is no accounting for tastes!"

16

After interviewing Frochot, Aristide had thought to visit the Palais-Égalité for a few hours, to lose himself amid the glitter and bustle of that hectic pleasure garden, but as he crossed the Seine he realized the weather had turned mild, with even a suggestion of wan late-afternoon sunshine filtering through the cover of pearly cloud. He turned westward instead to the gardens of the Tuileries and wandered for a time through the overgrown shrubbery, pale green with the first tiny, lacy leaves of spring.

The gardens, once the preserve of the fashionable and restricted to those who were sufficiently well dressed, had been thrown open to all since the Revolution. The revolutionary government having little time or substance to spare on public gardens, however, the boxwood hedges had long since lost their neat clipped appearance and instead thrust bent and spiky branches into the well-trodden pathways to snag unwary passersby. The small fenced-in yard, its grass now untrimmed and lank, that abutted the former palace had, five years ago, been reserved as a playground for the dauphin, the king's son, but little Louis-Charles had been in his own grave a year and a half. A dozen ragged urchins fought shrilly over the sole swing, which dangled from an overhanging branch.

Despite the neglect that prevailed in the gardens, a few marble statues of gods and nymphs still stood here and there, appearing suddenly like pale ghosts at the junctions of footpaths. Aristide suspected the wooden folding chairs that once had dotted the paths and grottoes had long since been stolen, but the stone benches remained, too heavy to steal, and the overgrown hedges and shrubs provided a sanctuary for lovers. He passed the whispering, giggling couples with scarcely a glance, meaning to find his way along the hedges to the terrace that ran along the northern border of the gardens, and on to the back streets that would take him to Rue Honoré.

On a bench on the Terrasse des Feuillants, near the entrance to the Manège, the former royal riding school that had served as the hall of the National Assembly for three years, he thought he spied a familiar figure. As he approached he found he was not mistaken; the seated woman, who was staring fixedly into the trees, stiff as one of the weathered statues, was Laurence Dupont.

He could guess, after a little thought, why she was there. He had loitered in the same spot himself, waiting for the Assembly's sessions to end. Mathieu had often arranged to meet him near that same marble bench.

"You used to wait for your husband here, didn't you?" he said at last. She looked up, startled, and gazed at him without expression for a moment before mutely nodding. "I often met Mathieu here." He gestured to the bench. "May I?"

She shrugged and moved to the far end of the bench as a few birds chuckled and twittered in the trees.

"I wonder how it was we never met before this?" he added, seating himself at the other end, with plenty of space between them. "If Mathieu and your husband were as close as you say."

"Does it matter?"

"Not really, I suppose."

"If I hadn't liked Citizen Alexandre so much," she said abruptly, "I would have hated him, for taking Aurèle away from me so often. They were always kind, always jolly—but I felt as if I was the intruder when we three were together. And I was his *wife*! If we'd had more time—we were married barely three years—but then he . . . I never even had the chance, as you did, to say good-bye."

"It wasn't for my own sake, believe me, that I went to that place," Aristide said, remembering the chill rain, and the blood trickling among the cobbles.

"It was so *sudden*," Laurence continued, as if she had not heard him. "Aurèle simply—never came home."

"On the ninth of Thermidor?" he said, remembering the stifling summer day on which Robespierre and his closest associates had lost their hold over the cowed and servile National Convention, when the resentful, fearful deputies had risen against him and shouted him down. Laurence nodded.

"He'd gone to the City Hall late that evening, after they heard Robespierre was under arrest, and then that he'd been set free and was planning insurrection. . . . Aurèle said he had to go. So I went with him, as far as the Place de Grève, and it was complete chaos there; you could see that nothing was organized, nothing was going to stand up against the National Guard when the Convention sent troops in to crush them. Aurèle could tell that at a glance, just as I could. I begged him to leave with me, told him he'd be throwing his life away, but he was like a madman; he insisted his place was there, beside Robespierre."

A pair of shabbily dressed men strolled past, occupied in an argument, and she lowered her voice, with a swift glance about her to be sure no potential spies were listening.

"If Robespierre lost, he said, then nothing mattered any more, anyway; then everything they'd done, the good and the bad, had been for nothing. And he kissed me and made me promise to go straight home, and he gave a few sous to a man who'd been slinking away, to get me home safely, and then he went into the Hôtel de Ville. . . .

"The man walked me home and I waited. . . . I waited all night, I couldn't sleep . . . and the next morning we began to hear things, all kinds of rumors, that there had been fighting, that some people had been killed or wounded, and finally that everyone had been captured . . . and then silence. And he didn't come home."

She paused and drew a long breath. A few pigeons strutted toward them, hopeful for crumbs, but she ignored them. "Then by afternoon everyone was saying Robespierre was outlawed and sentenced to death.

And still I couldn't learn anything . . . so I went out, because I had to know; I went to the Law Courts and waited outside the courtyard, and finally they came out, in the executioner's carts, and he wasn't there. I could have fallen to my knees and thanked God, if I hadn't known it was the end for Robespierre, for everything he'd tried to do, everything he'd wanted to do."

"You knew him yourself?"

"Barely. Aurèle knew him, though not well. I hope Aurèle never saw him on that last day, covered in blood, in such dreadful pain. . . ." She quickly wiped away the tears that had begun to trickle down her cheeks. "But I couldn't help rejoicing that Aurèle wasn't there, that he wasn't among the condemned. Until we heard in the streets, the next day, that the executions weren't over, that everybody from the Commune who'd supported Robespierre was outlawed, too. So I went to the Palais de Justice again, praying, praying, but I knew, because we'd heard nothing from him. Dozens had been condemned, they were saying."

"Yes."

"Nine carts. I counted them. I'll never forget it. I looked at each one, at men I knew, men who had dined at our table, who were going to die, tied up like cattle while the crowds were screaming abuse all around me, and finally I saw Aurèle."

"How hellishly familiar it sounds," Aristide murmured.

She squeezed her eyes shut for an instant, swallowed, and continued. "He never saw me. I would have followed them, to be near him, to let him see somebody still cared, but I think I fainted. . . . I came to myself in the refreshment room at the Law Courts, where someone had carried me. They thought they were being kind. I wish they had let the horses trample me. It was the first time in my life I'd fainted. . . . I was expecting."

Aristide slowly nodded. With no trace or mention of a small child at the Dupont house, he could guess what had happened.

"Then I lost the baby," she said, echoing his thoughts. "A miscarriage . . . from the shock, I suppose. So Aurèle was gone, and the baby was gone, and I had nothing at all."

She fell silent. After a few minutes she sucked in a breath, blew her nose, and straightened. "I don't know why I'm saying all this to you. Please forgive me. I scarcely know you."

"Sometimes it's easier to unburden yourself to a stranger," he said, "rather than to someone you have to face every day." He banished thoughts of Mathieu, with an effort, and fell in beside her as abruptly she rose and strode toward the river. "I think you Duponts have all been living together far too long, under your father-in-law's thumb, and you're all fearfully weary of each other's company. You—you're wretchedly unhappy there, aren't you?"

Laurence walked on without replying, head down, until they reached the quay. A sharp breeze rose from the river, whipping at their hair with the briny tang of water and weeds and fish. She pulled her cloak more snugly about her shoulders and stood gazing into the murky green shallows of the Seine, past barge workers unloading firewood and sacks of flour and winter vegetables.

"I hate it so much that I sometimes feel as if—as if my blood is on fire," she said at last. "And it's not that I'm mistreated—nobody is deliberately unkind, and I do no more work than anyone else, and I get the same miserly dress allowance as Magdeleine and Charlotte. . . . I've nothing to complain about."

"But you can't leave."

"That's it precisely. I can't leave. I feel like a prisoner there. And I have no money, no family, nothing beyond what they see fit to give me."

"No family at all?"

"I'm an orphan. The Duponts are distant cousins on my mother's side. I've known them since I was a child. And I feel as if soon they're going to stifle me." She drew another deep breath and shook her head, as if to clear it.

"At least the Palais-Égalité is only a few minutes' walk away," Aristide said. She turned, baffled.

"What has that to do with anything?"

"Don't you go there with a friend now and then, even Charlotte, perhaps, for some amusement, some distraction?"

"No, of course not."

"Why on earth not?"

"It's not a place where decent women should be seen."

"Oh, come now!" he exclaimed, nearly laughing. "Who told you that?"

"Everybody says so. I'd never go there except to shop for a few necessaries. And never after noon."

"Who's 'everybody'? Granted, after dark the Palais-Égalité becomes rather . . . undisciplined . . . but that's no reason why you shouldn't visit during the day, enjoy yourself a little. Surely you visited some of the restaurants with your husband."

She shrugged. "Gervais goes, from time to time . . . to the Comédie, and he says there are other little theaters there, so I suppose he knows people. And I did go to a restaurant or café a few times, with Aurèle and Citizen Alexandre. But Aurèle would always say it wasn't a place where decent women should go alone after eleven o'clock in the morning, and the Old Man was forever telling us all that the Palais-Royal—the Palais-Égalité, I mean—was just a nest of whores and thieves, waiting to fleece the unwary."

Suddenly incensed at the entire Dupont family, Aristide seized her arm and turned her about. "Enough of this. I'm already weary of hearing what that old tyrant used to say. Come on."

"What?" Laurence exclaimed, balking, as he tugged her forward. "What are you doing?"

"Taking you to the Palais-Égalité, of course."

"But—but you can't!"

"Why can't I?" he said, without breaking stride along the path.

"Because . . ."

Her voice trailed away and he paused and turned to face her.

"Do you know what I see when I look at you, citizeness? I see somebody who has stumbled along, day to day, paralyzed by grief and uncertainty, for so long that she's forgotten how to live. I won't molest you, you know, or lead you into a den of iniquity. Why not come with me, see the sights, have a glass of extremely poor wine because that's all I can afford, and remember what it's like to enjoy yourself? You did enjoy yourself, didn't you?"

"Yes, of course," she said. She drew her arm from his grasp and retreated a pace. "We went to—to Méot's to dine once. No, twice. They pointed out all kinds of important people to me. And we went once to the Café Mécanique, I remember, the one with the tables that pipe the coffee and hot chocolate right into your cups. That was fascinating." She smiled suddenly, fleetingly. "Mathieu—Citizen Alexandre—he was just like a small boy with a new plaything, watching the mechanisms work."

"Then remember how you enjoyed yourself at the Palais-Égalité with your husband," Aristide told her, "and then, for God's sake, say farewell to him for once and for all."

"How can you tell me to forget—"

"I didn't say to forget him. Only to set the past aside, and begin looking toward the future. Because if you don't start to look toward the future, you'll never get out of that prison you're in."

"You are impertinent," she snapped. "And how do you expect I'm to leave the Duponts when I have no money—"

"I don't mean the Dupont household," he said. "That's only a physical prison, though you ought to get out of that, too. I mean the prison you've built around yourself, stone by stone. You've walled yourself in with your grief and now you no longer know how to escape it."

Laurence glared at him, the color rising in her cheeks. "You—you are the most impertinent, discourteous—"

"We're not talking about me here, citizeness; we're talking about you." He thrust his hands in his pockets and took a step toward her. She recoiled but found herself backed up against one of the hedges. "Do you know what I think of when I look at you," Aristide continued, "now that I know a little about you? I can only think of something that Charles d'Orléans, the poet, wrote back in the fifteenth century."

She stared at him and he quoted softly:

"A dangerous thrift it is to amass
Only a treasury of regrets.
He who holds them too close to his heart
Suffers justly, and nothing forgets."

"Now you might imagine," he continued, "that that verse would apply more accurately to an old miser like your father-in-law, who grows rich by neglecting to enjoy living, but when I see you, festering in your unhappiness here, clinging to your shreds of the past, able to think of nothing but your dead-and-gone Aurèle—"

"Stop!" she cried. She dodged aside, wrenched her shawl from the grasp of the gnarled boxwood branches at her back, and hurried away across the muddy lawn. Aristide followed her, matching her pace. At last she whipped about and shouted, "Stop it! Let me alone!"

"You know I don't mean you any harm, citizeness," he said. "On the contrary; I want to help you."

"You know nothing about me! What business is it of yours how I live my life?"

"But you *don't* live it. Listen, citizeness, you may think what you like about me, but if you take a long, hard look at yourself and your existence, you'll realize I'm merely telling you the truth, whether you want to hear it or not." He paused and they glared at each other for a moment before Aristide abruptly turned and began to walk away. "Now, if you choose," he added over his shoulder, "you can walk home by yourself to Rue des Moulins, and go back to the crypt you've retreated into, and revert to being a walking, talking corpse; or you can come with me to the Palais-Égalité and remember how to live, by seeing something besides the four walls of that damned house, and the faces of your noxious in-laws."

She opened her mouth but did not utter a word, her cheeks still crimson. He looked at her an instant more, then, supposing he had failed to persuade her, strode away. Suddenly, behind him, he heard the last thing he expected: a peal of laughter.

"Stop! Wait! Oh, please, do, do stop."

"Citizeness?" he said, turning about.

"My 'noxious in-laws'!" she repeated, and laughed again, her whole body shuddering with it, and reached out a hand to him. "Wait—please—" She caught her breath and, without warning, burst into tears.

Aristide had never quite known what to do with weeping women. If she had been his sister, Thérèse, he thought, he would have drawn her into his arms and held her until she calmed; but Laurence he scarcely knew, and she would have thought it an unpardonable familiarity. At last he took her by the elbow and guided her to the nearest bench. She sank down onto it and continued to sob.

"Damn you!" she burst out suddenly. "Oh, damn you, damn you, damn you . . ."

He thought at first she was addressing him, but a glance at her, as she stared straight ahead of her at some phantom only she could see, tears running down her cheeks, proved that she was not thinking of him in the least. He moved a few yards away, in order not to intrude upon her grief.

At last, after several minutes, she raised her head and grimaced at her limp, crumpled handkerchief. Spying a fountain not far away, he dampened his own handkerchief, then silently handed it to her. She wiped at her face with it and pressed it against her swollen eyes before giving him an abashed glance.

"I loved Aurèle so," she murmured, her voice low and hoarse, "but he always loved his ideals and dreams more than he loved me, and in the end they destroyed him. He could have come home—it must have been such chaos, he could have slipped away while there was still a chance, before anyone knew he was at the City Hall, but he chose to follow Robespierre. . . . His wife and his child meant less to him than an *idea* . . ."

"I think," Aristide said at last, "you had better have something stronger than a glass of wine." He took her elbow again and raised her to her feet. She did not protest. Leading the way out of the gardens, he paused by the first spirit seller he found and bought a measure of eau-de-vie.

Laurence obediently sipped the brandy, though Aristide suspected it must have been vile, little more than raw spirit, and after a moment some color returned to her face. "Better?" he said. She nodded. "Good." He dropped the pewter cup to swing on its chain, and took Laurence's arm again. "Come along."

17

A quarter hour later they entered the Café Février. For an instant
Aristide wondered if Aurèle Dupont had taken Laurence there,
and if such memories would be painful for her, but she allayed his fears
by gazing about with the beginnings of lively interest. The Février,
though it lay below ground level in the cellars, was one of the more elegant cafés at the Palais-Égalité, hung with crystal chandeliers whose
gleam was reflected in touches of gilding and a dozen tall mirrors.

"Do you see that table in the corner," he said, pointing, "where the
fat man in the red coat is reading a newspaper? That's where Lepeletier-
Saint-Fargeau was assassinated."

"That very spot?"

"Yes. Of course, they don't advertise the fact." Lepeletier had been a
minor aristocrat who had adopted revolutionary principles and voted for
the death of Louis XVI. His assassin, a fanatical royalist, upon hearing of
the king's condemnation, had gone hunting for the first deputy he could
find and had skewered the unfortunate Lepeletier with a rapier, then escaped in the uproar. "I saw it happen, you see, quite by chance."

"You did? They never caught the man, did they?"

"No." A waiter approached them and he ordered coffee for himself
and a large glass of Cognac for Laurence.

"Drink," he told her when it arrived. She meekly obeyed. Soon her cheeks were flushed—she had eaten no more than he at the Duponts' table, he remembered—and the brandy had loosened her tongue.

"You're with the police, so you know quite a lot about murder, don't you?" she said suddenly.

"I suppose I do."

"It must have been you, you and Commissaire Brasseur, who investigated the murders on Rue du Hasard last autumn?"

"Yes, we did that."

"They caught the person who did it, didn't they?"

"Yes."

"It must have been exciting, hunting down a murderer."

Exciting?

He recalled all the corpses he had seen, lives cut short, some—he could not deny it—deserving their premature end, others a tragic waste of life.

"You've had a murder in your own household now," he said, without looking at her. "Do you think it's exciting?"

"No, it's frightful, wondering . . . I see what you mean; it's not a game. Was it very distressing?"

"Yes."

"What I meant to say is, you've got to find out who poisoned the Old Man," she added, leaning toward him, eyes bright with urgency. "You've *got* to. Do you know what it's like, knowing one of us is a murderer and yet nobody knows who? The others pretend they're sure Jeannette did it, but I know she didn't and I want to look over my shoulder at every step."

"How do you think I might best gain Charlotte's confidence?" Aristide asked.

"Charlotte?" Laurence hiccuped and bent her head to stifle a giggle. "Why? You don't think *she* did it? She—she's the *last* person—"

"I think she knows more than she's saying about old Martin's death. Yet from everything you and the others have told me, I can't believe she could have murdered him herself. How can I induce her to be frank with me?"

"Go with her to that appalling charlatan Cavalcanti," she said instantly, pronouncing the words with great care, "and attend one of his séances."

"I think she's already hurried off to seek his advice. She left the house immediately after dinner, and she mentioned his name."

She nodded sagely. "Then offer to accompany her the next time she visits him. He seems to hold a séance nearly every day, in the mid-afternoon or evening. Pretend you're swallowing everything, and I guarantee Charlotte will open her soul to you. Although," she added, "you may run the risk of being talked to death!"

"Thanks—I'll try that. Perhaps you should come with us? She may be more forthcoming with somebody she knows well."

"I doubt it," said Laurence, shaking her head. "Charlotte must know what I think of her Signor Cav—Cavalcanti, and she wouldn't discuss him with an unbeliever. You, on the other hand, are an unknown quantity. And you saw what Magdeleine was trying to do at dinner, I'm sure."

"By placing me next to Charlotte? Yes. I didn't imagine I was there by accident. Nor that she had you opposite me without a reason."

"Me!"

"Citizen Frochot seems to think Magdeleine would happily marry off either one of you, if not both."

Laurence giggled again and took another cautious sip of her brandy. "Nobody is going to marry me. I'm thirty-one and plain, and I haven't a sou of my own. Would *you* marry me?"

"I'm not looking for a wife," Aristide said.

"Well, that's a diplomatic answer!"

"Surely someone would marry you, if you wished to remarry. Obviously Aurèle Dupont thought well enough of you to marry you without a dowry, didn't he?"

"I never quite understood what Aurèle saw in me," she admitted, gazing down at her glass. "He was handsome enough, with fine-enough prospects, to have any woman he wanted. What was so special about me, really?"

"Well," Aristide said, summoning a brief smile, "you're not as hideously ugly as you seem to think you are, you know; and people who measure others only by their appearance aren't people worth knowing.

And you're quite intelligent, and you're obviously capable of great loyalty and affection, and you have a strong sense of justice. Such qualities would recommend themselves to many men."

Laurence shook her head. "None of them mean much without a dowry to go with them. You don't know very much about the marriage market, do you?"

"I confess I don't."

"Why haven't *you* married?"

"Personal reasons . . . private reasons."

He looked away for an instant. When Aristide was nine years old, his father had murdered his wife and her lover, and had died on the scaffold for the crime. Worse than the pain of loss, almost, had been the shame of bearing the name of a notorious murderer for more than a dozen years until he had escaped to the anonymity of Paris. Yet he had never changed it, never attached a second, meaningless surname to disguise the one that still raised eyebrows in Bordeaux almost thirty years later.

"Aside from the fact," he added, "that I have no prospects of inheriting any money, and I don't earn enough to keep a wife and family."

"So you find a woman with a fat dowry, don't you? Like everybody else."

Aristide shook his head. "I fear I wouldn't make a good husband."

"All a man really needs to do to be a good husband to a woman," she said abruptly, "is to keep his wife from starving or freezing to death, and to refrain from beating her. A woman should be grateful for anything beyond that, shouldn't she?"

He eyed her, curious at her sudden bitterness, guessed it was the brandy talking, and said nothing.

"Aurèle was a good husband to me. He was kind, and thoughtful. He would never have raised a hand to me. And he was delighted, overjoyed, when I told him I was expecting a child." Laurence paused and blew her nose. "He was so good to me," she insisted suddenly, her voice trembling. "He really was."

"I'm sure he loved you very much," Aristide said, for want of something to say.

"You think that?"

"I only—"

"He never loved me!"

She gulped down another swallow of the brandy before straightening in her chair and looking him in the eye. "There. I've had too much, haven't I? But that's the truth. He was fond of me, to be sure, but it wasn't love. Not the kind that I felt for him. I would have cut out my heart and offered it to him on a platter if he'd asked for it!"

"Did he have a mistress, then?" Aristide said, sensing she needed to talk to someone, anyone who would listen.

"Perhaps. If he did, I knew nothing about her."

"Some men prefer to keep such matters very private; if they're fond of their wives, they won't wish to hurt their feelings by—"

"I think, really, the Revolution was his mistress. He loved it more than he could ever love a human being. Why else would he have chosen Robespierre's side—against such terrible odds—over me, and his own child?" Laurence paused, stared at him for a moment, and hurriedly gulped down the last of the brandy.

"Ravel—is that how men behave? I'm very ignorant about such things. I think perhaps he only married me because his father was nagging him to marry a respectable woman and give him some grandchildren. Aurèle was nearly forty, you know, just a couple of years younger than Gervais. But even that doesn't explain why he should have chosen *me* among all the other women he might have married."

"Why did you love him?" Aristide said.

"What a question to ask!"

"I'm perfectly serious. Why did you love him? When you seem to have admitted to yourself that he didn't truly love you."

She thought about it for a moment, then shrugged. "Why does any young woman fall in love with a man? Aurèle was clever, amiable, charming, extraordinarily handsome. . . . He had a sort of magnetism about him. I was always in love with him, since my early teens. He was enough older than I was that he seemed like a god, the way dazzling, unattainable people do when you're young."

Aristide nodded, remembering a few adolescent infatuations of his own, and let her continue.

"When I was fourteen he was twenty-eight, and handsome as an angel. He had the most remarkable black eyes, and a beautiful smile. Once you saw him, you couldn't take your eyes off him."

"I remember he was handsome. But good-looking young men are widespread enough, really. What made him special?"

"He talked well. I suppose that was it, what I found so intriguing about him when I grew up and began to know him as an adult. He spoke so well; he could make his point in a few sentences, and do it with wit and style—really the most delicious, subtle wit. And we shared so many things. Of course, he believed in what I believe: reform and justice, and liberty and equality—all the principles of the Revolution."

He stole a glance at her and found her eyes shining and her face alight with the idealistic fervor he had grown to recognize in countless salons and cafés, during the early years of the Revolution. Could a shared passion for social justice, he wondered, truly form the basis of a marriage? It had been enough for Laurence, but evidently not for Aurèle Dupont.

"It's growing late," he said, turning to the gilt clock on the wall. "I'd better take you home before they begin to wonder where you are."

She shook her head. "I doubt they'd notice. Tell me, is the rest of the Palais-Égalité like this? So refined and elegant? I've only seen some of the shops, and the places I told you about."

"Well, not all of it. Some of the establishments here look far more elegant on the outside than the inside. Though even the brothels are expensively outfitted."

"Brothels?" She clapped her hand over her mouth to suppress a guilty giggle. "Do you know so very much about brothels, then?"

"I work for the police," Aristide said. "The police see everything, and nothing shocks them."

"Show me about," she demanded. "Please. I want to see more."

"Including the brothels?"

"No, not the brothels! But the Palais-Égalité isn't nearly as wicked and debauched as I imagined it would be."

"If you wish." He led her outside and they wove their way through the passersby and the lamplighters who had come out to stave off the dusk. With the sunset, the pleasure-seekers had begun to spill in, crowding the long arcades, peering in shop windows and dallying in the half-dozen cafés, pausing to gossip with friends equally as stylish and jaded. Most flaunted the latest outré fashions, the men with exaggerated coat-tails, long undressed hair, and cravats tied so high they covered the chin, the women with enormous bonnets above scanty, diaphanous muslin gowns and Grecian sandals.

Laurence stared with frank curiosity at the prostitutes who leaned out of mezzanine windows or loitered in corners and beneath the trees. Some were little more than children, thirteen or fourteen, the daubs of scarlet rouge grotesque on their smooth cheeks. A few recognized Aristide—the Palais-Égalité was part of Brasseur's territory and the girls knew the commissaire and his associates well—and acknowledged him with a wink or a boozy wave.

"How about a good time, citizen?" demanded one tall, deep-voiced, heavily painted woman, emerging from the shadows. She wore an out-moded gown, trimmed with torn and tarnished lace, over full panniers, and an elaborately curled wig that had long since gone a dingy yellow beneath its powder. "You can do better than a skinny piece like that, can't you?" Aristide turned toward her and the vision snickered.

"Oh, it's you. Didn't recognize you, without the commissaire beside you."

"Do mind your own business, Nicolas," Aristide said, without pausing. Beside him, Laurence sucked in a breath.

"Was that a *man?*"

"Yes."

"Wearing a *gown?*"

"I fear so," said Aristide, with a faint smile he hoped she could not see in the treacherous half-light.

"But who would want—"

Aristide said nothing as she abruptly fell silent, allowing her to draw her own conclusions, and strolled on to show her the Café de Foy, where the Revolution in Paris could be said to have begun on the twelfth of July, 1789.

At length, after pointing out a few more places of interest, he turned their steps toward the side passage that led out of the gardens to the narrow Rue Montpensier and another close, covered passage leading out to Rue de la Loi beyond. The night was overcast and starless, lit only by the firefly glow of the lamps swaying overhead from their ropes. They did not speak until they passed the corner of Rue des Moulins and were nearing the Dupont house. Laurence suddenly stopped and pointed toward the entrance to a back alley. "This way."

"Why not the front door?" Aristide said, following her.

"If I use the front door, someone inside is sure to see me. And I don't think it's anyone's business where I've been or how long I've been gone."

Brava, he said to himself. Could it have been nothing more than his rather heated and overhasty words that had prompted Laurence into taking charge, at least in that trifling fashion, of her own life?

Only the last deep-blue vestiges of daylight remained above them to guide them through the alley. Laurence seemed to know it well enough, however, and soon stopped at a door in the high wall on their left.

"Does this lead into the garden?" Aristide inquired.

"Yes. Usually Thérèse forgets to bolt it."

"I'll bid you good night, then."

"Wait—" She reached out and found his hand in the dark. "You needn't go."

"I doubt the rest of the family will be pleased to see me again, at this hour of the evening," he said.

"Who cares about the rest of the family?" Laurence retorted, in a fierce whisper. "To the devil with them. Citizen Ravel . . ."

"Yes?" he said, when she seemed to falter.

"Would you . . . come inside? No one has to see you. There's a door into the scullery that leads directly to the back staircase. You can come in without anyone knowing you're here."

"And go where, citizeness?" he said, suspecting he knew what she wished to say.

"Upstairs . . . with me."

In the darkness he heard her gasp, then let out a long sigh. He could imagine how difficult such an offer had been for her to make.

People who knew him well, François in particular, called him a monk; it was true that his appetites for the usual pleasures of men were moderate enough. He had not been with a woman for a fortnight (though it was not for lack of trying on the part of his landlady, who flirted with him on every available occasion) and suddenly he felt a quick stirring of desire.

He did not, he reflected, feel a whit of attraction for Laurence beyond what he might feel for any healthy young woman with all her teeth and hair; he pitied her more than he admired her. *But this*, he thought an instant later, *this is nothing to do with me, and has all to do with Laurence.* Laurence who, in taking a stranger to her bed, might at last exorcise the ghost of that adored, dazzling husband who had never loved her. No doubt Aurèle Dupont had done what was expected of a husband, dutifully shared her bed from time to time for the sake of getting a child on her, but probably she had never known true passion.

She would never have made such an offer to him, he knew, had he not plied her with brandy, and he felt a momentary stab of compunction at the thought of taking advantage of her tipsiness. He pressed her hand, wondering what to say to her, and felt her fingers close tightly around his, warm in the evening chill, just perceptibly trembling. Feeling like a character in a third-rate comedy, where lonely widows were invariably in search of consolation, he suppressed a sudden urge to laugh and instead bent toward her and with his fingertips found her cheek in the darkness.

"Come, then," she whispered.

"Don't take such a risk," he said, hanging back as she stepped forward. "What if someone should discover us? My room's not far away."

"No . . . *now*. Before I change my mind."

She tugged at the handle and pushed at the gate, pausing with a hiss as the damp wood gave a shriek of protest. "I don't understand. Something's blocking the latch."

"Let me try," Aristide said. He tried the door handle, but it would not turn. Feeling farther in the darkness, he found a rough surface that did not belong there. "What the—there's a rope tied to the handle."

"What do you mean?" Laurence whispered.

"It's tied to the handle and appears to go up and over the top of the gate," he told her, feeling up along its length. It seemed peculiarly taut.

"Why would—"

Suddenly apprehensive, he wrenched at the handle and put his shoulder to the gate. At last it opened, but sluggishly, as if a heavy bundle were attached to the other side.

"Should something be hanging from the inside of the gate?" he asked, cautiously stepping onto the garden path. The garden was in profound shadow, the only illumination from a lamp shining faintly somewhere in the kitchen beyond. Something immensely tall and jagged barred his way, a deeper black against the starless sky, and he drew back for an instant before remembering the ancient walnut tree.

"No—oh!" Laurence let out a stifled shriek. "On the back of the gate—it's *soft*—"

Straining to see in the darkness, Aristide felt at the dark mass and found something that was not wood, but folds of cloth. Cloth, with something beneath, soft and yielding as—

Now he could see it all, though dimly. A rough wooden ladder lay on the muddy earth beside the wall. Above it hung a dreadful shape, dangling perhaps a foot above the ground, the whole slowly swinging in the evening breeze as the rope knotted about the woman's neck squeaked gently against the gate.

18

Laurence sucked in a sharp breath and Aristide turned about and seized her by the shoulders. "Keep hold of yourself! You're too sensible to scream and faint. Run to the kitchen and find someone, Gervais for preference—"

"He's probably at the theater—"

"Anyone, then! And send someone for the police. Get Brasseur, no matter what, even if they have to fetch him at home."

She raced down the path and hammered at the kitchen door. A moment later he saw it open. Shadows and silhouettes wavered in the thin light of a kitchen candle.

He turned to examine the body. Was there the remotest chance she was still alive? He fingered the knot, shrinking back from the touch of chill flesh, but the rope was taut and he had no hope of untying it. She had knotted it to the handle on the alley side of the gate, he realized now, and flung it over the gate to dangle on the side of the garden. Then she had climbed a rung or two of the short ladder that leaned against the wall, fixed the noose about her neck, kicked the ladder away. . . .

Footsteps pounded through the house. Charles Jullien appeared at an upper window. "What is it? What's going on here?"

"You!" Aristide shouted, gesturing to him. "Come down here and help me. There's been a—an accident." He turned back to the body and tried to support it, to take the terrible strangling tautness from the rope.

"Death of the devil," Jullien muttered, joining him in the darkness of the garden a moment later. "Some accident! Could she still be alive? Who is it?"

"I think it's Charlotte. Can you catch her as I lower her?"

Jullien thrust a pocketknife into his hand as Aristide lifted the ladder and braced it once more against the wall. He climbed up and struggled with the knife for a moment but at last managed to hack through the rope. The body dropped into Jullien's arms and he grunted irreverently at the weight. Aristide sprang down from the ladder and rejoined Jullien, taking hold of the woman's shoulders, and together they carried her into the kitchen and onto the scrubbed wooden table.

It was Charlotte, her face crimson and distorted, tongue protruding. Aristide bent over the body and feverishly worked at the knot in the noose encircling her neck while avoiding the grotesque gaze of her wide-open, bulging eyes. At last the knot came loose and he tore the rope from her throat before shaking her and slapping at her cheeks.

"It's no good," Jullien told him softly, after a moment. "She's past help, I think. Feel her flesh!" he added when Aristide paid no attention. "She's growing cold."

Aristide would not believe him. *Poor foolish Charlotte—*

He went on shaking her, searching for any signs of life. At last, after an interminable few minutes, he gave up.

It seemed forever until Brasseur and his men arrived, though in truth it was perhaps a quarter of an hour. Brasseur felt her pulse and shook his head. "Prunelle'll be along shortly, I hope, but I don't need him to tell me she's dead. Who found her?"

"I did," Aristide said. "Laurence Dupont and I. We were coming into the garden from the back alley." He threw himself on the nearest chair and glowered over at the corpse. "Heaven help us, we ought to have been able to prevent this. Damn, damn, *damn*. This poor, silly woman—and here we were suspecting her!"

"Could be suicide, of course," said Brasseur. "Like you suggested, she did the old man in; and then remorse got the better of her. When did anybody see her last?"

"I saw her run out of the house at about quarter past three." Aristide sprang to his feet again and strode restlessly across the stone-flagged kitchen floor, making a wide detour around the table. "Oh, she could have hanged herself, certainly . . . if you ignore everything you know about human nature. This poor creature was no killer. And she was a deeply religious woman, or she used to be. That sort of teaching stays with you; she wouldn't have taken her own life."

"You found her outside? Where'd she get the rope? Is there a gardener's shed?"

"Yes, a little shack in the corner. But if she did do it, why hang herself in the garden, and run the risk of being interrupted? Why not do it quietly behind a locked door in her own bedroom, from a lamp hook?"

"You think the suicide could be a fake?"

Aristide nodded as he took up the rope, fingering the coarse hemp, and forced himself to look more closely at the angry red line on Charlotte's neck. Brasseur fetched a candle and together they bent over the body.

"Look," Brasseur said after a moment, pointing to the mark the rope had left, deep in Charlotte's flesh. "Do you see that, or am I imagining things?"

Aristide peered closer. Imprinted below the wider mark of the rope was a narrower, darker line.

"She didn't strangle from any hanging," Brasseur said after a moment. "Somebody stood behind her and pulled a cord around her neck. Quick, simple, and brutal. The same somebody who poisoned old Dupont, I suppose. I wouldn't bet much that it's just a coincidence." He straightened, sighing. "Let's keep this to ourselves for now, Ravel. Let them think poor Aunt Charlotte hanged herself; let the murderer think he got away with it."

"Perhaps allow them to believe the obvious conclusion you stated a moment ago, that she poisoned Martin and then killed herself out of remorse?"

Brasseur nodded. "Exactly."

"And sooner or later, thinking he's safe, the real killer will make a mistake. He's an amateur, Brasseur, like all domestic murderers— someone who'd never strangled anyone before, or seen the body of someone who died that way, or he would have known the marks could betray him." Aristide thrust his hands in his pockets and glanced again at the mark of the cord before quickly looking away. "He's not a doctor, either. A doctor or surgeon ought to know that, which probably lets Citizen Hébert out."

"You've seen more of these people than I have; who's strong enough to have done this?"

"I've been saying 'he,' but I suppose a strong woman could have strangled her with a cord, if Charlotte didn't put up too much of a fight. Certainly Gervais, Claude, Jullien . . . even Étienne. I don't think Magdeleine or Ursule have the strength, but Claude and Magdeleine might have been in it together, and so might Ursule and Charles Jullien. The cook might be strong enough—she's a big, strapping woman—but what possible motive could she have had?"

"And Laurence Dupont?"

"Laurence was with me from six o'clock until the moment we found the body, a little after eight."

"She might have done it anytime between half past three and six, then."

"In broad daylight? And with what motive? From the feel of the body, I would guess Charlotte died within an hour or so of our finding her. That certainly lets Laurence out."

Brasseur sighed. "And the most obvious question: why kill Charlotte?"

"Why indeed? Of course, she was due a third of Martin's estate, but she hadn't any heirs except for her brother and sister."

"Well, brother Gervais needs the money, and now that money'll be divided up two ways instead of three. . . ."

"I don't see Gervais as a man who would brutally murder his own sister for the sake of a little more money in the pot, not unless he was truly desperate. So . . . unless we discover something damning about

Gervais, I think we'd better follow the assumption that she knew something dangerous and had to be silenced. . . . Probably she knew or guessed who really murdered old Martin?"

"Well," said Brasseur, "she's not telling anyone about it now."

Dr. Prunelle soon arrived and, after a brief examination, pronounced Charlotte dead of strangulation, death having occurred at approximately seven o'clock in the evening.

After ordering all of the family into the salon, where a uniformed guardsman waited stolidly at the doorway to ensure that no one slipped out, Brasseur retreated into an antechamber that he had requisitioned as a headquarters. While he conferred with the police surgeon, Aristide retreated to a corner of the salon to lean against the wall, arms folded. After a few silent minutes Laurence joined him.

"Poor Charlotte."

"Yes."

She sniffed and impatiently rubbed away a tear. "It's odd: I found her intensely annoying, and I had nothing at all in common with her—but it's so pathetic that she's dead. She never really had a chance to live."

He nodded, thinking of Charlotte's youth spent in the strict confines of the religious life, of additional years spent in the dull routine of a bourgeois household, running errands for a domineering sister and a tyrannical old man. No wonder she had turned to the thrilling mysteries of the unknown by way of a plausible scoundrel.

Someone in the room was softly weeping. He turned to glance over the gathering and discovered, to his surprise, that it was Magdeleine, who sat crying into a handkerchief while her husband distractedly and ineffectually patted her shoulder. Laurence followed his gaze.

"Magdeleine tends—tended—to order Charlotte about, because that was the only way you could get her to concentrate her mind upon something; but she was devoted to Charlotte."

"I wouldn't have thought it," Aristide said.

"Well, Magdeleine is twelve years older, and Charlotte was still quite small when their mother died. I suppose Magdeleine has always felt very motherly toward her, and she hasn't any children of her own."

"I expect Charlotte was the sort of person who needs protecting all her life," he said, thinking of various swindlers and confidence artists he had known, and suspecting the shadowy Cavalcanti was much the same, smoothly soliciting "contributions" from the credulous and the desperate. Laurence's response was a bitter smile as Magdeleine continued to weep.

At last Brasseur emerged and beckoned Laurence and Aristide into the antechamber. "First of all," he said, "before we start on this very distressing business, I have a bit of bad news for you, citizeness. I'm afraid the examining magistrate put Jeannette Moineau under arrest on suspicion of murder and theft."

"But that's iniquitous!" Laurence burst out.

"The evidence was against her, you'll have to agree. If we hadn't found the stolen goods. . . ."

"Someone entrapped her, Commissaire. Someone deliberately made her the scapegoat for this."

"Yes, you believe that, citizeness, and I'm inclined to believe it myself, but the magistrate didn't. He can only go with the evidence shown him. However, the sooner we discover who really poisoned old Dupont, the sooner she'll be set free. She's been sent to the Maison Lazare, if you want to take her some linen or meals or whatnot. Now, if you please, tell me how you came to find Citizeness Charlotte's body."

Laurence related their discovery of the body, and Aristide corroborated her account.

"Citizeness," Brasseur said when they were done, "you told us earlier that nobody except her brother and sister would profit materially by Citizeness Charlotte Dupont's death? You've not yet read Martin's will?"

"No. Citizen Frochot was going to discuss that after dinner on Sunday, but then . . . the household has been in such confusion, of course."

"Frochot's in charge of Citizen Dupont's personal affairs?"

"Yes; he and the Old Man had known each other for ages and I think they even went in together on some investments. He drew up the will, and has charge of it."

Brasseur and Aristide exchanged glances. "You'd better see Martin's will before you come to any conclusion about Charlotte's death," Aristide said.

"But—she hanged herself," said Laurence. "Didn't she?"

Aristide involuntarily glanced at her and slowly she nodded, comprehending. "I see."

"Do you?" said Brasseur. "You're far too clever, citizeness. Well, keep it to yourself. As far as the police are officially concerned, Charlotte committed suicide."

Brasseur quickly scrawled a note, beckoned a junior inspector over, and sent him off to call upon Frochot. "All right," he continued with a sigh after the inspector had hurried out, "I suppose we've got to question everybody in the household all over again. . . ."

Questioning the household proved vexingly unprofitable. The family had been about their usual business. The curtains were always drawn at dusk, of course, and had been drawn that day just as usual at about half past six, and no one had seen anything. Thérèse, who might have observed something in the garden from the kitchen windows, had been far too busy at the hearth to pay any mind to what might go on outside her domain. Charlotte, everyone agreed, had left the house immediately after dinner, at quarter past three, and no one had seen her since.

"So Charlotte went out," Brasseur said after he and Aristide had finished interviewing everyone, and were alone once more with Dautry in the antechamber to the salon. He leaned back in his chair and tapped a finger on the transcript Dautry had made. "And Magdeleine Bouton says she intended to visit this Italian fellow with the crackpot cult."

Aristide nodded. "I was present when Charlotte said that. She seemed very distressed about something. Evidently she thought this Cavalcanti would be able to reassure her; she seemed to regard him as a sort of spiritual adviser."

"But distressed about what? If she did in her father, then why did somebody do *her* in?"

"Gain, revenge, jealousy, self-preservation, love," Aristide said, ticking them off on his fingers. "Gain: possibly. Revenge? Unlikely. Jealousy?"

"Jealous of what?" Brasseur said with a shrug. "Money, power, position, love. She didn't have any of those things, as far as we know."

"Fanny thinks she was in love. Possibly she was someone's rival, though it seems far-fetched."

"That leaves self-preservation," said Brasseur. "Which brings us back to where we started, with Martin Dupont's death. She must have known something damning to someone. But who, and what?"

It was nearly half past eleven by the time Frochot arrived with the returning inspector. "Dear lord, what a tragedy," he said, taking the chair to which Brasseur gestured him. "First Martin, now poor Charlotte. What sort of devilry is going on in this house, Citizen Commissaire?"

Brasseur grunted. "Perhaps you can help clear this up, citizen. I understand you handle the family's legal affairs?"

"Yes. Your inspector intimated that you wished to see old Citizen Dupont's will. I have a copy of it, of course, but he insisted on keeping the actual document himself. It might be better if I were to locate the document before revealing its contents."

"I think your copy will do, Maître. If you'd acquaint us with the basic provisions of it, that's all we'll need for today."

"I'll have to have the actual will before Dupont's affairs can be tended to, of course; I shall need to search through his papers—"

"All we need tonight, Maître, is the essence of it," Brasseur said, with an impatient glint in his eye. "Your copy will do very well."

Frochot sighed. "If you insist, citizen. This is most irregular, coming as it does before an official inventory of Citizen Dupont's effects has taken place . . . but I suppose it's immaterial to you how many waist-coats and writing-desks he may have owned." He permitted himself a small dry smile and took a folder from a leather satchel.

"So Charlotte must have inherited her share of old Dupont's property?" said Brasseur.

Frochot coughed. "The situation is, er, rather peculiar. This will is a new one, revised within the past year in fact, and I did try to convince

Citizen Dupont that it was a most inappropriate dispersal of his estate, sure to be promptly contested in the civil court and declared invalid, since it flatly contradicts the law of the seventeenth of Nivôse, Year Two, which provides for equal shares to the decedent's children—"

"Well?" Brasseur interrupted him as the flow of legal jargon threatened to go on without ceasing.

"A sum of ten thousand livres in various assets was provided for his wife, Ursule Dupont, née Armoncourt, as specified in the marriage contract, if he should predecease her, as seemed likely; this was agreed to in lieu of what would ordinarily be her right to half the property her husband had accrued during the period of their marriage. . . . This provision is common enough in prosperous households in which the marriage has taken place in an area of marital community property—"

Brasseur coughed and Frochot glanced up from his papers. "Forgive me, Commissaire. The pith of the matter is that—though it contradicts the current law of inheritance within families and is sure to be contested—as stated in Martin Dupont's will, the remainder of his estate, including the house, goes to Laurence Fauconnet, widow of Aurèle Dupont, absolutely, to dispose of as she wishes."

"*What?*" Aristide exclaimed. They turned to stare at him.

"Citizeness Dupont told me more than once," he said slowly, "that she didn't have a sou of her own, and knew of no way to obtain any money. She couldn't have been expecting Martin to leave her anything in his will, much less his entire fortune."

"Nevertheless," said Frochot, shaking his head, "against my advice, and my explaining of the new inheritance laws to him, and my appeals to consider his other children, he certainly did. He states that since she is the widow of his beloved late son Aurèle Dupont, and also a woman of intelligence and character as well as a generous disposition, he has chosen to leave her what he would have left his late son, to dispose of as she pleases, even though Aurèle left no issue. If you ask me," he added suddenly, with a faint twitch at the corner of his lips, "I suspect he did this purely in order to vex his children."

"Well, well," said Brasseur.

"Commissaire, I ought to inform you that I believe Laurence

Dupont knew about this legacy. Martin told me that he intended to tell the citizeness that he planned to leave her a large sum at his death. I'm sure she must have known about it."

Brasseur glanced at Aristide. "That does change things, doesn't it. Gives her a nice motive we didn't know about before, even if she'd be facing a legal battle over it."

"Whatever the case," Aristide said quickly, "Prunelle said Charlotte died at about seven o'clock, and Laurence was with me then, right until we found the body together at about eight."

"Fancy her, do you?"

He cast Brasseur an incredulous glance. "No, I don't. But I like her, and I don't think she is a poisoner." He rubbed his eyes and rose to his feet. "Citizens, it's been a long and exhausting day and I can't see that we'll learn anything else at this hour. I am going home. Good night."

19

Clotilde Prieur, Aristide's landlady, never lit fires for her lodgers after the first of March unless the weather had turned extraordinarily cold. His dressing gown flung crookedly over his clothes for warmth, Aristide was halfway through his meager breakfast of watery coffee and coarse bread that tasted faintly of mold when a rap on the door interrupted him. He opened it to discover Laurence.

"I need your help," she said before he could say a word. Coffee bowl still in his hand, he gestured her in. She was still shrouded in black, as was proper for mourning a member of the family, but her gown was of better quality and more elegantly cut than the one she had worn on the previous day.

"Forgive me, but what are you doing here, citizeness?"

"The commissaire gave me your address after I badgered him a bit," she told him impatiently, brushing past the maidservant who had shown her upstairs to his door. "What on earth do you think the Old Man did? I don't know what to do! It's the last thing I would have expected. He left me his entire fortune, *and* the house!"

"I gather Maître Frochot has paid a visit to discuss Citizen Dupont's will," Aristide said. He returned to his seat at the writing-desk and resumed eating his breakfast. "Pardon me while I eat, but I'd rather the coffee didn't go cold—"

"You *knew* about this? Martin's will?"

"Yes, Frochot told Commissaire Brasseur last night. It was scarcely something we could discuss with you. Why are you so upset over such good fortune?"

Laurence let out an exasperated little sigh and sat down in the nearest chair. "But the Old Man must have been mad! First of all, Maître Frochot says that the whole thing is illegal because property has to be divided among the children, that the will is certainly invalid, and of course the family is furious—Gervais, Magdeleine . . . Magdeleine has never liked me much and now she *loathes* me. But that's not the point." She paused for breath and he seized his opportunity.

"Did Citizen Dupont ever tell you he intended to leave you such a legacy?"

"No, of course not! I never dreamed of such a thing. He didn't owe me a sou, legally or morally."

"Frochot says that Martin was planning to tell you."

She quickly shook her head. "He never told me. Not a word. But if he thinks Martin must have told me, then soon enough all the rest of the family will think so, too, and they'll think *I* poisoned Martin!"

"Yes, I expect they will."

"And so will the police! You know, and the commissaire knows by now, that I had nothing of my own until—until this happened. And now I have the perfect motive for murder. Citizen Ravel, what am I to do?"

"Well," he said, "*I* don't believe you poisoned Martin. If you had killed him, you wouldn't have sprung so quickly to Jeannette's defense. And Brasseur is an intelligent man; he'll come to the same conclusion. But to clear your name of the slightest imputation, we'd better find the real murderer, hadn't we?"

"But how do we do that?" She jerked to her feet and began prowling about the room, lifting objects at random, inkwell, candlestick, a soiled coffee cup.

"I apologize for the clutter," he said. "I wasn't expecting visitors."

"What? Oh." Laurence stared down at the candlestick in her hand as if wondering how it had arrived there. "I hadn't noticed . . . how do you suppose we're going to find the right person?"

"It's only a hunch, but I think we ought to take a look at Charlotte's Signor Cavalcanti."

"That frightful impostor? Why?"

"Charlotte knew something she wouldn't talk about, and he is the one person whom she seemed to trust implicitly. I gather she might have asked him for advice about matters she wouldn't have dared to discuss even with Magdeleine."

"Yes, I expect you're right."

"Well, he may be the last person she spoke with, aside from her killer; and she may have asked for his counsel about what was distressing her, which might have had to do with Martin's death. Do you know where we can find him?"

Laurence nodded. "I went with Charlotte to a few of his séances, ages ago. Magdeleine and I thought we'd better learn what sort of scoundrel he was. He seemed harmless enough; at least it didn't look as if he would swindle her out of more than her pocket money. He holds his ceremonies or whatever you want to call them in a house in the Marais."

"Shall we visit him now, then, and startle him into plain speaking?"

"I can't. I have to go back to the house; Martin's funeral is at half past ten."

"Well then," Aristide said, consulting his notes, "Charlotte would leave home at half past five to attend Cavalcanti's séances, so let us do the same, and pretend to be eager converts. I'll meet you across the street from your house at half past five and we'll go on to the Marais."

"All right."

He thought she would leave then, but she did not. She fidgeted for a moment more and suddenly inquired, "Have you seen Jeannette since the judge sent her to prison?"

"No. I thought I might visit her today, ask her a few more questions."

"How do you suppose she is? Do you think she's all right?"

"How do you imagine she is, locked up with whores and criminals and accused of murder?"

"I didn't imagine she was enjoying herself," she retorted. "But I wish I could *do* something!"

"You *are* doing something. We may learn something valuable from this Cavalcanti."

"I mean something beyond that. I wish I could help Jeannette right now, make her life a little easier."

Aristide glanced at her. "Have you forgotten you're an heiress now?"

"What?"

"Look, all you have to do is ask Maître Frochot for a small advance on your inheritance. That's a perfectly reasonable request. Even if Citizen Dupont's will is declared invalid, in order to settle matters amicably you'd probably get the one-tenth of his fortune that the testator may leave to anyone he chooses."

She laughed. "Good lord, it never occurred to me! I've been so short of money all my life that I can't quite believe it now that I actually have some, or will have some. That is," she added dryly, "if they don't arrest me for murdering Martin in order to get hold of it."

"Simply ask Frochot for a hundred livres, or fifty, if you're shy about it," he told her, ignoring her last remark. "That's probably a tiny fraction of your tenth. Then use that money as you like to send Jeannette some meals, or even to pay for a private cell and some bedding if you feel like being extravagant. I promised myself I'd send her some decent food when I could, but I'm rather short at the moment, and clearly you're not."

Laurence smiled briefly. "Well then, I'll ask Maître Frochot this morning. . . . I believe he'll be joining Martin's funeral procession with us . . . and I'll arrange with a caterer to send Jeannette some dinner."

"One dinner?"

"Every day," she said with a jerk of her chin, "until this is resolved and they let her go."

"Splendid," he said. "I'll meet you on Rue des Moulins at half past five."

She turned to go, then paused in the open doorway and glanced over her shoulder. "Thank you."

"Why did you come to me?" Aristide inquired suddenly. "I'm not a police official."

"Because . . . of last night." He raised an eyebrow as she blushed and quickly looked away. "I know nothing happened between us last night, or is likely to happen now; but you were kind yesterday. And you made me think very hard about myself, and my life. I . . . I feel I can trust you, I suppose."

Aristide nodded. "Good day, then, citizeness; until half past five."

He found himself thinking about Laurence as he pulled on his usual everyday coat of shabby black. His brief, intense, and unconsummated attraction to Rosalie Clément during the Montereau murder case had left him in no fit state of mind to attempt a liaison with another unhappy young woman, or indeed anyone at all, for a long time to come. Yet he did like Laurence, and pitied her too, though he suspected she would not want his pity.

He glanced at his watch. There was little point in calling upon Brasseur so soon after their last meeting, and he doubted the Duponts would wish to see him at Martin's funeral.

Perhaps he would indulge his curiosity and make some inquiries unrelated to the murder of Martin Dupont, regarding certain ideas that had come to him since the previous evening at the Palais-Égalité. If he was right in his suspicions, he thought, he might free Laurence from the demon that had been tormenting her for three years and more— though how to tell her the truth was another matter entirely.

20

Edmé-Antoine-Philippe Feydeau de la Beyré, a young man of fashion whose function in society seemed purely decorative, lived in an elegantly appointed flat on Rue Caumartin at the corner of the Boulevard, not far from the Place Vendôme. His manservant glanced dubiously at Aristide's untidy suit but at last relented and gestured him into a small antechamber by the door. "I'll see if the citizen is receiving."

Aristide spent fifteen minutes admiring a small landscape that hung above a side table, and a set of small porcelain figures representing the characters from the Italian comedy, before Feydeau deigned to receive him, still in his exquisitely patterned dressing gown of aquamarine blue silk, undressed fair hair hanging to his shoulders. "Citizen Ravel?" He peered at Aristide, puzzled. "I feel I should know you. Have we met before?"

"Yes, citizen, four months ago," Aristide said, remembering that Feydeau was not the brightest of men. "In connection with the murder of Célie Montereau."

"Oh, lord, yes," he exclaimed, throwing himself into an armchair. "Have a seat, won't you? Coffee? You're up and about damned early, I must say. I'm only just up myself. What time is it?"

"Twenty minutes past ten."

"Is it really? People who can manage to do *anything* before noon amaze me. You don't mind if I take my breakfast, do you?" He rang a bell and requested two bowls of white coffee from the manservant, then turned back to Aristide. "Don't, if you please, tell me this visit is related to that frightful murder—I thought the trial was over and every-thing sewn up."

"It was, citizen," Aristide assured him.

"You see, I've really no desire whatever to testify again in a criminal case!"

"This is merely a personal matter," Aristide said. "I hope you'll for-give me for being so bold, and inquiring into matters of a most private nature, but . . ." He trailed to a stop, unsure how to go on tactfully.

Feydeau stared at him for an instant, blinking, before his full mouth curved into an amused smile. "Oh . . . I *see*. Wouldn't have thought it, somehow, but . . . what do you want to know, then? The address of a certain very discreet house of pleasure, which caters to men of . . . er . . . different tastes?"

Aristide found himself blushing. Carnal intercourse between one man and another, and certain private activities between men and women, all of which the Church and the state had lumped together under the vague term *sodomy*, had once been punishable in France by burning alive, though the law had rarely been enforced; the National Assembly, however, had legalized all such practices except pederasty six years ago, though violent prejudices still remained.

"No, thank you," he said when he had regained his composure. "I fear my, er, predilections . . . are quite conventional. But I came here in the hope that you might be able to shed some light on the behavior of a certain person who may have shared your tastes. The circle of men in the more exclusive levels of society is quite small, I suspect."

Feydeau blinked. "It is, rather; I suppose I might know him. But why on earth should I give the game away? It won't do his family any good to know the truth, I promise you. Best keep it quiet."

"For the sake of his wife. His widow, I should say. Who loved her husband very much, yet never truly saw her love returned."

"Oh . . . I see." Feydeau looked away and for a moment Aristide saw, beyond the façade of the amiable, vacuous young man-about-town, a flash of genuine pain and loneliness in his countenance. Perhaps, he imagined, Feydeau had once found himself falling silently in love with a man who could not or would not reciprocate. "What was his name?"

"Aurèle Dupont. He was a member of the Commune of Paris, before Thermidor."

The servant returned with a tray and Feydeau pushed one of the coffee bowls in Aristide's direction. The milky coffee was excellent and he gratefully sipped at it while Feydeau searched his memory, brow furrowed.

"No," Feydeau said at last. "I can't say I've ever heard of him. But I don't know *everybody*," he added, tapping his forefinger to his chin. "Hmm . . . Maurice might know . . . yes, I'm sure he would." He leaned back in his chair and beamed at Aristide. "Yes, you really ought to call on Maurice Roquefeuille. He knows everybody worth knowing in our crowd: gentry, politicians, artists, whoever you like."

"Where might I find this Citizen Roquefeuille?" Aristide inquired when Feydeau returned to his coffee without divulging anything further.

"Oh! Yes. The faubourg St. Germain, of course. Corner of Rue de Varenne and Rue du Bac. Only the very best address for Roquefeuille. I'll introduce you if you want."

Armed with a letter of introduction, Aristide proceeded southward to the quieter streets of the faubourg Germain, where fine stone apartment houses stood beside the immense, gated *hôtels particuliers* that once had belonged to the former nobility and now were often the property of wealthy speculators, grown rich from the upheavals of the Revolution. He presented Feydeau's letter to the supercilious footman who answered the door of the apartment on Rue de Varenne and looked him over with a dismissive glance. Shabby, unsmiling, lank-haired young men, it seemed, did not often call upon Citizen Roquefeuille. But the letter seemed to allay the man's doubts about Aristide, for he left him in an antechamber sumptuously appointed with the very latest in brocaded furniture and carved wall paneling in pale blues and grays. A portrait of a rosy-cheeked woman by Greuze hung on the wall in a massive gilded frame.

Twenty minutes later the footman reappeared and led him through a salon, elegantly understated in soft teal green, to a small library that was apparently Roquefeuille's private sitting-room. Roquefeuille rose from a desk to meet him, with a glance at the letter.

"How may I be of service to you, Citizen Ravel?"

"It's something of a delicate matter," Aristide said, sitting in the chair to which Roquefeuille gestured him and glancing about him. Roquefeuille was clearly a man of wealth, breeding, and taste. His bookshelves were lined with hundreds of leather-bound volumes whose gilt-stamped titles gleamed in the pale light from the windows. The man himself was perhaps sixty, tall, slender, and distinguished-looking. His graying hair neatly powdered, he was clothed in irreproachable style in a fawn-colored silk suit with an embroidered dove gray waistcoat.

"I'm known for my discretion, citizen," said Roquefeuille, with an urbane smile. "Pray proceed."

"Well then, Citizen Feydeau de la Beyré informed me that you are acquainted with a great many people. . . ."

"I move in many different circles. If you would be more precise, citizen?"

Aristide drew a breath and decided to plunge onward. "In the circle of men of a certain level of society who . . . who prefer the company of men."

"Sodomites, you mean?" he inquired, without a flicker of emotion.

"I would not use such a demeaning expression."

"We don't consider it so. It's merely—a word that distinguishes us."

Though Aristide had often claimed the police of Paris saw so many varieties of human deception, decadence, and debauchery that nothing could shock them, he found himself floundering. As the son of a convicted murderer and the victim of vicious prejudice and bigotry himself in his youth, he had always attempted to be free of prejudice of any sort, but six years at a boys' boarding school run by Oratorian priests had left their mark; childhood lessons about certain mortal sins died hard. He gulped another deep breath and began again.

"Citizen, I'm seeking knowledge about a man who is now dead, but whose widow deserves to know the truth about him, and why he would not, or could not, return her love. I suspect that he was fond of her as much as he was able, would have loved her if he could, but that he was unable to feel for women what he felt for men. Citizen Feydeau said that you knew everyone who mattered, and that you might be able to assist me."

Roquefeuille slowly nodded. "The man is dead, you say?"

"Yes. He was executed at Thermidor, with the Robespierrists and members of the Commune of Paris."

"Ah." Roquefeuille nodded again, pensive, his thoughts suddenly far away. "I think I know to whom you're referring."

"Aurèle Dupont."

"Yes, Dupont . . . a good man, and a charming dinner companion. I've dabbled in politics now and then myself, you see, nothing obvious, just a bit of meddling behind the scenes, if you like. . . . Dupont was a splendid fellow and a true patriot. Perhaps a little overearnest and narrow in his political convictions, but that's no crime in itself."

Aristide abandoned caution and blundered ahead. "Citizen, was he . . . did he share . . . ?"

"I have your word you'll keep this to yourself? Ah, no, you say you're inquiring for his wife's sake. Well then, your word that this will go no farther than you and Dupont's widow?"

"Word of honor."

"Very well . . . yes: Citizen Dupont preferred men to women, though he hid it well." He smiled wryly and Aristide guessed he was thinking about his own discretion in revealing his true self. "He wasn't . . . he didn't behave like a nance; but you must have known that. Many of us don't, you know, despite caricatures in the gutter press."

"You're quite certain of this?"

"Completely. I knew a man who . . . well, in short, I believe there was a brief affair, long before Dupont married."

"Thank you," Aristide said. "It will be hard for Citizeness Dupont to learn the truth, but all the same I think it will be better for her to know it was not her fault that her husband was unable to love her as she deserved."

"I believe I met her once or twice," said Roquefeuille after a moment's reflection. "Intelligent young woman, but a bit naive, I expect; plainly she had no inkling what Dupont might be up to when he spent an evening away from home. Then again, it's usually better that way."

"Do you think so?"

"Don't most women want only a comfortable home to run, children, their wants taken care of?"

Perhaps so, but Laurence Dupont is not most women, he thought as Roquefeuille continued.

"If a lady is hungry for affection and her husband's interests lie elsewhere, she can take a lover where she pleases. Nothing new or startling there."

"But if the woman wants no other lover than her husband?" Aristide said.

"Then she's no worse off than any other person, man or woman, who suffers from unrequited love. Dupont himself was pining after some fellow who didn't seem to be interested."

"A man who—preferred women, you mean?"

Roquefeuille straightened in his chair and eyed Aristide, his gaze piercing and sardonic. "Indeed not. Citizen Ravel, perhaps you're under the impression that all men who prefer the company of men are shameless libertines like Villette, and care nothing about affection?"

Aristide felt himself blushing again at the mention of the prodigal Marquis de Villette, who had been one of the most infamous libertines of the half century before the Revolution, notorious for sexual license, a tendency to public lewdness, and what the police discreetly called "intemperate behavior." Villette had consorted with actresses and prostitutes but was better known for haunting the gardens of the Tuileries and the Luxembourg after dark, as did many others, to pick up likely male partners; he had indulged in hundreds of well-publicized affairs and encounters, sometimes with women, but more often with men.

"Not all of us," Roquefeuille continued, "wish to copulate like rabbits with a new partner every night."

"I ought not to make unwarranted assumptions," Aristide said. *A Catholic upbringing,* he thought, *truly dies hard.*

"I grant you there are more male brothels than you'd imagine, and that little suppers behind closed doors, gentlemen only, usually conclude in the bedroom, but we're not so debauched as you probably think. Many men who desire other men—at least as they grow more mature—are no libertines; they wish only for a liaison like that between any ordinary man and his mistress. We are, I assure you, perfectly capable of falling in love, and as capable of being disappointed in love, as anyone else."

Aristide nodded. "I stand corrected, citizen. Please continue."

Roquefeuille nodded. "I have it on good authority that Aurèle Dupont became infatuated with a certain young man in our circle, someone with whom he'd been thrown together often in the course of his political life, and that the other young man, while on the most easy and friendly terms with him, had no desire for a liaison. A universally common situation, alas." Roquefeuille paused, rose, and crossed the room to a decanter that sat on a silver tray on a side table. "Citizen?"

Aristide declined and Roquefeuille poured himself a splash of brandy, though it was not yet midday, and returned to his chair. "Well," he said, after a brief silence, "if you're seeking to learn about Aurèle Dupont, you had better know all of it. I know of no evidence to support or deny it, but it was rumored Dupont had a hand in the fellow's eventual arrest. The young man was moderately active among the inner circle of the Brissotins; he wasn't arrested with the Brissotin leaders on the second of June, but in August or September, I believe."

Roquefeuille took another sip of brandy and Aristide gazed off at the painting behind him, a fine still-life of flowers and fruit. He remembered the second of June very well. Scarcely four months after the king's execution in January 1793, the factions that had briefly united to create the Republic were already splintering and threatening to tear it apart. The radical Mountain had accused the moderate, idealistic followers of Brissot, sometimes called Girondins from the *département* from which several of them came—his own home *département*— of plotting to destroy the Republic. In truth they had been guilty of no more than impracticality, and moderation at a time when audacity was needed, but that had been enough to destroy them as a political force.

On the second of June, 1793, armed men from the municipal forces had surrounded the National Convention and demanded the expulsion and arrest of twenty-two Brissotin deputies. Aristide had not been present in the spectators' gallery to observe that shameful hour, but Mathieu had been among the crowd of representatives, of course, and later had told him what had taken place. Mathieu had been more than a little nervous, for his own sympathies had lain with Vergniaud and the other deputies from the Gironde, men he had known at home in Bordeaux as well as in Paris. Fortunately he had often agreed with Jacobin policies and so was not unliked among the more radical faction, which had probably saved him from arrest that day, though his turn had come in August.

Aristide jerked upright and stared at Roquefeuille. Could it be? *Mathieu?*

"Something seems to have startled you?" Roquefeuille inquired, imperturbable.

Aristide settled back in his chair and found his hands were trembling. "Citizen, I pray you," he began, and the words spilled from his lips in a strangled croak. "I pray you," he began again, "what was this other man's name?"

"Perhaps I've said too much," Roquefeuille said, suddenly wary.

"I may have known him. Please. As we said before, nothing goes farther than this room."

Roquefeuille eyed him for a moment, then seemed to come to a decision. "The man was a deputy to the Convention, from the Gironde. Mathieu Alexandre."

"Dear God," Aristide said before he could stop himself.

"You knew him?"

"We were friends from boyhood."

"You had no idea?"

"No!" Aristide sprang to his feet and glared down at him, wanting to shout, "No! It's not possible—Mathieu wasn't a nance! I would have known!"

"He was married, had a child," he muttered at last, knowing it was the lamest of arguments. Nearly everybody married at one time or another, for convention's sake, unless they were steadfast bachelors like himself, without the resources or the desire to become family men. And yet . . . and yet Cécile had not really been the vivacious girl he had always imagined Mathieu marrying; she had been Mathieu's second cousin, good-tempered, practical, and unimaginative, affectionate but not possessive, the sort who would calmly accept the fact and ignore it if her husband took a discreet mistress. She had dutifully and inconspicuously mourned his death and remarried fourteen months later.

Precisely the sort of undemanding woman, he realized abruptly, whom a young man who secretly desired men would choose for a wife, when a wealthy and autocratic father badgered him into settling down and producing some heirs.

How, all those years, could I have been so blind?

"So am I," said Roquefeuille, breaking into Aristide's chaotic thoughts. "And I am quite fond of my wife, but we understand one another. One marries as a matter of business, you know, an alliance between families and interests, and finds love where one likes as a matter of pleasure. You may accept what I tell you or not, as you like, but I assure you Citizen Alexandre was sometimes found—most discreetly—in the company of men whom I know, and it was rumored that Citizen Dupont had a hand in his arrest. Though Dupont, I think, could not have foreseen that the Brissotin deputies would be sentenced to death; I remember he looked ghastly for weeks afterward."

Suddenly Aristide needed time to himself to reflect. He muttered something suitably courteous by way of thanks and made for the door before Roquefeuille could ring for the footman.

21

*D*amn *the vestiges of a monkish education,* Aristide told himself as he strode the length of the lively Rue du Bac, past fashionable promenaders, toward the bridge that led to the Right Bank. He had been indifferent, at best, to the Church for most of his adult life; why should its narrow-minded dogma influence his thoughts now?

And what great crime was there in sodomy, he wondered abruptly, that offended society so? Pederasty was one thing—children's innocence should not be corrupted by leering adults who sought only their own pleasures. But men who desired other men, and pursued their amusements, like anyone else, decently behind closed doors—what about that should make them worse than any others?

But Mathieu . . . I never would have suspected . . .

Had Mathieu merely been pretending to be something he was not when, as schoolboys, they had eyed pretty girls together and, like all teenaged boys, whispered filthy jokes back and forth behind their Latin books? Had he been pretending on that extraordinary, never-to-be-forgotten day when they had lost their virginity to a pair of jaded waterfront whores in a rundown brothel near the wharves of the river Garonne? Had he always kept a part of himself back, a closely guarded secret, for fear of what his best friend might think, for fear Aristide might recoil in disgust?

Mathieu had not recoiled, as so many boys and their parents had, when he had learned Aristide was the son of a man executed for murder. Instead he had offered him his friendship, his protection. Had Mathieu exhibited such unexpected tolerance because he knew he, too, had a secret that would elicit contempt, if not horror, from most pious, respectable folk?

That afternoon at the brothel . . .

He had been sixteen, Mathieu eighteen. Just a trifle old, if you thought about it, for the pampered, worldly son of a wealthy merchant to have his first woman. Had Mathieu's initiation by a plump, red-haired trollop been only pretense, once again, to hide his true self?

Laurence would learn nothing of this, he decided, until he knew more of Aurèle Dupont's friendship with Mathieu. Could the crumbs of evidence that remained tell him whether or not Aurèle had truly been responsible for the events that had led to Mathieu's death?

And then what will you do? the mocking voice in his head inquired. *If Dupont did it, he is now beyond repentance or retribution.*

He stepped off the bridge, crossed the busy quay past shouting peddlers and cursing hack-drivers, and strode into the Tuileries gardens, beneath the battered, bullet-pocked façade of the palace. An instant later he stopped and swung around sharply, staring up at the windows of the hall where the National Convention had met—where Danton had roared, where the Brissotins had been arrested, where Robespierre had fallen at Thermidor.

Thermidor?

Aurèle Dupont, during the crisis of Thermidor, had chosen to go to Robespierre and fight for a doomed cause. Had he, perhaps, chosen to follow his leader to the guillotine out of remorse, to atone for a crime committed in the heat and despair of frustrated, unreciprocated love?

And did it matter any more to anyone, now that they were dead and gone, forgotten like all the rest by people who only wanted to put the horror and fear of 1794 behind them?

It matters to those of us who can't let go, he thought, remembering Laurence and her words to him only the day before on the rutted footpath that lay a few yards away. *It matters. Didn't I tell her to set the past aside, and start looking toward the future? Perhaps I should heed my own advice.*

Finding that he was nearing the corner of Rue Honoré and Rue Traversine, he turned, by long habit, to the door of the Butte-des-Moulins section commissariat. Unfortunately, Brasseur and Dautry were out overseeing a rancorous paternity case and it was Didier who faced him in the outer reception chamber.

"He's not here," Didier snapped upon seeing Aristide.

"Is the Moineau girl still being held at the Maison Lazare?"

"I imagine so. What do you want with her?"

"I still don't believe she's guilty of poisoning anyone."

"The justice of the peace thought our case against her was sufficient," Didier retorted.

"That was before the second murder, wasn't it?" Aristide smiled politely and strode out.

It was past noon and a fine rain had begun to fall. He paused for a quick luncheon of soup and a glass of watered red wine at a crowded table in a cheap eating-house nearby. The wine was harsh enough to burn one's throat, the bread was gritty and sour, and the meat that lurked in the soup, whatever it might have been (he suspected he might be chewing the stringy remains of the dead cart horse he had passed on the previous morning), was scanty enough but the broth was thick with turnips, onions, and garlic. As he finished, he wondered if Laurence had been able to obtain an advance on her inheritance and order meals for Jeannette. Otherwise, poor Jeannette, being penniless, would be fed nothing but the vile prison fare—gruel, moldy bread, and the occasional half-spoiled turnip, potato, or cabbage. He paid for a generous portion of soup served up in an earthenware crock and set off with it through the rain-slick streets.

The turnkeys at the Maison Lazare, formerly St. Lazare Prison, had no objection to an agent of the police questioning Jeannette Moineau and soon he was following one of the jailers down a foul, ill-lit corridor to the common cells where the lowest and poorest of the female prisoners were herded together. "That her?" the man said, pointing at a slight, huddled figure in a dim corner.

"Yes. Bring her out; I want to see her in private."

He beckoned Jeannette out of the room and gestured them into a tiny, close chamber where a pair of guards were lackadaisically playing cards at a rickety table. "Out, lads," he said. "The citizen wants to question her *in private.*" A wink and a leer made it clear that he had no doubts as to why Aristide wished to be alone with the girl.

Aristide gave them each a few sous to get rid of them and pointed to a stool. Jeannette's ordeal was already showing in the blue-black shadows beneath her eyes. "Are you hungry?"

She nodded. He planted the crock in front of her, removed the cover, rummaged in his pockets for the spoon the cook had lent him, and said, "Eat. Go on."

She did not need to be told twice. She wolfed down the soup in a few minutes, scarcely pausing to breathe, much less talk. He sat opposite her and occupied the time and his hands by playing a round of patience with the spare pack of grimy cards the jailers had left him when he had produced another sou from his pocket. At last Jeannette slowed and looked up at him.

"Thank you, citizen."

"Are you all right?"

She shrugged thin shoulders. "Could be worse, m'sieur."

"Well then, talk to me."

"About what, m'sieur?"

"First of all, about Charlotte."

"Charlotte?"

He considered telling her Charlotte was dead, but decided the news would only distress her. "What can you tell me about her that you haven't already told me? Fanny thinks she was in love. Would you know anything about that?"

"No, she never talked to me much except about the housekeeping. She was kind and all, but she was off in her own world, if you know what I mean."

Aristide nodded as he laid out the cards for another round. "So she never spoke to you about anything other than ordinary household matters?"

"No. Just everyday things. You know: how hard it was to buy sugar, and how expensive everything's grown, and so on. She used to complain a lot that the master was so tightfisted about the housekeeping, and how it would be nice sometimes to spend money on a few little treats. But Citizeness Bouton, she would always take the old gentleman's side and say they had to watch out for their money."

Aristide sighed and gave up on Charlotte. Clearly she had not said anything important in front of Jeannette, and the girl had been in jail well before Charlotte's unexpected demise.

"What about old Citizen Dupont? Didn't you tell me he spoke kindly to you sometimes? What else did he say to you?"

"Oh, he never said much, m'sieur. Nothing important. I didn't see much of him, except when I took his breakfast up to him mornings, of course."

"But you did spend quite some time with him once," he said suddenly, looking up from the cards on the table. "The day he died. You spent all day with him in his room, nursing him as best you could. Was he conscious?"

"Was he what, m'sieur?"

"Was he awake? I know he must have been in great pain, but could he talk? Did he speak to you at all?"

"Yes, a bit. The pain, it would come and go. He'd be all right for a bit, just weak, and then suddenly he'd go white as the sheet, and groan and double up, and clutch at his belly, like this. . . ." She demonstrated, wrapping both arms about her abdomen and hunching her shoulders with a grimace. "And then sometimes he'd vomit, but it wouldn't help. It must have been dreadful." Her eyes filled with tears and she wiped at her nose with a grimy sleeve. "I never did nothing to him, I swear it. I only tried to help him."

"When the pain wasn't as bad, did he talk to you, Jeannette? To pass the time, to distract himself?"

She nodded. "He talked a lot, about his family mostly. About his son—the one that's dead, you know, and how he was worth three of the other one, the play-actor. And how his daughters never gave him any peace. 'One's a featherheaded fool and never shuts her silly trap,' he said, 'and the other's a sour-faced shrew who I believe's more of a skin-flint than I am myself.' He said how he knew they were all waiting for him to die." Suddenly she paused and frowned. "Then he said, 'But I've got a surprise in store for them, one that'll give them a little trouble . . . and in any case I'm not going to kick the bucket just in order to please my ungrateful children,' and he laughed. It wasn't a very nice laugh; more gloating, like. 'And especially not to please—' "

"Please whom?" Aristide said when she paused.

"I don't know. He had another attack right then, you see, a bad one, and he let out a howl and he was thrashing about the bed and groaning. It lasted a good long while and for a minute I thought he was gone. But then it passed and he lay back, breathing hard like, and he got a spot of color back in his cheeks and he said again that he wasn't going to die just so they could all get their paws on his money. Then he laughed again and he said, 'Want to see something, girl?' I said, anything he liked, and so he told me to pull out a box from under the bed, and I did, and he gave me a key he had on a string round his neck to open it, and he told me to take a look."

"What was in the box?" Aristide inquired, though he thought he could guess.

"Money, m'sieur. Lots of money, in gold!" Her eyes grew round at the memory. "I guess they was all louis. Hundreds of them. I haven't never seen so much money before."

He could well believe she had not; an uneducated servant girl like Jeannette would have earned, beyond her room and board, perhaps five or six livres a month in salary, a total of little more than two louis in the course of a year. He himself had rarely seen more than a dozen gold louis together at one time since the introduction of the paper assignats.

"What happened to the gold?" he said.

"Oh, Citizeness Bouton, she came in while the old gentleman was showing it to me, and she rapped out sharp enough, 'Father, you oughtn't do that in front of the servants; it'll give them ideas,' and she made him lock the box up again and give her the key, for safekeeping. So she took away his keys and I pushed the box back under the bed like Citizen Dupont told me to. It was too heavy for Citizeness Bouton to carry away with her, you see."

He wondered who might have taken charge of Martin's strongbox. Gervais, he supposed, as head of the family, though Charles Jullien was undoubtedly still keeping the old man's papers in order.

"All right," he said. He gathered up the cards in front of him. "Do you remember anything else from that day?"

Slowly Jeannette shook her head. "No, I don't think so. He took worse then, and we didn't have time for talking, and then he fainted, the poor old gentleman. He didn't say much after that, before he died." She gazed over the table at him, worried. "Is that any help to you, citizen?"

"I don't know. Perhaps." Aristide rose and took charge of the crock, which he would have to return to the cook at the eating-house. "Jeannette, I can't promise anything, but I think Citizeness Laurence is going to have some decent meals sent you, at least. You keep up your strength and try to remember anything you can that might help us find whoever killed Citizen Dupont."

She nodded and bobbed him a curtsy. "Yes, citizen. I'll try."

"Good girl." He left her in the guardroom and quit the prison, pausing on his way out to inform the clerks that a cook would send daily meals in to Jeannette.

22

I've been thinking," said Brasseur. He wiped up the last of the gravy on his plate with a morsel of bread, finished his wine, and tossed his napkin aside onto the caterer's tray that sat on a corner of his desk. "Ever try to drag a hundred-and-fifty-pound body at the end of a rope?"

"I can't say I have," Aristide admitted, stretching long legs out before him and adjusting his overcoat over a chair so that it would dry better in the heat from the hearth in Brasseur's office.

"It's not easy. Even just heaving Charlotte's body up a foot or two would take a good bit of effort. I've been hunting now and then with my brother-in-law and once we had to hang a deer in a tree and come back for it, and it was no picnic, hauling that weighted rope over a branch. Rope's rough and it catches like mad on anything else that's rough, including the top of a gate."

"So you're saying that the person who hung Charlotte on the gate would have to be fairly strong."

"Yes indeed. And I'm thinking the strongest person in that household is probably Gervais Dupont. Want to have another chat with him?"

"Papa's at the theater," Fanny told them when Brasseur inquired for Gervais at the house on Rue des Moulins. "He left half an hour ago. Aunt Magdeleine said it wasn't right that he should be running off to the theater when we're in mourning for Grandfather and now for Aunt Charlotte, but he's pressed for time because they're rehearsing a new production of *Monsieur de Pourceaugnac,* you see, which is going to open in six days exactly, and they also have to break in a new actor who's going to play Cléante in *The Miser* because they'll be doing another performance day after tomorrow and—"

"Fanny!" Magdeleine snapped as she passed. Fanny dimpled and curtsied.

"I'm sorry, Citizen Commissaire, Citizen Ravel. My aunt says I talk too much. Are you going to find Papa?"

"Yes, I expect we'd better," said Brasseur.

"I'll come with you," she said instantly, and vanished, only to return in a moment with a shawl. Aristide and Brasseur exchanged glances. It was scarcely customary for the dignity of the law to be accompanied by a talkative twelve-year-old girl.

"I think she likes you, Ravel," Brasseur muttered.

Fanny preceded them, chattering about everything and nothing, along Rue Anne to the Boulevard. Some had recently begun to call the broad, tree-lined carriageway and foot promenade the Boulevard des Italiens because of the theater, the Comédie-Italienne, that stood near it. Built a century ago along the foundations of Paris's demolished medieval walls, the Boulevard was a fashionable spot to be seen walking or driving a smart carriage, but few carriages were out on such a gray, drizzly March afternoon. The leafless trees swayed sadly, sprinkling droplets of rain, in the damp breeze.

"Have you been to Papa's theater?" Fanny asked them as they crossed the Boulevard. "It's very pretty—much nicer than those awful places," she added. She waved a hand at the ramshackle buildings, some of them no more than open-air stages, deserted still in early spring, that stood among grand new apartment houses along the roads that led away toward the distant customs barriers. Before the Revolution, when the Comédie-Française had monopolized plays that could be mounted on the Parisian stage, dozens of ragtag, fly-by-night companies had presented everything from ballets to pantomimes to puppet shows—anything that could excuse itself as not being a genuine play or opera—in tiny, rickety theaters just beyond the city's official boundaries.

"The theater's lovely inside," Fanny continued. "Lots of green velvet and gold paint. Of course, backstage is dreadful, but backstage is awful in every theater, isn't it?"

"I suppose you've been all around it?" Aristide inquired.

"Oh, yes. I saw it while it was being fixed up. Papa was always taking Mamma and me out to see it. Mamma said if he wanted her to leave the Comédie, he would have to have a theater for her that was worth acting in. So he made sure she would like it."

She led them to the theater, a small but solid wooden structure with a neoclassical portico, and went straight to a side door. "See, I can get you in right away," she announced as she tugged at the bell-chain. "They might not have been very friendly to you. Everybody loves actors *on*stage, but plenty of people hate them *off*stage. Papa says the police used to give actors a lot of trouble. It's not fair."

A surly-looking stagehand answered the bell and, upon seeing Fanny, became instantly cordial. Fanny strutted inside and gestured Brasseur and Aristide in behind her with a jerk of her head. "Where's my papa?"

Upon being informed that he was onstage, rehearsing, she beckoned them onward. They followed her through an ill-lit and hazardous maze of corridors and scaffolding, musty in the damp, where the smell of painted canvas and the faint tang of old smoke from a hundred charcoal braziers, used for heating the dressing rooms and the curtained boxes, lurked in the corners. Aristide heard Gervais's voice as they emerged onto the stage and found themselves facing half a dozen backs.

"No, no, *no*! Cléante, you're passionately in love with her, and you've just heard your father intends to *marry* her! I want a *reaction*! A reaction broad enough that they can see it and laugh at it up in Paradise!" Gervais flung a hand toward the highest, cheapest rank of seats, above the top boxes. "All right? Let's try again. 'Who? You? *You?*' Give me a grimace, boy, a bit of broad business! Clutch at your heart—clap your hand to your brow—*something*!"

"Citizen," Brasseur said, "if I might have a word?"

"What the devil?" Gervais exclaimed, turning. "This is a rehearsal, not a spectacle for prying trespassers. Get out."

"Police, citizen," Brasseur said imperturbably. "A moment of your time, if you please."

Gervais squinted at him in the dim half-light from the windows high above and the sputtering, smoking tallow candles stuck in saucers about the edge of the stage. "Oh, good lord, Commissaire, what is it now? I've given my statement. What else do you want from me?"

"Well, citizen, in your statement you claimed you were here at the theater yesterday at the time when your sister met her end. Perhaps some of the citizen actors here could corroborate that?"

"Papa says he'll let me play Élise or Mariane when I'm old enough," Fanny declared, edging to Aristide's side and eyeing the two actresses who sat on stools in the wings, yawning. "Citizeness Taillebot's almost *thirty-five*, Mamma says, though she makes up well. She's too old— Mariane's supposed to be about seventeen! I'll do it when *I'm* seventeen and don't have to put paint all over my face to look young and pretty."

"But what will you do when you're thirty-five?" Aristide inquired as they descended the steps from the stage and sat on the nearest bench in the pit. It was chilly in the dim, unheated theater and he rubbed cold hands together.

"Oh, I'll play old parts, like Frosine or Arsinoë. Frosine's supposed to be comic, you know. Actually Citizen Imbert's been pestering Papa to let *him* play Frosine. Citizen Imbert usually plays La Flèche, and he's wonderfully funny at it because his arms and legs are just like india-rubber, but I think he would be even funnier if he were to get into a gown. He does women awfully well. That's him," she added, pointing to a slender, loose-limbed actor who was now capering about the stage, glibly reading a long list from a roll of paper. "He does that bit so well. Have you seen him play La Flèche?"

Gervais called a halt to the scene and immediately began shouting again at the hapless young actor playing Cléante. The other actor strolled away, jumped nimbly down from the stage, and approached Fanny. "Good day, darling child!"

"I'm not a *child*," Fanny retorted, with a flirtatious pout.

"No, of course not," said Imbert. "My, who's your friend?"

"Ravel," Aristide said, rising and bowing.

"He's with the police," said Fanny. "He's friends with the commissaire over there."

"Oh, I suppose this is about Hauteroche's father again?" Imbert inquired, without interest.

"And my aunt Charlotte," Fanny said. "She's dead. She *hanged* herself yesterday!"

"Saints alive," Imbert said. "Nasty for you, *chérie*. But she wasn't much loss, from what I've heard. . . ." he added in an undertone, to Aristide.

"You must hear most of the backstage gossip," Aristide said. Imbert smiled.

"I imagine I do. All the dirt on everyone—you can't keep secrets for long when you spend as much time together as a troupe of actors does."

"So what's particularly juicy?"

Imbert pondered a moment, then turned to Fanny. "*Chérie,* did you know that Fabienne Borel has a new costume? It's the most luscious thing, all ribbons and lace. I expect she'd let you try it on if you asked her. You're growing so tall, you're almost the same size."

Fanny needed no second invitation and immediately vanished into the wings. Imbert dropped onto the bench and raked Aristide with a sardonic gaze.

"Not quite the thing, perhaps, to spill the dirt on her famous father while the precocious Fanny's sitting right here, is it?"

"That depends on the dirt," said Aristide. "Why don't you tell me?"

"Well . . . first of all, *if* he's really her father . . ."

"Is that the gossip?"

Imbert shrugged eloquently. "The boy's his, certainly; you can tell by one look. But none of us is so sure about Fanny. Gervais and Sophie were living together for years before 1790, of course, but I wouldn't say that prevented Sophie from accepting gifts from a few rich old men, if you know what I mean."

Aristide nodded. Probably, he thought, Gervais had married his Sophie shortly after the National Assembly had given actors, together with Jews and executioners, full civil rights.

"So both the children were born out of wedlock," he said.

"Oh, dear, yes. I expect he made it legal to please his father . . . not that it helped much," Imbert added. "You know, I've heard the late Dupont senior was rolling in money, and that our dear Gervais had the devil's own time getting the old man to cough up a sou toward buying the theater. Wouldn't you think a man that rich would pony up a bit to help his own son? Well, not a chance! He *lent* it to Gervais, you know."

"Yes, I knew that."

"About the only favor the old screw did him was to allow him a favorable rate of interest, I understand."

"Yes, we discovered that, too; none of this is anything we didn't know. Gervais borrowed plenty of money elsewhere, too, but debts don't mean so much when you're paying them back in assignats."

"Ah," Imbert said, wagging an arch finger at him, "but you've still got to have the chink in your hand, don't you, to live high? That's where the whole debts-don't-count matter falls flat. Once the shopkeepers refuse to give you any more credit, you still need the money to keep your wife in gowns and bracelets and face powder. And the lovely Sophie has expensive tastes, you see, and living under the same roof as Gervais's grisly sisters isn't to her liking one bit." He cocked an inquisitive eyebrow at Aristide. "I don't suppose Sophie could possibly have poisoned the old man herself? She'd dearly love to get her hands on his money."

"I hear she's touring at present, in the South. Were we misinformed?"

"Oh, yes, *touring*. Well, it started out as a tour, I suppose."

Aristide eyed him, studying the amused, derisive little smirk that hovered at the actor's lips. "Are you implying that Citizeness Dupont has left her husband and children?"

"Well, my goodness, it's the only explanation, isn't it? Gervais never talks about her any more. And it used to be, you couldn't get him to shut up about her; you'd think she was the goddess Aphrodite herself. Completely besotted. That's why he spoils the little brat rotten, of course; even if she isn't his daughter, and even if he knows she isn't, she reminds him of her mother."

"Yes, I guessed as much."

"But I imagine Sophie finally decided she could do better for herself than an out-of-pocket impresario with a tightfisted old skinflint, who was *never* going to die, for a father. She's off playing on a swansdown mattress with a stinking-rich banker, is my guess, and to hell with life in the theater. For all we know, she could be living it up half a mile away in the faubourg Germain as we speak."

"Citizeness Larivière hasn't been at the Duponts' for weeks," Aristide said, "and at that household, someone would have seen her."

"She could have persuaded somebody to do it for her, couldn't she?" Imbert suggested. "She's quite adept at getting what she wants."

Aristide briefly considered the idea of the actress seducing a lover—Jullien, Claude Bouton, even the valet Antoine?—into poisoning Martin while she herself was at the other end of France, but abandoned it. Sophie Larivière, he imagined, as he thought he understood her, would not wish to place herself in anyone's power.

"Which brings us back to Gervais Dupont," he said softly.

He gazed up at the stage, trying to imagine the genial, volatile Gervais in the grip of an obsession, willing to murder his father in order to obtain the money that would lure his selfish, shallow, bewitching wife back to his side before she divorced him for the sake of a more advantageous marriage. "You know him; do you think he's capable of it?"

Imbert shrugged. "Oh, citizen, we're all capable of murder for one reason or another, if suitably provoked. Now as a student of human beings, I could tell you a certain man isn't capable of committing something like theft, or rape, or treason, for any reason whatsoever . . . but murder? There are so many reasons why you might do it, and it's really terrifyingly simple. You must know, as a member of the police, that we're all still alive merely because none of our friends or relatives has decided to knock us over the head or slip a little rat poison into our dinner!"

"Yes," Aristide said, "murder's easy; it's getting away with it that's hard."

"So certainly Gervais is capable of it, if it's a matter of what he wants most in the world. So am I; so are you."

"You ought to be in the police," said Aristide. "So what are *you* capable of committing murder for?"

Imbert's only answer was a burst of laughter as he sprang to his feet, at an impatient sign from Gervais, and hurried back onto the stage. Aristide eyed him, wondering if the thing Imbert would commit murder for was to keep his sexual inclinations secret. *Not likely*, he thought a moment later; nearly anything adults might do together in private was legal now, and actors had such a low reputation already that such rumors would scarcely affect them.

But in politics it would be a first-rate scandal. . . .

If a boulevard actor fell in love with another man, few people would care; but if word got out that a rising young politician was a secret sodomite, it might be the end of his career. As Roquefeuille had surmised, Aurèle Dupont had probably made advances to Mathieu; had he then, in the shame and fury of rejection, and the fear of betrayal, himself betrayed Mathieu and soon found he could not bear the guilt of it?

He thrust away these speculations as Brasseur approached him. "Learn anything?" his friend inquired. "I got a lot of talk and nothing useful. Half a dozen actors and scene-shifters swore Gervais Dupont was here yesterday by quarter to four, rehearsing, and didn't stop until quarter past six, when he made up, and by seven he was onstage, where three hundred people saw him as Roggerio the Bandit King. It won't wash. He couldn't possibly have killed Charlotte."

"It doesn't eliminate the possibility that he might have poisoned his father, though," said Aristide. "Let me share some gossip with you."

23

Aristide returned to Rue des Moulins at quarter past five and waited across the street from the Dupont house, staring into the draper's window opposite at stacks of colorful bolts of muslin, linen, and India cotton. At half past five Laurence appeared, dressed for walking, with a warm shawl about her shoulders and a modest black bonnet. He raised his hat to her.

"Ready?" he said. "We'd better hire a fiacre; it's a long walk to the Marais." She nodded and they walked the short way to busy Rue de la Loi, hailed a passing fiacre, and settled onto the grimy leather seats.

"Have you learned anything more?" Laurence inquired as the carriage jolted its way toward Rue Honoré.

"A little. Did you know Martin kept quite a lot of gold in a strongbox under his bed?"

"Oh, yes. He was always boasting about it."

"He wasn't afraid of being robbed?"

"In a household of a dozen people, plus the servants? If any of it vanished, it would have to be one of us, wouldn't it? No housebreaker could get in without being seen, or overpowered."

"Who has charge of the gold now?"

Laurence's mouth curved in a brief sardonic smile. "Gervais has the strongbox, but Maître Frochot has the key. Magdeleine sent for him as soon as Martin died, the very same evening, and gave him Martin's keys for safekeeping as he suggested, until the Old Man's affairs could be wound up."

"I see. Not a great deal of mutual trust between Gervais and Frochot, I imagine?"

"Between an actor and a notary? Neither understands the other, nor do they wish to. They trust each other about as much as a pair of beggars defending their territory." She sighed and looked out the window for a moment as they rattled along eastward. "I did ask Frochot for some money. He hemmed and hawed a bit, but finally he gave in when I told him it was for Jeannette. Evidently lawyers and notaries aren't quite as stonyhearted as we imagine." Abruptly her face lit up and she turned to him, with a smile. "Oh, and what do you think! Magdeleine's actually succeeded in hiring a new servant."

"Has she?"

"Yes, his name is François and he turned up at the door this morning after I'd left, looking for work, saying he'd heard we were shorthanded. The possibility of being poisoned didn't seem to bother him. Though he's rather a disreputable-looking character," she added. "But Magdeleine said his letter of reference was all right, so I suppose we won't be knifed in our beds."

Aristide nearly smiled at her description of a "disreputable-looking character" and guessed it would elicit a hoot of laughter from François when he repeated it to him.

"I sent him over to a caterer near Saint-Lazare whom he said he knew," she continued, "to order dinner to be sent every day to Jeannette. So that's taken care of."

"That was kind of you," Aristide said.

"It's the least I can do—especially when I seem to have profited so much from the Old Man's death, and poor Jeannette has suffered by it."

They fell silent. Twenty minutes later they alighted near the Hôtel d'Albret, in the heart of the Marais, where two carts could barely pass each other on the narrow streets and the sand-colored courtyard walls of two-hundred-year-old mansions loomed above them, high and blank as cliffs.

The ancient quarter, thick with the great *hôtels particuliers* of sixteenth- and seventeenth-century nobility, had seen better days; for the past half century, the most fashionable had preferred to live in the faubourg Germain, across the Seine from the gardens of the Tuileries. But the Marais still boasted a wealth of opulent, though slightly shabby, town houses that now could be purchased or rented at bargain prices by the social climbers and adventurers who had flocked to Paris during the Revolution.

Cavalcanti held court in a fine old mansion not far from the Place de l'Indivisibilité. From the outside it looked like any other of the grand houses, with porte-cochere leading to a cobbled courtyard. The ground-floor foyer, too, with its facing of smooth cream-colored marble and broad, curving staircase to the main floor, seemed little out of the ordinary.

A handful of well-dressed women milled about, gossiping. Most were fashionably clad in light classical draperies most unsuited to early March in Paris, despite the addition of carmagnole jackets, high-fronted bonnets, and long cashmere stoles, the latest rage. People who had too much time on their hands, Aristide thought, eyeing them, and far too much money.

A thin, intense woman with feverish eyes inspected Aristide and Laurence for a moment and then stepped toward Laurence. "Do I know you, citizeness? Perhaps we've met before, here at the Master's altar?"

"Possibly," said Laurence, taken aback. "Though I've not come here for quite some time."

"Oh." The woman paused and gazed sorrowfully at her. "Have the unbelievers kept you away?"

"Really, I only came a few times to accompany my sister-in-law, who—"

Aristide seized Laurence's hand and pressed it before she could say more about Charlotte. She gave him a quick glance and nodded once. The thin woman seemed not to notice, however, and began to ramble on about the miracles the Master had wrought.

Above them, a clock struck the hour. As the silvery chimes ceased, a small, dark-skinned, turbaned manservant glided forward to greet them, bowed, and gestured them with a flowing motion toward the staircase. "I gather you've not been here before, citizen?" the thin woman whispered to Aristide as they climbed to the main floor. "That's Mustafa. He's a mute. Signor Cavalcanti found him during his travels in Egypt. He had had his tongue cut out because he had profaned some mystery or other, and Signor Cavalcanti rescued him, and now Mustafa is his most devoted servant."

"How remarkable," Aristide said. He glanced back at the servant, who was silently ushering in a plump lady flaunting the very latest in pseudo-Grecian style. He looked less like a typical Arab than like an ordinary Frenchman or Italian whose complexion had been darkened with a careful application of walnut juice. The man would probably betray himself, Aristide thought, with a Provençal or Savoyard accent the moment he opened his mouth. Or had his close association with the police made him oversuspicious and dubious of all extravagant claims?

They climbed the staircase to an imposing hall and a wide, curtained doorway. A dozen people were already milling about in the hall, exchanging greetings, waiting to be invited into the sacred chamber. The thin woman, who seemed determined to take them in hand, clutched at Aristide's arm in an ecstasy of excitement. "There!" she exclaimed, pointing at the doorway. "The shrine—that's where we gather, and we speak with those we've lost. . . ."

A muffled gong sounded from beyond the heavy velvet curtains. Mustafa reappeared, bowing and drawing the curtain aside, as he gestured the assembled company inside the open doors.

Though the large, circular room beyond had undoubtedly once boasted the usual decoration of carved and painted wood that framed large paintings set into the panels, perhaps accented by a gilded scroll or cupid, nothing of its previous baroque ornament remained. Here was an Eastern fantasy worthy of a sultan's seraglio, scented with sandalwood incense, swathed with silks, hung with pierced brass Moorish lamps that provided a dim light in place of the shuttered and curtained windows.

When all the congregation had seated themselves at the round table, an expectant hush fell. The gong sounded again. At the opposite side of the room, a pair of black silken draperies parted, to the reedy sound of a pipe. More incense billowed from behind the draperies and through the smoke a tall figure appeared, red-robed, turbaned, arms crossed and palms pressed against its chest.

"All those who believe are welcome here."

The voice was deep and commanding, a baritone rumble that seemed to echo in the bones, made beguiling by traces of an exotic, unidentifiable accent. A few of the women around the table uttered ecstatic whimpers and shivered with excitement.

After a few moments of portentous silence, Cavalcanti moved, with a majestic sweep of his robes, to the empty seat at the head of the table and enthroned himself. After another precisely calculated period of silence, while he looked slowly about the table and fixed each rapt devotee with an intense, piercing gaze, at last he spoke again.

"Speak, my children. What do you wish of me?"

A woman half rose from her seat, stretching out a hand in supplication. "Oh, please, Master—let me speak to my daughter again!"

He closed his eyes for a moment before replying. "As you wish, child. Let the congregation join hands and open their minds, to receive the force of the dark powers who rule the passage between this world and the next." A soft, faraway sound, the shiver of a cymbal perhaps, echoed as they clasped hands about the table.

Cavalcanti closed his eyes and let his hands rest on the tabletop. Softly he said, "Lucienne . . . Lucienne, child, are you there?"

"Mamma . . . Mamma . . ."

The treble voice that piped from his mouth startled Aristide almost into believing that a ghost was truly speaking through the man. It was high, thin, the voice of a child of eight or ten.

"Oh, my dear," exclaimed the mother, breaking the circle and clasping her hands before her, "are you happy? Are you safe?"

"I am well, Mamma. . . . It doesn't hurt any more. It's a beautiful place. I wish you could see it."

"Oh, Lucie . . ."

"But you don't belong here yet. Someday. We'll see each other again. I promise, Mamma."

"She has gone," Cavalcanti murmured in the silence that followed, broken only by the mother's soft weeping. "Never fear, child, she will return. Come back again and she will always be waiting for you."

"Thank you, signor, thank you. . . ."

"Is there another who would speak to those in the twilit realm?"

The thin woman timidly raised a hand. "Signor . . . I fear my lover is tiring of me—and I'll die if he leaves me! I scarcely dare to ask it, but if I could ask the advice of one of the great lovers of history . . . Cleopatra, or Héloïse . . ."

"You ask a great deal, Daughter," Cavalcanti said, smiling benignly. "Those souls crossed to the other world a long time ago, and are not so easily summoned."

"Oh, please, signor," the woman begged him, "do try. For the sake of my happiness."

"I shall try, for your sake. Though perhaps an offering to the dark powers might appease them, might make the passage easier. . . ."

"An offering?" the woman echoed him. After an instant's thought she unclasped a gold bracelet from her wrist. She crossed the chamber to a low, lamplit altar and dropped it into the ornate brass bowl that sat at the center between a pair of matching incense burners. "Will this do, Master?"

"We shall see if the powers accept your gift. Join hands, my children." Cavalcanti closed his eyes once more and slowly raised his hands, palms outward, in invocation. "Héloïse . . . passionate soul . . . come to us, across the centuries, and comfort one who suffers, as you did, for love. . . ."

Aristide was scarcely surprised when the spirit of Héloïse duly spoke through the prophet. Though she had been dead for six hundred years, she used remarkably contemporary French to offer advice to the lovesick. But the thin woman seemed satisfied and comforted. He watched her from the corner of his eye and wondered if Cavalcanti and others like him really did much harm. Surely their posturings were, essentially, little different from those of any priest!

At last, as Héloïse faded away into the twilit realm, Laurence stirred beside him and whispered, "Master?" Without looking at Aristide, she swiftly pressed his hand, then rose and hurried over to the brass bowl to drop a coin—a gold louis, he saw, astonished—into it.

"Please, Master—you *must* help me!"

His serene gaze turned her way—with a swift glance at the louis d'or lying in the bowl—and he reached out a hand toward her. "Child . . . child . . . you have returned. It has been a long time. I sense a fresh tragedy hanging over you . . . a new wound . . ."

"Master, it's been far too long since I visited. I allowed unbelievers to convince me I'd been deceived. But now I need your help. Terrible things have happened!"

"Yes," he said, "I sense you have lost another dear to you since we last invoked the spirits."

Now that was far too simple, Aristide said to himself. Charlotte would surely have told him yesterday about Martin's death; such plausible frauds learned their miraculous knowledge by any and all means. Much could be learned from a solid understanding of human nature, together with careful observation and the employment of their equally shady servants as spies, who might gossip with maids and valets, or even sift through household refuse to find old letters that had injudiciously been cast away or sold as scrap paper rather than flung on the fire.

"My—my father-in-law," Laurence said, her voice cracking into a sob. "He d—he died three days ago. We had quarreled and I never had the chance to make it up to him. Please, Master, let me speak to him!"

"Never fear; those who have only just left us will not be far away. Close your eyes, child, and imagine your father-in-law as he was before illness struck him down, while we join hands once again to summon the dark forces."

Laurence stifled a rather theatrical sob but did as she was told. "Who is there?" Cavalcanti said abruptly after a few moments of tense silence. "Which soul demands my attention? . . . Ah, yes. Your daughter in spirit is eager to speak to you, friend."

"Father-in-law?" Laurence said, voice rising in a breathless squeak.

A new voice spoke, not the voice of an old man, but neither was it Cavalcanti's deep baritone.

"Daughter . . ."

"Father-in-law, is that you?"

"Yes, Daughter, it's I. My dear . . . my dear . . ."

"It's Laurence, Father-in-law!" she exclaimed, outwardly eager and earnest, but Aristide did not doubt she found it amusing to prompt the ghost.

"Laurence. My dear."

"Father-in-law!" she burst out, sniffling. "Oh, *Father*! Is—are—are you in a better place?"

"Yes, child. Don't weep for me. I am very well where I am now. And I am with those I loved . . . my wife, my son. . . ."

A muscle jumped in Laurence's cheek at the suggestion that her beloved Aurèle's spirit was hovering nearby, waiting to speak to her at the beck and call of an astute swindler with a gift for mimicking voices. For an instant Aristide thought she might erupt in outrage, but she collected herself, though he could see she was violently trembling. "Father-in-law," she whispered, staring wide-eyed into the twilight surrounding them, heavy with incense fumes, "I know we parted on bad terms, but I did mean well, always. . . ."

"Of course, Daughter-in-law. When you cross the threshold, the old life no longer matters. Someday you'll understand."

"Father—in the other world—are you happier? It's a better world, isn't it?"

"Yes, child; this is a world of eternal youth. I am young again, without ills or sorrows. There is no pain or trouble here."

What claptrap, Aristide thought. Surely Martin Dupont, from what he had learned of the old miser's gruff and rigidly pious character, could scarcely have been capable of producing such sentimental drivel.

"Here we can forget all our earthly sorrows, Daughter. We can forget our woes and forgive everything. I am in a better world, a blessed world. Fear nothing, and go in peace."

She gulped back another sob. "Oh, Father, thank you!"

"Where is my daughter Charlotte?" the voice continued. "Let me speak to my dearest Charlotte."

You don't know everything, do you, Cavalcanti? Aristide said to himself as Laurence produced a fresh flood of tears.

"Oh, Father-in-law, Charlotte has passed over to the other world! Isn't she there with you? Can't you see her? I wanted to speak with her!"

For the first time, Cavalcanti seemed a trifle flustered. "Charlotte . . . Charlotte has not yet come to me," said the old-man voice, with less assurance than before. "I shall seek her out. She will be here when you return, I promise you."

Silence fell. Someone stifled a cough at the far end of the table. "He has left us," Cavalcanti said, rather hastily. "Are you comforted, child?"

Laurence beamed. "Yes, signor—oh, yes. Thank you, signor. God bless you." She settled into her chair and gazed into space, a rapt smile on her face.

At last, after several more conversations with departed loved ones, the séance ended. Half a dozen babbling women clustered about the medium and Aristide overheard him say, "Yes, yes, child, of course. You shall be beautiful always, for a small fee. Say a little word to Mustafa and you shall have the salve."

"And me, Master?" said another woman. "The elixir you promised me?"

"Yes, Mustafa has it ready. Remember, three drops only in your lover's wine, and he will see nothing but you." With another boom of the gong, a billow of smoke, and a swirl of his heavy robes, Cavalcanti retreated into the shadows whence he had come.

24

The straggling members of the flock dropped money—gold and sil-ver as well as assignats—into the brass bowl as one by one they mutely slipped away. Aristide turned to find the thin woman gazing at him with mild expectation in her expression.

"I'm afraid I have little money with me," he murmured, acutely aware of his empty pockets. "It's dangerous these days to carry too much on you."

"Oh! You mustn't worry about *that*," she assured him, in a hasty whisper. "Signor Cavalcanti *never* asks people for money! We contribute what we can. I'm sure you'll make it up when you come again," she added brightly. She bade them farewell with a brief, nervy smile and vanished down the marble staircase.

"The scum!" Laurence hissed, when the last of their companions had left and they found themselves alone in the first-floor hall. "I thought it was harmless—this fooling about with sham voices for foolish people—but it's not! It's obscene!"

"It's certainly lucrative," Aristide said, thinking of the brass bowl and its contents, and wondering how much money Cavalcanti earned from selling his quack remedies.

"It's an obscenity," she repeated. "Fleecing maudlin idiots who delude themselves into believing that man can bring back the dead for a nice chat! Mouthing reassuring nonsense and platitudes!"

"You did manage to rattle him. I didn't think he could have known already of Charlotte's death."

"So what do we do now?"

"Rattle him some more, I think." He turned and eased open the door to the shrine. The servant Mustafa was within, snuffing the lamps and dousing the incense burners. Aristide tiptoed up behind him and seized both his arms, at which he let out a startled yelp.

"So you do have a voice," Aristide said pleasantly. "I'm sure your master is responsible for such a miraculous cure. Where is he?"

Mustafa vigorously shook his head. Gesticulating and pointing, he made it clear that Aristide ought to go back the way he had come, but Aristide held onto him. "Kindly don't waste my time with this rubbish. Where's Cavalcanti?"

Mustafa pointed again to the door. Aristide got a better grip on his arms and shook him. "Listen, you! I'm not one of those sentimental idiots who can be deceived by a few theatrics. Do you want me to have the police on you for fraud, or are you going to take me to Cavalcanti right now, without any more fuss?"

Mustafa sagged in his grip and resignedly pointed toward the black draperies. Laurence had followed them inside the shrine and Aristide gestured her along, without loosing his hold on the servant.

Cavalcanti, divested of his robes and of much of the rest of his clothing as well, was reclining on a cushioned divan in a comfortable little sitting-room just down a corridor from the layers of draperies. He was not alone. The girl he had been fondling gave a squeal upon seeing them and belatedly attempted to cram her ample flesh back inside the front of her corset. The medium hastily adjusted his open shirt and turned with a thunderous scowl toward the doors.

"What is the meaning of this?"

Mustafa hung his head and began to express himself in a series of elaborate signals, but Cavalcanti swung himself to a sitting position, shoved away the girl, and gestured impatiently. "Enough!"

"Master, they came barging in—" Mustafa began, with an accent straight from the docks of Marseille. Aristide thrust him aside and strode up to Cavalcanti.

"All right: I know what you are, so let's not waste time. Talk to me or I go straight to the commissaire of this section and tell him what kind of swindler is duping silly women out of their jewelry."

"And their money," Laurence snapped, behind him. "I'll have that louis back now, if you please."

"Ah," Cavalcanti murmured, gazing at her, "I should have known. I knew you for a doubter from the first."

"But you just couldn't resist a little more gold, could you?"

"Gold? What is gold but an earthly thing, of no use but—"

"Enough of this!" Aristide said. "All of us here know what you are—unless this young lady is one of your flock, perhaps?"

"My flock believes me chaste as a novice," he said smoothly. "All right, Cyprienne, get out. Now," he continued after the girl had snatched up her gown and scuttled away, "what do you want, citizens?"

"Whatever you can tell us about Citizeness Charlotte Dupont. What did she wish advice about, yesterday afternoon?"

Cavalcanti shrugged as he rose and pulled a scarlet silk dressing gown around broad, muscular shoulders. He was tall—perhaps an inch shorter than Aristide—and well made, a fact that could not have lessened the attraction he held for susceptible women. "You must be mistaken. The citizeness never came here yesterday."

"Of course she did!" Laurence snapped. "How else would you have known today that her father was dead, if she hadn't told you yesterday? News doesn't travel across half Paris *that* fast."

"You had better tell us the truth, for your own sake," Aristide said. "She was upset yesterday at dinnertime, and she said she had to consult you. What did she want to ask your advice about?"

Cavalcanti licked his lips. "I assure you, citizens, she never called upon me. Perhaps she set out to visit me, but was diverted—"

"I sense you have something to hide, signor."

"I? What should I hide? The woman never came to see me and that's all. Besides," he added, "if she's dead, then she can't claim that I lie, can she?"

"Yes," said Aristide, without moving, "Charlotte is dead; she was murdered, and so was her father."

"Murdered!" Cavalcanti exclaimed.

"We found her dead last night," Aristide told him, watching the color slowly ebb from his face. "Was it you, perhaps, who strung up that poor woman from the gate in her own garden?"

"Saints have mercy! You think I, *I*, Cavalcanti, would commit such wickedness?" He rapidly crossed himself, with a pious glance heavenward. "No, no, citizens, even if you could think I would do such a thing, it is impossible. I conducted two séances yesterday. A dozen respectable citizens, and my servants, can swear I was here in my chambers all afternoon and evening."

"I see," Aristide said. He pulled his little notebook from his coat and scrawled a few notes. "Would those be the mute servants, citizen?"

They could get nothing more out of him. Probably, Aristide thought, Cavalcanti knew little else, though he could swear the man was lying about never having seen Charlotte the previous day. Cavalcanti returned Laurence's louis d'or to her with an oily smile, undoubtedly willing to give up the gold in order to be rid of two such troublesome intruders, and the sullen Mustafa showed them out.

"Now I wonder if it was Cavalcanti himself with whom Charlotte was in love?" Aristide said, thinking aloud, after they had found another fiacre and were rolling back along the cobbled, twilit streets toward the Palais-Égalité.

"In love?"

"Fanny thinks she was infatuated with somebody. She's a very perceptive child."

"That certainly would have been a reason for Charlotte to keep it secret," Laurence mused. "The Old Man would have recognized Cavalcanti right away as the worst kind of fortune hunter imaginable."

"Although everyone knew, or would learn quickly, that Martin would give her no dowry, that any husband of Charlotte's would have to live on Martin's grudging handouts, as Claude Bouton does, until Martin died." Aristide frowned. "I'm not sure it makes sense."

"But if she poisoned the Old Man so she could get her inheritance immediately, then perhaps Cavalcanti egged her on to it."

Aristide nodded. "Yes, I expect he could have twisted a credulous, sentimental, love-starved woman like that around his little finger."

"And if he's mixing up beauty salves for those silly women," Laurence continued eagerly, "and claiming to be an alchemist, he must know something about herbs and poisons and so on. . . ."

"And Charlotte had the best opportunity to put something in that porridge," Aristide said. "But, as all of you have insisted repeatedly, she was far too kindhearted to hurt anyone. Do you really think she could have poisoned her father, even for the sake of marrying a man she was infatuated with?"

"Let's say she did. So they poison Martin, and now Charlotte gets her share of the fortune—at least that's what they would have expected—"

"That's where I find myself baffled," Aristide said. "Then the man murders Charlotte immediately afterward, without marrying her, thus completely depriving himself of her dowry or any inheritance. It still makes no sense."

"Perhaps something went wrong and he panicked and decided to cut his losses by shutting her mouth for good." Abruptly Laurence gasped and he saw her eyes grow round in the faint light of a candle lantern that swayed from the roof of the hack. "Or . . . do you think— perhaps they were already married! Maybe Charlotte had secretly married Cavalcanti, and when the furor over the two deaths dies down, he'll come forward with proof of their marriage—"

"And immediately make himself the obvious suspect. Besides, I'd wager that Martin, if he hadn't decided to make trouble by leaving everything to you, would have arranged that Charlotte's property couldn't be inherited by a spouse, only by any children she might have. So a secret marriage and a quick murder wouldn't benefit anyone. I don't know. . . . I think your first idea, that he panicked and killed her for fear she would expose him, is a better one."

"There's still the matter of how the soup on Sunday was tainted," Laurence said thoughtfully. "That must tie in to all this, but I can't see how. Charlotte certainly didn't do that; she was upstairs locked in her bedchamber all day. And who hid the powder in Jeannette's room, and the bits of jewelry? That was sheer cruelty, you know."

Aristide nodded. "Even if we find the murderer, it may not be easy to clear Jeannette of the charge of theft."

"I'll pay for a good lawyer to represent her. I can at least do that."

"Do you know any?"

"Any what?"

"Good lawyers."

"I'm sure Maître Frochot does. He's been very helpful."

"Yes, I expect he can advise you."

They fell silent and rode for a while in the darkness, glancing out behind the blinds at the shuttered streets.

"How close were your husband and Mathieu Alexandre?" Aristide said suddenly, feeling it was as good a time as any to broach the subject in privacy.

"What has that to do with anything?"

"I'm merely curious. Because Mathieu rarely mentioned your husband to me, yet you say they were good friends."

"Well, don't people like to keep their friendships separate, sometimes?" She sighed. "Actually the three of us were practically inseparable. We used to go out, all of us together, and endlessly talk politics in cheap cafés."

"Not at the Palais-Égalité?" he inquired dryly.

"Not very often. I told you, Aurèle used to say it was a sink of iniquity and I'd be better off not visiting it. And he liked to visit the cheaper cafés because then he would get a better idea of what ordinary people hoped for from the Revolution."

Aristide nodded in the twilight. Aurèle Dupont had probably had other, unmentioned reasons for not taking his wife to the arcades of the Palais-Égalité; at certain hours they, like the Tuileries and Luxembourg gardens, became a favorite haunt not only of prostitutes, female and male both, but also of roving sodomites seeking a furtive, anonymous encounter. No doubt Aurèle had taken care not to bring Laurence to any place where he might be recognized as something other than a respectable young official in the city government.

"We had such fun," Laurence continued, paying no heed to his silence. "We often went to the theater, of course; Gervais used to give us plenty of tickets to his own performances at the Comédie, on condition that we be as enthusiastic as possible! And Aurèle and Mathieu were always talking about all the wonderful things the Revolution was going to do for France. . . . There was a glamor about it, it was . . . *intoxicating* . . . being young and daring and seeing our dreams unfold before us. Especially for me—I, who had been just a poor relation, a girl with no looks or money or prospects, there I was with *them*, two extraordinary young men who'd suddenly been blessed with power and influence. I adored them both. I think, if I'd not been so in love with Aurèle, that I could easily have fallen in love with Mathieu."

"He was married, you know," Aristide said.

"Oh, I know. He never talked about his wife much, though."

No, he never did talk very much about Cécile. How could I not have recognized such a marriage of convenience?

Aurèle Dupont, too, had evidently chosen the path of least resistance; he had married a naive, orphaned cousin who, without fortune or beauty, had been more than willing to marry a charming young man with such prospects and ambitions. But Laurence, Aristide thought, suddenly smiling to himself, had proved to be much more than a docile housewife; she had brains and a strong personality of her own, and a capacity for passion—more than mere physical passion—that Aurèle had probably never discovered.

"Did your husband and Mathieu spend a good deal of time together?" Aristide said. "Alone, I mean, without you."

"Of course; at political meetings, and so on. I admit, sometimes I grew a little jealous, that he seemed to spend more time with Mathieu than he did with me." She paused and abruptly her voice took on a harsher edge. "What does all this have to do with anything? What business is it of yours?"

"Mathieu was my friend," he said, shrugging, hoping he sounded offhand.

"That's not everything. What are you insinuating?"

"Tell me," he said, without answering her, "when did they part company? When did you sense their friendship seemed to be over?"

"In the middle of 'ninety-three. Aurèle said they had disagreed about the king's trial, and other matters."

"Aurèle had been against the death sentence?" Aristide said, surprised. Anyone who had been a member of the municipal government in 1793 and '94 had surely been a faithful Jacobin, promoting the radical, antiroyalist aspirations of the Left, and would never have entertained the thought that Louis XVI had been anything but guilty of high crimes against the nation.

"No, he was for it. He didn't like the death penalty, but he said sometimes it was necessary."

"But Mathieu voted for the king's death. What could they have disagreed about?"

"No, he didn't—"

"I assure you, he did." Mathieu had sat in the Convention with the moderates from the Gironde because they were people he had known for years, but his sympathies had always been a trifle more radical than theirs. "We had some very long, soul-searching conversations about it. Mathieu took a long time to make up his mind, but at last he voted for death. It's a matter of public record."

"Aurèle told me," Laurence said slowly, "that Mathieu had voted against the king's guilt, and against the death sentence, and that was why he had finally broken off their friendship that summer. Because they were growing apart in their beliefs."

"Then—forgive me—he was lying to you. If they quarreled, it wasn't over politics. That must have been just a convenient, believable excuse."

"But what else could they have quarreled about?"

"Personal matters . . ."

"I don't know what you mean," she insisted. " 'Personal matters'? You mean a woman? They certainly wouldn't have quarreled over *me*, God knows. We were the best of friends, but I told you, Aurèle never loved me. He—"

Abruptly she fell silent. Aristide fixed his gaze on a corner of the seat, where the straw stuffing was poking through a broad split in the dirty leather, and said nothing.

"Please tell me," she said, after a long, icy silence, "that a woman was involved, whom they were both infatuated with. Aurèle's mistress? Mathieu's?"

He slowly shook his head. "I think your husband was in love, but not with a mistress."

"*No.*"

"It's the only reasonable conclusion. And someone—"

"*No!*" She twisted about and hammered on the side of the cab. "Stop. Stop! Let me out now!"

A glance outside told Aristide they were nearly at the gates to the Palais-Égalité, and that she would be safe enough walking the last few streets home. He did not attempt to follow her as she scrambled out of the fiacre and slammed the door behind her.

25

A ristide arrived at the commissariat early the next morning to discover François lounging in the antechamber under Didier's cen-
sorious eye. While Didier would never deny that spies provided
indispensable services to the police, he had never taken pains to con-
ceal his contempt for them.

A moment later Brasseur beckoned François and Aristide into his
office, where they huddled about the hearth, warming cold hands. "So
you've managed to get yourself a situation with the Duponts, eh?"

François nodded. "Easy as winking. The Bouton woman was that
desperate, I could have been a drunk who smelled like a barnyard, and
she'd have taken me on. Got any orders for me, Commissaire?"

"Learned anything?"

"Well . . . the old man isn't universally mourned, his daughter's a
prize shrew, the actor's a piece of work, and the cook is a lot better in
bed than I thought she would be."

Aristide rolled his eyes and said nothing. Only François could have
managed to seduce Thérèse on his first night in the house.

"Did Thérèse whisper anything useful to you across the bolster?"
Brasseur inquired, with a chuckle, as he returned to his desk. "Any ten-
der thoughts about rat poison, for instance?"

"She did gossip about the family calamities, of course. And she swore up and down that she's never kept rat poison in the house, and Citizeness Bouton wouldn't either. Nasty dangerous stuff, she says; if they need it they buy just enough, and put it down the mouse holes, and they never have any left over where the children might get at it. So you can forget about anybody finding it in the back of a cupboard and using it. Somebody deliberately went out and bought it."

"Well, that's something," said Brasseur, scribbling a note. "Anything else?"

"Give me another couple of nights. Servants know everything; you know that."

"Has Thérèse said anything at all about Charlotte Dupont?"

"That's the one who hanged herself? No, not much, except that poor Ma'm'selle Charlotte ought to have had a husband. That kind of female needs a man to look after her."

"Charlotte might have had an admirer, maybe a fiancé," Aristide said.

François shook his head. "Thérèse never said a thing. Charlotte must have kept her mouth shut about that, though I gather she never kept her mouth shut about anything else. So what kind of questions should I be asking?"

"Just let them talk."

François grinned broadly. "Too bad there aren't any more girls with cold beds."

"You are incorrigible," Aristide said.

"Well," said Brasseur, after François had left them, "it's time we took stock of where we are." He thrust a letter at Aristide. "I've heard back from Prunelle's friend and he says he's as sure as he can be about the stuff in Dupont's stomach. Also a couple of tiny grains we found in the Duponts' tureen and one of the soup plates."

"So it *was* arsenic."

"Probably. It's not much of a test, though—ever see it done? You take a bit of what you've got and burn it for a minute or two between a couple of pieces of red-hot copper. Then you sniff the vapor it gives off and compare the odor with the smell of a little genuine burned arsenic."

"Someday, I hope, some enterprising apothecary will develop a more reliable test." Aristide pulled a chair toward the desk and dropped into it. "All right then, it couldn't have been rat poison from the household. What about the apothecaries in the neighborhood?"

"My men have been to every one of them and nobody sold arsenic or any other deadly poison to anyone connected to the Duponts. And this Citizen Thierry wasn't much use; he only confirmed what Laurence and the girl told us: that he examined the kitchen when they complained of tainted soup, and couldn't find any traces of poison, much less smell burned arsenic in the fire. Nothing to incriminate the maid, at any rate." He stretched and sighed. "I've sent them to the nearby sections, but I don't have high hopes. If some apothecary bent the rules a bit, he's not going to own up to it."

Aristide nodded. "I swear to you, Brasseur, I can't see Jeannette Moineau having the cunning to buy poison from an apothecary on the other side of Paris. This is an ignorant peasant girl, not Madame de Brinvilliers."

Brasseur chuckled sourly at the mention of the infamous poisoner of the previous century before settling back to his papers. "As far as other useless errands go . . . Inspector Thomas found the two other servants; they hadn't gone far, and I can't see they had anything to do with this. Zélie told him, and very indignant she was about it, I gather," he added as he glanced at the inspector's report, "that she was a chambermaid and lady's maid to the four women of the house, not a scullion, and the kitchen was none of her affair. She took her breakfast at half past five and was about her business upstairs before they began cooking anything." He turned to the second page. "Same for young Antoine. Took his breakfast, then began his duties, cleaning up the hearths—not that there's too much to be done at the hearths, with the stingy little fires they keep!—and polishing brasses and cleaning shoes and suchlike. Not much of his work took him into the kitchen."

"What about old Dupont's other countinghouse, the one on Rue du Renard?"

"The man I sent says it looks like a dead end. Old Dupont had a clerk there, of course, and the clerk says everything was business as usual, nothing much out of the ordinary. One or two angry threats from a couple of drunken layabouts, but as you said, it's not likely they'd try to murder the moneylender by poisoning him. Somebody in his house did that, and we're no closer to finding out which of them it was."

"Motive, Brasseur: motive, motive, motive."

"Then *you* tell me who did it." Brasseur pulled the dossier of the case toward him and extracted a sheet of paper covered in his own large, untidy handwriting. "There's everybody: opportunity and motive. Everybody who could have poisoned both Martin's breakfast and the soup the next day, and had a convincing reason to do so."

1. Gervais Dupont (called Hauteroche)

Opportunity to poison Martin Dupont: might have poisoned the porridge in the first-floor hall while Charlotte's back was turned
Opportunity to poison soup tureen: none
Motive: inheritance from a father living too long
Opportunity to strangle Charlotte: none
Motive: none known, unless he poisoned the porridge and thought Charlotte knew it

2. Ursule Dupont, née d'Armoncourt

Opportunity to poison Martin Dupont: might have poisoned Martin's breakfast in his room, while he was otherwise occupied
Opportunity to poison soup tureen: none—doesn't stoop to help with the cooking
Motive: legacy as spelled out in marriage contract, and/or marriage with C. Jullien
Opportunity to strangle Charlotte: none (she and Jullien were playing and singing at her clavichord all evening; corroborated by all who heard them)
Motive: none known

3. Magdeleine Bouton, née Dupont

Opportunity to poison Martin Dupont: none
Opportunity to poison soup tureen: while preparing Sunday dinner
Motive: inheritance? (unlikely, since she's as stingy as he was)
Opportunity to strangle Charlotte: none (and she was devoted to
    Charlotte)
Motive: none

4. Claude Bouton

Opportunity to poison Martin Dupont: none
Opportunity to poison soup tureen: none, unless in collusion with
    Magdeleine
Motive: Magdeleine's inheritance?
Opportunity to strangle Charlotte: could he have slipped out of the
    house? But why do it in the garden when it would have been easier
    in the house?
Motive: none known

5. Charlotte Dupont

Opportunity to poison Martin Dupont: could have poisoned his
    porridge or his coffee while bringing him his breakfast
Opportunity to poison soup tureen: none
Motive: inheritance, and/or the possibility of getting a better dowry
    from her brother in order to marry?
But who murdered her???

6. Laurence Fauconnet, widow Dupont

Opportunity to poison Martin Dupont: could have poisoned his
    breakfast in the kitchen
Opportunity to poison soup tureen: while preparing Sunday dinner
Motive: inheritance, if she knew Martin had changed his will in her
    favor as Frochot claims, and believed she somehow would get the
    money
Opportunity to strangle Charlotte: none

7. Étienne Dupont

*Opportunity to poison Martin Dupont: might have poisoned the
porridge in the first-floor hall while Charlotte's back was turned*
Opportunity to poison soup tureen: none
*Motive: his father would presumably inherit Martin's fortune, and
Martin would no longer be ruling the household, allowing Étienne
to go away to school*
*Opportunity to strangle Charlotte: claims he was in his room,
reading, all evening; no witnesses*
Motive: same as Gervais

8. Félicité (Fanny) Dupont

*Opportunity to poison Martin Dupont: might have poisoned the
porridge in the first-floor hall: admits she saw Charlotte on the
stairs with the breakfast tray*
*Opportunity to poison soup tureen: unknown, but possibly while
Sunday dinner was prepared*
*Motive: inheritance; she takes after her mother, who seems to know a
soft spot when she sees it*
Opportunity to strangle Charlotte: none (not physically strong enough)

SERVANTS AND EMPLOYEES

9. Charles Jullien

*Opportunity to poison Martin Dupont: might have poisoned Martin's
breakfast in his room, while he was otherwise occupied, possibly in
collusion with Ursule Dupont*
Opportunity to poison soup tureen: none
Motive: marriage with Ursule Dupont
Opportunity to strangle Charlotte: none (see Ursule Dupont)

10. Thérèse Huteau, cook

*Opportunity to poison Martin Dupont: while breakfast was being
prepared*

*Opportunity to poison soup tureen: none—was in her room,
recovering from the vapors*
Motive: none known
*Opportunity to strangle Charlotte: could have met her unseen in the
garden*
Motive: none

11. Zélie Nicolay, maidservant

Opportunity to poison Martin Dupont: none
Opportunity to poison soup tureen: none
Motive: none known

12. Antoine Bernardin, man of all work

Opportunity to poison Martin Dupont: none
Opportunity to poison soup tureen: none
Motive: none known

"You don't seriously think *Fanny* could—"

"She had more opportunity than some," Brasseur said bluntly, "and
I've seen twelve-year-olds who bashed other children's heads with bricks
in order to steal their clothes. Not that I really suspect her. If the poison had
been in the house, you never know . . . but no apothecary would have sold
that stuff to a kid. Frankly, Ravel," he added, "the person with the greatest
motive, and the opportunity to poison both dishes, is Laurence Dupont."

"*If* she had known Martin was going to leave her something, and if
she thought the family would give up the money without a fight."

"And Maître Frochot says she did know about it."

"Only because Martin told him he was planning on telling her.
That's hearsay, and Martin may have changed his mind. Thought he'd
leave it as a nice surprise for her. And how likely is it that the family
would roll over and let her take it?"

"She'd still probably get a tenth of it, which wouldn't be chicken
feed," Brasseur said, gazing at Aristide across the desk. "You want Laurence Dupont to be innocent of this, don't you?"

"I don't say she's not capable of murder; I can see her committing a crime of passion—over something that outraged her, perhaps—quite easily. But she'd snatch up a knife or a pistol in the heat of the moment—not something as coldblooded as poisoning, and not for money. And I'm certain money is what this affair is about."

"All right," said Brasseur, thumping a massive fist on the list of suspects, "let's go through it again. Who gains by old Dupont's death, and who *thought* they would gain by it? Laurence, first of all; then Gervais, Ursule, Magdeleine, and Charlotte directly, and Claude and the children indirectly. But Charlotte's dead, and we don't even know why. No more than we know why somebody wanted Jeannette Moineau blamed for the poisoning, other than that she made a convenient scapegoat."

"Something she knew, perhaps?" Aristide said suddenly. "I talked to her yesterday. . . ." He rapidly leafed through his little notebook. "It didn't seem very illuminating at the time. . . . Wait a moment, Brasseur, listen here: Martin, on his deathbed, kept saying he didn't intend to die just to please his family. His ungrateful children, were her exact words. 'And especially not to please' . . . somebody else. He broke off there, when he had another bad attack of stomach cramps, and Jeannette didn't know whom he meant."

"One of the children, do you think? Or maybe not—somebody he did business with?" said Brasseur, brightening. "Somebody he was getting the better of?"

"Yes, that could be it. . . ."

"So how does that person benefit by Dupont's death, if he's not an heir?"

"Someone who owed him money," Aristide said promptly, "but that won't wash; we've been through all that before, and he'd still owe Martin's estate. Someone he was extorting money from?"

"Still, money in assignats doesn't mean much," Brasseur said, with a grimace.

"Yes, but—look—a common debt is one thing; it can be paid in notes. But an extortioner dictates his own terms," Aristide told him, suddenly excited. "Don't you recall, in the Montereau case, Louis Saint-Ange demanded his hush money in gold? And if the victim didn't have any gold, he asked for fifty times as much in assignats? Either way, it was a sum people could ill afford. Perhaps something of the same sort is going on here."

"But we've never had the barest hint that Dupont dabbled in extortion," Brasseur objected. "Everything he did was legal, even if it wasn't strictly ethical." He shrugged. "All right, say somebody he was getting the better of wanted him out of the way. But if he wasn't living in the house, how did he murder Martin? And why the devil murder Charlotte? What did she have to do with it? What could she have known that was so important he had to silence her?"

"That—that *she* had poisoned Martin," Aristide said abruptly as the pattern fell into place before him.

"*What?*"

"You heard me."

"*Charlotte?*" Brasseur riffled through his notes and at last looked up at him suspiciously, staring across the heap of reports on his desk. "Have you been drinking?"

"You know I don't drink."

"Damn it, Ravel, every one of the family swore poor Aunt Charlotte couldn't—"

"Hurt a fly. Yes, I know. Nevertheless, I think it was Charlotte." Aristide rose and reached for his hat and coat. "I'll be back, with proof."

26

He took a fiacre to the Marais and rang the bell at the gate to Cavalcanti's house. When no one answered, he rang again, more loudly, confident that the din at quarter to nine in the morning would provoke complaints from wealthy neighbors who preferred to sleep till noon. At length the servant Mustafa opened the side door a crack, peered through, and hastily withdrew at the sight of him. Aristide was prepared for that, however, and shouldered his way past the door.

"I want to see him," he told the spurious mute. "Now."

Mustafa shook his head sorrowfully and raised his hands, palms up, with an eloquent shrug, before recollecting himself, grimacing, and muttering, "Sorry, citizen, he's gone out."

"At this hour of the morning?" Aristide said, glancing up at the second-floor windows. "I can think of so many amusing ways to pass the night in the comfort of my own house . . . women, wine, opium. . . . Why don't we join the party?"

Mustafa pointed again to the gate but Aristide was growing impatient with his charade. "I am an agent of the police," he said, pulling his police card from his pocket, "and if you don't let me inside and upstairs to see Cavalcanti right now, I'll go have a chat with the local magistrate. . . ."

The threat worked again, as he suspected it would, and Mustafa scowled and gestured him inside with a jerk of his head. He led Aristide upstairs to the same little parlor and paused at the closed door, behind which issued squeals and titters, a few muted thumps, and the occasional luscious slap of flesh on flesh. Aristide threw open the door and strode in to find Cavalcanti supine on the carpet by the hearth, fingering the intimate anatomy of the squirming, giggling brunette from the day before, who was straddling him among a litter of velvet-covered cushions and what Aristide thought might be a fur cloak.

The mystic was far too distracted to notice a visitor. Aristide slammed the door shut with a bang and Cavalcanti jumped and struggled to sit up.

"You!" he exclaimed. His face was flushed from the heat of the fire behind him and, to judge from the number of empty bottles lying beneath chairs and in corners, from the wine he had drunk. "What do you want? Get out of my house."

"I want the truth," Aristide said. "I think you can spare me a quarter hour for that."

The fur draping Cavalcanti's lower half wriggled and another girl emerged from beneath it, wiping her mouth. She uttered a sharp squeak as she saw Aristide and Cavalcanti pushed her away.

"Ladies, why don't you go and fetch us a few more bottles of wine? Don't run away, though!" he added as, pouting, they retrieved crumpled peignoirs that had been flung over the furniture. "Or get dressed!"

When the prostitutes had left, he drew the fur cloak higher about him and glared at Aristide. "All right, what is it now? I told you, I never saw that Dupont woman after her last visit to a séance. And if you think I killed her, I repeat—I was holding a séance at the time."

"Oh, no doubt you were," Aristide said. "And do you also have such a convenient alibi for the poisoning of her father?"

He was gratified to see the high color flee Cavalcanti's cheeks, leaving his handsome face suddenly as pale and flabby as the belly of a dead skate in a fishmonger's stall.

"P-poison?"

"Poison," he said, relentless. This sort of brazen adventurer was capable of endless bluffing and only a severe shock and a good fright would jolt him into telling the truth. "Arsenic. A large dose of it."

"Oh, sweet Heaven!" Cavalcanti slumped backward, sweat glistening on his brow, the bluster gone from him. Aristide pressed on.

"Look, I *know* Charlotte came to consult you about something. Stop wasting my time pretending it didn't happen. What was it she needed to ask you?"

"She—she . . ."

He's scared out of his wits about something, Aristide thought; from the way the man was avoiding his gaze, he was clearly grasping at time enough to fabricate a convincing story. Another piece of the puzzle fell into place and suddenly Aristide realized why Cavalcanti persisted in claiming he had not seen Charlotte the day before. If he admitted that Charlotte had come to him, he would have to grope for a credible reason why she had sought him out in such distress, for the truth was far too dangerous to him; no, no, much better to deny she had ever arrived.

"You sold something to Charlotte last week, didn't you?" Aristide said. "Some kind of magic powder or potion like the ones you were peddling to those women after the séance?"

"I never—"

"You'd better not try to deny it. The police can question your servants, you know, and all those silly people who think you're the prophet Elijah. They'll tell us all about those quack medicines and elixirs you concoct. One of your servants is bound to know something about Charlotte, and eventually is going to talk."

"All right, all right!" he cried. His manner abruptly altered—his speech, Aristide noticed, had lost the accent that had added to his exotic aura—and he was no longer the man of mystery but merely a compelling rogue who seemed unable to choose between bluffing and cringing his way out of a tight spot. "Yes, I deal in elixirs for any malady. Why should I deny it? What of it?"

"What did you sell to Charlotte? What was it she wanted?"

"What they all want! A few potions to bring her youth back, to make her irresistible to the opposite sex! What do you think?"

"And what else?"

"Nothing else," he said, far too quickly.

"Of course there was something else. You'd not be so frightened if it was merely some fancy salve to freshen a lady's complexion. What kind of poison did you sell her?"

"I never did! I don't deal in poisons, citizen. Never poisons!"

"But you do deal in magic elixirs, made of the devil knows what?"

"Harmless concoctions!" he sputtered. "Little more than spiced spirits of wine, or perfumed tallow with a few herbs in it, or rice powder with a bit of glitter added. The strongest mess I sell has a few drops of laudanum in it, no more. I tell them my medicines and salves will cure them, or make them young and beautiful again, and the silly creatures swear they work. Just believing in the stuff is half the battle."

"Just as believing you can communicate with the dead makes your flock eager to trust whatever 'the dead' may say?"

Cavalcanti smirked. "Belief—the power of suggestion over credulous people—it's a wonderful thing, citizen. Why should the Catholic Church be the only entity to get rich from peddling miracles?"

"So you admit you're quite as much of a fraud as Cagliostro, Mesmer, or Casanova?"

"I protest," he said, with a flicker of indignation. "Mesmer is a man of science, just as I am—"

"Mesmer was no more above taking the money of the gullible when it suited him than you are, Cavalcanti. But I'd say you're much more a mountebank than a man of science."

Cavalcanti glared at him and then suddenly seemed to deflate like a pricked bladder, shoulders slumping. "Mountebank, fraud—anything you like," he admitted. "But I'm no poisoner. Search this place all you want; you won't find any poisons."

Aristide was inclined to believe him; such men did not take unnecessary risks. "So what *did* you sell to her? Don't try to deny it. You sold her something recently, something that worried her. And I'm sure the police will find a record of it, in your account books, perhaps."

Cavalcanti glowered at him for a moment and at last rose heavily to his feet, wrapping the fur snugly about him. "All right, then, have it your own way. You'll see I've done nothing wrong." He tugged at a bell-rope and shouted, "Mustafa! The accounts! Bring them in here."

A few minutes later the servant appeared with a thick ledger in his arms. Cavalcanti opened it and thrust it before Aristide. "There. You see? Eight days ago. 'Two ounces of pearl powder, sold to C. Dupont.' Nothing but rice powder mixed with a bit of powdered sugar and set to sparkling with a pinch of crushed pearl and mica. Perfectly harmless stuff. You could eat a pound of it and feel nothing except grit between your teeth."

"And what was it supposed to be for?"

He attempted a weak grin. "Ah, pearl powder is useful for so many things, citizen."

"What did Charlotte think this powder was for?" Aristide insisted.

"She begged me for something to sweeten her father's disposition. The old buzzard was a tyrant, I gather, and the silly creature was infatuated with some man and wanted Papa's approval—"

"And old Dupont was supposed to swallow down your concoction," Aristide interrupted him, "and believe in its powers as thoroughly as Charlotte did, and suddenly become a paragon of benevolence?"

"Of course not. Charlotte was to give it to him secretly; ideally, to mix it with his soup or his porridge, where a bit of grit at the bottom wouldn't be noticed. It wouldn't do a thing to him, but dear woolly-headed Charlotte is so—was so convinced of my powers, and was so sure it would work, that she would take any flash of good humor from the old man as a sign of success." He edged away from Aristide, grabbed the nearest wine bottle, and took a long gulp from it. "I tell you, citizen," he added with a sigh of relief, "people believe what they want to believe. They like to be soothed and reassured and told that everything is in the hands of a higher power, because they can't bear the brutal truth that the world is random, that both good and evil happen to both the good and the evil, and that nobody up in Heaven is looking out for them."

"You are a cynic, Cavalcanti," Aristide murmured. He nodded.

"Yes, citizen, I am. Never underestimate the gullibility of the average man or woman and you'll go far."

"So you sold Charlotte this magic powder . . . how long ago? What was the exact date?"

"The seventh of Ventôse," he said, with a glance at the ledger. "February twenty-fifth."

Aristide nodded. "Good. We're making some progress here. But we're digressing from the point. Once again, *what did Charlotte want your advice about yesterday?* Something to do with the powder she'd given to her father, wasn't it?" He paused and stepped forward until they were less than an arm's length apart, face-to-face, and Cavalcanti squirmed beneath his scrutiny. "Wasn't it?"

At last Cavalcanti threw up his hands in vexation. "Yes! In the name of the devil, let me be. If I tell you the honest truth, will you leave me in peace?"

"After you've given your statement to Commissaire Brasseur."

"Commissaire—"

"That is not negotiable. You come with me now and you tell him the entire truth, and you keep yourself available to give your testimony to a justice of the peace, and to the criminal court."

"No questions about my business!"

"Cavalcanti," Aristide said, "as far as I'm concerned, you're no more than a particularly creative apothecary. Tell us about the powder Charlotte bought from you, and what she said to you later, and we'll forget everything else. Now get dressed. And if you don't waste time making a fuss about it," he added, as Cavalcanti opened his mouth, "you can be back here in a couple of hours to get your money's worth from those girls. They must be worn out; why don't you tell your cook to give them a nice little breakfast while you're gone?"

27

Aristide returned to the Section de la Butte-des-Moulins in another fiacre, Cavalcanti silent and sullen beside him. He left the medium in the outer chamber of the commissariat, with an inspector gloomily watching him, and went on to Brasseur's office. Settling himself comfortably by the fire, he recounted his visits to Cavalcanti's house. "I warn you," he concluded, "this fellow is a very glib, clever charlatan who knows how to look out for his own interests. He'll lie himself black in the face unless there is absolutely no risk to him in providing us with the truth."

Brasseur nodded. "Well, let's have him in and hear his story." He shouted down the corridor and beckoned Cavalcanti inside.

"So you talked to Charlotte Dupont on the afternoon she died, did you?" he said, looking Cavalcanti over, much in the way he would have eyed a pile of horse droppings in the street.

Cavalcanti puffed out his chest and began gesticulating dramatically.

"I assure you, Citizen Commissaire, I never did a thing to her! I held a séance that afternoon, not half an hour after she left me—I could not have been on the other side of Paris murdering her—"

"Do calm down, you blockhead," Aristide snapped. "Nobody's accusing you of murdering anybody. We just want to know what Charlotte said to you." Cavalcanti eyed him and scowled, but said nothing.

"She was frightened and upset, wasn't she," Aristide continued impatiently, "because she thought the magic powder you sold her must have gone wrong. She told you it must have gone bad, been too strong, whatever you like, because instead of improving her father's disposition, it had killed him!"

Cavalcanti glanced warily from Aristide to Brasseur and back again, without a word. "What if she did?" he said at last. "It's not my fault!"

"What was it she said to you?" Brasseur growled. "It'll be much better for you if you talk, you know."

"The woman came to me all in a flutter," Cavalcanti said sullenly, "and burst into tears. Said she gave her father a dose of the powder just as I'd directed her, but she must have given him too much, or else I must have sent her the wrong powder, or made it too strong, because now the old man was dead. And one of their maidservants had been arrested for poisoning him, and she was terribly afraid the wretched girl was going to suffer for it, but of course she was too frightened to own up to the fact that it was she who had put the stuff in the porridge."

Aristide nodded, remembering how agitated Charlotte had become at dinner when he had introduced the subject of Jeannette's probable guilt and punishment. "Go on."

"There's nothing more to tell you!" he exclaimed. "I regret the man is dead, but what was *I* supposed to do about it? It wasn't *my* fault. I repeat, citizen, I don't traffic in poisons. I keep nothing in my laboratory that could have harmed him. Nothing, but nothing, I could have given her could have done the least harm to anybody. It was she who made the mistake, not I. I wash my hands of it—I am not responsible."

"Was that what you told Charlotte?" said Brasseur.

"Not in so many words, but yes. 'I'm sorry your father is dead, but the mixture I gave you could not possibly have killed him, and I will take no responsibility for it.' She went off, sniffling into her handkerchief, and I never saw her again."

"So how do you explain Martin Dupont's death?"

Cavalcanti shrugged. "I imagine that harebrained woman was perfectly capable of confusing a packet of what I sold her with a packet of rat poison. It wouldn't surprise me at all. Or else the servant made an error!" he added.

"What servant?" Brasseur and Aristide exclaimed, almost in the same breath.

"The servant she sent to pick it up."

"A servant came to fetch it?" Aristide said. "Not Charlotte herself?"

"Yes, a lackey of some sort," he said dismissively. "I was prepared to listen to her vaporings for half an hour . . . the usual, 'Oh, Master, I simply *must* have your advice; the gentleman I love finds me pleasing, but after all you *know* I'm not nine*teen* any more . . . and I wonder if you could provide me . . .'"

The voice issuing from his lips, and the self-conscious titter that interrupted the sentence, were such a pitilessly perfect imitation of Charlotte's breathless tones that Aristide started.

"This voice of mine," Cavalcanti said, preening a little, "—a talent I was born with. It was Nature, citizens, or a Supreme Being, whatever you like, that gave me this gift, to imitate any voice I hear. And who am I," he added, in a deep voice that uncannily imitated Brasseur's own, "to reject the blessings Nature bestowed upon me?"

"The servant," Brasseur persisted, unamused, "he said he came from Charlotte?"

"Yes indeed. Said she had sent him to fetch a certain preparation for her, and had brought the money to pay for it. So I let Mustafa—my valet—settle the matter with him and returned to more amusing diversions with my chambermaid."

"This lackey: what did he look like?"

"I really couldn't tell you," he said, after a moment's thought. "Nondescript."

"Was he young?"

Cavalcanti shook his head. "No. Forties, maybe more."

"Antoine Bernardin's twenty-six," Brasseur muttered, and savagely slashed his pen across the note he had made.

"This man, he was no twenty-six. Middle-aged, balding on top. I tell you, he made little impression on me. The sort of colorless servant one barely notices. Perhaps an errand runner hired off the street. Such people are careless," Cavalcanti continued, warming to his theme. "The man is sent out on several errands, one of them is to get some rat poison, he buys little packets from the apothecary as well as from me, he confuses two of them. Why not?"

"Yes," Aristide said, "why not? Or else your harmless powder was deliberately replaced, or added to, in its packet by something not so harmless."

Brasseur scrawled a few notes and turned back to Cavalcanti. "What about this man she was in love with? Who is he? Did she ever mention his name, tell you anything about him?"

Cavalcanti shook his head. "Not a word. Just 'the gentleman I love' or 'a certain person' or, once or twice, 'my fiancé.' For a woman who never stopped talking, she was very secretive about him. He must have made her keep it quiet."

Brasseur tried a few more questions, but Cavalcanti could not, or would not, tell them anything more. At last Brasseur rubbed his hands together and nodded. "That'll do. That's very good indeed, citizen, very useful. You can go now, but don't think about leaving town; you'll be asked to come repeat your statement before the justice of the peace when we have this fellow behind bars."

"You realize, don't you," Aristide said when Cavalcanti had slunk away, "that this opens up the field to all of Paris?"

Brasseur groaned. "Don't I know it! But d'you think it's remotely possible *he* was the one she was in love with, maybe?"

"Cavalcanti? It's unlikely. He's running far too profitable a racket to risk losing everything by something as dangerous as this. He's quite happy to make his fortune in a way that's just this side of legal, by fleecing the credulous . . . while murder carries a death sentence. Why chance it?"

"Wait—wait a moment—what about the family friends: Frochot and Hébert?" Brasseur leafed through the dossier of the case and paused at a page of interrogations set down in Dautry's neat handwriting. "They called at the house a lot, I gather. Either of them could have charmed Charlotte."

"Hébert?" said Aristide, recalling their visit to the surgeon's rooms. "He's stout and bald and looks older than his years. Not in the least romantic, though you recall he admitted readily enough that he found Charlotte appealing, in a domestic sort of way . . . and some men do like them plump. . . ."

Brasseur, whose wife, Marie, was certainly rosy and plump, allowed himself a guffaw before settling back to business.

"I imagine," Aristide continued, "he thought she'd make a good housewifely sort of wife for a modest professional man like himself."

Brasseur nodded. "I know the type. He'd put up with her gushing for the sake of her cooking and mending and a tumble every night, and patiently wait for the day when she came into something from her father. But why kill her, then? He gets nothing unless he's married to her."

"Laurence suggested that the man may have panicked, fearing she'd crack, and chose to stop her mouth for the sake of his own safety."

"Perhaps." Brasseur searched further through the papers in the folder and took up a page. "What about our smooth lawyer friend, Maître Frochot?"

"Frochot is more likely—at least he's good-looking, for his age—but, once again, how on earth could Martin's death, followed by Charlotte's death, benefit either of them? Frochot may even lose by Martin's death; he was Martin's man of affairs, but now the heirs may choose to go elsewhere for advice on their financial and legal matters."

"And why not just marry Charlotte, if it was the inheritance he wanted?" Brasseur mused. "He's a widower, you said, free to marry her, if he could stand her."

"And I don't see how Martin could have disapproved of him," Aristide said, nodding. "A respectable, prosperous professional gentleman, sober and fiscally responsible . . . he ought to have been Martin's model son-in-law." He abruptly fell silent, sorting through snatches of conversation remembered, trivial things observed. "Unless . . ."

"Unless?" Brasseur said impatiently, after a moment.

"Well, it's just an idea of mine. You know how I work, Brasseur. Do you still know any of the clerks at the Hôtel de Ville?"

"Blanchard ought to be cooperative if you mention my name. What's all this about?"

"I'll let you know if I'm right," Aristide said, with a fleeting smile, and left Brasseur scowling behind him.

Aristide crossed the river to the Latin Quarter and knocked at the door to Frochot's apartment. The manservant Pierre answered the door and began to tell him that Citizen Frochot was in conference with a client, but Aristide interrupted him. "It's not Frochot I've come to see. I merely wanted to ask you how long you've worked for him."

"How long?" the man echoed him, puzzled. "About a year and a half, citizen."

"Any other servants?"

"My wife and I, we look after him."

"So naturally you've both been employed here for the same amount of time?"

"Yes, citizen. Maître Frochot came back to Paris after a long journey abroad, he said, and took up new lodgings with new domestics."

"Thank you," said Aristide, passing him a ten-livre note. He descended the staircase, the valet staring after him.

It was another twenty minutes' walk to the City Hall. He strode unchallenged through the high, vaulted marble corridors, past busy city officials and clerks hurrying past, to the office where records of Parisian births, marriages, and deaths had been kept since 1792, when such matters had been taken out of the hands of parish priests. The clerk Blanchard, bored and ready enough to escape his desk for a few minutes, led him to a high shelf of registers. "Which section was it you wanted again, citizen?"

"Théâtre-Français."

"Hmm, Théâtre-Français . . . there we are."

Aristide took the heavy volume and laid it open on the nearest table. "I'll need to look through this for a while, if I may; probably the records from September 1792 to, oh, sometime in the Year Four."

"Suit yourself, citizen." Blanchard hauled down another volume from the shelf and left him to pore over their dusty pages.

———

"Well, you look like the cat that got into the cream jug," Brasseur said when Aristide returned, as the clock in his office chimed two. He gestured to the carafe of red wine on his desk. "Have a glass? Were you looking up records at the Hôtel de Ville all this time?"

Aristide rubbed his eyes and brushed a cobweb from his cuff. "Does it show?"

"So what have you learned? That Frochot was secretly married to Charlotte?"

"No. Nobody was married to poor Charlotte. That's what I can't understand. Nobody but her brother and sister is going to inherit Charlotte's portion of Martin's fortune." Aristide poured a splash of wine for himself and topped off the glass with water. "Oh, I've learned a few things, of course: I've learned Frochot lied to me about a matter that shouldn't ordinarily have been a matter to lie about, and why he wouldn't have married Charlotte. But I still don't know why he would possibly have wanted Martin dead. If he *had* married Charlotte, he would have had a motive for hurrying Martin along, so Charlotte would inherit. But since he *didn't* marry her, what use would Martin's death have been to him? I think I'll just go quietly mad, Brasseur. Nothing seems to make sense."

"What you need," said Brasseur kindly, "is some dinner."

They took a late, hasty midday meal at the same eating-house where Aristide had eaten the day before. The stew today was no better and the meat was mostly gristle and bone, but it was thick and filling. Aristide went over his interview with Jeannette in his mind as they ate, trying to grasp at something she had mentioned to him. Something about Martin on his deathbed, talking feverishly to pass the time and distract himself from the pain . . . something about his strongbox, he thought, that box full of more gold than most people had seen in years . . .

"I want to talk to Jeannette again," he said to Brasseur when they had finished their meal. "She may know something more than she thinks she does."

"Popular girl, that one," remarked the prison clerk at the Maison Lazare as he noted down Aristide's name.

"How do you mean?"

"Any number of visitors she's had," he said, shrugging. "She's only a scullery maid or whatnot, isn't she? First you, yesterday, then the lawyer this morning, then the man from the caterer delivered her dinner today. Not that he really counts as a visitor; they don't get past the gate. And now you again."

Aristide went on to the common cells, holding a handkerchief to his nose against the stink of misery, of unwashed bodies and filthy privies, but a turnkey told him Jeannette had been transferred to a private cell by order of a benefactor who had paid for it. Laurence, he supposed, smiling to himself, had arranged for both the cell and the defense counsel. The friendless little kitchenmaid was not as friendless as she had thought.

"Somebody ought to go and tell old Peltier that something in his soup was off," the man remarked as he led Aristide up a tight spiral staircase to the private cells, where the stench was not so heavy as below. "You can't have a caterer poisoning the whole neighborhood, now can you?"

"Poisoning?" Aristide echoed him sharply. "What do you mean, poisoning?"

"Why, the girl, maybe half an hour after she ate the soup, she said she had stomach pains. Something awful they were, to look at her, dead pale like. And pretty soon she vomited it all right up again."

"Oh, my God," he whispered. He seized the man's arm and spun him about. "How is she now? Has a doctor seen her? What—"

"We had the prison doctor take a look at her when she started bawling," the turnkey said. "Kept vomiting and crying that the pain was awful, though she's quieted down now. Doctor said she'd probably had a bit of spoiled meat in the soup, or something rotten in the bread—God knows what they're putting in bread these days—"

"Half an hour after eating it? You fool, nobody comes down sick from bad food that quickly, not in cool weather! Where is she?"

"Here, citizen." The turnkey paused before the last door at the end of the corridor and fumbled with his keys. "The doctor said—"

"I don't care what the doctor said! Go fetch him again—and—and get me—" Aristide racked his memory as he tugged open the spy hole and tried to see inside the room. Arsenic—for it had to be the same poison that had killed Martin Dupont—what did you give to someone suffering from arsenic poisoning? "Milk! Get me a jug of milk now!"

The man gaped at him. "Milk, citizen?"

"Milk!" Aristide shouted. "At least a pint!" He thrust the guard back down the corridor and fought with the clumsy key. At last the lock gave way and he flung the door open. The narrow, cold room was thick with the sour reek of vomit.

Jeannette lay on the cot, face haggard, breathing slow and labored. The candle on a rude table beside her had burned down to a puddle of tallow and gone out. Beside it lay a tray bearing a covered tureen, an empty bowl, and a basket in which a few bread crumbs still remained.

"Jeannette—"

She did not move. He seized her shoulders and shook her, gently at first, then harder when she did not respond. Her flesh was chill and clammy in his hands. "Jeannette, wake up!"

Part of him knew she was unconscious, that his efforts to revive her were probably as useless as his previous efforts had been with Charlotte, but still he persisted. He shook her, cradling her head in his arms, repeating her name, but there was no sign of life in her besides that slow, harsh breathing.

A quarter of an hour later the doctor appeared, a stooped, middle-aged man with snuff stains on his cravat, rheumy eyes, and two days' growth of beard. "What's the matter with her now?" he inquired, without interest. "I told them, it was just a gastric fever that—"

"Gastric fever?" Aristide snapped. "This girl has been poisoned, you unspeakable fool! She's dying!"

"Poisoned?" He let out a wheezing sigh, heavy with the harsh odor of eau-de-vie, and bent over her. "Hmm . . . sweating, skin cold, pupils fixed . . . breathing labored. You may be right. I suppose some milk is in order, or possibly an emetic, though if it's only a gastric upset after all—"

"For God's sake," Aristide said, turning away from him, "get out."

The turnkey arrived shortly afterward with a jar of milk, complaining of the cost, and Aristide tried to spoon a little of it past Jeannette's lips, but she could barely swallow, and an hour later she died.

28

Aristide trudged back through the darkening streets, glistening with rain beneath the solitary street lamps, to the Butte-des-Moulins section. He paused as he passed the Mint, drawing deep breaths to steady himself, and found he was still shaking with anger.

Before going on to Rue Traversine and Brasseur, he decided, he would tell Laurence; however painful it would be, she should know of the latest calamity. He retraced his steps once more to the Dupont house and tugged at the bell-chain.

François answered the door and gave him a quick grin, but the grin died on his lips. "Here, what's up?" he whispered as he gestured Aristide inside. "What's the matter?"

"Jeannette Moineau is dead," Aristide told him. "Keep it to yourself for now, please. Could you—could you show me to Laurence's room? I don't know which it is."

François nodded and wordlessly led him upstairs to the second floor. The house was dark and still as a churchyard, save for the faint strains of a violin. "Where is everybody?" Aristide murmured.

"The widow's in her room, probably regaining her strength after a bout in bed with the secretary. Bouton's scraping away at his fiddle—hear it? Citizeness Bouton said she was feeling ill—she looked like death warmed over—and took off to her bed."

"Good God, you don't think—" Aristide began, but François shook his head.

"*She's* not poisoned, if that's what you're thinking. She's been looking like hell ever since her sister hanged herself, Thérèse says. Let's see . . . Citizen Dupont—Hauteroche, that is—he's upstairs conferring with the notary about business; I think Jullien's with them. They've been palavering for hours. Thérèse sent me up with a supper tray for them about ten minutes ago. The kids are in the kitchen, helping with the crockery and scrounging food from Thérèse, last I saw."

He pointed to a door. When he had discreetly slipped away, Aristide rapped a few times and called Laurence's name.

"Who is it?"

Laurence's voice sounded listless and dispirited. Could she possibly have learned already, he wondered, of Jeannette's death?

"It's Ravel, citizeness. May I speak to you a moment?"

She opened the door to him and stood silently gazing at him, her eyes dark hollows in the faint light of a single candle that stood on a table behind her. "I have been thinking all day about what you said," she said at last, her tone still lifeless. "I didn't want to believe you. I didn't want to think it was possible."

For an instant he had no idea what she was talking about, then remembered their last conversation together in the fiacre, coming home from Cavalcanti's house. "Citizeness," he began, "I have to tell you—"

She held up a hand to silence him. "No. Please. Let me finish before I lose my nerve. I thought about Aurèle and—and what you said about him . . . and—I don't know much about such things . . . but I have some letters. I found them under the floor of the wardrobe, af-ter . . . after his death. I didn't understand what they meant."

She turned and reached for a small pile of letters on the table. "He was your friend, too. I suppose you have the right to read them."

Aristide nearly said that he had scarcely known Aurèle Dupont be-fore he realized she meant not Aurèle but Mathieu. He took them and sat down to look at them in the quavering candlelight.

The letters were in two different hands; he recognized Mathieu's sprawling writing on half a dozen of them. The rest, two or three dozen, were in a firm spiky script and addressed to a Citizen Berthier, undoubtedly an alias, in care of a grocer's shop near the Hôtel de Ville. None of them bore any salutation or signature other than variants of "your affectionate friend." They were discreet and prudent in their language, but transparently clear to anyone who had guessed the truth.

Mathieu's letters were open, warm, though not fervent. Aurèle's to Mathieu, however, were more amorous; here and there the suppressed passion showed through the careful phrases. Aristide glanced through them, not daring to read them, though an occasional phrase caught his eye: "saw you yesterday and my heart ached that we could not spend an hour together"; "cannot allow our beloved L to suspect anything"; "Remain assured, my dearest friend, that I shall always be yours alone."

"I am 'L,' of course," Laurence said, speaking from the shadows. "What a lot of pains they must have taken to avoid hurting me."

He looked again through the letters, noting the dates. The last one was in Mathieu's hand.

My dear friend,

    It is with the deepest regret and sorrow that I must return your letters. I have treasured them as tokens of a friendship such as few can have shared. But I have reflected long and hard upon this matter, and I find I should be unjust to you if I were to pretend that you, and you alone, hold my heart. You know of what I write; now I find that, since I cannot have, and can never have, that which I so ardently desire, I wish no other and cannot give you what you desire of me. Let us part as friends, as we ever were, with fond memories of our shared times together.

    Your affectionate friend and most obedient servant.
    This 19th July, 1793.

Aristide thought back as well as he could to the summer of 1793. Yes, he recalled, Mathieu had seemed extraordinarily distracted on the rare occasions when they had seen each other. But Aristide had been more than usually busy that summer between police matters, and Delphine, and the "errands" he had sometimes performed for Danton and others high-placed in the Committees of Public Safety and General Security. He had had little time to spend with an old friend.

"They were in love," Laurence said softly. "And I never guessed a thing. I—I've heard some men feel that way toward their own sex . . . women, too . . . Gervais says a lot of actresses . . . but I would never have believed . . ."

"I suspect it was Aurèle who was in love, not Mathieu. But neither of them ever wished to cause you pain."

She drew a deep, shuddering breath, let it out again. "I think I would rather have known then, that Aurèle was in love with another man and could never have loved me, no matter what I did. To spend almost three years missing him so acutely that it felt as if some part of me were gone, three years building a—a whole framework of fantasy about his memory—and then to discover that everything I believed about him was a lie?"

"I think you exaggerate," Aristide said. He looked away from her, into the shadows. The room was a small one, narrow and ill-lit; it could not have been the chamber she and Aurèle had shared during the years of their marriage. "He cared for you, and kept the truth from you only in that one matter. He was still a good man, a decent man, who cherished his ideals. Mathieu wouldn't have liked and admired him otherwise."

As soon as he had spoken he remembered Roquefeuille's words, that Aurèle Dupont was rumored to have been responsible for Mathieu's arrest. Surely it had not been a cold-blooded gesture of self-preservation, the retaliation of an ambitious man with a reputation to shield. No, the man who had written those ardent letters had more likely been mad with the grief and anguish of rejection. Perhaps he had even arranged Mathieu's house arrest with some misguided idea that it would keep Mathieu out of public life for a time and bring them together once more.

He raised his head. "I must say what I came here to tell you. I fear I have sad news. Jeannette is dead."

"Dead?" she echoed him. "But—how?"

"She was poisoned. Probably by Martin's murderer."

"Oh, lord." She sat heavily on a corner of the bed. "You know who murdered Martin, then?"

"No, though we know who must have fed him the poison."

"How . . ." She thought a moment, then nodded. "Oh, I see. Charlotte? She didn't know what she was doing?"

"Yes."

"Somebody told her some nonsense that of course she believed, and she put the poison in Martin's food, thinking it was something else, and then . . . and then this person murdered her to stop her mouth."

"I fear so."

He waited a moment in silence, but she made no other sound. Somewhere nearby, Claude Bouton's violin scraped incessantly, slightly off pitch.

"Please," Laurence said at last, "I'd rather be alone."

"Of course." He found he was still clutching Mathieu's letters. He replaced them on the table and left her.

29

"How the *hell?*" Brasseur thundered. "How in the name of all the saints did the poison get into that meal? It *was* the soup from outside?"

"I don't know what else it could have been," Aristide said. He pushed the lank, wet hair from his face and sat down to lean forward, elbows on his knees, staring at the threadbare rug on the floor in front of him. The clock on the mantel chimed eight, as if mocking him. "They say she ate nothing else except the prison gruel this morning; and everybody had the same gruel from the same kettle. It had to have been the soup that Laurence had sent in to her from the cookshop."

"Nothing to do with Laurence Dupont, I suppose?" Brasseur said, eyeing him through the half-light of the four tapers on the pewter candelabrum beside him.

"She never went near the place; she sent François to arrange meals for Jeannette, and it was a caterer he knew in the quarter, named Peltier, who knew nothing about it."

"Then—"

"I went to the cookshop, of course. Peltier said François had ordered one good meal a day until further notice, to be delivered to the Maison Lazare by Peltier's errand boy, and had prepaid for three days' worth. But a man had shown up around midday and said Citizeness Laurence Dupont had sent him to prepay for another *décade's* worth of meals, and while he was there he would fetch Jeannette's dinner and deliver it. Peltier pocketed the money and thought nothing of it."

"What man?"

Aristide shook his head. "No idea. Peltier has his stew pots to worry about and barely noticed him. An inconspicuous-looking fellow, he says, nothing remarkable about him. Ordinary, shabby clothes. Might have been anybody: a servant, or a clerk down on his luck."

"The same errand runner who fetched Cavalcanti's magic powder, you think?"

"I wouldn't be at all surprised."

Brasseur groaned and rubbed at his eyes, smarting in the greasy smoke from the candles. "Why kill the wretched girl anyway, for God's sake?"

"She must have known something," Aristide said. "Or the murderer thought she did. I went to ask her about that strongbox of Martin's."

"What about it?"

"She said it was full of gold. More gold than she'd ever seen." He frowned, trying to remember everything she had told him. "Martin Dupont was a miser, we know that much. He probably loved gold for its own sake more than for what it could buy. Jullien told me he preferred to make his income from financial transactions rather than from investing in land. . . . A few acres of dirt can't compare to the feel of a handful of gold louis to a man like Martin."

Brasseur nodded. "So where did all that gold come from? Over the past five years you'd think the total would have dwindled a little, just from normal expenses. You have to come up with some gold or silver now and then to satisfy somebody, say the local official whose palm you're greasing, or just the tiler who mends your roof, or a peasant who absolutely refuses to take assignats for his cabbages."

"Exactly. If Martin was spending some of his gold in the normal way, where was it coming from to keep that strongbox so full? Nobody pays off his debts with gold if he can possibly help it."

"So we're still missing something."

"I still think," Aristide said, gazing over Brasseur's shoulder at the sagging shelves of dossiers that lined the wall behind him, "that this affair is a matter of motive. Learn 'why' to all the unanswered questions, and you'll learn 'who.'" He sat up straighter and ticked the questions off one by one on his fingers. "First: Why murder Martin at all? Unfortunately there are still plenty of good motives to go around, so we'll have to lay that one aside for the moment. Two: Why did somebody drop a couple of pinches of arsenic into the soup the next day, just enough to make everybody sick? If we know anything, we know Charlotte *didn't* do that, because she had no opportunity whatsoever to do it."

"And why," said Brasseur, "was Citizeness Bouton so damned positive it was the servant girl who'd done it?"

"Yes, that's question number three." Abruptly an answer slid into place as neatly as a piece of inlay in a surface of fine wooden marquetry. "Of *course*! Brasseur, Magdeleine was determined to blame Jeannette because she'd done it herself—poisoned the soup, I mean."

"Eh?"

"Magdeleine was devoted to Charlotte. She looked upon Charlotte as her child more than her sister; several of them said so, and even the appallingly precocious Fanny said Charlotte was no more than an overgrown twelve-year-old herself."

"Now we're pretty sure it must have been Charlotte who put the arsenic in the porridge, even if she didn't know it was arsenic," Brasseur muttered, thinking aloud, "and so . . . Magdeleine found out, and she's been shielding Charlotte all this time?"

"Exactly! *That's* why she was so determined to throw suspicion on someone else, someone who didn't matter. And—so it must have been Magdeleine who tainted the soup. Charlotte was locked in her room having hysterics all afternoon and went nowhere near the kitchen or the dining room, and had no opportunity to do it; Magdeleine did it to divert suspicion from her. She must also have planted a bit of the arsenic, and those gewgaws, in Jeannette's room where the first searcher would find them, in order to show that Jeannette had a motive to poison the household."

"Pretty cold-blooded of her," Brasseur grunted, "to lay all that on a servant who'd never done her any harm."

"I don't suppose Magdeleine sees it that way. To her, nothing is important but Charlotte, her naive little sister who's always had to be sheltered and protected from the merciless outside world. Ask a she-wolf if anything matters except the safety of her cub."

"But now Charlotte's dead anyway. And so is the wretched girl."

"Yes. And Magdeleine is looking ghastly, I'm told. She knows Jeannette was innocent, and she no longer has any reason to shield Charlotte, but she's afraid to come out and admit to what she did. Deliberately making false accusations isn't something the police just overlook."

Brasseur sighed. "This is growing uglier by the minute. All right, Ravel, let's find whoever it was put Charlotte up to dosing the porridge, and let's be done with this filthy affair!"

"What about Magdeleine?" Aristide said.

"Yes ... I think we'll have Citizeness Bouton in for a talk. I wonder if the public prosecutor could charge her with false witness, malicious denunciation, something of that sort." Brasseur reached for a bell to summon an inspector but abruptly paused and instead scraped back his chair. "No, on second thought, we'll pay her a visit. Take along a couple of inspectors to impress her and give her a good fright; that should shake her into telling us the truth. Want to come along?"

"Of course."

They collected a pair of junior inspectors on their way out and walked the few short streets, through a clammy evening mist, to Rue des Moulins. François answered the bell and did himself credit by showing not a particle of recognition as he ushered them inside to the larger salon.

Magdeleine soon appeared in the salon, her pale complexion now looking pasty and unhealthy in the candlelight. "Citizen Commissaire? It's rather late; have you any news for us?"

"Yes, citizeness, I do. We know who poisoned your father."

Magdeleine swallowed. "You do? That—that's very good news."

"It was your sister, Charlotte, citizeness, and you know it."

"I?" she said, in a strangled whisper. "I—I don't know what you mean."

"Yes, you do, citizeness. You guessed Charlotte had done something she shouldn't to that porridge, and you did everything you could think of to shield her, including laying the blame on an innocent servant. There's such a thing as bearing false witness."

Her fingers convulsively clutched at the folds of her dingy black wool skirt. Abruptly she broke down and sank to her knees on the floor, hiding her face in her hands and weeping. "Oh, dear lord! I—I—please, Commissaire, please understand—when Father died—I couldn't let her be arrested! She's only—" Her voice failed her and she dissolved into heaving, raucous sobs. After a few minutes she collected herself, grabbed at the nearest chair and dragged herself to her feet, and stood wiping at her reddened eyes.

"Citizen Commissaire," she said at last, "my sister was as foolish and transparent as a little child. When Father died so suddenly, and I felt it couldn't be natural . . . I knew at once Charlotte had had something to do with it. She was shocked, like all of us, but more than that she was confused and frightened . . . and she was the one who'd taken his breakfast up to him. . . . Of course, she denied everything when I confronted her, but I knew. But what could I do? Let them arrest her and throw her in prison and guillotine her for murder? She couldn't have known what she was doing, I swear it!"

"So you callously chose to let Jeannette Moineau be arrested and imprisoned instead?" Aristide said, more harshly than he had intended. "If Charlotte hadn't died, I suppose you would have been quite content to let them guillotine Jeannette in your sister's place?"

"Well, why not?" she demanded with a flash of anger, raising her head to meet his stony gaze. "What difference would it make, and who would care? What sort of life is that stupid girl ever going to have? Twenty or thirty years as a kitchen drudge, or wife to some lump of a peasant? I'd rather be dead!"

She wrenched the door open, her mouth set in a hard line, and strode out of the room before Brasseur could respond.

"Perhaps," Aristide said softly, as the door slammed behind

Magdeleine, "she was content, in her simple way, to be a kitchen drudge for the rest of her life." Brasseur turned to him with a sigh.

"Well, Ravel, that's two of your questions answered quick enough. What have we left? The identity of Charlotte's mysterious lover, and incidentally the murderer of her father?"

Aristide paused for a moment, thinking. "You realize, of course, this lets out the rest of the family? Cavalcanti said most definitely that she had wanted the magic powder because she wanted to get married and because her lover had suggested it. Now she couldn't very well have been carrying on a love affair with her brother or her nephew. And if it had been Claude Bouton who was the object of Charlotte's affections—not that he's much of a catch, and he couldn't marry her unless he divorced Magdeleine—I think Magdeleine would have known immediately. Nothing much gets past that woman."

"What about the handsome secretary?"

"Jullien's got a good thing going with the widow Dupont; why spoil it? Why would he want to burden himself with Charlotte when the lovely Ursule would be just as wealthy, and far more attractive, at her husband's death?"

"Ha," said Brasseur, shaking a finger at him. "What about this: Jullien's been warming Ursule's bed for some time and wants to marry her, not to mention the money she'll come into at Martin's death. Maybe he gets tired of waiting for old Dupont to kick off; so he pretends to make love to Charlotte simply in order to get her to do anything he wants. He gulls her into poisoning Martin, then kills her to shut her up. It wouldn't do to leave a foolish, worried woman like her alive to talk. But it's Ursule's inheritance he wants, not Charlotte's, so marrying Charlotte never has to come into it."

Aristide thought about it for a moment, frowning. "That's a very good case against him, I grant you. He's young and handsome and a lonely spinster of forty-odd would find him most attractive. However . . . I saw Charlotte attempt to flirt with him in a very inept, simpering, old-maidish way. I doubt she was devious enough to flirt clumsily in order to cover up a genuine affair."

"You may be right; but I think I'll have him in and see what we can startle out of him." Brasseur scribbled some notes and sent Dautry out to find the secretary. "It if wasn't Jullien," he resumed, "then who else might it have been? You don't meet too many eligible bachelors if you're a dowdy, silly old maid with no dowry to sweeten things, and a cantankerous old father who's likely to live forever. You don't suppose she could have been carrying on a passionate affair with the local grocer or baker, do you?"

"It scarcely seems her style," Aristide said. "She was too romantic and flighty to fall for somebody as prosaic as a petty-bourgeois trades-man. Charlotte would have been smitten by a man with a certain élan, a certain finesse to his wooing. An attractive, urbane man she could spin sugarcoated dreams about. And a man with wit enough to go along with, and use, her credence in Cavalcanti's mystical claptrap."

They turned as the door opened and Charles Jullien sauntered into the room. "You wished to see me, Citizen Commissaire? I hope it won't take too long; I'm still wanted upstairs."

Despite Jullien's nonchalant air, Aristide could sense unease in the way the young man watched Brasseur while fidgeting with his watch chain. "Maître Frochot," Jullien continued, with an attempt at flip-pancy, "is discussing urgent money matters with the great Hauteroche, who doesn't know an annuity from a letter of credit, and Gervais needs me to translate for him."

"Does he, now?" Brasseur echoed him, with a genial smile. "He's not much of a man of business?"

"Only where his own interests are concerned. Of course, he doesn't trust lawyers and financiers an inch, and he's positive that Frochot is go-ing to cheat him blind if given half the chance."

"But he trusts *you*, evidently. I imagine old Citizen Dupont placed great faith in your honesty and competence."

Jullien smirked. "I suppose so, citizen."

"And Gervais holds the same confidence in you that his father did."

"Well," said Jullien, his tense stance relaxing a trifle, "he trusts me more than he trusts lawyers. Yesterday he swore to me that Frochot just wants to get his hands on old Dupont's records and pinch a few bonds and contracts and so on for himself, and told me I should never let the fellow out of my sight when he's in this house."

Brasseur looked up from his notes, his smile vanishing. "So, citizen, how easy did you find it to seduce Charlotte Dupont, in order to convince her to poison her father?"

Aristide recognized the bluff, one of Brasseur's favorites. Abruptly spring a frightful accusation upon a suspected malefactor in a way that implies the police know all—it often reaped excellent rewards. This time, however, it produced little result. Jullien's response was an expression of the utmost astonishment. He goggled at Brasseur for a moment before he found his voice and exclaimed, *"What?"*

"Lonely, middle-aged old maid . . . it couldn't have been hard, could it? She must have been on her back in about a minute and a half."

"Citizen Commissaire," Jullien insisted, "I don't know what you're getting at, but I swear to you on all that's holy that I never had any sort of traffic with that poor cow. Why on earth would I want to?"

Brasseur scrutinized him a moment longer, his eyes never leaving Jullien's, before turning to glance at Aristide. Aristide assessed Jullien's bearing for an instant. Though the young man had paled, he had not flinched beneath Brasseur's accusing gaze.

"No," he said, "I don't think so."

"Too bad," Brasseur grumbled, with a sigh. "It was a good theory while it lasted. All right, Citizen Jullien, you can—"

A short, harsh cry and a shattering crash abruptly drowned out his last words. Brasseur and Aristide leaped to their feet, but not before a series of heavy thuds followed the crash.

They exchanged a single glance and made for the door, Jullien just behind them. Outside on the stone floor of the foyer, at the foot of the narrow staircase and surrounded by the remains of a china coffee service, Magdeleine Bouton lay sprawled, unmoving.

30

In the shocked silence, Laurence came running down the stairs to drop to her knees beside her sister-in-law.

"*Magdeleine!*"

Aristide sped to Laurence's side and gently raised Magdeleine's head. Her gaze was fixed, mouth hanging open in blank surprise. As he eased his arm beneath her shoulders, her head sagged backward at a painful, unnatural angle.

"Is she . . ." Laurence whispered. She was ashen. "Is she dead?"

"I fear so," he said. He lowered the body to the floor once more and rose to his feet. "Did you see her fall?"

"No, I was just coming down the stairs from the second floor. I—I heard her scream. She must have tripped on a step . . . or . . . or on the edge of her skirt."

"Good lord!" Maître Frochot exclaimed, appearing on the upper landing. "How did this happen?"

Raised voices babbled from all directions. Fanny came running toward them down the long hall from the kitchen.

"What's the *matter*? What was that awful noise?"

"Get out of here, Fanny," Aristide began, but he was not quick enough. She came to a sudden halt, clapped her hands to her mouth, and screamed.

"Oh, sweet Heavens!" Thérèse exclaimed, close behind her. Fanny continued to scream, frozen in place, barely pausing to draw breath between shrieks. Aristide grabbed the cook, thrust Fanny at her, and shoved them both toward the kitchen.

"Tend to her!" he told Thérèse. "And fetch Citizen Bouton!"

Thérèse paid no attention to him but stood gaping at Magdeleine's crumpled body. Laurence suddenly stirred into life, seized Fanny's shoulders and shook her, and then, when shaking produced no effect, slapped her smartly across the cheek. Fanny stopped in midshriek, gasped, and burst into noisy sobs.

"What the *devil* is going on here?" Gervais roared from the landing above them, behind Frochot. "Can't a fellow sit in his own study—"

"Papa!" Fanny wailed. She wrenched herself from Laurence's arms and fled upstairs into his arms as Claude at last appeared from the second floor, still clutching his violin and looking bewildered.

"*Silence!*" Brasseur shouted. "All right," he continued, in the sudden icy hush, "I want everybody in the salon. No questions, no exceptions. Children, servants, everybody! You too, Maître; and you, Citizen Bouton."

The inspectors whom they had brought with them soon herded everyone, including the weeping Claude Bouton, away and into the salon. Brasseur and Aristide silently faced each other over Magdeleine's inert body as the rich bitter scent of fresh coffee filled the air. Aristide bent to drape her skirt more modestly over her legs and, in doing so, nudged the ring of keys she wore at her waist. Who would carry the household keys next, he wondered. Ursule? It hardly seemed likely. Or perhaps Thérèse? More than one loyal, kindly despot of a cook or housekeeper had become the de facto ruler of a bourgeois family.

"Well," Brasseur said at last, "I suppose this is justice, in a way." Aristide nodded, without speaking, still gazing at the keys.

Brasseur nudged the debris of broken crockery aside with his foot from the splatters that still faintly steamed in the cold foyer. "The coffeepot was full," he added. "She must have been going upstairs with it. Probably to Gervais and Frochot, at a guess."

"Brasseur, wouldn't you say it's harder to tumble down a flight of stairs when you're going up than when you're going down? Even in skirts?"

"Yes, I expect I would."

The inspectors returned from the salon and, at Brasseur's instructions, carried the body upstairs on a shutter to a bedchamber. When they had gone, Brasseur turned to Aristide again.

"Four deaths! Don't tell me this one isn't related to the others."

"No," Aristide said, "it's no coincidence." He drew a deep breath. "I think I know who did it, Brasseur."

"You know who murdered Citizeness Bouton?"

"I know who murdered all of them, and why. I just need to know one thing more."

"How the devil did you come to that?"

"Keys," Aristide said. "Magdeleine's keys."

"*Magdeleine's* keys?"

"Which led me to thinking of the keys to Martin's strongbox and his files. I know we looked at plenty of those records," Aristide added, raising a hand as Brasseur opened his mouth to object, "but there was one box we didn't look through. When we wondered who benefited financially from Martin Dupont's death, the heirs and the debtors and the owners of annuities and so on, the one thing we didn't think about was whether Martin, in the past, might have purchased a life annuity or two for himself."

"By God, the box marked 'Annuities.'" Brasseur snapped his fingers. "Slipshod of us, Ravel, very slipshod. We assumed—"

"Never *assume*!"

"—that they were records of people who'd bought annuities from him. But that box could also contain records of annuities he owned himself." He paused, scowling. "But so what if he'd taken out an annuity from the government? He might have, I suppose, but he'd be getting worthless bits of paper as interest now, like everybody else."

"No. *Not* from the government. From an individual, a banker or a speculator like himself. You couldn't dictate your own terms with the royal annuities. But with a financier who wants to get rich from you by guessing you'll die soon . . ."

Brasseur frowned. "But if Dupont was drawing interest from an annuity of his own, no matter who issued it, he'd still be getting paper."

"Then where did all the gold in his strongbox come from? Think over everything you've learned about Dupont's character. Let's get that box and take a look, shall we?"

Brasseur returned shortly, the box marked ANNUITIES under his arm, and sat down with it on the high-backed bench in the foyer. The lock, well made and intricate, for a quarter hour resisted his attempts with a pick-lock, but at last gave way.

"Dated October ninth, 1786, all official and watertight," said Aristide. He lifted a candle for a better look and studied the contract, ornamented with its bright red blob of sealing wax and dangling white ribbons, that Brasseur had extracted from a file at the back of the box. "I think that's enough proof. Don't you?"

"But why not just marry the woman instead of going through all this rigmarole?" Brasseur objected. "Surely they'd have worked something out if he'd become Martin's son-in-law."

"He couldn't. Martin wouldn't have allowed it."

"Why on earth not?"

"Because," Aristide said, "the Duponts keep to the old calendar."

"Eh?"

"Think it over."

Brasseur frowned and glanced about him for a moment, his eyes at last coming to rest on a small crucifix on the wall, and brightened. "Ah. And you went to the Hôtel de Ville this morning to look up something in the records. Yes . . . very likely."

When two of the inspectors returned from the second floor, Brasseur and Aristide strode into the salon. The inspectors took up positions beside the doors. Aristide glanced about him at the Duponts, their faces pale ghosts in the shadows lit only by the weak firelight. Ursule and Jullien stood together by the fireplace, discreetly clasping hands, uneasy but not unduly distressed; Magdeleine could have meant little to either of them. Gervais, Fanny beside him, sat on the sofa, his forehead puckered in a worried, disbelieving frown. Claude, oblivious to everyone, sat hunched, face buried in his hands, at his other side. From time to time Gervais awkwardly clasped Claude's shoulder, in an ineffectual gesture of sympathy.

In a corner, Étienne leaned against the wall, hands in his pockets, his handsome face sulky and eyes narrow with suspicion. Nearby, Frochot perched on a side chair, wig and coat immaculate, expression betraying nothing. François stood with his arm about Thérèse's shoulders as she sniffled softly into a handkerchief.

Laurence, who was standing between the shuttered windows, turned her head a fraction and met Aristide's eyes for an instant before she turned away again and continued to gaze into the meager fire that flickered on the hearth. Her expression was empty of all emotion, as wooden and indifferent as the faces of some of those whom he had seen on their way to the guillotine during the Terror, those almost too stupefied to comprehend what was happening to them.

He spotted a pair of pewter candelabra on a buffet at the other side of the room, fetched one, and lit a few of the candles at the hearth. Gervais stirred.

"For the love of Heaven, burn them all!"

François took a burning candle and began lighting the rest. The shadows retreated. Brasseur cleared his throat and the sound echoed in Aristide's ears like a pistol shot in the silent room.

"Citizens . . . I suppose by now you're all sick with fear, wondering if you have a madman among you, and dreading that you may be the next one in this household to die. Well, that stops now. Nobody else here is going to die unless it's by natural causes . . . except for one."

"All right then," Gervais said, rising to his feet and planting his fists on his hips, "who the devil poisoned my father?"

"Your father, citizen, was poisoned by your sister Charlotte."

A whisper of incredulous gasps rose about the room.

"*Charlotte?*" Gervais exclaimed. "Rubbish! Charlotte couldn't have hurt—"

"I know, citizen. Charlotte couldn't have hurt a fly. Nevertheless, it's the truth. It was Charlotte who—"

"You're saying," he demanded, "that poor muddleheaded, sentimental Charlotte poisoned the Old Man and then hanged herself in remorse? I don't believe it! My profession, Citizen Commissaire, my profession is all about the understanding and interpretation of motive and character, and I tell you again, my sister was completely incapable of committing murder—unless, in a moment of rage, she'd thrown herself on some ruffian whom she'd caught setting a stray dog on fire!"

"If you'll let me continue, citizen, I was about to say that while it was Charlotte who poisoned Martin Dupont's porridge, she had no idea what she was doing. She thought she was giving him a magical drug to sweeten his disposition and make him more agreeable to the idea of her marrying."

"Marrying!"

"Yes. Your sister, like any normal, healthy, affectionate woman, wanted to get married, didn't she? That's how the murderer did his work—by promising Charlotte marriage, probably after seducing her, and convincing her to do whatever he asked."

"I *told* you," Fanny declared to nobody in particular. "I *said* Aunt Charlotte was in love, and nobody listened to me!"

"But who could it have been," said Gervais, "and why on earth would he want to poison Father? Father wasn't against the idea of Charlotte marrying; he only wanted to be sure she didn't run off and marry some fortune-hunter who was only after his money. That's why he wouldn't give her a dowry."

"We considered that," Aristide said. "But the murderer didn't kill Martin for the sake of Charlotte's dowry, or even her inheritance. He didn't care about a dowry, any more than he cared about Charlotte. She was simply a means to an end, an easy cat's-paw. I imagine he always intended to kill her after she'd served her purpose."

"You mean Charlotte didn't hang herself?"

"No, of course not. We've known that from the start."

All eyes shifted irresistibly again toward Brasseur, who nodded. "We had to let you think the obvious, citizens. But Charlotte didn't kill herself. Somebody strangled her."

Gervais muttered something unintelligible and returned to his seat on the sofa. Aristide glanced about the room and continued.

"So—Charlotte put something into Martin's porridge, and he fell violently ill and later died. Now, Charlotte must have had at least enough sense to realize that her father died suspiciously on the very day she'd put the 'magic powder' into his porridge. Remember how worried and distracted she was, and how uncomfortable she was with the thought of Jeannette being tried and condemned for murder? She was frightened and remorseful because she suspected something in that powder had disagreed with him. So she went out to get advice: first from Signor Cavalcanti, who had sold her the magic powder, but who told her in no uncertain terms that his powder could not have killed Citizen Dupont. Then, I think, she went to her lover, the man who had actually handed her the powder, and confessed her fears and doubts, and he reassured her before he escorted her back to the house . . . and once in the garden, out of sight in the dark, he strangled her. Then he hoisted her up with a bit of old rope from the garden shed and made it look as if she had hanged herself from the gate."

"But who *was* her lover?" said Ursule, speaking unexpectedly from the hearthside. "Not this Signor Cavalcanti she kept talking about?"

"We suspected him, of course. As a self-declared magician and alchemist, who sold salves and potions to his faithful flock, he was the most likely person to give Charlotte a magic powder that she would unhesitatingly accept as such."

"But why would this Cavalcanti want to murder my husband? If, as you say, it wasn't a matter of money, and he didn't care about Charlotte or her dowry or her inheritance?"

Aristide shook his head. "It wasn't Cavalcanti. That sort of charlatan doesn't commit murder when he can make a fortune through far less dangerous methods. True, he sold Charlotte something he called a magic powder, but he told us himself that a servant had called for it. Now since Cavalcanti had little motive for murdering either Martin or Charlotte, we suspected the servant immediately. It wasn't your man Antoine, so it might very well have been the lackey of the man who was using Charlotte . . . or the man himself."

"Easy," Brasseur interposed. "Just put on a shabby old suit of clothes, old shoes with strings to them instead of buckles, leave your hair undressed, announce you're here to fetch a purchase for Citizeness Charlotte Dupont, and who's to know? Nobody looks twice at a domestic."

"All right," said Gervais, eyeing Aristide, "you've convinced me this far. Charlotte was fool enough to let some plausible fellow hoodwink her. But, as Madame my stepmother points out," he added sardonically, "if he didn't want her dowry, if it wasn't a matter of money, what *did* he gain by Father's death?"

"Oh, on the contrary, citizen; it *was* a matter of money. A very great deal of money, and his own personal ruin." Gervais frowned, puzzled, and Aristide continued. "Old Martin, besides lending money at exorbitant rates, made a practice of issuing life annuities to people, didn't he? It's a simple enough arrangement: on receipt of a certain sum of money from an individual, you agree to pay back a certain percentage of that money as guaranteed income, every quarter until that person's death. It's a gamble—you're wagering the person will die before you've paid back all the money. Just as the person who purchases the annuity is wagering that he or she will live long enough that they'll get back more than they originally paid. Otherwise, they might as well just live on the capital."

"Very well put," said Jullien, with the faint condescension of a schoolmaster whose dullest pupil had dutifully repeated the day's lesson, "but why would anybody kill the man who was paying out the income?"

"Well, you see, it occurred to me that, while Martin did his own profitable business in annuities, he might have bought a few life annuities of his own, trusting in his own excellent health to make it worth his while."

"But annuities are scarcely worth anything these days," Laurence protested. It was the first time she had spoken and Aristide turned, surprised. "I heard the Old Man cackling about it often enough—how assignats had made him even richer."

"Exactly," Jullien agreed. "Most of the annuity contracts he issued to people were before the Revolution, or at least before 'ninety-two or so,

and they simply stated, 'On receipt of a lump sum of so many livres I contract to pay So-and-so a guaranteed annual income of five percent; that is
to say, so many livres per quarter.' And what happened was that assignats
became worthless; he was paying out paper, just like everybody else. So if
Citizen Dupont had bought an annuity from someone else, on his own
life, he's the one who would have lost by it, not the issuer."

Aristide shook his head. "Not if the contract clearly stated that the
income was to be paid in gold."

31

G old!" Gervais exclaimed.

"Who'd let something like that get past him, these days?" said Jullien.

"Oh, I don't imagine anyone was foolish enough during the past couple of years to issue an annuity that had to be paid in gold. But Martin purchased that annuity years ago, before 1789. No one could have foreseen that the government would issue paper money that would lose its value."

"So why would anyone have demanded gold," Laurence interrupted him, "when we had no other money than coinage before the Revolution?"

Aristide shrugged. "Who knows? Perhaps he simply loved gold for its own sake, and demanding gold, even over silver, had become a habit with him. Perhaps it was to make sure no one tried to pay him off with bonds or shares or land instead of good solid metal. And the issuer of the annuity agreed to it, thinking it was merely the harmless eccentricity of an old miser. But when gold grew scarce because everyone was hoarding it, it began to ruin him. All he could do was hope Martin would hurry up and die—Martin was seventy-three when he purchased that annuity."

"But when Martin showed signs of living on and on," Laurence said slowly, "the issuer decided to murder him before all his gold was gone and he was bankrupt."

"Yes. Because if he had no more gold, he would have had to default on the debt, which would have ruined him forever, even if he had been able to survive on whatever assets he might have had left. Imagine his desperation as he saw his hoard of gold inexorably shrinking, and as he watched old Martin gloating about how clever he was, and how good his health was."

"We've looked in Citizen Dupont's files," Brasseur said, "and we found half a dozen records of his having bought an annuity for himself, all but one of them from the government. It was that one that interested us the most."

"Then came the third death," Aristide said when Brasseur said nothing more. "Not the one you're thinking of—not Magdeleine just now. I'm speaking of the poisoning of Jeannette Moineau."

Someone drew in his breath with a sharp hiss. "Jeannette?" Ursule repeated, frowning. "You mean the kitchenmaid?"

"Yes. Perhaps you had all forgotten about her?"

"Of course not," Gervais snapped. "Magdeleine was so sure she was the one who'd dosed the soup. . . ." His voice trailed off as he considered the matter from a new angle. "But if *Charlotte* had put the stuff in Father's porridge?"

"Magdeleine guessed that Charlotte had had something to do with Martin's death and, because she cared for her sister's safety and happiness as if Charlotte had been her own child, she threw suspicion on Jeannette instead, in order to divert attention from Charlotte."

"But what do you mean, Jeannette was poisoned?"

"Jeannette was poisoned this afternoon in prison, in the food Citizeness Laurence had had sent in to her, and died a few hours later."

"Laurence!" Ursule exclaimed, glancing narrowly at her. Laurence returned the glance with an icy stare and said nothing.

"Laurence had nothing to do with that," Aristide said. "Out of sheer kindness, she sent François here to a cookshop he knew of and ordered meals to be sent to Jeannette in prison. And don't look at François, either," he added quickly as Thérèse pulled away from him with a gasp. "François is one of our men."

"A police spy!"

"Yes, and a very able one. François, why don't you tell them the gist of your conversation with Peltier?"

François shrugged. "Not much to tell. I went to Peltier's shed like Citizeness Laurence asked me to, and gave him a bit of chink up front for three days' worth. Told him he was to send in a good nourishing dinner, soup or stew or such, to the prisoner Jeannette Moineau in the Maison Lazare, until further notice."

"And Peltier said?"

"He said fine, one of his boys would deliver it every day around midday, and that was all."

"Now when I questioned Peltier after Jeannette's death," Aristide continued, resuming the tale, "he told me a man, a servant, had stopped in at the cookshop that noon and claimed he had come from Laurence Dupont. He said he was taking a few items to Jeannette and that he would take in her dinner at the same time; he also gave Peltier some additional money to pay for another ten days' worth of dinners. So Peltier gave him the tray and the tureen of soup and thought nothing more of it."

"Was it the same servant who'd bought the powder stuff for Aunt Charlotte?" Fanny inquired.

Clever child, Aristide thought; she had put it together before her elders did. "We can't be sure, but Peltier's description, or lack of it, could describe the same man. A shabby, inconspicuous, middle-aged fellow."

"But all this is getting you nowhere," Gervais declared. "You still don't know who this so-called servant was, do you?"

"Yes, Citizen Dupont, I think we do. Because Jeannette's death led to more questions. Why murder Jeannette, who was no more than a scapegoat in all this? Did she know something that would have betrayed Martin's killer? I talked to her the day before she died and I believe the only time she could ever have learned anything important to someone else, and dangerous to herself, was when she spent those hours nursing Martin. And what did Martin talk about as he lay dying? The things that mattered most to him: his money and his family. He even did a bit of showing off; he gave Jeannette a peep at the gold in his strongbox. And he began to say something like, 'I don't intend to die just in order to please my ungrateful children, and especially not to please'—somebody else. He never finished the sentence, but it set me to wondering who, besides the family, would benefit from Martin's death, and in what way, and also how all that gold had arrived in Martin's treasury."

"But how could this person have known what Jeannette knew?" Laurence demanded. "She was in prison, for Heaven's sake."

"Yes. She was in prison. And the only person who saw her there, besides the turnkeys and the other women prisoners and I, was the defense counsel you sent to advise her."

"What of it?"

"Did you ever meet this defense counsel?"

"No, I asked Maître Frochot if he knew one who might be willing to take Jeannette's case, and he said he did, and he would ask the man to go—" She abruptly paused and looked at Aristide, the question in her eyes.

"Precisely. A lawyer went that morning to the Maison Lazare to advise Jeannette about her situation. I don't know what he told her, or what she told him, though I can guess; because by the time I went to see her, later that afternoon, she was unconscious and dying of arsenic poisoning. Now anybody can claim he's a lawyer, of course . . . but you'll be most convincing if you really are a lawyer. Perhaps not a criminal defense lawyer, but at least a notary. . . ."

"Are you referring to *me*?" Maître Frochot inquired, speaking for the first time. He rose to his feet and turned to Brasseur. "Commissaire, I must protest. This—this associate of yours is drawing an incredible conclusion from a very simple fact. I did visit the poor girl at the Maison Lazare, just as Citizeness Laurence Dupont asked me to. I thought I should have the story from the girl's own lips before I asked a fellow advocate to take her case."

"That was most generous of you," Aristide said, feeling a sudden swift anger churning his vitals, "when you had a hand in sending her there. I expect she told you everything she'd told me, about Martin's ramblings and the gold and so on. You realized she knew too much and had to be silenced. Then you remembered that Laurence had asked you for an advance on her inheritance to send food and necessities in to Jeannette." He stole a glance at Laurence; she was paler than ever and her fists, half-hidden in the folds of her skirt, were clenched.

"Yes, she did, but—"

"It probably wasn't very hard to find the right cook; it's common sense to hire a caterer who's closest to the destination of the food, so it doesn't get cold while it's being delivered. You only had to go, in your disguise as a shabby errand boy, to a couple of cookshops nearest to the Maison Lazare, and announce that you were to pick up Jeannette's dinner. The right one would hand it over to you without a second thought. You made your story even more convincing, of course, by handing him extra money. Then it was only the work of a moment to stir a couple of spoonfuls of arsenic into the soup tureen, and take it to the prison gate like any other deliveryman."

"This is nonsense!"

Frochot had paled, though he had not lost his composure. Étienne, who had been standing closest to him, stared at him in fascinated loathing.

"No, Maître, it's not nonsense. You're a man of business. I think, when Brasseur and his men search your office, they will find more than one annuity contract in your files; what could be more natural for a man like you than to speculate in annuities with various elderly clients and acquaintances? But you made the mistake of gambling with the life of a man who was both very hardy and very, very clever."

"None of this is proof," Frochot said calmly.

"Who was experienced in legal documents and contracts, and who dabbled in a little speculation, and who might very well have issued some annuities to his elderly, wealthy clients? You. Who was an attractive, unmarried man of respectable profession and means, well-known to the family, who could have charmed vulnerable, silly, sentimental Charlotte into telling him anything he wanted to know, and doing anything he suggested to her? You. Who was the one person who tried to pass off Martin's death, and the poison in the soup the next day, as mere tainted food, so no suspicion would lead toward Charlotte? You. Who was a notary, an accredited lawyer, who would be admitted without question into a prison to confer with a client? You."

"What of it? I had a perfect right to visit the girl in prison."

"Yes, of course you did. But it will seem a little strange, I think, when the various guards at the prison gates identify you as both the lawyer who came to advise Jeannette and the errand boy who delivered her dinner a couple of hours later. Peltier, the cook, will identify you as the servant who picked up the dinner. And Cavalcanti will identify you, too, as the servant who paid for Charlotte's magic powder. Because it *was* you, wasn't it, every time? In an old secondhand suit and without your wig, and with the demeanor of a weary, middle-aged domestic, you'd be completely nondescript. But not so nondescript that a man who makes his living taking people's measure wouldn't remember your face."

Aristide paused and glanced at Brasseur. "Then, of course, the ultimate proof: the sealed and witnessed contract between you and Martin Dupont, dated 1786, regarding the annuity he had purchased from you on his own life, to be paid only in gold coin. He must have secretly laughed at you, these past few years, knowing that contract was just a few steps away from you whenever you visited the house. Once he was dead, it must have been your dearest wish to get at it, to break into that box and burn the contract so no proof would remain of your motive to murder him. That's why you wanted to go looking for Martin's will in his study, isn't it? Because you were the one person who might have had access to all his papers after his death, if only you could get into that room."

"I *said* he was trying to steal Father's papers," Gervais growled, "didn't I? Never trust lawyers!"

"Martin Dupont never let his keys out of his sight," Brasseur said. "Isn't that correct, Jullien?"

"Yes. He wore them on a string about his neck."

"Jeannette told me herself," Aristide continued, "that Martin wore the key to the strongbox on his person. Then I should have noticed that she also said Magdeleine had taken away the *keys*, plural, when she chided her father for showing off his gold to the servants. Of course, Martin had more than one key; he had one to the strongbox, and at least two or three more for various cabinets and drawers and so on. Correct?"

Jullien nodded. "There were four."

"And Magdeleine gave them to you, Frochot, the evening Martin died."

"Yes," said Laurence, "I was in the room; I saw her do it. She gave him all of the Old Man's keys. He told her it would be the wisest thing to do, so no one in the household could try any pilfering from the strong-box or the records before the will was read. He had the keys all right. And he knew all about my plans to send some decent meals in to Jeannette," she added, with swift, mounting anger, "because I went to him myself, like a fool, trusting him, and asked him for the money to do it!"

Gervais suddenly sprang to his feet and strode over to Frochot. "You! You bastard! My father, my sister—*both* my sisters—you murdering swine—"

"You—" Claude cried, rising in the same instant. "You murdered my *wife*! My Magdeleine! What—what am I going—" His voice cracked and he slumped onto the sofa again, weeping once more.

"Wait!" said Frochot, rising to his feet as Gervais towered above him. "Wait, I pray you. This is all very clever, but it's ridiculous. If I had been able to seduce Charlotte and persuade her to do anything I asked of her, then why should I have committed murder when it would have been far easier and safer for me simply to marry her, and come to some agreement with Martin?"

"Because your 'late' wife is alive," Aristide said, meeting his gaze, "and you knew Martin would never let his daughter marry a divorced man."

"Divorced!" Laurence said.

"Yes. Henriette Frochot, née Cauchon, is very much alive." He pulled his notes from a pocket, squinting over them in the candlelight, and read out the jottings he had set down at the Hôtel de Ville. "She and Robert-Louis Frochot were divorced, citing irreconcilable differences, on the seventeenth of Floréal, Year Two—otherwise known as the sixth of May, 1794, for those here who keep the Christian calendar and continue to be faithful, as Martin was, to the Catholic Church. The state may say that Citizen Frochot is no longer married to Citizeness Cauchon and is free to marry anyone he chooses, but the Church does not and will never recognize divorce. And although Martin might have relaxed his principles just far enough to consider allowing a daughter who was once a nun to marry, he would never have allowed her to marry someone who was a bigamist in the eyes of the Church. Were you afraid he'd find out, Maître? Or did Martin already know everything about you?"

Frochot slowly resumed his seat. He had gone very pale. "My wife—my ex-wife—and I agreed to keep the matter quiet, for the sake of my professional reputation. However—"

"Yes," Aristide interrupted him, "you kept it very quiet. Your wife went away, home to her family in the provinces, I suppose, and you put it about to people in Paris who knew you that she had died. But it wasn't for another year and a half after your wife's supposed death that you moved into a new apartment in a different quarter of Paris and hired new servants who knew nothing about your previous life— servants who could swear, to the best of their knowledge, that you were a widower, because you had told them so. It was then, wasn't it, knowing you couldn't take the easy way out and marry poor Charlotte, that you'd already decided to murder Martin Dupont if he didn't die soon. Charlotte, like everyone else, believed you a widower and was overjoyed when you began to pay her court, ever so discreetly. You took your time, didn't rush matters, but you always meant to kill Martin, and then Charlotte, too, when she'd fulfilled her purpose. . . ." He paused and drew a breath, meaning to continue, but found that anger was choking him. He glanced at Brasseur, then again at Frochot, in disgust, and turned away.

Brasseur stirred. "Robert-Louis Frochot, I order you, in the name of the law, to follow me before the justice of the peace to answer questions in relation to the death of the citizen Martin Dupont, the death of the citizeness Charlotte Dupont, the death of the citizeness Jeannette Moineau, and the death of the citizeness Magdeleine Dupont, wife of Bouton."

"Magdeleine Du—" Frochot exclaimed indignantly. "But this is absurd! I never touched the woman!"

"So you admit to causing the deaths of Martin Dupont, Charlotte Dupont, and Jeannette Moineau, but not that of Magdeleine Bouton?" Brasseur said, gesturing the inspectors over.

Frochot went a ghastly shade of white. "I—no! That's to say, I reserve my right not to be forced to give evidence against myself—but I never touched Magdeleine! You can't fix that on me!"

Brasseur sighed and glanced over at Aristide, as if to say, *Why do they bother?* Aristide studied Frochot for a moment, thinking, and then turned to Gervais.

"Citizen, I understand Citizen Jullien and Maître Frochot spent much of this evening with you in your study, discussing matters of business?"

"Yes, they did," Gervais said, frowning.

"Who left the room first?"

"Frochot did," Jullien said. "He excused himself to go to the privy." Gervais nodded in agreement.

"And how soon afterward did you hear the crash when Citizeness Bouton fell down the stairs?"

"Just a few minutes," said Gervais. "Time for a visit out to the garden and back."

"Magdeleine knew Charlotte had put the poison in Martin's porridge," Aristide said, turning back to Frochot. "Who's to say Charlotte didn't confess everything to her, including the name of the man who had induced her to do it? Perhaps Magdeleine was extorting payment from you, Maître, or simply threatened to denounce you for the murder of the father and sister whom she loved?"

"You'll never prove it," he said sullenly as the inspectors took hold of his arms.

"It's enough," Brasseur said. "You might wriggle yourself out of that one for lack of evidence, Frochot, but I doubt you'll be able to get off so easily with the other three charges. Take him to headquarters," he told the inspectors, with a jerk of his head.

The door closed behind them. At last Brasseur cleared his throat. "Well then. You'll all be summoned to give your statements before the justice of the peace. So mind you don't go anywhere. If you have anything else to tell us, you know where the commissariat is." He laid a hand on the door handle and turned back toward Aristide. "Ravel?"

"I'll be by in the morning," he said.

"Good night, then, citizens."

32

When Brasseur had gone, the others began to stir, shaking off their shocked silence, and one by one slipped out of the room.

"Well," said François, to no one in particular, "I suppose I'll stick around long enough to help Thérèse with the morning chores. Got to have a bed for the night anyway."

After he had gone Aristide turned to Laurence. She gave him a swift questioning glance and quickly looked away again, unsmiling.

"So," he said. "It's over."

"Yes . . . it's over." She heaved a long sigh, closing her eyes. "All for the sake of money. Not even to get hold of more money, just to cling to the money he already had, and was terrified of losing." She paused, thinking. "All the gold in the Old Man's strongbox . . . that was his, wasn't it? Frochot's?"

"Some of it must have come from that annuity, certainly."

She shivered. "I feel—filthy. I don't feel as though I can accept it."

"Do you imagine Gervais is going to have any compunctions about accepting *his* inheritance, especially now that the other two heirs are dead and he'll get it all?" Aristide said.

"He can have it. I'm not going to fight him in court. It would be a losing battle . . . and I don't think I want it. Not *that* money."

"It was legally obtained. Unscrupulously perhaps, but Martin had every right to it, and so do you, at least to your share; they'd probably award you the tenth that Martin was free to give away, if you demanded it. Or would you rather take the house as your share?"

"Ugh! I couldn't live in this house any more."

"Too much death?"

"That . . . and too many memories." She hugged herself, shivering again, and moved closer to the fire. Aristide followed her.

"Laurence . . . Frochot didn't push Magdeleine down the stairs, did he?"

She turned and looked at him, and said nothing.

"Magdeleine never confronted Frochot with the truth. Charlotte had denied everything, had never admitted that someone had put her up to it. Magdeleine didn't know who was ultimately responsible for the poisoning." He paused but Laurence remained silent and he continued.

"I think you realized, just as I did, that Magdeleine must have accused Jeannette in order to shield Charlotte. You were nearest to her—the first to run to her side after we all heard the crash—just at the top of the staircase, I believe, while Frochot must have been farther down the upstairs hall. It was you who exacted justice on Magdeleine because she had been the indirect cause of Jeannette's death, and because you knew justice would never be visited on her in any other way."

Laurence turned away and gazed at the hearth. The fire abruptly flared and then dwindled as a log collapsed into ash, and she bent and laid another stick on the dying flames.

"After you told me Jeannette was dead," she said at last, "and that it must have been Charlotte who had given the Old Man the poison, I worked it out. So I found Magdeleine and confronted her with what she'd done. At first she denied it, but finally she admitted she'd done it for Charlotte's sake. She had guessed Martin's illness was worse, much worse, than just a bout of tainted food . . . and she knew something was wrong with Charlotte—she looked guilty and bewildered and terrified all at once—and Thérèse had mentioned that Charlotte had taken his breakfast to him that morning. Magdeleine found the powder in Charlotte's room in the first place she looked—the silly little fool had rolled the packet up inside a clean chemise."

"And then Citizen Dupont died," said Aristide.

"Yes," she continued. "Then Martin died. And Magdeleine knew Charlotte was responsible, though Charlotte wouldn't admit anything, or tell her why she'd done it. So she told Charlotte to go to her room and lock herself in and cry all she wanted. Magdeleine would spread it about that she was hysterical with grief over the Old Man's death and was best left alone for a while. Then she put a pinch of the powder into the soup in the kitchen, when nobody was looking. Nobody could say Charlotte had done that.

"I asked her why she then had to fetch in the police and accuse Jeannette; why not just pass everything off, even Martin's death, as tainted food? After all, people fall ill from bad meat all the time. But she said Citizen Hébert had insisted it was very fishy, this poisoning coming so soon after Martin's death. I heard him myself; he told us something about some relative of his who'd been poisoned by his cook. Magdeleine said she had to go along with it, had to do something, blame someone, or else he'd have thought it was suspicious that she did nothing. So she planted the valuables in Jeannette's room, as well as the packet she'd found in Charlotte's drawer."

Laurence paused and added fiercely, "She told me everything as if she was proud of what she'd done, because she'd protected Charlotte. She was *proud* of it! She didn't care in the least what might happen to Jeannette. Frochot will be guillotined for murder, I suppose; but the only real punishment Magdeleine would ever have suffered was a pricking conscience. And I don't think it would have troubled her very much. She was so completely single-minded about Charlotte."

She glanced quickly at Aristide. "I didn't plan it, you know. It was just chance. A while later, I met her on the staircase, and I saw her. . . . I saw it in her hateful, self-righteous face, that she wasn't sorry for Jeannette at all, that she still felt everything was justified for her darling Charlotte's sake—I knew right away that she wouldn't really care when she learned Jeannette was dead, not the slightest remorse—and then, well . . . I just reached out and did it. No one saw us. It was so easy."

She drew a deep breath and squared her shoulders. "So what are you going to do about it?"

"I?" Aristide said. "What should I do about it?"

"Isn't it your duty to—"

"I'm not a police official; only one of their agents."

"You might as well tell the commissaire the truth. I don't care what happens now."

Aristide leaned on the mantel and stared for a few minutes into the fire, thinking of another woman he had known who had grown so weary of living that she had coolly committed murder and confessed to it in order to be free of her bleak existence.

"It wasn't just for Jeannette's sake, was it?" he said. "It was because of Aurèle, and Mathieu, and realizing that so much you had believed about your husband had been no more than a daydream. It's a terrifying thing, when your safe, cherished world—even the world inside your memories—is snatched away from you and leaves you nothing to cling to."

He saw her swallow and suddenly squeeze her eyes shut for an instant, as if fighting back tears. "It's time you broke free of that, left it behind you," he added. "Time to start afresh."

Laurence studied him for a moment, a little crease between her brows. "Is this some sort of . . . proposal . . . or a threat? Do you want hush money from me? Or something else?"

"Good lord, no," he exclaimed. Realizing she might misunderstand him, he hurried to correct himself. "What I mean to say is . . . I like you, Laurence, and I think you're an extraordinarily fine and decent person, no matter what you might have done in one instant of honest rage. Knowing the circumstances, I might have done it myself. And if I hadn't meddled in your private affairs and destroyed your treasured illusions, perhaps you wouldn't have felt yourself in so intolerable a situation that you didn't care what might happen next; so I'm not entirely guiltless in this matter, and I don't see what right I have to reproach you. Personally, I think justice has been served." He shrugged and turned away. "I want nothing from you, unless it's to see you break free of this house and your memories and find a new life for yourself."

Laurence drew a deep breath and nodded, but said nothing. At last she went to the door.

"Stay here."

She returned a few minutes later, Aurèle's letters in her hand. She separated a few from the rest and held them out to him.

"These are Mathieu's," she said. "Perhaps you want them." She knelt by the fire and slowly, one by one, fed the others to the flames. When she was done, she rose, dusted off her skirt, and looked at him once more. "Well . . . what now?"

"I suppose you have two choices," he said. "You can get out of this house and come with me to the commissariat and tell Brasseur everything, and oblige him to do his duty according to the law by locking you up and charging you with murder; or we can forget that this conversation ever took place and let the world assume that Frochot murdered Magdeleine. You can come with me and tell Brasseur only that you've had enough of inertia and dreariness and that you're going to leave the Duponts and will need to earn your own living, and start doing the sort of work I do."

"Spying, you mean?"

"Gathering information in a way the police can't. Think of it, if you want, as serving justice."

She smiled bitterly at that and he continued. "There's always room for one more police agent who has brains and ingenuity and who isn't afraid, when it's necessary, to be ruthless. I think I would rather enjoy working with you."

"I see."

Laurence slowly walked to the door but turned back to him as she reached for the handle. "Has it occurred to you," she said, "that what Mathieu spoke of in his last letter, 'since I cannot have, and can never have, that which I so ardently desire, I wish no other and cannot give you what you desire of me,'—oh yes, I know them by heart—that what he wanted, and knew he could never have, was your love?"

She went out and closed the door behind her with a soft click of the latch. Aristide gazed after her, remembering a host of shared smiles, of school holidays full of earnest talks and bottles of cheap wine, of walks along the riverside and among the flowerbeds in the public gardens of Bordeaux. All the times when, no longer boys, they had opened their hearts to one another, all the times Mathieu had talked of politics and philosophy and he had talked of—what?

That summer, the summer Mathieu wrote that letter, he thought, *I scarcely spoke of anything other than Delphine and how I adored her.* And by the time Delphine had turned him down with no more than an apologetic shrug, Mathieu was already under arrest in his own lodgings, soon to be on his way to prison and the Place de la Révolution.

Could Mathieu's last silent words to me, he thought suddenly, *have been words he had never dared to whisper until that final moment before the scaffold?*

Could they have been simply "I love you"?

He looked down at the letters in his hand, at the handwriting he knew so well, and closed his eyes for a moment at the sorrow and the tragedy of it all, of the illicit love and hidden longing that had led only to loss and regret.

At last he knelt at the hearth and dropped Mathieu's letters into the embers where Aurèle Dupont's letters lay in ashes. He watched them flare up and blacken and curl away, the traces of sealing wax hissing and sputtering in the flames, then rose and stood a while again by the mantel, remembering.

A long time later, or so it seemed, François came in, pausing at the sight of him. "You're still here?" He began blowing out the candles that stood about the room.

"Citizeness Laurence and I had a few . . . final matters to discuss."

"I thought she might still be in here," he said, pinching out all but one flame on the last candelabrum. "They're having cold supper in the kitchen, them who want it. She hasn't been in."

Aristide suddenly thought of Charlotte hanging from the garden gate, and of starving pensioners dangling from the roof beams of their garret rooms, and felt the fear clutch at his vitals. "Come with me—quickly."

They sped up the stairs to the second floor and he fumbled at the door to Laurence's bedchamber. It was unlocked. He threw the door open and stepped inside, fearful of what he might find in the darkness and silence. François swung his candle about, its tiny flame throwing flickering shadows on the walls.

"Empty."

Aristide waited a moment for his heart to stop pounding, then glanced about. The bare little room looked no different. François glanced about him before muttering "Huh" to himself and pulling open the wardrobe door.

"Ravel, there aren't any clothes here."

Aristide drew out the drawer beneath, meant for stockings and chemises. It was empty.

"I think she took off," François added. "Where do you suppose she's gone?"

Aristide wondered briefly if he would find her in Brasseur's office the next morning, and what she would be saying to him. Then again, he thought, perhaps she was done with choosing the conventional, predictable paths.

"I don't know." He gestured François out of the room and closed the door behind them. "But I imagine she'll turn up; don't you?"

HISTORICAL NOTE

The 1781–86 cause célèbre of Marie-Victoire Salmon served as the starting point for this plot. Victoire Salmon, like Jeannette Moineau, was a servant girl who had taken up a new job in a bourgeois household. A week after she began working for the Huet-Duparc family, Monsieur de Beaulieu, her mistress's elderly father, who lived with them, suddenly died of a severe gastric upset. The following day Madame Duparc and others in the family claimed they had been taken ill after eating soup that Victoire had prepared; they accused the girl of trying to poison them.

After the Duparcs also accused her of poisoning Monsieur de Beaulieu, Victoire was arrested. An autopsy proved the old man had indeed died of unnatural causes, and some mysterious powder was found in Victoire's pockets, where it had probably been planted.

Her unfortunate situation was compounded by the fact that Revel, the local royal prosecutor, had known her previously and had evidently made improper advances to her (or perhaps even raped her). Prerevolutionary criminal law made no concession to the possibility that prosecutors might abuse their positions in order to silence an inconvenient witness to wrongdoing. With Victoire unexpectedly in his power, Revel wasted no time in seeing her tried, found guilty (with the barest evidence), and condemned to death for the murder.

It was only through the efforts of one Maître Lecauchois, a lawyer who took up Victoire's defense and prepared an appeal to Louis XVI, that Victoire was saved from being burned alive. At last, after nearly five years of legal wrangling, while Victoire remained in prison under sentence of death, the case reached the highest court of France, the Paris Parlement, which reversed the decision and freed her. Victoire Salmon was luckier than Jeannette Moineau; her case had become so famous that, upon her release, she became an instant celebrity.

No member of the Huet-Duparc family was ever prosecuted for the murder of Monsieur de Beaulieu.

ACKNOWLEDGMENTS

As ever, I owe a huge debt to Johanna, Berenice, and Kristi for their support, as well as for reading and criticizing the work in progress. Another round of thanks goes to the members of the Hudson Writers' Roundtable for their help and their patience. And I must not forget Barbara L. Smith and the talented cast of *The Miser* at Columbia Civic Players, who provided me with some marvelous inspiration for aspects of the tale.

Merci to the following scholars for their kind assistance: Professors Suzanne Desan, for answering my numerous questions about the finer points of dowries, inheritance, and civil affairs; Jean-Laurent Rosenthal, for information about eighteenth-century economics; and James Mall and Gary Mole, for tips on medieval French poetry.

SELECT BIBLIOGRAPHY

Brown, Frederick. *Theater and Revolution: The Culture of the French Stage.* New York: Viking Press, 1980.

Carlson, Marvin. *The Theatre of the French Revolution.* Ithaca, N.Y.: Cornell University Press, 1966.

Cobb, Richard. *Death in Paris, 1795–1801.* Oxford: Oxford University Press, 1978.

Emsley, Clive. *Policing and Its Context, 1750–1870.* London: Macmillan, 1983.

Emsley, Clive. "Policing the Streets of Early Nineteenth-Century Paris," *French History,* 1, no. 2, pp. 257–82. Oxford: Oxford University Press, 1987.

Hillairet, Jacques. *Connaissance de Vieux Paris.* Paris: Editions Payot & Rivages, 1993.

Merrick, Jeffrey, and Bryant T. Ragin, Jr., editors. *Homosexuality in Modern France.* Oxford: Oxford University Press, 1996.

Minnigerode, Meade. *The Magnificent Comedy: Some Aspects of Public and Private Life in Paris, from the fall of Robespierre to the coming of Bonaparte.* New York: Farrar & Rinehart, 1931.

Restif de la Bretonne, Nicolas-Edmé; Linda Asher and Ellen Fertig, translators. *Les Nuits de Paris or The Nocturnal Spectator.* New York: Random House, 1964.

Robiquet, Maurice; James Kirkup, translator. *Daily Life in the French Revolution.* New York: Macmillan, 1964.

Stead, Philip John. *The Police of Paris.* London: Staples Press, 1957.

Williams, Alan. *The Police of Paris, 1718–1789.* Baton Rouge, La.: Louisiana State University Press, 1979.

Wills, Antoinette. *Crime and Punishment in Revolutionary Paris.* Westport, Conn.: Greenwood Press, 1981.